ADVANCE PRAISE FOR *ROMANOV*

"*Romanov* will cast a spell on readers and immerse them in a history anyone would long to be a part of."

—SASHA ALSBERG, #1 *NEW YORK TIMES* BESTSELLING
AUTHOR OF *ZENITH: THE ANDROMA SAGA*

"I am obsessed with this book! *Romanov* is a magical twist on history that will have Anastasia fans wishing for more. I loved every detail Brandes wrote—from the Romanovs' daily life in Ipatiev House to the conflicted Bolshevik soldiers to the mysterious spell ink that Tsarevich Alexei desperately needed. If you love magic and Imperial Russia, you want *Romanov* on your shelf!"

—EVELYN SKYE, *NEW YORK TIMES* BESTSELLING AUTHOR OF
THE *CROWN'S GAME* SERIES AND *CIRCLE OF SHADOWS*

"If you think you know the story behind Anastasia Romanov, think again! What Brandes has done with this tale is exquisite. The perfect blend of history and fantasy, *Romanov* takes a deeper look at the days leading up to the family's tragedy, while also exploring the possibilities behind the mysteries that have long intrigued history buffs everywhere. Brandes weaves a brilliant and intricate saga of love, loss, and the power of forgiveness. Prepare to have your breath stolen by this gorgeous novel of brilliant prose and epic enchantment."

—SARA ELLA, AWARD-WINNING AUTHOR
OF THE *UNBLEMISHED* TRILOGY

PRAISE FOR *FAWKES*

"Historical facts, along with captivating characters and quick dialogue, make for an extremely enjoyable novel. A great read for fans of *The Gentleman's Guide to Vice and Virtue*, *Fawkes* brings new life to the Gunpowder Plot of 1605."

—*SHELF AWARENESS*

"Engrossing historical fantasy."

—*Booklist*

"Set against the backdrop of the infamous Gunpowder Plot but with a paranormal parallel reflecting the real-life Protestant and Catholic conflicts of the day . . . A satisfying tale."

—*Publishers Weekly*

"Allegorical promise and imaginative recasting . . ."

—*Kirkus*

"Brandes successfully blends magic into history . . . A recommended purchase."

—*School Library Journal*

"*Fawkes* is the perfect mix of history and magic. I was up late in the night reading, waiting to get to the fifth of November to see how the plot would actually unfold, and it did not disappoint. An imaginative, colorful tale about choosing for yourself between what's right and what others insist is the truth."

—Cynthia Hand, *New York Times* bestselling author of *My Lady Jane*

"Hold on to your heart as this slow-burning adventure quickly escalates into an explosion of magic, love, and the truth about loyalty."

—Mary Weber, bestselling author of the Storm Siren Trilogy

"A magical retelling of the seventeenth century's famous Gunpowder Plot that will sweep you back in time . . . Deft and clever, *Fawkes* is a vibrant story about the search for truth and issues relevant to us, still, today."

—Tosca Lee, *New York Times* bestselling author

"*Fawkes* is a tale full of spiritual depth, tragedy, and hope. A beautifully written allegory for the magic of faith, with an achingly relatable hero who pulls you into his world heart and soul. A must-read for all fantasy fans!"

—Lorie Langdon, author of *Olivia Twist*

ROMANOV

ALSO BY NADINE BRANDES

Fawkes

OUT OF TIME SERIES
A Time to Die
A Time to Speak
A Time to Rise

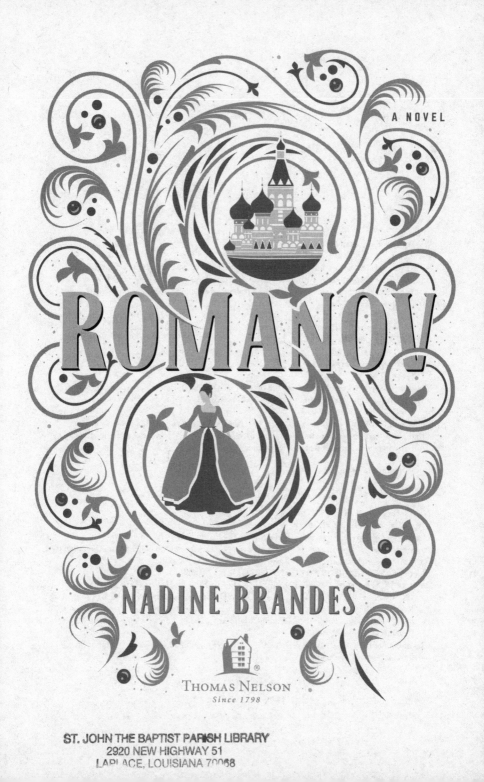

A NOVEL

ROMANOV

NADINE BRANDES

THOMAS NELSON
Since 1798

ISBN: 978-1-4041-1165-3 (custom edition)

Library of Congress Cataloging-in-Publication Data

Names: Brandes, Nadine, 1986- author.
Title: Romanov / Nadine Brandes.
Description: Nashville, Tennessee : Thomas Nelson, [2019] | Summary:
Anastasia "Nastya" Romanov must choose between using the ancient spell her father, the exiled tsar, trusted her to keep safe, or trust Zash, a handsome Bolshevik soldier.
Identifiers: LCCN 2018060690 | ISBN 9780785217244 (hardback)
Subjects: LCSH: Anastasia, Grand Duchess, daughter of Nicholas II, Emperor of Russia, 1901-1918--Fiction. | CYAC: Anastasia, Grand Duchess, daughter of Nicholas II, Emperor of Russia, 1901-1918--Juvenile fiction. | Exiles--Fiction. | Kings, queens, rulers, etc.--Fiction. | Magic--Fiction. | Forgiveness--Fiction. | Soldiers--Fiction. | Soviet Union--History--Revolution, 1917-1921--Fiction.
Classification: LCC PZ7.1.B75146 Rom 2019 | DDC [Fic]--dc23 LC record available at https://lccn.loc.gov/2018060690

Printed in the United States of America

19 20 21 22 LSC 5 4 3 2 1

To all those who have experienced hurt,
and then dared to hope, dared to forgive, dared to live.
You are proof that light will always prevail.

ASIDE

My blood is my crime.

If you look at it, it's still red. If you touch it, it's still wet. But if you listen to it, it speaks a single name in a pulsing chant.

Romanov.

Romanov.

Romanov.

For that name alone, bound to my blood like a Bolshevik is bound to the Russian Revolution, I am destined to die.

Because not even royal blood can stop bullets.

APRIL 25, 1918
TOBOLSK, RUSSIA

I watched my diaries burn.

Pages curled in on themselves, like spider legs accepting death. My past—my stories—turned to ash and tendrils of smoke. But I would not weep for them. The Bolsheviks could take far more precious things from me. I would not give them my tears.

I shoved another diary into the white-tiled stove that filled the corner of the bedroom I shared with my three older sisters here in Tobolsk. Here in exile. A photo slipped free from between two pages, as if putting forth a last attempt to escape its fate. I picked up the black-and-white portrait.

Tired, hooded eyes, a long, dark beard, and his hair parted meticulously down the middle: Grigori Rasputin. Our friend. Our spell master. He healed Alexei, he counseled Mamma, and he had been about to teach me spell mastery . . . until they shot him. The

Bolsheviks shot him as easily as they threw back a shot of vodka at the end of the day. Or the beginning of the day, depending on how many deaths weighed down their hands.

Now they were coming for us.

I threw Rasputin's photo into the fire. That photo, more than any other, could get me in the most trouble if the approaching Bolsheviks conducted a search. Evidence of our connection with the spell master would work against us. And they were searching for any reason to condemn Papa, no matter that he'd abdicated the Russian throne.

I snatched my book on spell mastery from my bedside table and shoved it on the bottom of our small bookshelf with the other volumes. It was a German translation—one the Russian guards likely couldn't read—and I'd rebound it with the cover from a German book of folktales. Still, they'd find it if they tried hard enough.

The *clip, clip, clip* of Papa's polished boots sounded down the hallway. They passed my door, stopped, and then returned. The door opened, and his calm beard-and-mustached face turned toward me. "Nastya. They're here."

I shut the stove door and stood. Papa held himself straight and regal, despite his short stature. We walked down the chilled corridor together. In silence. Ex-tsar and ex-princess. We passed Alexei's room and I glanced in. My thirteen-year-old brother lay thin and haggard on his bed, his skin yellow and eyes like dark bulbs in his skeletal face. He didn't look at us as we passed by.

I balled my fingers into fists. I would heal him. No matter the Bolsheviks' quest to murder all spell masters or if they searched us or if they sent us back to St. Petersburg. I would study spell mastery and find a cure for Alexei.

Noise came from the entryway and I focused forward. The

strain of the Bolsheviks' arrival was overshadowed by the anxiety of not knowing *why* they were coming.

We joined our guards—the ones who had been with us the past year and become our friends—in the entryway. The weathered rug cushioned our weight once we stopped.

A new man stood in the doorway, filling it like a giant shadow. He was tall with pale skin, black eyes, and an angular face beneath a mass of curly dark hair. I'd seen his type before, at the few lavish balls and parties Mamma had allowed us to attend. The type who stood on a pedestal in his mind. Usually those types were the scheming grand dukes or political leaders more interested in social climbing and control than dancing or conversation.

For some reason they never seemed to like me.

The warped windows into the courtyard distorted—but did not conceal—the lines of Bolsheviks standing at attention and waiting. Our chickens pecked at their valenki boots, tearing off bits of grey felt. The Bolsheviks didn't even blink. There had to be over a hundred of them! Why so many?

Papa strode toward the dark-eyed man and extended a hand of greeting. "Welcome to Tobolsk, Commandant."

The commandant did not shake it but instead announced in a loud voice, "I am Yakov Yurovsky. By order of Lenin's Central Committee, the Romanov family is to be relocated."

Relocated? Could it be that they were going to send us home? We'd been holed up in this cramped house for a year, unable to enter town or breathe more than a few hours of fresh air every day. I longed to be free in the forests again, picking *opyata* mushrooms, growing a life . . . dabbling in spells.

I cupped the small flare of hope in my palms and waited for more explanation.

Papa lowered his unshaken hand and asked calmly, "Where?"

"That is to be decided." Yurovsky's flat monotone caused the spark of hope simmering against my skin to wither.

"When?" Papa asked.

"Immediately."

Mamma sat at the edge of the room wrapped in thick blankets and a steely expression despite her own illness. She straightened in her chair. "But our son is too ill to travel."

"I am ordered to remove the former tsar without delay." Yurovsky clipped his heels, sending mud from his boots to the entry rug. "The rest of the family is not my concern."

I gasped and it echoed across the room until it turned Yurovsky's gaze toward me. He would take Papa *without* us? Our only solace during this time of exile had been our union. Our strength as a family. The bonds of our Romanov blood keeping us from despair.

Please. Please no.

Papa lifted his chin, and the guards in the room who had come to respect him all seemed to stand taller. He resembled a tsar again. "I will not be separated from my family."

"Then you will be taken by force." Yurovsky did not need to gesture to the Bolsheviks outside. We were outnumbered. "You may bring traveling companions, but we will leave by morning. The rest of your family will follow once the boy is . . . well." He almost said *dead*. That word hung heavier in the room than any other.

Leave. Tomorrow. By force.

Yurovsky's words were final. My control slipped through my fingers, threatening to break out in the form of a scream. They couldn't separate us! Why? Why must they take Papa away so urgently? And without telling us *where*?

Yurovsky turned on his heel and addressed three Bolshevik soldiers. "Oversee the packing."

There was no search. I'd burned my diaries for nothing. Instead they were tearing us apart. With Alexei ill and Mamma's health declining . . . this might be the last time we were all together.

Perhaps Papa sensed my rising outrage, because he took my arm and steered me away. "Come, Nastya."

"They cannot separate us," I hissed as we left the Bolsheviks behind. "You cannot let them!"

"This is not the time to resist."

"But where? Where are they sending you?"

"Probably to Moscow for trial."

My throat burned hotter than the scorched pages of my diaries. "Curse those Bolsheviks. I ought to poke holes in the soles of all their boots!"

A smile entered Papa's voice, hidden by his mustache. "That is why *you* must stay, Nastya. To cheer everyone up with your impish mischief."

I ground to a halt. "I am to stay?" He'd made up his mind already?

"There are things I need you to do here—"

"Nikolai . . ." Mamma caught up to us, her composure held together by only the clasp of her brittle fingers on her worn handkerchief. Papa went to her.

I stomped away from them, from the pain, leaving him to make the necessary arrangements and decisions he needed to focus on. None of which involved stitching up the gash in my heart.

But I wasn't the only one with a gaping wound inside. We would all have to carry this pain.

I found myself entering Alexei's room and plopping by his bedside as he coughed—a weak, wheezing thing. But that was much better than the violent hacking last week that had caused a hemor-rhage and damaged his kidneys.

Alexei had saluted death before. His hemophilia never prom-ised him a long life. But when Rasputin had been alive, he could heal Alexei's injuries with a single word, even from a different city through the telephone line.

Now there was nothing to save Alexei except his own will to live.

That would change if I could learn more about spell mastery. I itched to pick up that German spell book and read it right under the Bolsheviks' noses.

Alexei's coughing subsided and he blinked his hollow eyes toward me. "You look gloomy."

I smiled, relieved by the one family member who understood that banter could dispel even the darkest mood. "It's because you're being so lazy, staying here in bed. I've had to do all your chores."

"Lucky. Being lazy is incredibly boring." He winked, but it seemed tired. "You've likely killed my poor chickens by now."

"They had a hearty breakfast of boot felt."

"Poor creatures. To be under your care is a frightening thing." He nodded his chin toward the door. "What's happening out there? I know the Bolsheviks arrived, but no one has told me anything."

Every time Alexei was sick, the family avoided negative con-versation around him. I understood the concept—that despair could affect his will to live or might send him into a gloom that slowed his healing.

But Alexei and I had a mutual understanding never to keep things from one another. We understood that being left in the dark was far more despairing than dealing with the weight of dark news. "They're taking Papa away."

Alexei, having spent time with soldiers on the front line when Papa was still tsar, took in the statement with a deep breath. It turned into a cough and I handed him the glass of water from his bedside.

"What . . . what about me?" he finally managed. "I must go, too. I am the tsarevich."

"You're not well enough." I held back my wince.

Steel entered Alexei's features. His body. His will. "Not yet. But I will be."

And *that* was why he would have made a brilliant tsar. "They are likely sending him to trial in Moscow. Papa will leave tomorrow morning and we will follow once you are well." I fixed him with a stern gaze. "The Bolshevik commandant thinks you'll die. Survive so you can spit in his face."

Papa's voice came from the corridor. I shoved myself to my feet and hurried out, but not before I caught Alexei's whisper. "Come back and tell me everything."

Papa and Maria—my partner in mischief and only two years older—spoke quietly in the hall. Maria paled beneath her long brown hair, but she gave a brave nod and then headed toward our room.

I hurried to take her place at Papa's side. "What is the decision?"

"Your mamma will join me," Papa finally said. "Maria will come as her companion."

Not me.

He must have been able to see the resignation on my face, because he cupped my cheek with his hand and it sparked the fuse that led to the burn of tears. "Tatiana will manage the household in my absence. You have your own role to play."

So it was decided. As simple as that. Like a surgeon slicing a heart in two. My heart pumped a broken rhythm. Everything was happening too fast. I was about to be left behind. There were too many unknowns.

I grabbed his sleeve. "Is there no other way?" My plea might as well have been a shout to the corridor of guards. But I had no reason to hide my love for my family.

Papa sounded equally as desperate in his reply. "I cannot see one, *shvibzik*." He guided me up the hallway, away from the guards. "When Alexei is well enough to travel, you and your sisters will join us."

I opened my mouth to protest—how I loved protesting—but Papa added a seemingly unrelated question. "When was the last time you read Pushkin's novels?"

My jaw snapped shut like the bite of a nutcracker. Pushkin. *Pushkin.* A brief moment passed as though he wanted to be sure I understood the undertones of his question. So much of my family's conversation these days consisted of hidden messages and code words.

Pushkin meant "secrets."

The burn of my tears was snuffed. I couldn't hold back the sly grin that crawled onto my face. "I was planning on reading one today." As soon as he left, I would slip to the library and find whatever secret he'd hidden there for me.

Papa glanced over his shoulder. No guards in sight. We stopped. "Nastya, you know the most about spells. I did not trust Rasputin as Mamma did, but I know he instructed you and he likely did it well." Code words were abandoned.

"He only ever had time to show me the basics." And hardly even that.

"That is still more than your siblings. This is why you must guard the family Matryoshka doll and bring it with you when you join us."

My throat cinched. Thirteen years ago, I'd watched Mamma and him open a layer of that painted doll and release the now-forbidden spell that brought us Alexei. I'd not seen the doll since. "Dochkin made that doll." Vasily Dochkin, Russia's most respected and skilled spell master.

"*Da*. Do not let the Bolsheviks take it."

My mind raced through questions and answers. After Rasputin, the people grew too suspicious of spell masters, convinced they could control minds. So the revolution began—forcing Papa off the throne and hunting down spell masters one by one.

"The Bolsheviks would use the doll to find Dochkin and kill him," I surmised. "I must protect him." The revolutionaries were fools. They knew nothing about spell masters. Spells from the old artists of Russia were now forbidden. I liked forbidden things.

"That is not why I am entrusting it to you." Papa glanced over his shoulder. "This doll, Nastya. It may be our family's only salvation."

A familiar thrill twirled in my chest. Papa was depending on me and not my eldest sisters, Olga or Tatiana, because he knew I could do it. I was sneaky—they were too honest. "I will not fail you, Papa."

He kissed me on the forehead. "You never do. Now go help Maria pack."

I spun on my heel and strode down the hallway of the Tobolsk governor's house as though I was, once again, Grand Duchess Anastasia Nikolaevna back in the Alexander Palace.

I could pretend away Papa's abdication.

I could pretend away our exile.

And now that Papa had given me a mission, I could—for the moment—pretend away the fear of never seeing him, Mamma, or Maria again.

I entered the bedroom that my sisters and I shared. Maria stood staring at her brown valise, looking far too vulnerable and unsure for her stocky eighteen-year-old frame.

I sighed and crossed the room. "You *had* to volunteer." I pulled books from our shelf and stuffed them into Maria's valise, making sure she had the essentials—Tolstoy, Dostoevsky, Turgenev, Chekhov. I tried to set my envy aside—I wished *I* were going. But then who would Alexei have?

Maria snapped out of her helplessness, as I knew she would if I forced literature on her. She took the books out and replaced them with a beaded gown. "I could not let Mamma face Papa's trial alone."

I tried to slip in two of the discarded volumes. How did she expect to dispel the boredom on the train ride without books? "You'll not need an evening gown at a court trial, Maria." Nor, likely, ever again. Why she'd brought the gown to Tobolsk in the first place made sense only to Maria's flirtatious mind.

If we were lucky, the trial would allow us—the last Romanov family—to disappear into a quaint Russian village and live out the rest of our lives as the common people did.

"It is *Moscow*," Maria stressed. "I would rather have a flattering gown on hand than old dusty books." She dumped the volumes out and I managed to catch all but Dostoevsky, which slammed to the ground, spine up. My soul cracked right along with the crisp pages.

I picked it up. "Did you know Dostoevsky was exiled to Tobolsk for a time?" I held out the book. "It would be a bad omen to leave him behind."

"Then *you* can bring the book when you join us."

I screwed up my face, not caring that pouting was far beneath the maturity I should be showing as a sixteen-year-old princess. Well, *ex*-princess. "Whenever that might be."

"We will see each other again, shvibzik."

Her use of my pet name—"imp" in Russian—did nothing to ease my building dread. "You must write to me."

"If they will let me." Maria's hands stilled. She leaned over the valise as though curling in pain.

"You need only smile at them and they'll let you do whatever you wish." I shoved parchment into the bottom of the valise, filling the role of the strong one. That was how we sisters worked. When one was weak, another picked up the strength. "You and Papa will befriend these Bolsheviks as you have the soldiers here in Tobolsk. Papa may have abdicated the throne, but we are still royalty. We are Romanovs. The bond of our hearts—"

"—spans miles, memory, and time," Maria finished.

Our beloved Russia had filled the people's heads with propaganda—painting Papa as a weak, careless tsar who discarded Russian soldiers' lives. That was proof they didn't know Papa at all. Our only defense was to show the Bolsheviks otherwise. Since arriving in Tobolsk, we'd grown to love our guards. I believe they grew to love us, too—or at least to see us as we truly were. Not as the revolution painted us.

But things were changing. We were separating. Though the people had overthrown Papa, the Bolsheviks had now overthrown the provisional government. Vladimir Lenin was in charge of Russia, and no one knew what he'd do. I was afraid. Our voices were losing power.

No one could outshout a revolution.

Maria clicked the valise closed. "Alexei feels this separation is his fault."

I flopped backward onto my cot, staring up at the chipped paint on the ceiling. "Fault lies with the Bolsheviks. If they would simply acknowledge that we're no threat to our beloved Russia, we could go live in peace in a small village somewhere."

"That's what this trial will finally decide."

───※───

No one slept that night.

We took in the dawn with tired, red eyes and wilted wills. Olga—the mother of our sibling group at age twenty-two—went to check on Alexei. Tatiana spent the morning with Papa, gathering any last information she might need for dealing with the Bolsheviks. Maria and I had a breakfast of silence in our bedroom. A single word would break the dam holding back the tears. We needed to be strong today.

Maria hoisted her valise off the bed with one hand. I didn't offer to help—I was born with all the mischief and she with all the muscles. We made our way to the entrance, where my emotional armor threatened to crumble. My family formed two lines on the entry rug.

Those who were leaving: Papa, Mamma, and then Maria.

Those who were being left behind: Olga, Tatiana, myself, and Alexei sitting in his wooden wheelchair and wrapped in a blanket so thick I could barely see his face beneath his mop of copper-colored hair.

All of us had to say good-bye.

A third line of bodies watched our farewells. Tobolsk soldiers. Papa went down the line and shook their hands. Every man looked somber—as though equally distraught to see Papa leaving. He handed out a few cigarettes and laughed about a recent card game with one of them.

Near the door stood a clump of Bolsheviks. The ones taking Papa away. I paid them no mind. This was *our* moment. My gaze met Papa's. His eyes shone with the same heartache currently shredding my innards.

I hugged Mamma good-bye first. Then I faced Maria. She wept openly, which guaranteed that my eyes stayed dry. "You must write to me, too, Nastya."

I hugged her stocky frame. "You will have to write first and tell me where you are staying."

I approached Papa last. He crushed me to him and pressed his face into my neck. Never had I received such an endearing embrace from him. A sob broke free—shattering my resolve. *"Ya tebya lublu."*

"I love you, too, shvibzik." He did not remind me about the doll. I did not mention it.

"Take care of Alexei," Mamma implored as Papa steered her away from her line of children she might never see again. *"And take care of our secret,"* was what she didn't say. Even now, amidst fear and separation, we were to keep Alexei's genetic illness hidden.

Alexei, though currently too weak to rise from his chair, piped up. "Perhaps *I* shall be the one taking care of my sisters."

We all grasped on to the weak attempt at humor. It filled me with enough strength to watch Papa, Mamma, and Maria walk away into the crisp April air. Alexei shivered, and a word barely escaped my lips before the servants steered his chair back to his room.

Mamma had looked at me when she bid us to take care of him. Like me, she had been the second youngest. Her own brother had suffered from hemophilia. But hers had died.

Mine would not.

Even though Olga and Tatiana had tended soldiers during the war and gained healing knowledge, the bond between Alexei and me brought the true healing he needed.

I entered his room just as he drew a sleeve across his eyes. Dr. Botkin took Alexei's pulse. He squinted at his pocket watch through his round glasses, his balding head shining beneath the single electric lamp. Alexei showed no shame over his tears. His weakness banished mine. I would be strong again.

"Well, Nastya. This might be my last time seeing them." His blood disease was always threatening to take him from us. Life expectancy for someone with hemophilia wasn't very high. Slightly higher if that someone was royalty with a devoted doctor.

I folded my arms. "You certainly *won't* see them again if you continue to ride your toboggan down the governor's stairs." That had been months ago and Alexei was *still* recovering. I think he'd hoped he wouldn't survive the ordeal. At this point, with no throne to inherit, a time of exile, and endless days of painful recovery, I could understand why he had trouble finding reason to live.

Dr. Botkin patted Alexei's knee. "You shall be reunited, Tsarevich."

Alexei and I shared a grin at the doctor's assurance of something no one could control. But even empty promises could fill a heart for a moment.

Dr. Botkin applied the Fohn apparatus to Alexei's joints and muscles to help keep back any atrophy.

"I can do that, Doctor," I interjected, catching a cursory glance from Alexei.

The doctor glanced between us. Alexei nodded, so Dr. Botkin allowed me to spread the apparatus over Alexei's legs as it warmed.

Then he gathered his things and left the room. The moment the door closed, Alexei asked, "Do you have a spell, Nastya? I want to get better as soon as possible."

I reached into my skirt pocket and pulled out a small tin. "Only one. I used the last of the spell ink on this, and I don't know how to make more." I was lucky I'd found a bottle of spell ink in this abandoned governor's house in the first place.

I unscrewed the tin. At the bottom, against the thin metal, a single painted word glimmered like a rainbow through a spattered window or like a bubble under sunshine. I had seen many lovely things in my life, but spell ink would always be my favorite.

Oblegcheniye—the only spell I knew how to make. *Relief.* "This will ease the pain, but not heal it."

Alexei nodded. "It allows my body to relax. It will still help."

I sent a furtive glance toward the door before I slid a finger along the bottom of the tin until the word squirmed and attached to my skin. I transferred the word to Alexei's skin—a snail trail of glimmering ink.

Alexei clenched his teeth under the brief pressure of my touch. *"Oblegcheniye,"* I whispered.

The shimmery ink sank into Alexei's skin. Alexei expelled a pent-up breath and sank against the pillows. I shoved the empty tin back into my skirt, my heart pounding. No Bolsheviks caught us.

"That'll last a few hours. Be patient. Soon you'll be well enough to travel." I smiled, glowing beneath the rebellion of using a spell right under the enemy's noses. "It won't be long now."

"We were still left behind." Alexei sighed. "I am a burden."

"Tishe." I flicked his shoulder with my pinkie. "You're not fat enough to be a burden."

He rolled his eyes and I knelt on the ground beside him.

"Imagine this." I adopted a mysterious tone. "Mamma and Papa have left us behind for secret tasks instead."

Alexei's head lifted at our game. "Tasks of spying."

"Tasks of mischief."

"Tasks of adventure."

"Tasks of . . . *magic*."

His grey-blue eyes widened. "And imagine this: We are, in fact, soon to be their rescue. As we speak, Dr. Botkin is incapacitating the Bolsheviks."

"Bravo, Dr. Botkin!" I applauded, and we both giggled at the image of our dear doctor wielding his stethoscope as a weapon.

Almost as quickly as the giggles came, Alexei sobered and his face fell. "But imagine that I never get strong enough to travel . . ."

I took his hand. "You're breaking the rules, you know." His fingers pressed against mine, a mere breath of a squeeze. I was careful not to return it too firmly. "You have been weak before and it has passed. Every time you think it's the last time. And every time you regain your strength. This is no different."

But it was.

This time the Bolsheviks were waiting to see the verdict after Papa's trial. Once that judgment came, our fates would be decided. Then the Bolsheviks would take us where they willed. I much preferred the soldiers who let us play cards with them. Who shared their smokes with Papa and sat through my Sunday-night plays of silliness.

"We won't be separated for long." I stood. "In fact, I'm going to pack." I left Alexei's room at the same time his spunky little red-and-white spaniel pattered into the room. I glanced back long enough to see Alexei's face brighten considerably as Joy plopped her two front paws on the side of his bed.

Then I went to the library.

The library of the Tobolsk governor's house was a candle stub compared to the chandelier of the Alexander Palace library. Still, it was a place of light for me, no matter the size of the flame. Papa would read to us every evening in here.

Tonight, that wouldn't happen.

No fire blazed in the hearth to combat the chill. The only fires lit were in the bedrooms. And even then, they were never enough to abolish the ice in our bones. Like St. Petersburg, Tobolsk was willing to release a heavy snowfall in any month of the year. The Irtysh River hadn't even thawed yet.

No soldiers filled the library, but I browsed the shelves in any case, maintaining a constant posture of innocence—one of my more prized talents. I stopped at a book of poetry and flipped it open, scanning the words but thinking only of Papa's departure— No. Of Papa's *mission*. I would not think of the fact he was gone.

I would *not*.

We would be together again.

I snapped the poetry book closed and strode to the case that held Pushkin's works. My fingers tingled, though I let them hang by my side while I searched with my eyes first. Nothing appeared different about the set of spines, but the bookshelves were deep.

I slipped one book from the shelf, glancing into the dark space behind it. Red and gold paint resisted the shadow. A shimmer of secrets. Of hope. Of adventure.

The Matryoshka doll.

I dipped my fingertips into the shadow.

"You should not be in here unattended."

My nerves scraped against my skull at the sudden voice, but my body did not react—trained to resist reflexive surprise. Everything within me wanted to snatch my inquiring hand back and pretend I'd seen nothing. Instead, I lifted my head and slipped on a smile. "Is reading so dangerous?" I almost choked on the last word when my gaze landed on the source of the voice.

Soldier.

Stranger.

Bolshevik.

He wasn't one of the kind guards. This was a man who didn't know us, didn't know Papa. He stood stiff in his Bolshevik uniform, sporting the red star badge with a hammer-and-plough emblem in the center. He appeared hardly older than me, though I couldn't quite make out all his features beneath his budenovka felt cap. The elegant shape of his eyes told me he came from Eastern Russia. Somewhere local, maybe? Old eyes in a young face.

"You must be new." I tried to sound friendly. Every new soldier—or Bolshevik—was a new mission to show them *us* and not the revolution's portrayal of us. But with the departure of half my family, I wasn't sure I could manage it today.

His gaze went to the shelf. "Find anything interesting?"

I had a feeling he wasn't talking about books. "I find every book interesting." I slid the Pushkin volume from the shelf, subtly scooting the Matryoshka doll deeper into the shadows with the tips of my fingers. The Bolshevik didn't smile, but that wasn't unusual. Emotions were private—even the fake ones. We Russians weren't required to share any amount of emotion we didn't want to.

The Bolshevik passed through the doorway and approached me, stepping into the dim light.

"What's your name?" I asked to contrast the tense silence.

He stopped a few feet away and held out his hand for the book. I swallowed hard. Had he overheard Papa's instructions?

I handed him the volume. "Pushkin."

"Everyone likes Pushkin." He said it in a way that made me feel as though I was shallow. Average. Common.

We couldn't have that. "Allow me to make a different recommendation." I placed a children's book of fairy tales in his hand. I meant it as a joke, but he glanced at the cover with the same indifference he'd maintained since he stepped into the library.

That was the last of my cordial energy. This Bolshevik might take some time to soften, but I would get through to him. After all, what else was there to do in Tobolsk?

I snatched Pushkin back from him and plopped onto a sofa to read. Hopefully he'd go away, or at least be satisfied that I wasn't doing anything dangerous. But he stood there, flipping through the book of Russian fairy tales.

"My name is Zash." He shut the book and returned it to its place on the shelf.

There. Was that so hard? "I'm Nastya." I knew *he* knew my name. Up until a year ago, he would have bowed to me. Still, I wanted him to understand I expected no formalities. The first step of getting through to a soldier was to show them I was human and that I did not expect grand duchess treatment.

"I know who you are. I know what your family has done. Do not expect that I will fall for the cheap friendliness with which your father has brainwashed the other soldiers." He finally left.

I pretended to read. My eyes moved back and forth and I turned pages at a rate equal to my average reading speed, but my mind processed only the terrible itch to retrieve the doll. I focused on that and not the burn beneath my skin that lingered after Zash's insult to my character—to Papa's character. That bothered me most.

Zash believed the propaganda about Papa—that Papa was a

weak ruler, that he cared not for the people, that he threw parties while peasants starved, that his wife ruled over him. I couldn't blame Zash—how could he know any different? But it made me that much more desperate to set him and the other Bolsheviks right.

Eventually the candles burned to stubs. I finally returned the Pushkin book to its spot on the shelf. Then I glanced around the room . . . and slipped the Matryoshka doll into my sleeve.

2

A grenade would be safer in the palm of my hand than the Matryoshka doll.

I sat on my bed in my room, staring at the small wooden toy. A regular Matryoshka doll typically held layer upon layer of miniature dolls inside it. Did that mean this doll held layers of spells?

I turned it round and round in my hand, running a thumb over every inch of wood. No seam. Was there no way to open it to inspect the spells inside? Maybe it was filled with spell ink instead. I shook it and the inner layers rattled against each other. I tried to twist it open, but it didn't give.

This doll was made by Dochkin. Papa instructed me to protect it. He must know what was inside. So I let it be. Despite my nickname of *imp,* I respected Papa too much to toy with something he claimed might be our family's salvation. I placed the doll on the shelf across the room that held a display of candles, music boxes, and trinkets.

The best place to hide an item was on your person. But when you couldn't manage that, the next best place was to hide it in plain view. People searched there last.

"Any news?" A Bolshevik snickered as I passed. They'd been with us for two weeks and not one of them had softened. Fifty remaining Bolsheviks with guns who didn't care to know us.

Fifty men who laughed at me, knowing I'd received no letter from Maria. The calculations didn't add up. She should have arrived in Moscow within three or four days, and then a couple days for them to settle in and Maria to write, then three days for the letter to reach me.

Still, no letter.

I tried not to be concerned. The post took a long time. Besides, the Bolsheviks had to examine every piece of post. Perhaps the trial had kept her too busy. Maybe they weren't allowing her to write.

Longing spiked in me, but I shut it down. I wanted to be out of Tobolsk. Out of Siberia. I wanted to be *home*. At the very least I wanted permission to make a place our home—*any* place, as long as it was ours. Together.

My thoughts drifted beyond my control—to the unthinkable. That the train had been attacked on the way to Moscow, or that the revolutionaries had gone after Papa on his way to the trial, or that the Bolsheviks had pulled out their guns and—

"Has the post come?" Alexei asked weakly as I passed his room. He lay in bed, attached to the electrotherapy machines to stimulate his weak leg muscles. I was out of spells with which to help him. He had only just begun to sit up on his own.

I shook my head. Then I returned to my room and toyed with the Matryoshka doll again. Nothing had changed. Did I need to speak a certain word to prompt it open? My bottle of spell ink was dry, and Rasputin had never told me how to make more.

The doorknob creaked, and I barely returned the doll to its spot before my older sister Tatiana entered. Her short auburn hair flipped out elegantly above her shoulders. Always put together. Always beautiful.

"I have work for you," she said.

Always bossy. But I'd take any distraction I could.

She shoved a sewing kit into my hands. "Before she left, Mamma told us to dispose of the medicines."

Medicines was our code word for "jewels."

"We will do our mending in here," she said in a tone as crisp as the frozen leaves outside.

I plopped on the bed, grabbed the corset I loathed wearing, and set to work opening a seam. "At least there's *something* we can do to resist this revolution."

"Tishe," Tatiana hushed. She pored over her work as though stitching a soldier's head wound—something she'd done plenty of times during the war. It reminded me that this was a mission. I needed to remain on guard.

I tucked a strand of pearls between the ribbing of my corset, then threaded my needle. I pinched it too tightly as I shoved it through the material and it pricked me. We would not be able to pack any riches in our valises when we joined Papa, Mamma, and Maria. We would have to wear the jewels so that, should we escape the Red Army's hold, we had money with which to live on.

"Do you think we will join them soon?" Tatiana, at least, would give me a straight answer. She was like Papa in that way.

Tatiana shoved a diamond bracelet into the hem of her coat cuff. "It will likely be another few weeks."

I sewed a thick length of cloth over my seam. "We've received no news. Are you . . . concerned?" I pulled the stitches tight so they would withstand any upcoming travel.

"Double knot it." Her needle flew through the fabric. "Of course I wish we had news, but I think the Bolsheviks are keeping it from us. They will let a letter through soon."

"Accursed Bolsheviks." I knotted my thread so forcefully, it snapped. A prickle swept up my arms and I snapped my gaze toward the doorway.

Zash the Bolshevik stood there watching us. My hands stilled. How did he arrive so silently? And how much had he heard? His sneer of loathing told me he'd caught at least my muttered curse. I gave him a sheepish grin. "Can you blame me?"

Tatiana knotted her thread before giving him a more sophisticated response. "Do you bring news, sir?"

"You are to do your mending and recreational activities in the sitting room." He no longer wore his budenovka hat, and I took in his sweep of black hair. He stood out from the other Bolsheviks with his prominent cheekbones. The textured coloring of his skin spoke of many years spent beneath the sun. Not smooth and even like the men in the palaces. His was a soldier's skin. A wild skin. I quite liked it.

"In addition, doors to bedrooms are no longer allowed to be closed."

"What about for sleeping?" I exclaimed.

"Not even then."

I opened my mouth, but Tatiana rested a hand on my arm. "We will comply, of course." Her calm tone echoed Papa's heart. I snapped my mouth shut. Humility. Obedience. For Papa.

But leaving our doors open would release the small amounts

of heat we managed to keep in our sleeping quarters. It would be freezing. And no privacy! Not even to change clothing!

Zash stayed in the doorway until we'd gathered up our sewing. The "medicines" remained tucked in our baggage, waiting for us to take out piece by piece. I was lucky I'd gotten that pearl bracelet sewed up in time.

Tatiana led the way to the sitting room, but I took longer, releasing my irritation upon my corset and overcoat as I folded them. It wasn't Zash's fault. He was delivering orders, so by the time I'd gathered my mending, I was in a proper state of mind.

"Thank you for delivering the message." I gave him a bright smile.

He glowered. "You can drop the feigned kindness."

My eyebrows shot up. "It's not feigned. It's not *easy* either, but what is there to gain from animosity?"

He closed our bedroom door and strode down the hall. I jogged to catch up. "Do you enjoy your hatred of us?"

"You are no longer a grand duchess. I have no obligation to converse or bow to you."

My face warmed. "I am still a *person*. I do not expect conversation or bows. Just some cordial humanity!"

"You and your family destroyed our country!" he burst out, stopping in the middle of the hall. "Your father's one job was to care for the people. Instead, he hardly *knew* them. And because of your golden halls and fancy palaces, you have no idea what you've done to the citizens of Russia."

My jaw hung open. I had no argument. I *had* been raised differently. We weren't among the common folk much, but I knew Papa. I knew his heart. I knew how Olga and Tatiana had served soldiers. I knew our love for the people. Did they not know that we loved them? Had they never known?

Suddenly I wanted to know Zash's story. He wasn't an enemy. He was a confused Bolshevik who didn't understand me . . . and I didn't understand him. I reached for his arm and my folded corset tumbled to the ground. "Then tell me. I want to know."

He jerked away, seemingly taken aback by my response. "It's too late. Just . . . just obey our orders and stop . . . stop talking to me."

I picked up the corset and followed him the rest of the way to the sitting room. I wanted to understand him. But he was wrong about us, too. We'd slept on cots, made our own beds, worn simple Russian clothing, and adored the Alexander Palace filled with wood furniture and rustic necessities rather than the gold walls of the Catherine Palace. Papa and Mamma had raised us to love family, not luxury.

Papa didn't want his throne back. All we craved was to be released to build a cottage somewhere. But I gathered that Zash wouldn't believe that any more than he believed my kindness was genuine.

~

Maria's first letter struck our household like the blade of an ax to a fallen log.

We are not in Moscow.

Papa had no trial.

They have given us to the Bolsheviks.

I stared at it, jaw slack, voice clogged as though I'd swallowed a *pelmeni* whole. They didn't give Papa a trial? They didn't send us to a new quiet home. Instead . . .

"What does it say?" Dread hung thick in Alexei's question. He could see on my face that something was wrong. I didn't try to hide it. Not from Alexei. He'd remained frail—losing even more weight and unable to walk on his own. I tried not to be angry at his illness. It wasn't his fault, and yet it kept us trapped in this Tobolsk house. Trapped waiting. Wondering.

Abandoned.

"Bolsheviks." My mouth moved but my voice resisted, as though to say it aloud would speak it into existence. "There was no trial. They . . . they handed them—*us*—over to the Bolsheviks. For exile." The enemy. Those who wished us dead. I passed him the letter with a trembling hand.

Where I read only as much as I could swallow, Alexei scanned the entire letter, his eyes widening with each line. But he didn't stop. He charged through the fire of information, despite the burns on our hearts. And he filled in the blanks I hadn't been bold enough to read. Each sentence sliced like the swing of a pendulum.

Tick. "They are in Ekaterinburg." *Tock.* "They were sent by train." *Tick.* "They were searched upon their arrival." *Tock.* "We are to follow . . ."

His voice trailed off and his gaze dropped to his legs. His electrotherapy machines. As though summoned by his fear, a cough broke through his chest. Dry. Wheezing. Bending his body with a gnarled hand.

I didn't know how to comfort him. I couldn't heal him. The Bolsheviks were no longer just our guards. Now we belonged to them.

Alexei wasn't ready to travel.

Exile would kill him.

My corset poked and pinched, but I knew—as with any pair of new boots or rough collar—I would build up a tolerance to the discomfort. I would have to, for I'd rarely be taking off these jewel-lined underclothes.

Our trunks were packed with belongings and our hearts packed with memories. We would be leaving for Ekaterinburg once Commandant Yurovsky returned to gather us.

I prayed he would come swiftly so I could be with my family.

I prayed he would be delayed so Alexei could rest and heal as much as possible.

I replied to Maria's letter, telling her of our surprise at her news and our plans to join them as soon as possible. I wrote how Alexei was weak and thin, yet he seemed to be growing stronger through sheer willpower. All that remained was for me to pack the Matryoshka doll. I hadn't touched it—the more dust it gathered and the more it blended in, the less the Bolsheviks would suspect it meant anything.

Commandant Yurovsky arrived one week later. I followed Olga and Tatiana to the entryway so we could welcome him. "Behave," Olga said before we descended the stairs.

"Of course I'll behave." I would behave exactly as I always did.

"You will leave in the morning," Yurovsky announced the moment we three sisters entered. No greeting. No formalities. "All belongings will undergo inspection."

His Bolsheviks stood behind him, tall and stiff in freshly brushed uniforms. Zash stared at the back of Yurovsky's head as though it bore a shining crown.

The Tobolsk soldiers—our *friendly* soldiers—formed a separate clump, looking uncomfortable and out of place.

"Inspection?" I asked Yurovsky. "What are you hoping to find?

Perhaps we can help you." I smiled sweetly, enjoying the press of diamonds against my ribs. Olga pinched my arm. Tatiana sighed.

"I am expecting to find compliance." Yurovsky pulled a pocket watch from his coat lining, glanced at the face, then snapped it shut.

Olga, Tatiana, and I waited. He stared us down as though waiting for us to squirm. But I was no worm, and despite Olga's tender heart, she could brandish a tongue of fire hotter than a crackling hearth.

"You may begin," Yurovsky said to his stone-faced soldiers. They broke from their lines and panic blossomed in my chest. The doll. My gaze found Zash's. He appeared as moody as every other time we had interacted. It could have been my imagination, but it seemed as though he made a beeline for the hallway toward our bedroom.

"I will go pack," I said softly, but loud enough for Yurovsky to hear. I needed to make it sound like resignation, not desperation.

Two Bolsheviks entered Mamma and Papa's room. Another one entered Alexei's. Joy, the spaniel, stood guard between Alexei and the soldier. Olga broke from our threesome to accompany Alexei during the search.

I quickened my steps to catch Zash. I suspected he chose my bedroom because he mistrusted me. From the moment he stepped into the library he knew I was hiding something.

I entered only a few steps behind him and the Matryoshka doll seemed to glow from the shelf over to my left. So I gestured to the left—because to gesture *away* from my valuables would raise more suspicion. "My trunks are there." I pointed to the back right. "And those are Tatiana's and Olga's."

Zash surveyed the room for a moment. I waited for him to move toward one set of trunks or the other . . . or the doll. "You may go."

I was not accustomed to being sent out of my own space. I wanted to argue, but I imagined Papa's voice in my mind—urging me to be kind to the Bolsheviks. To show them who we really were and to reflect what we hoped Russia would become.

Humility. Ugh.

"Of course, sir." I bowed my head—and only my head, because my pride was a steel rod in my spine. I left, although walking up the hallway felt as if I strained against a current of resistance in my mind.

I could only pray that Zash did not find the doll. There was no reason for him to suspect it. There wasn't even a way to open it to find the spell Papa claimed it contained.

What did Yurovsky command the soldiers to search for? Jewels? Hidden spells? Diaries? I headed to the kitchens to see if the cook, Kharitonov, needed help baking the day's bread. I needed a distraction and was thankful he allowed us girls to help him. The heat from the baking oven warmed us beyond what the hearths upstairs could do.

But the kitchen was empty. No bits of food to snatch. Only a basket of eggs sat on the windowsill, likely never to be eaten by us since we were leaving in the morning. Who would eat them? The Bolsheviks?

Finally Kharitonov returned and we set to work. Olga joined us, too, her hair a nervous frizz. Tatiana was likely upstairs ensuring that Yurovsky had all the compliance he wanted. She was better at hiding her emotions than Olga or I.

We expelled our anxiety through stirring, chopping, and kneading. "Bread dough has seen many an anxious person through difficult times," Kharitonov remarked. "It is very receptive to abuse."

I punched my fist into the yeasty mass of dark rye.

"Precisely, Nastya."

Commandant Yurovsky settled at his new post—a desk in the entryway. Throughout the day, he stared at his pocket watch as though counting down the minutes until he could send us to exile.

We gathered with our servants for a farewell meal of borscht and hazel hen with rice. We also shared two bottles of wine that Kharitonov had kept hidden from the Bolsheviks and guards. Merriness bolstered our hearts, knowing we'd soon be on our way to our parents.

After hours, the soldiers finally finished their inspections. I tried not to run back to my room. My valise already held most of the necessities—a change of clothing, writing utensils, and three books: Pushkin for my sanity, the *Bibliya* for my soul, and the German book on spell mastery for my education. Likely they were ruffled from Zash's inspection.

When I entered the room, my gaze went straight to the shelf on the left wall. The dusty, glittering objects seemed untouched. But a gap of air sat between the music box and the jeweled figure of a ballerina as though it were an artifact in itself.

Papa's Matryoshka doll was gone.

3

He'd found it. Zash had found the doll. How?

I forced myself to fiddle with the valise buckle as though I was still packing, just in case Yurovsky or Zash were somehow watching for my reaction. But how could they? How could they have *known*?

Yurovsky had been here for barely a day. If he'd discovered that we were harboring old spells, he would have said something when he was here weeks ago. We'd have been confronted and punished.

It had to have been Zash. Somehow he'd known I took it from the library. Or maybe he saw it added to my room. I didn't know how—but it was him.

I had to get it back.

The question was *how*. It was nightfall, and to wander around the house in the darkness would arouse suspicion. But I was good at sneaking around. My best time to search for the doll would be in the morning—with the light as my ally. Although we were to leave early. I needed to buy time.

A delay.

My favorite grin slipped out—the one that preceded a particularly fantastic prank. All it would cost me was a basket of eggs.

I rose before dawn, dressed, and carried my belongings to the entryway. Commandant Yurovsky would have no reason to accuse me of noncompliance.

I was an angel.

A few soldiers patrolled the corridors, eyes red and postures askew. They'd been on night watch and seemed far less rested than usual. Probably because now that Yurovsky was there, they actually stood watch the entire night.

Yurovsky moved into the entryway as I plopped my valise by the door. I acted as though he wasn't there, but I felt his gaze and it boiled my skin. Thankfully he would not be accompanying us to Ekaterinburg.

I tried to look busy, and when the first startled cry broke the morning silence, I gasped like the rest of the servants. I must say, I almost convinced myself of my surprise.

Yurovsky tilted his head—a minor acknowledgment of the distressed person. When a second cry was followed by a third, I put on my most concerned face and strode toward the noise—toward the soldiers' hallway.

Yurovsky was right behind me.

I added a panicked little run to my steps. Yurovsky's methodical stride down the hallway did not increase or decrease. A clockwork commandant. I appreciated his lack of alarm, because it allowed me to burst into the soldiers' quarters a few seconds before him and take in the scene.

Several soldiers sat on their bunks with boot in hand. Strings of egg yolk stretched from their gooey socks to the boot interior.

"What is going on here?" Yurovsky demanded, halting behind me.

"Raw eggs!" one of the Bolsheviks exclaimed. "Raw eggs in our boots!"

The soldiers who had not yet slipped their feet into their boots dumped them over and, sure enough, eggs rolled out. Several of them chuckled. I scooted out of Yurovsky's way, but not before Zash met my eyes, a question in his.

He wore both his boots already, dressed and awake for duty. No egg debacle for him.

"Oh, is that all?" I said to the distressed room. "I thought someone was injured!" I turned on a heel and walked away, leaving Yurovsky to sort out the mess.

"You, go question the cook and find out who did this." Yurovsky showed a level of control that didn't surprise me from such a man as he. I didn't want to be in his path, because the calmest voices could carry the cruelest words. But the footsteps that strode down the hall behind me were not clockwork. They were quick—a soldier on an errand. And I knew just which soldier the commandant had sent.

Zash came alongside me. "Interesting that I was spared."

I shrugged and kept walking. "And why not? I would hate for you to track egg into the library. Or into my bedroom."

"That was extremely immature."

I rolled my eyes. "Those who cannot laugh cannot properly live."

"It was wasteful. Those eggs could have gone to the people."

Enough was enough. We rounded a corner and I faced him

full on, coming to a stop in front of the kitchen door. "Why did I receive no report of the items you confiscated when you searched my room? Commandant Yurovsky has said nothing to me—did you report the items to him?"

Zash's gait hiccupped and he straightened into official Bolshevik stance, as though affronted. My words implied that he had kept my items—my Matryoshka doll—for himself.

"I found nothing during my search of your rooms. Should I check again?" He sounded so serious. So confident. Even a little baffled.

That tiny glimpse of confusion made me pause. "N-No. I . . . I . . ." Oy, what to say. "I suppose I'm sensitive because of our swift departure. I feel so . . . out of sorts." That sounded like a nice girlish response. Perhaps he'd buy it.

"If you'll excuse me, I have duties to attend to."

I watched him go, stunned by his denial. My confidence flattened beneath the stampede of fresh panic. Zash claimed he hadn't taken any of my things. Liar. But usually I could detect lying. Maybe someone else had found the doll.

An icy finger of premonition slid down the back of my neck. I looked up the hallway toward the soldiers' quarters. Commandant Yurovsky stood at the opposite end. Watching.

Suddenly I felt exposed. Found out. Known. I didn't like it one bit.

I held his gaze—for my own sake. Not to be stubborn but because if I glanced away now, the needle of fear would pierce its way into my mind and the next time I encountered Yurovsky, I would be unable to find courage to defy him when I needed to.

With every heartbeat my confidence returned. I was the Grand Duchess Anastasia. I had snuck eggs into his soldiers' boots without them catching a single whiff of the prank, and I was going to smuggle a Matryoshka doll filled with spells out of this house and to Ekaterinburg, right under Yurovsky's or Zash's watchful eyes.

I would save my family.

I dipped into a curtsy, then strode up the hall, posture perfected by my jewel-encrusted corset. My grin returned, despite my quickened breath. When I finally turned the corner, I sprinted to my room on the pads of my feet.

I enacted one last search. The doll was definitely gone. Zash was lying—it was excellent acting. But a Bolshevik would lie only if he wanted to keep the item himself. I returned to the entryway where the servants hustled back and forth, packing belongings for themselves and whatever else they figured we might need.

Dr. Botkin helped Alexei into his thick officer's coat with its double-breasted gold buttons. It hung on him like a blanket. Alexei wore his tsarevich soldier uniform, standing tall with his papakha hat at a little jaunt on his head. He could not walk yet, only stand. Dark rings outlined his large eyes and painted his face like porthole windows in a white ship's hull.

Alexei wouldn't be able to stand for long, but at least he was showing his strength to the soldiers before we bid them all farewell. Papa would be proud.

My stomach lurched. We were mere minutes away from leaving and I'd yet to locate the doll. I would *not* lose this match!

I gathered an armful of towels and marched down to the soldiers' quarters, passing Olga as she tucked a sewing kit into her valise. "Nastya, what are you *doing*? Get your coat on!"

"In a moment!" I left the entry and hurried down the hall. Only two Bolsheviks remained in their quarters, tightening their belts and moving soggy egg feet around in their slimy boots. "I brought towels," I chirped.

One rolled his eyes and swept past me. The other snatched a towel and wiped his foot off before he pushed it into his boot, without so much as a thank-you. As he left he ground out a single word. "Shvibzik."

It wasn't said in the sweet nickname way my family said it. But it made me grin all the same. They knew I'd put the eggs in their boots. Served them right. If they couldn't even detect raw eggs in their boots, how could they protect the Russian people?

I dumped the towels on the ground once the room was empty and hurried to Zash's space. His belongings sat neatly on his cot—a folded bedroll beneath a smooth, buckled knapsack and a coat beside it.

This was more than an organized soldier. This was a soldier ready to leave. He was joining us on the train. I could search his belongings then. It took incredible willpower not to tear into his knapsack, but the best imps were the patient ones. Still, I patted it down and squeezed all the fat areas to see if there were any hard pieces in there. None of them felt round, but the doll was so small he could have snuck it into a sock.

Then I squeezed and met something firm. I glanced back toward the door, my senses on high alert. I couldn't risk losing the doll.

I unlatched the straps holding the fat pack together. Then I placed one hand on the outside where I'd first felt the hard item and sent my free hand through the bag's opening. I wove it carefully through the folded fabrics and past a small notebook. The doll was, indeed, wrapped in an extra set of socks. I pushed them aside with my nimble fingers until I finally felt smooth wood. I curled my fingers around the doll and pulled it out ever so carefully, pausing to listen toward the doorway.

Still no sounds.

Finally, I yanked my hand out with a relieved exhale. I'd done it. I'd retrieved the—

"No," I breathed, turning the item over in my hand. Brown and silver paint, a fat sphere, and a pointed stopper.

It wasn't the doll.

It was a bottle of . . . cologne? Perfume? I popped out the stopper and smelled. No scent, but the sphere weighed down my hand with its sloshing contents. I dipped a pinky in and met liquid. When I pulled it out, my breath caught.

Spell ink. Glistening, silvery-rainbow spell ink.

What was a *Bolshevik* doing with a bottle of spell ink in his pack? Spell mastery was illegal! If this had been an item found during the search, he would have turned it in to Yurovsky. Either he found it and kept it for himself, or he had brought it with him.

But Bolsheviks were hunting and murdering spell masters. This made no sense.

I gripped the traitorous bottle. It wasn't the Matryoshka doll, but at least it was something I wanted. Something I *needed* so I could help Alexei. Yet I was an imp. Not a thief. And no matter how badly I wanted this spell ink, I could not allow myself to sink so low as to steal it.

I was a Romanov. And I would represent that name honorably until my dying day.

I shoved the stopper back in and plunged the bottle back into the pack, making sure it returned to roughly the same location. I buckled the flaps and angled the pack against the end of the bed as I'd found it.

I left the room, glad I hadn't put an egg in Zash's boot. It had been awkward peering at his sleeping face last night to make sure the boots belonged to him, but if he thought I was an ally—or even just a flirt—he might show my family kindness. And if he didn't . . . I now had blackmail.

My shoes clipped up the hall. I knew who I'd need to search next. If Zash did not have the doll, that meant he must have turned it in to Yurovsky.

The entryway was a flutter of madness. People lugging suitcases, servants asking the Bolsheviks to help, Bolsheviks resisting, Yurovsky directing the chaos, and only half of the crowd listening to him. The front door hung open, letting in the cold. It was raining outside.

Yurovsky wore his coat, a shoulder satchel, and a firearm—enough attire to see us to the train station but not enough for him to travel along the spine of Russia with us. I located his quarters—a room to himself with hardly more than a water pitcher in it. His belongings lay folded but not packed.

I ran to them, stilling the thunder of my heart. He wouldn't come in here. Not right now, at least. I tore through his belongings, unfolding every shirt, turning out every sock, bending a fingernail on another pocket watch, slicing my thumb on the thin pages of a journal.

No doll.

No doll.

No doll.

For the first time I considered the fact I might fail. I might fail Papa. I might fail my family. Papa said the doll could be our salvation. Without it, we could perish.

I stuffed Yurovsky's belongings back into the pack as panic burned behind my eyes. No. No. No. Where was it? Who took it?

I had no new ideas.

I reentered the main room with the weight of defeat. I couldn't meet Yurovsky's eyes. Zash loaded our items onto the carriage that would take us to the train station in Tyumen. My heart threatened to still with the memory that we were going to Ekaterinburg. The city between familiar Russia and savage Russia. Nestled in the Ural Mountains and home to the most bitter Russians.

Impossible to be home to us.

I donned my long grey coat that had seen me from St. Petersburg to Tobolsk and would now see me to Ekaterinburg. I knotted the tie around the middle until it pinched and stoppered my emotions. Olga flitted about, searching for any loose items we were forgetting. Did she see all the threads of life we were leaving behind? The piles of memories we'd never revisit? The sheen of hope we were abandoning?

Her gaze landed on me and her eyes lost the anxious busyness and took on a soft tone. She lifted her hand, and suddenly I felt like the little sister. The small one who stood in a crowd, lost. A failure. I stumbled forward and took her hand, wanting to tell her I'd let Papa down but unable to own that fact yet.

"The bond of our hearts—" she whispered.

"—spans miles, memory, and time," I finished.

We moved past Yurovsky to the tarantass—a rustic, springless carriage meant to take us to the station. His hands rested in a way to intimidate—one on the holstered pistol, the other on the strap of his small satchel that held the orders to send us to Ekaterinburg. He drew out his pocket watch, tracking the seconds to make sure we would be exiled on time.

Tatiana entered the carriage with Dr. Botkin and Kharitonov—her own guard of Bolsheviks filling in the extra spaces in the carriage. We wore our wool kubanka hats and ducked our heads against the downpour.

My hand moved to my stomach, to press down the feelings of sorrow and to touch the bump of jewels. To remind myself that I was defying the Bolsheviks with every step. Olga's fingers twined the locket at her throat that held a photo of a soldier she'd mended during the war and fallen in love with. Alexei already sat in the carriage clutching his box of toy soldiers as though they were his last loyal army.

We were clinging to the memories—the good ones. The small comforts and victories.

As we climbed into the carriage and settled side by side, close enough to form a human blanket with Alexei across from us underneath a real blanket, I allowed my gaze to follow Yurovsky as he hoisted himself onto the seat with the driver, the collar of his coat turned up tall to block the rain.

My mind buzzed as it clicked clues together.

Olga held her necklace to check its safety. Alexei held his soldiers to keep them secure in his lap. I pressed my palm against the corset to check the jewels. And Yurovsky . . . Yurovsky had held his satchel the same way we did—as though *it* held something valuable.

Like a magical Matryoshka doll.

The carriage lurched to a start. My sorrow fled. Yurovsky moved his hand to the small bar at the edge of his seat for balance, leaving his satchel loose. It swung back and forth with the movement of the uncomfortable trundle through Tobolsk, sliding against the rain-slicked carriage side. He might lift it onto his lap at any moment.

I pushed at the rusty window lock with my knuckles. It came free and the carriage window dropped with a *clunk*.

"Nastya." Olga reached for me, but I ignored her. Hesitance

had cost too many imps their perfect opportunities. I would not hesitate.

For Papa.

For my family.

And, to be frank, for my own satisfaction in beating the enemy.

I reached for the satchel, but it was too far, so I pushed the front half of my body through the window. The wind nearly blew my hat off, so I tossed it back into the carriage. Rain pelted my face, its loud splatter drowning out even the splash of horses' hooves in the mud. Olga tugged at my clothes to pull me back in. But then I felt Alexei's gentle hand on my knee. Some people supported with their physical strength. Others supported with their emotions. Alexei's hand was the latter, steadying me with his heart since he couldn't steady me with his strength. I could almost picture him saying, "Imagine this . . . Nastya defeated the Bolshevik commandant at his own game."

With one hand I lifted Yurovsky's satchel so when I inserted my other hand, it wouldn't pull against his shoulder. I stayed as flat against the carriage as I could, so as not to alert his peripheral. The muscles in my abdomen burned and pinched against the stiff corset. I took advantage of the stiffness and used it for balance.

I picked at the tie. We hit a bump in the road and I plunged my hand into the satchel. My fingers searched, groping for the smooth, round piece of wood. They encountered papers, then something sharp, but did not recoil. Olga was pinching my leg now, too nervous to scream my name. Alexei's grip had strengthened, revealing his fear.

Then a kiss of wood on flesh.

My fingers wrapped around the small body. I wanted to pull it free and duck back into the carriage, but this was false victory. It would be an amateur move to forget caution now. In every prank, in every move of stealth, there are two victories: the false and the true. The first and then the final. The victory of achieving your desired goal, but then the true victory of getting away with it.

Impatience was the grim reaper of all true victories.

So I paused. I forced my tired arm to lift the satchel even higher, removing any tug or weight from Yurovsky's body. Then I slid the doll carefully out of the satchel. I slipped it up my sleeve with two fingers and then tied the satchel shut again.

By this point my body was trembling and icy, Olga was sobbing, and Alexei's hand clawed at my knee. I lowered the satchel slowly until it rested against the carriage once more. Then I ducked inside, my auburn hair filling the sitting space like a sopping pet. Joy moved from Alexei's lap and licked the rainwater from my cheek.

I slid the window back up, latched it, and checked my sleeve. The doll bulged against the seams.

I'd done it.

I'd located and retrieved the doll from the enemy.

I lifted my eyes to Alexei. He stared at me, his own wide and wondering, but he didn't ask. Olga remained silent with her handkerchief pressed against her face. We didn't speak, didn't explain.

Alexei knew I had a purpose to my mischief. Olga had simply given up on trying to scold me.

But this time . . . this time I think she'd have been proud. Still, I didn't tell them about the doll. If Papa had wanted them to know, he would have included them.

The bumpy ride pained Alexei more than the agonizing hours lying in bed. Olga and I spent most of the ride trying to massage his legs. All three of us exhaled relief when we arrived at the Tyumen train station. I let them exit the carriage first, then transferred the doll from my sleeve to the small space between my bosoms. I was not so endowed that my cleavage would fully conceal the item, but with my coat on no one could tell unless they embraced me. And I did not plan to embrace anyone. Least of all Yurovsky.

He made us all load our own belongings onto Special Train No. 8. We Romanov girls and Alexei were placed into a dirty third-class carriage with a group of Bolsheviks. Nothing like our Imperial Train.

Our servants and friends were loaded into the goods wagon and forced to sit on crude wooden benches. Tatiana protested once. The Bolsheviks didn't let her protest a second time.

I sat by the window, my heartbeat hammering the wood of the Matryoshka doll. I expected Yurovsky's hand to slip into his satchel at any moment. To notice the loss. To call a halt to our train.

"Come on," I urged the trembling locomotive. *"Bystro, bystro."*

The engine belched forth a warning whistle.

A lurch.

We inched away from the station. I could barely breathe. Yurovsky stood on the platform, arms folded, watching our departure. He would notice the lightness of his satchel soon enough. And he would know it was me when he saw his ransacked room. So when the train picked up speed and my window passed him by and his eyes met mine . . .

I winked.

4

I clung to the victory of retrieving the Matryoshka doll, wanting for the moment to think backward and not forward. But eventually my situation caught up with me. I could avoid the inevitable no longer.

Exile.

I would allow myself one day. One day to mourn the smothered hope for a quiet life, or the pardon from a trial, or the future of spell mastery.

I sat by the window, propped my chin on my hand, and unbuttoned my heart. The blurred countryside flowed in, halting my breath. It was too much—to watch the trees and fields and villages leave my view forever. Each trunk, each leaf, each pane of glass one breath farther from home. One breath closer to the unknown.

I felt, instead, that we were sitting still and the world spun beneath me. Leaving me behind and abandoning me to my fate. *Farewell, Grand Duchess Anastasia.*

Once the sun set, I rebuttoned my heart and closed the drapes. My new focus turned forward. I'd not mourn the lost good memories—I would apply them to my heart as a poultice every time it ached. That was what positive moments were for—to help heal the wounds of the future. As long as we chose to remember them.

Days later, we finally pulled into the Ekaterinburg station. My spirit hung like a soggy garment on a drooping clothesline. The train sat in the station for almost twenty hours. It was cold and frosty, and snow covered the ground. I shivered down to my very marrow until morning finally came.

Bolsheviks collected us, but they did not allow the kind soldiers from Tobolsk off the train. The Ekaterinburg Bolsheviks wore leather jackets and all carried weapons. I checked the cloth buttons on my dark coat to make sure each was fastened. The downpour still got through.

Each of us girls carried our own heavy valises across the muddy road to the open-carriage droshkies. Tatiana had her suitcase in one hand and her black French bulldog, Ortipo, under the other arm. Poor pup looked half-squished, half-drenched. One of our servants—a sailor named Nagorny—carefully carried Alexei to a droshky.

Mud soaked into my valenki boots, despite their leather soles, but I didn't complain and I didn't ask for help. A few people had gathered at the station to gawk at us. Their cold curiosity added to the frigidity in the air, but nothing could dispel our eagerness and excitement to see our parents. I couldn't restrain my smile even beneath absurd weather conditions.

I caught the gaze of one man—a bold revolutionary. But the longer he stared, the more his attempted indifference melted into something else. Pity? Guilt? His hand seemed half-raised, as though to wave or even reach for us. But then, as if struck by intense shame, he melted into the shadows.

The Bolsheviks shoved us into the droshkies. Most of the carriages were open with one long bench seat for passengers, but Alexei, Olga, Tatiana, and I were put in a covered droshky. Zash climbed in with us. I had not interacted with him on the train since he'd been in a different compartment.

He didn't have his pack with him. Did it still hold the spell ink?

Before the door closed, I saw only Dr. Botkin and Kharitonov through the downpour, climbing into an open droshky of their own. Nagorny got two steps out of the train carriage, his hand raised in a farewell, before a Bolshevik shoved him out of sight.

"Wait, what of our other servants? Our friends?" I asked.

"They're not joining you." Zash didn't meet our eyes.

"What?" Alexei lurched toward the window. "Wait! May we say farewell?"

The droshky trundled forward and Zash shut the door. "I am sorry." As though to cement the situation, he pulled the drapes shut.

Five sets of lungs released quickened breaths, mixing in the tiny space. I couldn't bring myself to inhale again. There was no air. There was no light. I gripped the curtain fabric with a shuddering breath like a lifeline, pulling it to let in a stream of dim light, but Zash grabbed my fist with his own.

He was gentle but firm, prying my fingers off. "It is for your safety."

"Since when do Bolsheviks care about our safety?"

He straightened the curtain. "Since our commandant ordered us to. Ekaterinburg is not pleased to have you. It is best if you are not seen by any other locals. It could incite a lynching."

I pressed back into the old cushions of the carriage seat and closed my eyes. In Tobolsk the people had brought us gifts and smiles and hope. But Ekaterinburg was all Bolsheviks and revolutionaries.

Alexei slipped his hand into mine. I wanted to press it to my heart, but he needed assurance as well as I. "How long to our new lodging?" How long to Papa? Maria? Mamma?

"I expect it is half an hour to the Ipatiev House."

"Who is Ipatiev?"

Zash shrugged. "The man who owned the house before the Ekaterinburg Soviet claimed it for your exile."

How typical of the Bolsheviks to steal a person's home for their purposes.

The half hour was the longest of my life. With no light and no fresh air, I felt buried. Alexei's breathing quickened like a young bird's. He hadn't handled the journey well, physically. Emotionally, however, he'd maintained a soldier's resolve. Mamma would be heartbroken to see his frail state. But soon he would be in a bed and a stable place . . . for as long as the Bolsheviks would allow us to stay.

To live.

I pressed a hand to the Matryoshka doll still shoved in my jewel-lined corset. We would survive. I had the key.

Zash peeked out of the curtains and then drew one open. The splash of light splitting the storm clouds rebounded off the snow and stung my eyes, but I gulped it in. "Here it is." He pointed.

The carriage passed through a palisade of sawed timber and telegraph poles, about twelve feet in height. The white stucco walls of the Ipatiev House, with carved doors and window frames, were classic Russian style. It was significantly smaller than the governor's house in Tobolsk. Linden trees shaded parts of the house and street, but a stiff rotation of guards tainted its natural loveliness.

We rolled to the entrance at 49 Voznesensky Prospekt. The heavy wooden courtyard doors slammed shut behind us. We had entered a fortress.

No one rushed out of the house to greet us. Instead, Zash led us in one at a time. First Olga went, then Tatiana, then it was my turn. Zash held open the door and took my upper arm to "lead" me into the house whether or not I wanted it. I would have dragged him behind me in my haste had I the strength.

We entered through a sentry of guards and then the door. Despite the chill outside, the house brought an immediate stuffiness. It seemed too dark, and I couldn't place the reason until I passed a window. I couldn't see out—the glass had been whitewashed.

A Bolshevik soldier patted me down. He was extremely thorough but avoided the bosom area, as was appropriate. Ah, the power of being a woman.

He straightened and looked me in the eye. "We received a telegram that you stole a magical item from Commandant Yurovsky in Tobolsk."

My jaw dropped as my tired and cold mind scrambled for a response. "Stole? Magical item? I don't know what he's talking about. I found one of my babushka's dolls with his belongings. It was sentimental to me."

"What happened to it?"

I thrust emotion into my voice. "The guards took it away when I was on the train."

"Which guard?"

"How should I know? One dressed as a Bolshevik."

His mouth thinned. "Your belongings will be searched thoroughly."

I swallowed. Nodded. Compliant. "Of course. Do what you must." Would they search the soldiers' packs? Zash's?

He shoved me onward and relief poured through my aching

bones. Yurovsky had telegrammed. He knew. But did he know what the doll held? Even *I* didn't know.

I never should have winked at him.

I stumbled up a set of narrow stairs, across a landing that smelled strongly of body odor, and finally entered a sitting room filled with voices. I saw first more whitewashed windows and how they made the house feel full of steam. Then a mahogany piano, a writing desk, and landscape art hanging on the papered walls.

Finally, I saw Papa.

He stepped out of an embrace with Tatiana and stood taller at the sight of me. I stumbled to him, flinging myself into his strong arms. He held me so tight, so securely, I felt as though I would never despair again.

"My little shvibzik," he muttered. I planted kisses all over his face—on his brow, his cheeks, his prickly mustache. My sweet, sweet papa.

Another set of arms embraced me and I moved to Mamma. I'd barely kissed her cheek when a squeal sent a burly bundle of delight crashing into me.

"Maria!" I exclaimed.

She felt thinner than three weeks ago, but her face glowed with joy. She grabbed both my hands and hopped up and down. "They told us only a couple hours ago that you were arriving! Oh, Nastya, what a time it has been."

Her face transformed from joy to weeping in seconds. This must have been terrible for her. To be trapped in this painted house with high walls around it, not knowing we were coming. Why did the Bolsheviks not tell them sooner? Didn't she receive my letter?

Alexei came in last, walking on his own with a disjointed, stumbling gait. He looked ready to fall at any moment. Papa strode across the room and swept his son into his arms. He embraced Alexei gently. Mamma hurried over, muttering, "Oh, my sweet boy."

Neither mentioned how much smaller he'd gotten since they last saw him.

"I wanted to walk in by my own strength," Alexei mumbled.

"Of course," Papa said.

And here we were, together again. A family ready to face whatever the Bolsheviks deemed "exile."

A middle-aged man with fair hair and a tiny mustache entered the room. He swayed a bit on his feet and wore a cavalry sword at his side. "I'm Commannnnant Avdeev." Definitely tipsy.

So *this* was our new authority . . . and the new target of my mischief.

He showed us our quarters. There wasn't much to see. Our group consisted only of my family, Dr. Botkin, Anna the maid, Trupp the manservant, and Kharitonov the cook. Our friends, committed to exile with us. Trupp brought Alexei's spaniel and Tatiana's two dogs. After his entrance, the house was closed up, but nothing could stop up our delight in reunion.

Our small crew of people and pups was confined to five interconnecting rooms with a bathroom on the landing and a small kitchen at the far end. The staircase was shut off by a locked doorway. We'd never been enclosed in quarters this small. Surely they didn't mean for us to stay in these five rooms throughout the days.

Avdeev left us to settle in, but we soon heard that he sent away all the kind, loyal soldiers who had been left on the train. Back to Tobolsk? To prison? We didn't know.

The Bolsheviks from Tobolsk stayed, joining those already at the Ipatiev House. They all seemed angry with us.

Commandant Avdeev and his aides had access to our rooms

any time they desired. Had Avdeev entered at that moment, he would have found us all gathered in the sitting room, kneeling together beneath the electric Italian glass chandelier with Papa leading us in prayer. More tears came from our eyes than words from our mouths. Papa always said that tears were the most fervent prayers, so I let them flow.

"We must show kindness to the soldiers," Papa entreated us. "Every day, show them forgiveness. We are a reflection of *Iisus*, and he was rejected by his own people just as we are. Love. Forgive." He kissed each of us on the forehead.

I was determined to be as he asked. To be humble. To be forgiving. To always hold to hope. We bid each other good night.

Papa carried Alexei to the small room designated for him toward the back of the house. It was a luxury in this tight space, yet I suspected Alexei did not wish to sleep alone just as I didn't. Through the open doorway, he looked over Papa's shoulder back at me. I forced a brave smile.

"I will dress on my own," Alexei announced to Papa.

Papa nodded and set him on his feet to change into sleeping clothes. Alexei was determined to prove he was healing and he was strong. But as he climbed into his bed, his socked foot slipped and he landed hard on his knee against the wood floor. He gasped at the impact and I was the first at his side. "Oh, Alexei."

He'd surely bruised it, and his hemophilia would keep that blood in his joints, sending pain for weeks. It would swell and keep him from walking.

Papa and I lifted him into his bed. Alexei grimaced and Mamma was in the room within seconds, fluffing his pillow. She swept me aside and Alexei gripped her hand. I left them alone. I let her care for him.

My sisters and I were to share a room. Not much furniture filled the space—a simple table, some chairs, and a looking glass on a stand. I rather liked the light floral wallpaper decorating the space. One could imagine we were stepping into a garden.

An oriental rug covered most of the linoleum flooring, upon which Olga, Tatiana, and Maria had created a pile of coats and blankets since our portable camp beds had not yet arrived from Tobolsk. I tucked myself into the nest, craving the press of their bodies and the security of family.

All night, I heard Alexei's moans of pain.

All night, Mamma stayed awake and held his hand.

All night, I cried.

I knew Iisus' heart heard me. And I was certain the fervency of my tear-prayers would surely break it.

5

MAY 24

Everyone woke at sunrise—not because we were rested and certainly not from the sun shining, for it couldn't penetrate the whitewash. We woke because we were together again. It was better than any birthday or Easter morning. We also knew that rhythm was a fierce weapon against despair.

Alexei stayed in bed, his knee already swollen to twice its size. Dr. Botkin bent over him with his tiny satchel of medicines. They wouldn't be enough. He needed healing spells. But Alexei's joy at being with Mamma and Papa again provided a small balm for his suffering.

This morning my mind was no longer in despair. Instead, my thoughts lingered on the bruise against my sternum. The press of a figure-eight piece of wood I'd kept on my person since Tobolsk.

I hurried into the main room where Papa sat in a chair beside a large potted palm, reading a newspaper. *"Dobroye utra,* Papa." Oh, how nice it was to say that again.

He flopped a corner of the paper down. "Good morning, Nastya." I kissed his cheek and then took a breath to speak, but Papa spoke first. Swiftly. "You should spend the day with Maria. She has missed you dreadfully."

I closed my mouth, reading his dismissal. His warning. Then I noticed the doors to the landing—and to Commandant Avdeev's office—were propped open. I picked up the hint and joined in so no pauses in conversation would implicate me. "Of course! I've missed her, too."

If I singled out Papa on the first day, that would rouse suspicion. Papa had been here for a month, which meant he had spent that time reading the soldiers and the commandant. He would let me know when it was safe to speak with him alone. I was much more used to the long corridors and private spaces in Tobolsk.

I needed to forget everything I knew. Everything I'd been accustomed to.

This was different. This was exile.

But the doll burned against my skin. I wanted to know when to use it. What it meant. What it contained. I wanted answers. Knowledge. But Papa asked for my patience without speaking a word. So I spent the day with Maria.

We breakfasted in the dining room, easily the nicest room in our quarters with enormous oak doors opening to a parquet floor and a room filled with dark, heavy furniture upholstered in leather. Maria practically pasted herself to my side. When I'd been stuck in Tobolsk, at least I had the companionship of my siblings. But poor Maria had no friends with her when she came to Ekaterinburg.

We were allowed outside after lunch, and we practically fled the house into the fresh air. Considering we had grown up more outdoors than indoors—boating, foraging, gardening—the Ipatiev House felt like a stifling box. And this was only the first day.

"I don't know how I shall bear being in that house," I confided to Maria.

She hooked her arm around mine and we took in the measly garden. It was barely a patch of grass with a few trees. Ninety paces long at most. I tried to be thankful and resisted comparing it to the governor's house in Tobolsk—which had still paled to the rolling grounds of the Alexander Palace. It had been so long since I'd been at the palace that the idea touched my memory like a different lifetime.

"They painted the windows only a week ago." Maria set a brisk pace and I matched it. I didn't know how long the commandant would allow us to remain outside, so we needed to get our exercise in while we could.

"Why?"

"Our arrival was supposed to be a secret, but when we got here there were riots at the station. We had to bypass it and then come to the house via a long road route. Only a couple weeks ago, our presence was announced in the *Ural'skiy Rabochiy* paper. After that, they painted the windows and increased the guards. I think maybe they're afraid we'll signal for help."

The dogs ran in circles—Tatiana sat on the grass tossing a ball to her two pups. But Alexei's sweet spaniel would have none of it. Joy sat by the door, wagging her tail in the sunshine and longing for her master.

"Poor Alexei," Maria murmured as we passed Joy. "If only we could bring sunshine back in to him."

"As if the guards would allow it. They seem stiffer than their own vodka bottles." Three Bolsheviks stood out in the garden, watching us. One in particular seemed to follow Maria's and my path with his gaze. I resisted the urge to check and make sure the Matryoshka doll was secure.

"Not *all* of them." A glimmer of sunlight entered Maria's tone. "They have not been as receptive as the soldiers in Tobolsk, but they are still good men. Papa says they are only trying to serve their country. The problem is, their country has branded us as enemies. That's not our fault. That's not the Bolshevik soldiers' fault."

I knew what Papa said. But Maria seemed particularly passionate. And when her eyes met those of the guard who watched us so closely, I knew why. Maria had been here a full month. And that soldier had a kind face. She'd found a friend in the only place she could.

Zash entered the garden wearing a freshly washed uniform and a rigid spine. He caught my gaze, but then he spotted the friendly Bolshevik. Zash's face broke into a wild grin and he spread his arms wide. "Ivan!"

He and Ivan crossed the garden to meet in a firm handshake. How did they know each other? Was Zash from Ekaterinburg?

Maria watched the exchange with a dreamy expression. I nudged her. "Now that you mention it, some of the guards out here seem particularly pleasant to look at."

Maria sighed. "His name is Ivan."

His name is Zash, I replied in my head.

Maria sounded weary. The friendships here must not have been easy to build. Nothing was more exhausting than putting forth kindness and receiving indifference in return. I waggled my eyebrows. "Have you broken out your beaded gown yet? That would fell all the Bolsheviks in one swish."

She lifted her chin in a mock sort of snootiness. "My stunning figure would be too good a death for them."

I laughed. She laughed. Neither acknowledged the tears that came with it.

"I've missed you," we both said.

The Bolsheviks watched us the way a wolverine stakes out a vole hole. Without blinking. Without softening. This went on for several days. It was said a wolverine could never be tamed. I suspected this was also the case for Bolsheviks.

"It's likely due to the change in rhythm and increase in guards," Maria said when I shared my thoughts. "They now have twelve enemies to guard instead of just Papa, Mamma, and me."

Due to their vigilant supervision, there was never a good time to speak with Papa alone. So I kept the Matryoshka doll solidly beneath my corset and busied myself with other things, like sending the guards kind smiles as Papa encouraged us to do. Like writing letters to friends back home that likely never got mailed. Like playing cards and dominoes with Maria and beating her soundly every time.

I read Alexei story after story, making all the voices and silly faces. I pretended not to notice the grimaces brought on by his swollen knee. We played with his toy soldiers, setting them up as the Red Army Bolsheviks versus the White Army loyalists.

I read my German book on spell mastery cover to cover but never once found info about how to make ink. Every day, Alexei seemed frailer. Dr. Botkin said that Alexei had lost fourteen pounds in the past month. Our current rations were not likely to help him regain that weight. Not for the first time, I snuck a peek at the Matryoshka doll. Nothing had changed. Perhaps I would have to smash it to release the spell.

Meanwhile, a bottle of spell ink was sitting, untouched, in Zash's pack. I started to wish I'd stolen it. The Bolsheviks had stolen our lives from us. It would have been a fair exchange. Yet Zash had it for a reason. I wanted to know that reason. Perhaps he'd share some. I wasn't too prideful to ask. I couldn't bear to watch Alexei wrestle with the pain, deprived of all sunlight.

"Have you seen any spells being used or hidden?" I asked Maria nonchalantly as we finished up a card game.

"Don't get involved in spell mastery, Nastya. Not here."

I shuffled. "It's for Alexei. For his knee." And for my sanity.

"I've seen nothing. But if there are any spell items, they'd probably be in Avdeev's office. Sometimes there are raids in the city and items are stored here."

In the late afternoon I joined the doctor as he tended to Alexei's knee. "Dr. Botkin, you used to use spells for healing, didn't you?"

He pressed gently on the swelling in Alexei's joints. Alexei hissed. "Only ones I could purchase. I never made them."

"Did you never ask how spell masters obtained their spell ink? How they made it?"

"Of course I asked. But those questions need to leave our minds now. The age of spell masters is over."

What a dull response. Life as a curious imp was *far* more exciting. "What's happening to the spell masters now? Are they . . . stopping their work?"

"The Bolsheviks are hunting them. Forcing them to either serve Lenin or die."

"What is Lenin going to do with them?"

"He's promised to make spells accessible to everyone. Someday."

I tilted my head. "That doesn't sound so terrible."

"It sounds like a good solution, *da*? Simple. Equal. But if the spells become free and distributed equally, who pays the spell masters? How do they live? How do they eat?"

The question was a challenge. Dr. Botkin, always the teacher. "Can they . . . use spells to provide for their needs?"

"Spells do not provide tangible resources. And the masters cannot sell them since the Soviet government is the ultimate distributor."

I started to see his point. "So the government will provide spell masters with food. But then . . . if the spell masters stop working, the new system fails. And in the end there is still one group of people—the Soviet leaders—who decide who gets what. Those who do not want to work take advantage of the system and those who work harder receive no gain for their diligence."

I was only sixteen and *I* could see the cracks in the proposed system the people claimed they wanted. "The spell masters must see this flaw."

"They do. And that is why Bolsheviks are hunting them."

"Murdering them," I grumbled. Like they'd done with Rasputin. "Perhaps the masters will rebel. Maybe they'll join the White Army and come rescue us." And maybe I could join them.

"Let's not discuss such dangerous topics while the tsarevich is still healing."

"The *tsarevich* is part of this conversation, too." Alexei folded his arms. "And just because I'm stuck in bed doesn't mean I'm a doughbrain. I like Nastya's idea."

Dr. Botkin heaved a sigh, but the crinkles at the corners of his eyes gave him away. "Do not strain yourself, Tsarevich." He pulled the bedsheet over Alexei's legs. "You must rest your knee even if you begin to feel better."

"I have spent more time resting than a corpse in its coffin. I'll be careful, Doctor, but I will do as I please."

"As usual," Dr. Botkin muttered, exiting the room, leaving Alexei and me with our thoughts.

"I wish there was some spell that could lead the White Army to us." Alexei toyed with one of his small metal soldiers.

The White Army was made of loyalists—those who wanted Papa back on the Russian throne. Those who knew Mamma wasn't brainwashed by Rasputin. Those who knew we loved our people. They wanted to save spell masters.

I didn't know how strong in numbers the White Army was, but they gave us hope. They were strong enough to force the Bolsheviks to hide us in exile. I brushed my fingers over the lump in my corset. "Perhaps there is a spell like that."

"I may not have sat in on all the conversations you and Rasputin had, but even *I* know such a spell is beyond you."

I sniffed. "What a doubter you are today. Have you learned nothing from my exploits?"

"I've learned that you're very good at sneaking eggs in soldiers' boots."

I flipped one of his toy soldiers in the air, then caught it right side up. "The White Army will find us, Alexei. Somehow . . . I'll help them." *And somehow I'll help* you.

I crossed the room to stand by the painted window as though I'd be able to see the sky and gauge the weather. I scraped at the glass with a fingernail, but the whitewash was on the outside. I let my eyes drift to the *fortochka* at the top of the window—a tiny ventilator window used mainly in winter. I glanced back at Alexei and then the door. No soldiers in sight. As casually as possible, I reached up and undid the latch on the fortochka.

"Nastya . . ."

"*Tishe.*" I pushed the fortochka open. It crackled, breaking through the messy whitewash that had dried over the outer edges. "You need fresh air."

A tiny puff of air made its way to my face, sending my heart wings aflutter. I breathed deep and cracked it a bit more so I could see the view below. My eyes took in the scene like an inhale of sweet spring. I caught the glimpse of the golden-domed skyline, glistening like jewels of promise beneath the sun. But the grandeur was interrupted by gunshots in the heart of the city. Controlled shots. Executions.

I could see over the palisade. Voznesensky Prospekt stretched out before me—wide and cobbled. No one walked along the main road through Ekaterinburg, but I could imagine life and freedom and bustle along that cold, packed street.

I imagined the White Army marching up the hill, climbing the palisade, and busting the door open. Taking us away to safety. To a new life.

I allowed myself only a few seconds, then slid away from the window. Best not to linger. I was in that dreamy middle ground where opening the fortochka was not yet forbidden so I could claim ignorance. But once it *was* forbidden, I'd be hard-pressed to open it again without getting punished.

Or shot.

6

MAY 31

"Death to the tyrant!"

"Hang them!"

"Drown him in the lake!"

I couldn't see through the whitewashed windows, but the shouts of the Russian people peeled away my resolve like the skinning of a potato. Our belongings had arrived from Tobolsk on the train yesterday. We were not allowed to see them until they were thoroughly inspected, pilfered, sold off, inspected again, stored in the outhouse, then inspected again.

"Those poor people." Tatiana stood at the window, listening to the cries. "They ought to have whatever they wish from our valuables."

"Whatever they wish?" Mamma lowered one of her hands from stopping up her ears. "Your cots and linens are in those trunks. And what of the tableware from the Alexander Palace or your papa's bath salts?"

"You truly think the commandant will allow us to use those

things?" Olga asked. "He already moved the piano into his office. He took our gramophone. He isn't going to let you keep your English eau de cologne, Mamma."

"It is not his to take!"

"Everything we have is his to take," I muttered.

Tatiana smoothed the wrinkles from her simple worn frock. "The people should have it."

"And what would they do with it?" Mamma huffed. "Pawn it off! They're not going to *use* it. Besides, they've elected their Soviet government that is supposed to make those decisions *for* them. They've sold their freedom."

Papa entered the sitting room from the yellow-wallpapered bedroom he and Mamma shared. His very presence carried an air of humility. "The Soviet government was not elected by the people. You've heard the gunshots every few days. Each one signifies the death of a Russian citizen who didn't comply with Bolshevik demands."

I'd heard gunshots. Was that really what instigated them?

"They are in need," Papa said. "Though we are no longer their tsar or royal family, their needs must always be our concern." He carried his daily Ekaterinburg newspaper to what had quickly become "Papa's chair" near the biggest whitewashed window and sat down to read.

Undeterred, Mamma asked, "What of my medical kit? If Alexei gets any worse, we will need what is left of our morphine supply." Her hand drifted to her head. Alexei wasn't the only one who needed—or used—the morphine. Mamma's headaches and weak heart were equally as crippling as his hemophilia.

"We may be exiled, but we can still make requests." Papa opened the paper and read it as calmly as he'd spoken.

I wished I could keep my peace the way he did. It was as though he bore no animosity. I tried to be like him, but sometimes I felt as though a small ball of hate lurked in the back corner of my heart—waiting to spring out and consume me.

Mamma returned to Alexei's room. Tatiana and Maria returned to the pups, and Olga returned to her mending—the only entertainment she had in this prison of ours.

Papa and I were alone.

With the Bolshevik soldiers busy dealing with the angry people and sifting through our belongings, an opportunity finally rested before me. Was it . . . time?

I watched Papa read his paper. Did the same turmoil exist inside his chest? He was too calm to show it. I was too stubborn to show it.

Seeing his form steadied my fire—his mustache quirked at an angle while he contemplated the contents of the paper, his legs crossed the way they always were when I would find him reading in the library. We were together again.

He finally looked up, and his mustache wiggled above the crack of a smile. His eyes went squinty and my heart melted all the way out my slippers. Papa folded the newspaper and patted his knee.

I was sixteen. An exiled princess. A child no longer. Still, I strode across the room and settled onto his lap, linking my arms around his neck. No amount of age, pride, or maturity could stop me from loving my papa with the heart of a little girl. I kissed his cheek and we stayed that way for several seconds, soaking in each other's company. Me wondering—for the hundredth time—how our beloved country could have missed his sweetness and demanded his abdication . . . and even his death.

"How is my little shvibzik?" Papa asked.

We'd exchanged little more than family talk since my arrival. *This* time was ours. "I put eggs in the Tobolsk soldiers' boots."

Papa dragged a hand down his face, but I still caught a glimmer of amusement. "What will I do with you?"

"You will let me stay on your lap and we will discuss the prose of Pushkin all the day long." My voice remained playful, but the slight tension in his posture told me he read the subtext.

I swelled with pride. Now he knew I'd succeeded in his mission for me. I wanted to tell him the entire story—the *why* behind the eggs in the soldiers' boots and how I hung out of a carriage and vexed Olga so severely that she burst into tears. I wanted to tell him how I winked at Yurovsky as we left the station with the Matryoshka doll snug in my corset.

But even without the details, he sought the story victory. "Did you bring any Pushkin novels with you?"

"Most of them are packed in our Tobolsk trunks that are being examined by the soldiers." I picked a piece of fluff off his linen shirt. "But I brought one with me on the train so I would not perish of boredom."

"That's my girl."

I plucked the newspaper from his hand, opened it, and blocked our faces from view of the hallway. "What now, Papa?" This, I whispered in German. From my repertoire of Russian, English, German, and French, I figured German was the language a common Bolshevik would least understand if he walked in during our conversation.

Papa peeked over the newspaper. I already knew no guards were in sight and the dogs were yapping, so we were safe. For the moment.

"You must keep it with you, Nastya. It was a gift to Mamma

and me when we were newly married from the greatest spell master, Vasily Dochkin. There used to be seven layers. Every layer holds a . . ."—he dropped his voice even lower—"spell."

"But how do you open them? And how many layers remain? And what is *in* them?" What made Papa claim it was our family's salvation?

"Each layer opens when the spell is ready. There are three remaining layers—"

"Citizen Nikolai!" Commandant Avdeev called from the doorway.

My brain startled with a zing, but my well-trained muscles kept my body still. My weight on Papa's lap kept *him* from startling too badly. Good thing I held the newspaper, because Papa would have crumpled it.

I lowered the paper casually, trying not to allow my disgust at Avdeev's informal title for Papa to show. "*Dobroye dyen*, Commandant," I said in Russian.

"Your trunks from Tobolsk shall be brought up shortly. I expect them organized by evening."

I hopped from Papa's lap, indignation singeing my tongue, but Papa rose and gave a little bow. "Of course, Commandant."

No. *No!* I wanted to push away Papa's humility, pull him straight again, and remind him how much more of a leader he was than tipsy Avdeev. But his humility was *why* he made such a good leader for our family. Wise. Humble. Papa.

An example to me.

I still didn't bow. I couldn't make myself. Not yet.

Avdeev held a bottle of liquor, possibly from one of our trunks. He stepped aside to let Zash and Ivan haul in a trunk of Papa's journals, then took the bottle with him to his office and shut the door.

Zash lowered the trunk carefully. His gaze burned my skin as he returned to the stairway for another trunk. It must have been difficult for him to load our belongings into our home of exile when it seemed like excess to a common soldier such as him.

But he didn't understand my life, needs, or upbringing.

And I didn't understand his.

But I intended to.

"Papa, how can you bow to Avdeev? You are above this man in so many ways—honor, kindness, bloodline . . ."

"Ah, but not stature. I am quite shorter than he is, you know." Papa kissed my forehead and went to open his trunk. "I remind myself that he is doing his duty. He is showing loyalty to the country and people I love. And that is something I can bow to."

Zash and Ivan returned with another trunk. The moment they disappeared down the stairs for a third, I knelt by Papa over his trunk. "Papa," I whispered. "When will the doll open for me? When do I use it?"

He thumbed through the spines of the journals but did not remove them. "Use it at the last possible moment."

"When is—?" I bit off my question as Zash returned with another trunk. Mamma entered the sitting room and directed them to the small kitchen. It took the remainder of the day for us to receive our belongings—or at least what was left of them. The Bolsheviks delivered barely half of what we'd originally packed. The rest, they kept for themselves.

JUNE 1

The next day Papa carried Alexei into the garden for the first time. Maria and I danced around him tossing little handfuls of yellow acacia flowers down upon him—bringing the garden to his lap. Joy tumbled among the lilacs, releasing what little pollen they held. Alexei sneezed. Winced. Then laughed.

I'd missed his laugh.

Mamma sat in her wheelchair, a broad-rimmed hat keeping the sun from beating upon her. It was stylish to be pale, but my sisters and I threw our faces to the sky and welcomed the tan. It painted our skin with freckles of freedom. Mamma lasted barely ten minutes before she had to retire due to her headaches. Olga went with her to read to her.

Better her than me. If I had a spell to heal Mamma's headaches, I would use it immediately. But since there was nothing to be done, I'd rather be outside while someone else tended to Mamma's discomfort. If I spent one second longer than necessary in that house, I feared suffocation.

Zash was one of the three soldiers on garden guard. Why did I always notice him? He muttered out of the side of his mouth with the guard Maria had her eye set on—Ivan. Since finding his friend, he seemed to look upon us with less loathing.

I allowed my stroll to take me past them so I could catch part of their conversation.

". . . surprised at these living conditions," Zash muttered.

Ivan nodded. "Wait until you've been here a month. It's terrible to watch."

I rounded the garden, unsure if Zash and Ivan were remarking on *our* living conditions or the soldiers' quarters. Maybe both. Maria chased Joy and ended up catching her right near the feet of Ivan. She stood slowly as Alexei called the spaniel back to him, leaving Maria with her Bolshevik.

Ivan brightened. Zash stiffened. I kept walking, observing. I liked that she'd found someone else who could bring her joy, but a twinge of warning pinched the back of my mind.

Commandant Avdeev entered the garden at a slight sway. He leaned against the outer wall, watching us with bloodshot eyes, but he did not order us inside. He didn't tell Maria and Ivan to stop talking. In fact, Papa struck up a conversation with Avdeev.

It was time I did the same with the Bolshevik soldiers. With Zash.

When I was just halfway across the garden, Maria spotted me and held out her hand. "Nastya, come here!"

I grinned and skipped to her side.

"This is Ivan." She laid a delicate hand on the sleeve of his Soviet uniform.

Ivan bowed cordially. "A pleasure to officially meet you." His eyes sparkled in sync with his bright smile.

Now *this* was a Bolshevik I could befriend. I could see why Maria gravitated toward him. "The pleasure is mine." Then, to bring Zash into the conversation before he escaped, I gestured toward him. "This is Zash. He was at Tobolsk with us."

"Ah, you've met this rascal?" Ivan chuckled.

"Only as was necessary," Zash was quick to add, as though not wanting Ivan to think of us beyond the roles of captor and captive.

Ivan gave Zash a side glance. He looked seconds away from commenting on Zash's brusque manner but then seemed to reconsider.

"How do you two know each other?" I pointed between the men.

But Ivan had tamed his playful manner, respecting his friend's obvious desire for distance.

A wooden groan split the air. The palisade gates opened and a Russo-Balt automobile drove in, shining black beneath its open cloth roof. Commandant Avdeev paled and then pushed Papa away from him.

A man in a Soviet uniform climbed out of the car. He squinted up at the house, the sun revealing a friendly face not quite thirty years of age. Then he spotted us, and whatever friendliness I'd caught on his round-cheeked visage melted into a cool indifference— one that appeared far more natural to him than friendliness.

Avdeev shook his hand, then pointed to each of us in turn, speaking low. He made no introductions but kept one side of his body pressed against the wall as though for support. Even in his mildly intoxicated state he seemed to know to put on a front. This round-cheeked man was important.

The stranger surveyed our family, glossing over each of us as though taking note of numbers and not humans. "How long have they been outside today?"

Avdeev muttered something in response, then gestured to the house. The new man nodded and they went inside. Mere seconds after they disappeared, Ivan spoke to Maria in quiet, gentle tones.

Zash had put a few more feet of distance between us. I closed the gap. "Do you know who that new man is?"

Zash stared resolutely forward, his chin high and spine straight. I made it a little more personal and gently used his name. "Zash?"

His gaze darted to me.

"Is he a new . . . guard?" I didn't like playing dumb, but I'd do what was necessary to get answers.

Zash pulled his pistol from his belt and held it between us as a barricade. As though I were posing a threat. "Return to your garden activities, Citizen."

I stumbled back, instinctively putting up my hands. "I'm . . . I'm sorry."

He looked fierce. Formidable. Like the other guards who had granted us not a single moment of softness.

"Oy, Zash!" Ivan hissed, bodily moving Maria to a safer spot away from the weapon.

Someone took my arm from behind and I spun. Papa led me toward the tiny group of birch trees against the palisade. "The new man is Alexander Beloborodov, the chair of the Ural Regional Soviet. He is likely here for a surprise inspection. He did the same thing a few days after your mamma, Maria, and I arrived."

So Beloborodov was the big shot. And with him on the premises we were endangering any Bolshevik soldier we dared to speak to with any familiarity. Zash was likely trying to protect himself. I darted my gaze to Maria and Ivan. She knelt and pruned wildflowers from the tiny garden corner while Ivan watched. Entranced.

Beloborodov did not stay long. But the moment he zoomed away in his automobile, Avdeev commanded us back inside. We didn't visit the garden again that day. I suspected his bloodshot eyes had bought him no favors with his superior. Alcohol was not forbidden to soldiers, but it certainly wasn't encouraged in large amounts. Particularly when you were guarding the Imperial family that one army wanted to rescue and another army wanted to murder.

~

Morning came with a summons from Avdeev.

We rose, changed from our sleeping clothes, and congregated in the sitting room. My sisters and I squished together on the sofa while Mamma, Papa, and Alexei took the freestanding chairs.

Avdeev stood inside the doorway with two soldiers on each side.

He clasped his hands behind his back. "From now on, you will rise at eight. You will be washed and dressed for breakfast at nine, at which time I shall be present to take roll. Your clothing will no longer be sent out for laundering—you can do that on your own. Lunch will be at one in the afternoon and dinner delivered at eight."

"And what of fresh air and exercise?" Papa asked with firm cordiality.

"One half hour of recreation in the garden will be permitted twice daily—once in the late morning and once in the afternoon."

"A single hour?" Papa asked, aghast. "May I ask the reason behind this sudden change in routine?"

"It is so that your life at the Ipatiev House more closely resemble a prison regime." Avdeev punctuated this with a hard stare. "You are no longer permitted to live like tsars."

I rose before eight the following morning and took a peek through my secret fortochka window. I sucked in a rebellious breath of free air and then released the breath toward Avdeev's office, as though taunting him.

In the main room I pulled the small cord beside the landing door and a bell rang on the other side of the wall. A soldier opened the door and escorted me to the bathroom. *"Dobroye utra,"* I greeted in Russian, trying to show friendliness. He didn't respond. I didn't try again.

Inside, I washed and ignored the rude political comments scraped on the wall by the nastier soldiers. An hour later, my family and I sat around the dining table for a breakfast of tea and black bread. *"No longer permitted to live like tsars,"* Avdeev had said. As though coffee and eggs were living like tsars! Beloborodov must have been displeased with his inspection.

Papa prayed over our food and we helped ourselves to the bread.

At least the tea was hot. Cold tea, even on a hot day, always left me chilled.

In a ridiculous contrast, our bread and tea were served on our fine china, bringing a semblance of our old life to this new dirty one. It felt pretend—like one of the plays I used to put on for the family. A fancy princess eating on fancy china . . . in a rotting prison cell void of direct light.

The mental image made me giggle. It wasn't a funny scenario, being too close to the truth. But I'd learned that when I felt like despairing, a well-timed giggle could infuse a measure of strength. It could also lead straight to tears if I wasn't careful.

This morning, I was careful. And I soaked in the smile that passed from me to Alexei to Maria to Tatiana to Papa. It skipped Mamma and Olga.

The click of Avdeev's boots mixed with the clink of small spoons on china cups, stirring the tea though there was no sugar or lemon to mix in. He stopped in the doorway and watched us for a moment. My giggling stopped, but Papa turned his smile to Avdeev. We all followed suit. We would show him that his new regime could not dampen the bond of our family.

Avdeev held the folded Ekaterinburg paper under his arm. His blond hair was mussed, as though he had slept poorly and then bypassed a mirror. Red eyes again. Avdeev was en route to poisoning himself into a grave.

"Ah, thank you, Commandant." Papa rose from the table to receive his paper.

Avdeev shook his head, which caused him to stumble briefly, but he caught himself on the doorframe. "No, Citizen Nikolai. You will no longer receive newspapers."

Avdeev's bloodshot gaze slid to meet mine. He held it. And

somehow I knew this had to do with the fact Papa and I had carried on a secret conversation behind the paper two days ago. Avdeev must have seen the guilt on my face, because he straightened. His message had been sent.

"I will, however, allow you to hear this morning's local announcement." He flicked the paper open. "'All those under arrest will be held as hostages.'" He looked up. *Those under arrest* meant us. The Romanovs. "'The slightest attempt at counterrevolutionary action in the town will result in the summary execution of the hostages.'" He snapped the paper closed. Then he entered his office and turned on the gramophone that used to be ours.

Not a breath. Not a word. Not a clink of silverware on china. Just that crackling record spinning in betrayal, sending out music that used to send us dancing. Mocking us.

Then the pop of a cork being yanked out of a cheap bottle of vodka.

We would be executed if anyone tried to rescue us. If there had been any members of the White Army hidden in Ekaterinburg, this surely would have silenced them.

I was the first to turn back to my dense black bread. I whispered, "I'm sorry, Papa."

JUNE 5

"What is our purpose in living, Nastya?" Alexei lay in his bed while the rest of the family went outside for the first excursion into the garden. I opted to stay inside and keep Alexei company—not because I didn't care for the fresh air, but because I cared for my brother even more.

I lifted Joy carefully onto his lap. She licked the toy soldiers that lay facedown on his sheet. "What do you mean?"

He shrugged and tugged a toy soldier from Joy's mouth, then wiped it clean with the corner of his sheet. "What am I now? Even if they release us and we live in a village somewhere, forgotten to Russia . . . what am I? I won't be tsar. I can't be a soldier because of all this." He gestured to his body. "Why is it important to survive?"

I tried to detect the deeper question, instead of simply despairing at the hopelessness in it. He asked it logically. Calmly. The least I could do was respond in kind. "I see why it's hard for you." He'd lost his throne. Everything he grew up learning and training for no longer applied to his life. "But what do your people—the Russian people—live for? They don't have thrones. Not all of them are soldiers. So what would you tell them their purpose is?"

He cocked his head to one side. "Very perceptive, Sister. I suppose they live to care for their families. To follow dreams." He rubbed Joy behind the ears and she curled herself into the blankets by his side. "I still have my family. And though I am ill—*always* ill—I can think of new dreams. If Papa can, I can."

"Papa's goal is to care for the Russian people . . . as a fellow citizen. Through love, forgiveness, and humility. Perhaps that is the sign of a true tsar. One that doesn't change whether he has a throne or not."

"*This* is why you're my favorite sister." Alexei winked and I laughed. He'd said that to all four of us sisters, but I liked to think he truly meant it with me. "Oh, and happy birthday."

I startled. "Birthday?"

"Well . . . according to the old style." He withdrew a small scroll of paper bound with a linen ribbon. "I suppose, under the new

Gregorian, calendar you don't turn seventeen for another thirteen days."

I'd wholly forgotten about my birthday. When Lenin changed the calendar from Julian to Gregorian, I'd abandoned keeping track of most dates. But today, on June fifth, I was now seventeen.

I took so long in accepting the scroll, Alexei finally tossed it into my lap. "I don't think I've ever seen you without a smart remark."

I raised an eyebrow. "Thank you, dear Brother, but I shall celebrate *your* birthday according to the Gregorian calendar, which now makes me thirteen extra days older than you." I slid the ribbon from around the thick paper, already detecting the nature of the gift as it unfurled. "A play?"

"One you've not yet performed because I snitched it on our first day in Tobolsk so as to save it for your birthday."

He'd brought it all the way here, to Ekaterinburg, even when so ill. I took in the gift—a one-act playlet farce. Alexei knew how I loved to make people laugh. "It's truly the best gift I've ever received."

"*Khorosho.* Good." He tapped the parchment. "You'll notice there are three roles. I demand that you include me in one of them."

"As if I would consider anyone else worthy."

Lunch was a simple serving of soup broth with small bits of meat, delivered to the gates from the Ekaterinburg Soviet. I didn't feel full once the entire day. And poor Mamma—a vegetarian—barely got any nutrition as she picked at the soup.

When Avdeev announced our garden time, everyone but Mamma and Olga rushed into the fresh air. I took up the rear. As the rest of my family descended the stairs at the lead of a Bolshevik, I took a detour . . .

. . . into Avdeev's office.

The space smelled strongly of cigarette smoke and alcohol. Boxes, papers, trunks, trinkets, and rubbish filled the room the way a rat might build its nest. I wrinkled my nose but scanned with my eyes. Where would a drunken commandant hide spell items?

I crossed to the cabinet beneath our gramophone. The small door was locked. A thrill struck my chest. This must have been it.

I glanced in his desk drawers—only papers. I riffled through a stack of boxes on the floor by his desk—more papers and empty liquor bottles. Then, beneath a chest of Papa's journals, I found a small rusted key. Why would he have left it lying there?

It fit perfectly into the cabinet lock. I gave it the slightest turn. *Snick.* The door opened and . . . vodka. Bottles and bottles of vodka.

No spell items. No spell ink. No books of spell mastery.

I shut the door, locked it, and returned the key to its spot on the desk with an exasperated sigh.

"What are you doing?"

I snapped my head up. Zash filled the doorway, arms folded, pistol glinting at his side. How had I not heard him? My senses had been on high alert. I tried to shrug off the situation, but I'd crossed a line. "Just a bit of mischief."

"This is more than mischief. This is rebellion."

I stood by the desk, running through excuses or lies, but this was too much. Too deep. And when improvisation couldn't rescue you, the best bet was to spill the truth. Honesty was the most efficient—and the most dangerous—rescuer.

"You're right." My arms fell limp to my sides. "It wasn't mischief. But I'm not trying to rebel. I'm trying to look out for my family."

"What, they can't handle the soldier rations like the rest of us?"

I could practically taste his bitterness. As my next words spilled forth, I didn't meet his eyes. "Alexei is ill. I was hoping to find a healing spell that could help him."

Talk of spells could send a bullet to my heart, but Zash had spell secrets of his own, so I forged ahead. "I know it's not allowed, but he's my brother. Everything has been taken from us." My throat tightened. "We have only each other. Can you blame me for wanting to do anything I can to keep my family from suffering?"

I expected to meet his stiff gaze again, but the coldness was gone. Zash released a long exhale. "*Nyet.* I cannot blame you for that. *If* it is the truth, that is likely the only thing you and I have in common."

I made my way slowly toward the door. He stepped aside to let me out, then he closed the door behind me. I held my arms out from my body. "If you need to search me, please do. I promise I've taken nothing."

He conducted a swift search, and the same unspoken rule kept him from examining where the Matryoshka doll rested. "I'm satisfied." He straightened.

I clasped my hands in front of me, truly humbled. I wasn't often caught in my mischief. "Will you . . . will you tell Commandant Avdeev?"

"It is my duty."

"But perhaps you don't need to tell him *immediately*, right?" I attempted a cautious grin. If I couldn't convince him to keep my secret, I might have to threaten to reveal his. But blackmailing a Bolshevik guard was my absolute last resort.

Zash seemed annoyed. "I am taking you to the garden."

"Of course." I followed him down the stairs, palms sweating at what might await me in the garden. Would he take me straight to Avdeev?

"Why is your brother always so sick? The doctor has plenty of medicines at his disposal."

A tiny little kit of morphine and a few other drugs were Zash's idea of "plenty of medicines"? All the same, I grasped at the conversation. "It is his blood. It does not clot, so any cut or bruise can be fatal. It is called hemophilia."

We stepped into the light of the garden and I breathed in the freedom. Zash stopped at the edge of the grass. I did, too. He frowned at me. "When did he contract such an illness?"

Oy. There was no going back now. "Since birth. It has been passed through our bloodline. My uncle died as a boy from the same illness. We . . ." I wrung my hands. Too much truth was coming out, but I couldn't seem to stop. "We kept it a secret from the public. Alexei was to be the next tsar. The people adored him, but they wouldn't understand that his weakness was in body only. If they had known, they would think him unfit to rule."

"You did not have much faith in your people."

I folded my arms. "Do you wonder why none of us four girls ever married or even courted? Because some nobility heard of Alexei's illness, and even though they did not know the details, they considered all us girls diseased. Infected. They denied us our futures because of their own speculation."

Zash raised an eyebrow. "Had you revealed the truth, they might not have."

"You are not very familiar with nobility." I sniffed.

"And you are not very familiar with the common folk."

I'd give him that one. "We always wished to be." I could reminisce about my life of traveling and palaces as fondly as I liked, but there had always been a layer of frustration shared between us siblings. Frustration in never being allowed *out*. Not allowed to know our people. Not allowed to attend parties. Not allowed to live or learn or explore beyond our own family life. All at Mamma's dictate.

"You'd best join your family before your time ends." Zash nudged me forward with his elbow.

So surprised was I by his touch that I practically bounded away from him. But not before sending a quick thank-you. "*Spasibo*, Zash."

"For what?" he grumbled.

I didn't answer. *For talking with me. And . . . for hopefully keeping my secret.*

Three days later, Avdeev had still said nothing to me. I could only guess that Zash decided not to share my trespassing. That meant I wouldn't have to blackmail him. And maybe it meant we were becoming . . . friendly?

The grumble of my stomach had stopped hurting, having accepted the new rations. But as I scraped the last of the broth from my lunch bowl, I still felt filled with little more than air.

"This is unacceptable," Dr. Botkin fumed. "Even under exile you should not be *starved*. The tsarina and tsarevich will never heal under these conditions."

Mamma no longer left her bed—not even to go out into the garden. This left her wooden wheelchair for Alexei to use. And as much as he enjoyed being pushed around the garden, Alexei grew more and more frail with each passing day. I needed spell ink. But I couldn't steal it from Zash, even if I wanted to, because of the mass of Bolsheviks everywhere. And Avdeev didn't have any.

The Matryoshka doll remained resolutely sealed. I felt so helpless.

Mornings grew particularly dull as we counted down the

minutes until eleven when we would be permitted outside. Papa read and reread the small stack of books that had arrived in his and my trunks. Sometimes he would read aloud, and I soaked in his voice the way I wished I could be soaking in the sun.

Maria, Tatiana, and I played the French card game bezique until I was ready to tear the cards to pieces and scream. Olga soothed Mamma by her bedside, and Alexei played with his tin soldiers on a small model ship that had been returned to his possession. Oftentimes I would join him simply because the tin soldiers were such a relief from the endless cards.

One morning we woke to the noise of sawing, hammering, and clunking. When we had our garden time we saw why. The Bolsheviks were building a second palisade of timber. Taller, longer, more secure around the small palisade. Zash helped haul logs and balance them in place while others bound them. I didn't know why they thought we needed a second barrier—we'd done nothing to warrant extra security other than grow thinner from our pathetic rations.

I continued to peek out the small fortochka window over the next few days, though more of my view was blocked by the new palisade. With no newspaper and no view, we could not know the state of the country or if the White Army had continued to resist the Bolsheviks.

But a couple days later, the gates cranked open and twenty new soldiers marched into the entryway. They carried their packs and settled into the already-cramped Ipatiev House, bringing their sweat and cigarette smoke into our space.

Extra guards? A second palisade? We posed no threat from the inside. That left only one logical reason the Bolsheviks would bring more security: there must be a threat from the outside.

The White Army was coming to rescue us.

7

"The guard rotation has changed." Maria waggled her eyebrows, sitting crosslegged with me on the oriental rug in our room. "With all the extra guards, they had to switch some things around, and guess who is now on duty on our landing every other day?"

"Hm . . . that's a tough one." I shuffled two decks of cards, not quite in the mood for bezique. "Ivan?"

Maria stuck out her tongue. The way she talked of Ivan went a touch beyond flirtation. She was entering dangerous territory, but I didn't know what to do about it. It could happen to any of us. The more starved we were of kindness, the more we clung to any crumb of it.

We needed to look out for each other. I needed to look out for her. "You be careful with that Bolshevik." I dealt out eight cards each and flipped the trump card.

"That's just it. I don't think he is one," she said in a hushed voice, picking up her cards. "He comes from the local factory same as this influx of new soldiers—they're *all* from the factory. None of them are actually soldiers. I think Avdeev is getting whoever he can."

I *had* noticed a decrease in hostility from the new soldiers, which encouraged more cordiality from the original Bolsheviks. That meant these new men probably took the position of soldier for the pay rather than because of loyalty. "How do you know they come from the factory?"

"I asked Ivan."

"Just don't get *too* friendly."

"Why shouldn't I?" She flicked a card into the center of our spot on the carpet, then dropped her tone. "If the White Army is truly on its way to free us, wouldn't it be best to have some of these soldiers sympathetic to our cause?"

My silence conveyed my acknowledgment. "All I'm saying is that we don't need a string of broken—or jealous—hearts in the chests of soldiers with guns." I outranked her trump card and picked up the trick.

Maria played her next card more forcefully. "Then we convince them not to use their guns." She stood with a huff and marched toward the landing. She rang the bell and Ivan opened the door. Maria left the room to visit the lavatory. Supposedly.

The next day brought rain and kept us out of the garden. I couldn't bear the idea of returning to our white foggy portion of rooms. My mind scrambled to latch onto some source of upcoming hope or joy. Back in Tobolsk and the Alexander Palace, this would have been a prank. Pranks here flirted too closely with noncompliance, especially with the increase of soldiers. But I could put on a play.

Like we used to in Tobolsk.

I now had a new playlet and tomorrow was Sunday. Plays were always better with more than one actor, so I hurried into Alexei's room with a grin. "Alexei, the time has come . . ."

"Mrs. Chugwater, I ought to stuff you in your trunk and give you to the luggage man!" I stomped across the floor wearing a dressing gown and putting on my best grumpy-husband face for the ending of our one-act play. Alexei played the role of the luggage man, dutifully following me around in his wheelchair with his lap full of parcels.

Maria—Mrs. Chugwater—folded her arms, wearing her beaded gown at last. "You're such a blockhead, I almost confused you with the luggage."

The audience snickered. I caught their amused smiles out of the corner of my eye—Papa, Mamma, Tatiana, and Olga. Even Avdeev and some of the guards had come to observe. I tried not to focus *too* much on Zash and Ivan, watching from the corner.

"And *that*, my dear Mrs. Chugwater, is why you can carry your *own* bags!" I threw the two empty suitcases at her feet and nearly toppled over from the momentum. My dressing gown flew up, exposing Papa's Jaeger long johns bunched up on my legs. I yanked the dressing gown down in mock horror and that was too much for the audience.

They howled and I soaked it in. Even Mamma laughed more than I'd seen her do in the past year. At last, I felt useful. Like I was helping heal my family, even if it was just their spirits.

We finished up our final lines, and the applause was the happiest sound that had struck my ears since Alexei's last healthy laugh. I bowed with an exaggerated flourish. Even Avdeev clapped.

As I straightened I caught Zash watching me. Since our conversation about Alexei, his posture and presence no longer screamed "enemy." Not like some of the others.

I thought of my warnings to Maria—not to get too attached to Ivan. But maybe she was right. Maybe being friendlier with some of the guards might make them sympathetic. It could help us survive this exile.

I smiled at Zash.

He smiled back.

And my stomach flipped.

Oh dear. That had been a terrible idea.

8

As we filed down the stairs out toward the garden once the storms had passed, I heard Dr. Botkin's voice coming from Avdeev's office. I couldn't make out the words, but he sounded adamant. Forceful, even. Was he in trouble with the commandant?

I broke from the line to press my ear to the door, but Papa—who brought up the rear—took my arm and steered me down the stairs. "Let it be, Nastya."

My imagination spun with all the possibilities—perhaps the Bolsheviks were going to get rid of us one by one. Starting with Dr. Botkin. Then Anna. And so on through the servants until they finally started on the Romanov family.

We entered the garden and I gulped in the sunshine, my heart already pattering in anxiety at the anticipated shout from Avdeev sending us back inside.

Just a while longer.

A minute longer.

Please, please, please.

I didn't care that the sun would burn my skin. I didn't care that the wind would tangle my hair. I didn't care that the people on the other side of the palisades might shout profanities at us. I just wanted the air. The breath. The freedom.

A gunshot echoed from the lower city. I heard at least one every time we visited the garden. An execution . . . of someone. For something. By a Bolshevik. The gunshots rang more frequently than the church bells.

Papa strolled, as though soaking in the freedom, despite the morbid sounds, whereas Maria wanted to exhaust herself in it and use up every tiny ounce. Papa had petitioned for more time outside. Avdeev said no. Then Papa asked Avdeev to allow him to help with the garden, with the wood, with the chores.

Again, Commandant Avdeev said no, in between his gulps of vodka.

It didn't make sense, except to torment us.

Another distant gunshot broke through the air from the city. I flinched. At first it had been hard to believe that each shot represented the death of someone not adhering to the Bolshevik demands. But the more it happened, the more I believed it. For all we knew, that could have been a member of the White Army on his way to rescue us.

"Papa, what is going to happen to us?" I suspected he also heard my unspoken question, *Will we be rescued?* We were quickly on our way to starvation. Even with the occasional morning cocoa, our bodies barely obeyed our commands when running on the diet of broth, cutlets, and bread.

We were fading—both from Russia's hearts and from our own mirrors. Mamma hadn't come outside for several days. She could barely gather herself from her bed due to her headaches and poor nutrition.

"Our only hopes are rescue or to soften hearts."

He believed the Bolsheviks—if they had their way—would keep us here until we rotted. Or would kill us before things got that far. Up until this moment, I had clung to the hope that maybe they would *still* send us to a deserted little village, stripped of riches and titles, but alive to end our days as peasants.

Even that shadowed dream was now fading. "Can their hearts be softened?"

"It's not up to you to soften theirs. It's up to you to keep *yours* soft. These soldiers are serving their country as they would have served me if I were still tsar."

I didn't believe that. Had they been loyal to Papa, they would not be partaking in his exile and looming death right now. I let my gaze drift to Zash. He and Ivan were on rotation between garden duty and upstairs landing duty. Zash watched us like a kestrel.

Perhaps after our exchanged smile yesterday he felt convicted to return to his stiff Bolshevik posture. Why was he so afraid of kindness?

I turned my face so he could not read my lips. "What of the doll? When will we be able to use it?"

No code words this time. I'd pulled the doll from its hiding spot in my corset this morning and still it wouldn't open no matter how hard I twisted it. The spell wasn't ready.

Papa stopped us in the far corner and I could feel the eyes of the guards on us. "Nastya, it is like the diamonds in your corset. The moment we use a spell shows we have been defying the Soviet government. It shows we are noncompliant. To *use* the spell might very well instigate our execution. This is why, even if it allows you to open it, you must use it only at the last possible moment."

I thought of Yurovsky, the commandant who had almost taken

the doll from me in Tobolsk. My hand drifted to my chest, ensuring the doll was still there and that Yurovsky was still far away in Tobolsk.

"The spell does not always do what we might expect it to. Mamma and I used one spell layer when she was pregnant with Alexei—asking for the baby to be a boy so I would have an heir. We did not expect to have a child with a degenerative blood disease who would likely not live long enough to rule."

"Colonel Nikolai!" Avdeev called from a window above our heads. It was the first time I'd heard him use Papa's proper title post-abdication.

Papa peered upward. "Yes, Commandant?"

"Keep walkinnn'. Annnn' . . . cease your conversation." Drunk again.

Papa gave a small bow. "As you wish." We resumed our stroll, but not before Papa muttered, "I suspect the doll will have a spell for you on the day the White Army rescues us."

He nudged me away. To avoid further suspicion I left him and joined Maria in the shade of one of the birch trees. She lay on her back, conveniently situated at the feet of Ivan and Zash. Ivan dropped little lilac leaves down on Maria, who tried to catch them between her fingers before they hit her face.

She giggled and Ivan wouldn't stop laughing. The more he laughed, the stonier Zash became. Without stopping his leaf dropping, Ivan nudged Zash. "If you cannot handle the fun, go guard somewhere else."

"I'm here to guard *you*," Zash snapped back.

Determined to maintain the playful mood, I lifted my hands like a boxer. "From what? Our bony little female fists?"

He turned away and gave no answer. My hands drifted down. I

was missing some sort of insinuation. Ivan rolled his eyes. "Zash is of the impression that your siren voices are *brainwashing* us."

I snorted. "*What?*" I laughed at the absurd superstition, but the longer Zash stood with a determinedly emotionless face, the more my humor leaked away. I took a gentle step toward him. "I don't exactly know what Ivan means, but . . . we have no power to do such a thing, Zash."

Where did he get such an idea? Was it because he saw me searching for spells in Avdeev's office?

Ivan wagged a finger at me. "Ah, that's exactly what a siren would say. Especially under the tutelage of—"

"Ivan." Zash's reprimand cut the playful air like a snap of thunder.

I fit the pieces together. "Because of Rasputin?" No matter how often Mamma drilled us not to use Rasputin's name, the people still knew of our involvement with him.

Maria sat up at this, all four of us now somber. "You think we can control your minds because of the spell master?"

"He was at your palace more often than the tsar himself." Zash raised his eyebrows, the implications clear.

A spear of injustice twisted in my chest. "That's what you think? That Rasputin brainwashed us? Controlled us? Taught us to control other people?" The garden seemed eerily quiet under the outrage in my voice. But maybe that was because I could hear nothing beyond the angry pulsing in my ears.

"He. Caused. The revolution!" Zash's face flushed. "Why do you *think* the people revolted? No one could trust your father to run the country anymore."

Maria sprang from her spot on the garden floor. "This is ridiculous. Come, Nastya."

The fact she was willing to leave Ivan told me just how upset she was. But I held my ground. "No. I want to understand. I thought surely even the common man knew that spell mastery does not work in that way."

"Then why was Rasputin always at the palace?"

"To heal Alexei from his injuries! He was the only one who could!" A burn of tears pushed from the inside, more from frustration than sorrow. How could Zash not see, especially after I revealed Alexei's illness to him?

"You truly believe he came only for your brother?" Zash's voice sounded sympathetic. "Your mother adored him. The papers published her letters. We saw what she wrote to him. Everyone knew she visited his residence. Alone."

I'd seen the letters. Zash's insinuations proved that gossip had become a more influential tsar than my wholesome papa. And there was nothing I could do to reverse that. "You read propaganda, Zash, but *we* lived there. We saw the day-to-day. And all we have are our voices to speak *truth* . . . if you're willing to listen to them without thinking we're trying to control your mind."

Everyone went silent for a long breath. Ivan wore a half smile, as though challenging Zash to respond to that.

When Zash spoke next, it was with a gentle tone, as if hoping I'd not get offended. "Perhaps, Nastya, you were too close to see what the rest of the country could."

I swallowed hard once. Twice. I would *not* let him taint Mamma's character. But arguing at this point would get us no further. So I took a deep breath and channeled all the humility I could muster. "I want to understand. I want to hear your side, Zash. Thank you for hearing mine."

By the time I finished, I actually believed my own words. Maria calmed and sank back to the grass, and Ivan's half grin turned into a full one. Zash gave me a nod and it was as though the stoniness had never happened. Another step forward. Another seed of understanding.

"How is Alexei?" Zash asked, attempting to soften the strained aftermath of our argument.

I shook my head. "Not healing. He barely sleeps because of the pain. Dr. Botkin's medicines are not enough." I let the insinuation hang between us like the weak birch branches swaying in the breeze. *I need spell ink.*

When Zash said nothing more, I joined Maria on the grass. Our garden time had expired long ago, but Avdeev hadn't called to us yet so I soaked in what more I could. I stared upward into the secret world of leaves and wind and slivers of blue. Maria linked her arms behind her head.

I wanted to say something light, to prove to Ivan and Zash that we could move on and not hold bitterness. The leaves spun above us. "This tree would make for a lovely swing," I said wistfully, wishing I could be as tossed and beset by the wind as the leaves were.

"I hardly remember what it is like to swing." Maria's tone held despair. She was still sensitive.

So I rolled onto my side and did what I knew would perk her up. "Ivan, what were your favorite summer activities as a boy?"

Ivan startled. I smiled and sent a flash of it toward Zash, who angled toward the conversation. That was better than nothing.

"I was a bit of a rascal," Ivan said. Maria brightened at that. Nothing made a soldier handsomer than hearing of his dangerous escapades. "When I was good, I would climb trees. Search for berries in the woods."

"We did that, too!" I sat up fully now, flooded with memories of our childhood at Alexander Palace.

"Ah, but Ivan wasn't surrounded by golden gates," Zash groused, draining my pool of swirling excitement.

I forced away a scowl and instead thought of where Zash might be coming from. "We were surrounded by gates, but Papa valued the wild and the adventure." My voice grew more excited as I recalled those days. "We camped and he taught us to build fires. We helped him chop wood for winter. We learned to cook and work and mend wounds."

I wanted Zash to know we never saw ourselves as above our people. "He raised us as best he could in our situation, as I'm sure your parents did."

"I had no parents. Do not assume to know my upbringing."

I clamped my mouth shut. Maria looked between Zash and me, took a deep breath, and continued the conversation with Ivan. "What about when you *weren't* good, Ivan?"

"I do not speak of such things in front of grand duchesses."

We giggled. Maria brushed her lovely brown hair away from her face, and the wind caught it in a way that would have sent her straight onto the cover of a magazine.

Zash relaxed his stance—almost as a physical apology for his irritation.

"Zash? Did you have any favorite summer activities?" I put forth my kindest and most interested tones in an attempt to convey that our reminiscence could transcend differences.

He took the bait, or rather he humored me and gave in. "Swimming. Fishing. Sharing a meal of *stroganina*. Spending the day on the beach of the river, cooking *shashlik* over the fire." As he talked, his speech grew more relaxed. Nostalgic. A pathway toward a childhood that sounded free and wild. How did he end up a Bolshevik? "That is summer for me."

"I've never made my own *shashlik* over a fire." My mouth watered at the idea of the thick mutton soaked in spices and then grilled on a stripped branch or skewer.

Zash smiled at some memory beyond my reach. "Then you've not yet lived."

"Back inside!" Avdeev hollered from the door of the Ipatiev House.

I darted my gaze to Papa. As expected, he rose obediently, scooping up Tatiana's two dogs. Tatiana pushed Alexei toward the house in Mamma's chair.

Ivan helped Maria to her feet. I scrambled up before Zash felt as though he would need to do the same. And we all retreated back into the house like shackled, obedient slaves. But instead of imaginary chains on my shoulders, this time I carried the spoils of victory.

Conversation hadn't been easy, but every time I interacted with Zash I understood a bit more why he was so angry with us. And once I could dispel those misunderstandings, I was certain we could form some allies to help us escape.

JUNE 11

"Dr. Botkin, you are a savior!" Mamma's frail voice bespoke all our hearts. Our beloved doctor had brought his professional concerns to Avdeev regarding our health, and Avdeev allowed Dr. Botkin to commission the sisters at the local convent for help with food.

Baskets of eggs, milk, cream, meat, sausage, vegetables, and

Russian pies arrived at the gate of the Ipatiev House, carried by the sweet sisters. Commandant Avdeev took most of it for himself and his guards, but every morsel we received was more precious to us than the jewels in our undergarments.

Papa prayed over every piece before serving out equal portions.

This became a daily occurrence, and I was so thankful to the sisters that I wrote them a lengthy letter of gratitude. I stood by the door to the landing for several minutes, not yet ringing the bell. Would Avdeev give them my letter? It was hard to imagine he would. Not much would be lost if he didn't, but it was worth a try. My encouragement could not be quelled today.

I pulled the bell cord. The door opened and I found myself face-to-face with Zash. "Oh!" I stepped back, my stomach performing a clumsy pirouette. "Hello."

"*Dobroye dyen,*" he replied. *Good day.*

I was so cheerful now with several days of proper nutrients pumping through my body that I practically beamed at him. "I have a letter for the sisters."

Something changed on his face—not a smile, specifically, but a layer of warmth. "They have been very generous."

I was sure he appreciated the siphoned goods as much as we did since Avdeev claimed his soldiers needed the sustenance as well.

"We are so grateful." I thought of how many of these soldiers were in their roles because they needed the rubles. How they were all crammed in the basement floors of the Ipatiev House—far stuffier than our five rooms. Even though we were under a prison regime, we likely still looked pampered to them.

I reached out and touched Zash's arm. "Thank you for serving our beautiful country of Russia. I know our positions might have labeled us as enemies, but I am as grateful for your loyalty as I am for the sisters' generosity."

The warmth fled from his face and he schooled his features into indifference once more, but I understood. Compliments were more difficult to swallow than the dry black bread we chewed every breakfast.

I remembered one of the verses Papa read us from the Bibliya—that a kind word turns away wrath. I wasn't very good at it, but when I did manage to squeak out a compliment or kindness, I always saw Papa's words in action.

In this moment I wished Zash to hear my sincerity and to know that I did not begrudge him for having to enact Avdeev's orders.

I knocked on Avdeev's office door, Zash at my side—standing guard as I tried to find his commandant. The door was locked. I knocked again and a grunt came from inside.

Zash turned me away and held out his hand. "I will give him the letter when he . . . when he is available." Meaning when Avdeev wasn't drunk.

"Thank you." I passed Zash the letter and turned to go back into our prison, but Zash's low mutter made me pause.

"Some items were recently brought into the commandant's office from a city raid. Perhaps . . . perhaps you should try searching again. To help your brother."

I stood, mouth agape, with my hand hovering over the door handle. Did he mean . . . Avdeev had spell ink?

"Maybe tomorrow," Zash finished, still not meeting my eyes. Then, in a louder voice, he said, "Now return to your quarters, Citizen."

I obeyed, not sure what I'd just heard. Not sure I believed those words came from Zash's mouth. And then suddenly giddy that they had. Papa was right—holding on to hope would always lead to surprises.

The next day I had the fidgets. Twisting my fingers. Twisting my napkin. Flipping book edges with my thumb if only to hear the *thrick* of pages. Wrestling with Joy until she was too tuckered to even lick my face.

Finally, the time came.

Ivan and Zash escorted our family into the garden and I took up the rear. Zash gave no signal, no assurance, but I'd heard the commandant's voice from outside, which meant his office was empty.

Like a shadow I slipped inside and cracked the door behind me. His office looked pretty much the same as the last time, only now it was filled with twice as many empty vodka bottles. I wasn't sure where to search. No new crates. No new barrels or boxes.

But then, as I scanned the messy shelves, I saw it.

A round wooden container with silver painting and a tiny stopper that made me think it held perfume. Zash's spell ink.

Avdeev hadn't collected any raid items. He probably didn't know about any of this. Zash . . . Zash had put his bottle of spell ink in here for me. For Alexei.

With my throat growing thick, I grabbed the bottle and slipped out of the office a mere two minutes after entering. And I wanted to cry. Because this kindness—Zash's kindness—undid me.

I could never thank him properly. He didn't realize I knew this was *his* bottle of spell ink. He didn't realize I knew he had risked his own neck by sneaking it into Avdeev's office for me. Why? Why would he do this?

Perhaps this was some sort of cruel setup. But with our raw-hearted frustrations and communication, it couldn't be. Zash had said the one thing we had in common was a willingness to do anything to help a loved one.

He'd seen Alexei's pain, and the sorrow it caused the rest of us. And even though we were captives under the guard of his gun, he still had compassion. He showed that to me today. And I adored him for it.

9

I painted the spell ink directly onto Alexei's knee. The rest of our family was finishing up supper in the dining room. This was the only spell I knew, so I made quick work of it. Alexei kept an eye on the door, holding as still as he could.

As I painted the word onto Alexei's pale skin, I hummed the small tune Rasputin had taught me and focused all my thoughts on the word for the relief spell. Fresh spells came from the right word paired with the right focus and the right music. Part of me considered trying for a new word—something that wouldn't just relieve some of the pain but would resolve the problem—but I wouldn't even know where to start.

I placed a palm over the word, closed my eyes, and kept humming. It was a short little tune—Rasputin always emphasized how spell magic was a blend of the ink and the master. Something awoke in me while I hummed. A delight to be *doing*. Helping. Learning.

If I couldn't be a princess, I wanted to be a spell master, now more than ever.

The ink wiggled like an impatient worm beneath my hand. Activated. Ready to be used. *"Oblegcheniye,"* I whispered.

I lifted my hand in time to see the spell sink into Alexei's skin. Alexei melted back against his pillow, a contented smile on his face. "Ah. *So* much better than Dr. Botkin's apparatus."

"It worked." I stared at the spot of skin, amazed that I was still able to create a spell. I wanted to learn others. To grow stronger. But the remaining spell ink was barely an inch deep in the bottle. Zash had removed—or used—some before planting it in Avdeev's office. It didn't lessen his gift at all, but it *did* lessen the amount of experimenting I could do. I needed to preserve it for Alexei's pain.

If we were going to be rescued soon, he'd need all the relief he could get.

"Maybe I'll go into the garden without the chair tomorrow." Alexei pushed himself to a sitting position.

"Now don't give me away," I scolded.

"You expect me to *fake* being in more discomfort than I am? Oh, Sister, you ought to know better than anyone that I won't do that."

I tucked the bottle into my pocket. "I had to try."

Alexei watched my movements with a frown. "Where did you get the ink?"

I raised my eyebrows in mock offense. "You expect me to reveal my secrets?"

"You and I don't have secrets."

"True." Could I tell him? *Should* I tell him about Zash? "I snitched it from Avdeev's office."

"Uh-huh." He knew I wasn't telling him the full truth. "Spit it out, shvibzik."

I let out a gust of air and rolled my eyes. *"Fine.* Zash got it for me. When we left Tobolsk he had some in his pack, but he doesn't know I knew about it. He tipped me off to search Avdeev's office and then I found Zash's bottle of spell ink in there. I think he put it there for me. For you."

"I thought he hated spell masters. And Rasputin. And all of us."

"He has some ideas about Rasputin. But . . . I'm still hoping to understand them more."

Alexei waggled his eyebrows. "Does Soldier Zash *liiiiike* you?"

I snorted. "Certainly not!"

"Oh. Well, excuse me for assuming that risking his life might be a sign of affection."

My traitorous pulse quickened. "It's not like that."

Alexei folded his arms and adopted a snooty tsar expression. "Until you provide me with a believable alternative, I will hold to my own opinions."

I feigned exasperation and left the room. But I dropped the banter act once I entered my own room. Maria was already climbing onto her cot. We kissed each other's cheeks and I changed into my nightdress.

I couldn't let myself hope for Zash's affections. Even I could tell my desire came from the strain of exile. It wasn't right. It wasn't safe. But then again, what if he *did* end up helping in our rescue someday? Should I allow myself to entertain the idea of affection?

I rolled over, my back toward Maria. My thoughts felt more private when she couldn't see my face. I redirected my pondering away from the dangerous waters of affection and back toward spell mastery. Back toward Rasputin . . . and what Zash had said about Rasputin and Mamma.

Maria breathed heavily in her cot beside me. I allowed myself to question. Even . . . to doubt. I had never doubted Mamma's loyalty to Papa. But she *had* spent a lot of time with Rasputin. When he visited us at the palace, Maria and I were often not allowed to be in the same room while she and Rasputin discussed Alexei's illness.

Rasputin never revealed how he had healed Alexei. He only ever informed me of the very basics of spell mastery—how to make the relief spell. How to apply it. But nothing more—no instruction regarding the history of spell mastery. No direction on how to make other spells or how to obtain spell ink.

Was he just soothing my curiosity? Keeping me happy so I would trust him?

I had seen Mamma's letters to him when they were published in the Russian newspapers. They were endearing. They were loving. The people called it a scandal. But we Romanovs *all* loved Rasputin. We *all* wrote letters like that. The public didn't understand.

Well . . . Papa never fully trusted Rasputin. Even Olga had disliked him on occasion. They never told me why. If there had been some sort of romantic tryst, wouldn't they have said something? Wouldn't they have *done* something?

The darkness took me into restless dreams, but I woke the next morning determined to ease my mind. I changed into my frayed black skirt and white blouse I'd worn day after day. We ate a quiet, tired breakfast.

Papa moved to his chair, reading a biography on Emperor Paul I that he'd probably read a hundred times already. Mamma stayed in bed, pale and wraithlike.

When the afternoon garden time came, I caught Olga's arm. "Let me care for Mamma. You go enjoy the sunshine."

Olga exhaled a gust of air. "Our little imp being an angel? What madness is this?"

I smirked and she rushed down the stairs after the rest of the family. I gathered a bowl of Mamma's lentil soup from the kitchen and brought it to her bedside.

"*Privyet*, my little one." Mamma sat up and her hand went instantly to her forehead. I waited for her headache to lessen enough for me to hand her the bowl.

Perhaps this wasn't the best time.

Mamma was always so ill. Besides, who was I to doubt her integrity? But if I was to engage Zash—or any other guard, for that matter—regarding their suspicions about Rasputin and Mamma, I needed answers.

"What a gift to have you by my side today."

I straightened her blanket as she sipped her soup. I could do this. "Mamma, I stayed inside because . . . some of the guards have been talking to me."

"Are they keeping their hands to themselves? They are not as kind as the ones at Tobolsk."

"They are not harassing me. They've just been . . . saying things that I wanted to talk with you about." *Spit it out!*

Mamma set her soup on the bedside table and rubbed a hand over her forehead. "What is it, Nastya? *Izvini*, but my headache is terrible today."

"It's about Rasputin," I blurted.

She stilled. Then, in a bitter voice, she said, "I can only imagine what shameful propaganda they are spewing."

"Why did you never allow us in the room with you two?" The garden time was already almost half gone. I needed to get to my questions. "Why did you visit him alone so often? Mamma . . . what happened? Forgive my prying, but I think I see why the guards were so untrusting and the people so suspicious. I don't know how to set them straight!"

I didn't think it possible, but Mamma paled more than her usual weak pallor. "What do you think of me, Nastya?"

"I don't know what to think!" My voice turned teary. "I don't think ill of you. I *love* you. I seek only understanding." She'd spent so much time with Alexei once he was born, hardly any of us sisters had more than a half relationship with her. We didn't know her deeply the same way we did Papa. Maria and me least of all.

"Grigori Rasputin saved your brother's life countless times. Do you doubt his goodness?"

She was affronted by the attack on *his* character? What about her own? "Nyet. I do not doubt his goodness. But tell me, Mamma. Why the visits to his home? Why the closed doors?" I hated being at unease. I hated the gnawing in my mind. I wanted to return to my confidence.

"Some secrets are not meant for you, Nastya. You must trust my words. I have never dishonored your papa."

So she chose to hoard her answers. "Perhaps not through intentions, but due to your secrecy the entire country thinks he was a weak-minded tsar who couldn't keep track of his own wife!" I gasped the moment the words left my lips. How dare I? I dropped to her side and clasped her hand. "Forgive me, Mamma."

She pulled her hand from mine.

Shame overwhelmed me, yet ought I be ashamed of speaking my heart? "I trust you, Mamma, but I do not know how to answer the soldiers when they tear apart my family's integrity. When they accuse Papa of being weak and you of . . . unmentionable things."

"Even if I shared my secrets with you, they would not be for you to tell the soldiers. It would not ease your predicament."

"It would ease my mind," I croaked. "It would ease my heart. This tortures me far more than our exile."

She fell back against her pillow, her soup abandoned. At this point I would usually go fetch some sort of medicine or Olga to read soothingly to her. Instead, I waited through her discomfort. Through her pain. Hoping—praying—that she would not withdraw her love from me.

I had crossed a line I'd no right to cross. I never should have stayed. I never should have asked.

"We are to die soon anyway," she mumbled beneath a frail hand, now a broken shell of a woman. "Do with my secrets what you must."

My heart tripped over its own rhythm. I overlooked her despair about our exile and waited for her to speak.

"Rasputin used . . . uncommon magic. We'd consulted countless spell masters and doctors about Alexei's condition. Only Rasputin could heal his episodes. But that was because Rasputin and I had an agreement. An agreement your papa did not condone."

Her voice turned as mechanical as a record on a turntable. "Rasputin's spell work alone was not enough to help Alexei. So I allowed him to draw from my health. It was an exchange. He channeled my good health into Alexei during the direst times. That is why I grew ill."

"But . . . how is that possible?" I breathed. "I've never heard of such spells."

Mamma shrugged. "I did not question his ways."

"Is that why you have a weak heart?" Rasputin did this to my mother? Spell masters were supposed to help the people. Heal them. How did I not connect her illness with his arrival at our palace?

"I demanded it, Nastya! It was a small sacrifice to keep my son alive. Any mother—peasant or royal—would have done the same."

Perhaps that comforted her, but instead of relief I felt only fear at such raw power. For the first time I understood the people's caution. They had known Rasputin had mysterious spell powers, and in their fear they destroyed the line of spell masters.

"That's why you never asked Rasputin to heal you." We'd begged Rasputin so many times to attend to Mamma's heart, but Mamma always refused. Because *he* was the cause of her weakness and headaches. "You didn't want us to know what you were sacrificing."

I forced myself to think from her position. To think about how she had anguished over Alexei's illness. How his hemophilia came from *her* bloodline. Wouldn't I allow a spell master to do whatever was needed if I thought it would help Alexei?

"Oh, Mamma." I embraced her gently.

She patted my back. "It is a small relief to have someone else know."

"Thank you for telling me." I tucked the information into the pocket of my mind, thankful I had it but not yet sure how to process it. In her attempts to save Alexei's life as future tsar, her secrets had cost him—and Papa—the throne.

~

The next day when eleven o'clock signaled our time to enter the garden, Avdeev did not come to get us. Instead, Zash opened the door, Ivan at his side. "We will escort you to the garden today."

Maria hung on Ivan's arm. We filed out of our rooms and followed the soldiers. I was behind Maria at the front and Zash took up the rear. The call of the outdoors sped up my heart. We burst into the sunshine, but Maria pulled up short a few steps in front of me. I skidded to a halt to avoid running into her.

She held Ivan's arm as she stared ahead into the garden. Ivan beamed as he watched her. I followed Maria's gaze toward our garden. Something was different in the tiny space.

From the branches of the birch trees hung a flat board attached to two thick ropes.

A swing.

We both squealed and ran for it. The board was thick and long enough for both of us to fit. During our race to the new amusement, I caught a small collection of guards grinning ear to ear. Taking in our joy. They clapped two soldiers on the shoulders—the first was Ivan, to whom Maria blew a giddy kiss as she plopped on the seat.

The other was Zash.

10

Avdeev had forbidden us from speaking in any language other than Russian. He'd forbidden us from signaling anyone outside. He'd forbidden us from opening windows. But nothing could forbid us from squealing like children as we swooped back and forth on our swing.

He didn't take the swing away. He might have even given permission for the soldiers to hang it for us. In fact, oftentimes he overlooked the fact that our half hours of exercise stretched to ninety minutes more and more frequently.

With each *whoosh*—back and forth, back and forth—my heart caught an extra gust of hope. The soldiers made us a swing. Many of them, beyond Zash and Ivan, seemed to relish our delight. They no longer wanted to kill us.

The Bolsheviks here were trying to keep us contained until the Soviet government decided what to do with us.

Papa took a turn on the swing and his boots flew high over his head. His laugh pierced the air, contagious as a revolution. Even the guards joined in. Alexei crossed the garden—sans wheelchair—and joined Papa on the swing. A few guards cheered.

I caught noise from behind us, near the giant gate. Guards in the opening with their rifles held in a threatening manner. "Walk on, Citizens, walk on. There's nothing to see here." They took a few menacing steps toward the street on the other side.

By now, all of Ekaterinburg knew the Romanov family was being kept at the Ipatiev House. I wasn't surprised our laughs had lured the curious passersby.

"Well, if there's nothing to see, then why can't we stand here if we want to?" came an irritated reply.

I snickered and turned back to the fun.

I caught Zash watching me out of the corner of his eye. My smile stayed wide as I moved his way. He stepped from the clump of soldiers, and I could sense him trying to school his features once more into something controlled and firm. He lost the fight.

We met by the wall of the house and stopped with a good amount of distance between us. I leaned against the warm exterior wall and beamed. "I don't know why you took part, but . . . thank you."

Zash dropped his gaze. "Perhaps it's hard to believe, but even as your guard, I—we—don't wish despair upon your family."

"I believe you." Grateful warmth flooded my chest. "Because of you, Alexei is walking on his own again."

A pause. "I am glad he is feeling better."

As though sensing us talking about him, Alexei made a little mock-kissing face at me while swinging back and forth. I flushed. But when Zash followed my gaze to Alexei, Alexei had the decency to drop the mockery just in time and send an honorable salute to Zash.

To my surprise, Zash returned the salute.

"He is grateful." I willed my skin to calm back to a regular temperature.

"I did nothing."

Let him think I didn't know. Let him believe his own lie. But I knew what he did for us. And it had crumbled a wall in my chest. "All the same. Thank you, Zash."

A breeze picked up, blowing dark clouds across the city and toward our prison. With visible effort Zash resumed the soldier face. "You'd best enjoy the garden while you can."

"Yes, of course." I left his side, our interaction now concluded with a formal air. Perhaps it was best that we stayed Bolshevik and exiled princess.

Neither of us seemed pleased with that.

The swing was our new savior. It broke the final thread of tension between us and the soldiers we interacted with on a daily basis. Even the pacing and rifles of the patrolling Bolsheviks couldn't keep the hope from slipping in.

We bottled every pinhole of light and sunshine as though they were spells of old—from a soldier's smile to a new tree swing to an extra five minutes outside. I had to make a daily list in my mind so when Avdeev was particularly drunk or when the unkind Bolsheviks pillaged our food, I still had encouragement to remind me that humanity and joy existed.

Summer heat blew the storms in, bringing gusts of torment with them. The heat pulled us outside into the shade of the poplars one moment and then the gale drenched us the next. "Everyone inside," Avdeev hollered, exiting his alcohol-ridden office.

"We don't mind the rain!" I threw my arms wide and embraced the drenching.

I hadn't taken in how drunk Avdeev actually was, because at my proclamation he stomped across the wet grass toward me, his face as thunderous as the clouds above. I backpedaled, but a strong hand gripped my arm from behind. "I will see her inside, sir."

I relaxed at Zash's presence, even though his voice was brusque. Avdeev nodded and then herded the rest of my family indoors.

I returned to the house with Zash at my side. Did Avdeev really have to cut our half hour short? Why couldn't we be out in the rain? It did us no harm.

As we ascended back to our prison cells, the sealed windows kept in all the cigarette smoke from the soldiers taking shelter from the rain. It also trapped the vile odors of the overused lavatory, which quickly mixed with the smell of lunch coming from our small kitchen.

No wonder poor Mamma never got well. She was breathing this in every moment of every day.

Avdeev stood in the doorway of his office with narrowed eyes, ensuring our reentry. With Zash at my side I felt bolder. "Please, Commandant, let us open some windows."

"And allow you to signal the citizens outside for help? Absolutely not." Avdeev shoved me into our room, severing the connection between Zash and me, and shut the door.

Not even a pause. Not even a flash of empathy.

Swine.

I was so angry, I stomped right through the dining room and into Alexei's room where I popped open the fortochka and breathed in the storm.

Wet boots from thirty soldiers and hot brows turned the house into a sealed, airless crate of stench. When Avdeev checked on us during breakfast the next morning, and it was still raining, I tried the meek approach. "Commandant? May we open a window, please? Just for a few minutes?"

He held my gaze for a long moment. "No."

No matter how many times we asked over the next few days, Avdeev would not allow us to unseal a window. How could he stand the smell? Did not he and the soldiers feel as encased and suffocated as we did?

The rain did not abate, nor did the heat. The humid air hung like airborne grime, attaching itself to our skin and bedclothes. The five-room tomb became a breeding ground for parasites. We cleaned our linens as best we could, trying to keep the filth at bay. But the dogs started scratching first. Then Tatiana and Alexei. And then me.

My scalp itched to no end, and no matter how many times I rinsed my hair or washed my pillowcase, the itching wouldn't stop. Finally, Mamma's maid, Anna, stepped into the room with an armful of linens. "Head lice."

I startled from my card game with Maria—one hand flying to my head.

"Lice have bred in this prison and I pray that the commandant feels their bites on his scalp more severely than any of you." Anna set the linens down and faced us with a grim set to her mouth. "But since you are infested already, there is only one thing we can do."

She held up a pair of scissors and a razor.

Maria burst into tears.

"You are still beautiful." I caught Ivan's gentle murmur on the other side of the door to the landing.

I'd come to ring the bell that would summon a guard—him—to

escort me to the lavatory. But apparently Maria was out there already . . . with him.

Maria sported the baldness best of us all. Her head shape was elegant and proportionate, but that brought her no comfort coming from me. I was her sister. Yet when her handsome Ivan asked, "Do you believe me?" Maria released a breathless whisper. "Yes, Ivan. I will always believe you."

Always. She would always believe him. She had let her heart go. If Avdeev saw them . . .

I rang the bell with a clang and burst onto the landing. Maria and Ivan jumped, but I saw how close they'd been standing. Inches apart. Barely.

I hauled Maria back into our room and shoved a pack of cards into her hand. "Shuffle these."

"I don't want to play bezi—"

I stalked back onto the landing, shut the door behind us, and went toe to toe with Ivan. "My sister is beautiful and you are handsome, but if you dare to touch her then you risk all our necks. I like you, Ivan. But I don't want to see you shot. Even more so, I don't want to see my *sister* shot because she kissed a guard."

Ivan's Adam's apple bobbed severely and he had the honor to look ashamed. It gave me no pleasure to scold him—but better him than Maria. Maria wouldn't listen to me. I liked seeing her happy. But not if it meant she would die.

I stepped away and only then spotted Zash at the top of the stairs. How much had he heard? He stared at Ivan and I thought about the words that had spilled from my lips—what if I'd endangered Ivan? Maria? What if *my* rash actions resulted in the danger I so desperately sought to avoid?

"I am here to relieve you of your post, Ivan." When Zash met my gaze, he looked kind. Understanding. He'd heard it all. But then I remembered my bald head. Heat flooded my face. I spun on my heel and shut the door behind me. What a silly response! What did I expect? That I could hide my haircut from him for the rest of our exile?

It didn't matter what he thought. If I told myself that enough, perhaps I'd believe it.

I leaned my back against the door, breathing hard. What was I doing confronting a soldier right outside the commandant's office? I closed my eyes and steadied my breathing. Voices drifted through the thin door.

"She's right, you know," Zash said quietly.

"Why shouldn't I be kind to Maria?" Ivan argued. "Why shouldn't I tell her she's beautiful? Their lives are miserable. *We* can leave this place if we wish. *We* have a future outside of this rotten house. They don't know whether they're going to live or starve to death. I almost hope the White Army gets them out of here."

"They are here because of the tsar and tsarina's actions." Zash sounded as though he was quoting a reason rather than thinking it on his own.

"Do you really believe that?"

I pressed my ear against the wood for Zash's response. "I don't know what to believe, Ivan. Neither side seems right to me, but this side seems safer. I am here to protect my family—to serve where our government tells me to serve. To be compliant."

"What a disgusting way to live." Footsteps denoted Ivan's attempt to leave, but Zash cut him off.

"Why are *you* here then?"

A pause. "At first, for the money. But now . . . for Maria." Ivan's boot clomps faded down the stairs.

Zash wasn't here because he supported the Bolsheviks. He was here to protect his family. But didn't he say he had no parents? Who was he protecting? And Ivan . . .

I pushed myself off the door and found Maria. She stood in front of the small wall mirror, trying to tie a worn string of lace around her head. I stepped up beside her and knotted the lace, finishing the bow. We were almost the same height. "You *are* beautiful, Sister."

Her chin quivered and her hand dropped from her head, but she gave no response. She'd always been more concerned with her appearance than the rest of us—probably because she was stocky and strong. She focused on that aspect of her build. But everyone—every relative and every male suitor—always commented how Maria was "the pretty one." Why did her ears never hear that?

She would be turning nineteen this month. Mamma had fallen in love with Papa at age seventeen. Maria likely feared never experiencing love.

I couldn't afford to fear or hope for love. Then I thought about Zash and how my heart desired his friendliness more than the other guards'. Exile was affecting my emotions. That frightened me.

I scratched at my dried scalp and compared my pudgy face and bulb of a head to Maria's gentle features. I tried to imagine what Zash had seen from the top of the stairs. I thought I'd read kindness in his gaze, but had it actually been pity?

Maria turned from the mirror and shuffled the cards for bezique. My baldness did not become me. Good. It would deter Zash from getting any ideas.

I laughed quietly at myself. As if *he* had any ideas of attraction. I was the one stirring that pot. Still, my face flushed in embarrassment at my sickly appearance. Was it so petty to wish to be rescued—or to die—beautiful?

When I joined Maria, I looked anywhere but at her—at the cards, at the dogs scratching themselves and chewing at their backs, at Papa trimming his mustache. It felt so wrong to tell my sister that happiness was dangerous and loneliness was safe.

But if the White Army was coming, we needed to be ready to leave everything behind.

Everything.

Even people we loved.

The White Army was near. I could see it in the fidgeting of the guards. I could smell it in the alcohol that soaked Avdeev's skin. Hope sat in my mouth like a pastila confectionery I couldn't bring myself to swallow.

I'd woken to another rainy day. Suffocating from the dimness, the heat, the imprisonment, the humidity. Everyone else still slept, so I crept to the fortochka to watch the sun rise and to inhale false freedom. As I slid to the small cracked window, I half expected to see the White Army marching through the town and advancing on the Ipatiev House.

But all I saw were the sisters from the convent on their way to deliver our daily basket of goods. *They* did not wish for our deaths. They were nuns. They were good. They were even walking through the pouring rain to bring us food.

An idea struck me as abruptly as one of the raindrops splashing my face. I watched the sisters. I thought of my family. My hope.

And I scrambled for a piece of stationery.

Avdeev wouldn't unseal the windows because he was afraid we'd signal people outside. All this time I'd had the small fortochka for fresh air, yet I'd never considered signaling for help or trying to send a message. If Avdeev was afraid of that, this meant that some people outside the walls were sympathetic to our cause.

What if I could somehow get a message to the White Army? What if I could tell them how many guards were here and where we were located in the house and what our routine was? They could rescue us. They could prepare adequately.

I could save my family.

I scribbled the details on the stationery, glancing up as the sisters approached. They were almost here. I wrote what I could, ink dribbling down my hand, smearing on the paper. I almost blotted it with my nightdress, but that would leave evidence or lead to questions. So I dabbed it with another piece of paper and then grabbed one of Papa's paperweights.

The sisters were at the gate.

I crumpled the letter of information around the paperweight, then tied it with one of Maria's lace hair ribbons. The sisters handed their basket of food to the soldiers and turned to leave. In mere seconds they would be passing by the palisade directly across from me.

My hands trembled.

I couldn't allow myself to think of the repercussions. Not with something as important as the lives of my family at stake. I would have to throw the weight over both palisades. I must not miss.

The rain lessened. The sun shone through a crack in the sky. Alexei stirred behind me. The sisters walked across from me, making the sign of the cross toward our windows. I pushed the fortochka all the way open so they'd see me.

Then I stepped back, thinking of the times Papa and I had thrown snowballs and he'd corrected my stance. I cranked my arm back and threw. The paperweight sailed through the window, arced over the garden . . .

. . . and fell inside the palisade, next to our swing.

It sat there for all the Bolsheviks to see. A crumpled white piece of evidence. My skin chilled. What had I done? Had any guards seen?

I poked my head out the window to glance down. To see if any guards stood watch against the wall below. Nothing. All clear. No soldiers in sight—

A gunshot.

Pain exploded in my face.

11

"*It is because the children* are suffocating! We all are!" Papa stood in front of Commandant Avdeev like Tsar Nikolai would have. Feet set firmly apart, spine straight. Leader. Protector. Papa.

I stood in his shadow, pressing a cloth to my burning cheek. A soldier had shot at me. The sill above my head had shattered and the bullet ricocheted into the plaster on the bedroom wall.

Right. Above. Alexei.

Until that moment I hadn't realized the Bolsheviks hid manned machine guns in the towers across from the Ipatiev House. The shrapnel scrapes on my face didn't burn nearly as hot as my remorse. Alexei could have been killed. *I* could have been killed, though that currently didn't bother me as much as the mental image of that note lying by the swing. At this very moment. Waiting to be picked up and read by one of Commandant Avdeev's soldiers. Then we'd be shot.

And this time, the Bolsheviks wouldn't miss.

"She was foolish." Commandant Avdeev—fully sober and rigid with anger—eyed me and I was glad that my face bore my shame. I needed him to see humility. Obedience.

Three Bolsheviks stood behind Papa and me. They were not our friends—I'd never seen them before and heat radiated off their uniforms, filling the already stuffy room. I imagined the barrels of their guns pressing into my spine. Blowing a hole between my shoulders. Papa weeping . . .

"Commandant, I implore you, allow us to open a window." Papa's tone remained submissive. "We cannot breathe. Nastya was desperate for air."

"And allow you to repeat this offense?" Avdeev waved a hand toward me. "You were warned repeatedly!" There was no sign of softening and I knew it was because of the Bolsheviks behind us. Avdeev had a position to maintain—a persona to uphold.

"Please, Commandant. Please put in a request."

A Bolshevik made a scoffing sound in the back of his throat from behind me. Avdeev lifted his chin and steeled his features. "Say it again."

Papa swallowed. He was reading the situation same as I was. He'd show the humility that would humor the soldiers behind us and save face for Avdeev. Because that was Papa. Humble. Selfless. "Please."

"Again."

"Please."

"Again."

My throat closed. My eyes stung. Papa lowered himself to his knees. Knelt before his captor in complete humiliation. "I beg you, Commandant."

"Again."

"Imagine this," I ground out to Alexei that evening at his bedside. "I steal a gun and make Commandant Avdeev bow to all of *us*."

Alexei didn't play along. "Did he agree to open a window?"

"No." I picked at the ruff of my dress collar. It needed mending. I was so tired of mending, I'd rather endure a frayed collar. Or chop it off altogether. "But he didn't say he wouldn't. I think he'll try."

"Was that really why you were at the fortochka, Nastya?" Alexei knew me too well.

I shook my head. The window had been resealed. I wanted to monitor the piece of paper still sitting in the grass outside. Because of the rain we hadn't been able to retrieve it. I prayed the water washed away any of the contents. But if a guard found it, we'd be ruined.

"I admire your courage," Alexei said.

I hadn't felt courageous. I'd felt only reckless. And because of that, *I* had opened the fortochka. *I* had disobeyed the rules and risked our lives. *I* had sent Papa to his knees, pleading with Avdeev until the Bolsheviks laughed and my heart screamed.

And I had failed.

I absentmindedly fiddled with Alexei's blanket. The relief spell had worn off after only a day. "Do you need me to write another spell?"

"I'd rather wait until I can't bear it, since we don't have much ink."

I nodded, my hands itching to do something helpful. To remedy the glaring mistake I'd made this morning.

"Nastya . . . do you think Avdeev would kill us?" Alexei asked in a small voice.

I had wondered this over and over, analyzing the way he humiliated Papa or how he took our belongings, our extra food, and our freedom. But still, he had laughed at our play. He had allowed the convent sisters to deliver food. He approved a swing to be hung in the garden even though that had been Ivan and Zash's idea. He stretched our time out in the fresh air.

"No, Alexei. I don't think he would."

<hr />

The sun didn't come out all day. I didn't sleep all night. I considered sneaking out to retrieve the letter, but had I been caught, that would have been even worse after my window episode. I'd also thought of asking Ivan—or even Zash—to retrieve it for me. But I couldn't trust them not to turn it in to Avdeev.

So I waited, tossing and turning all night, sweating in my monogrammed linens, and counting down the minutes. It was the worst night of my life.

I spent the morning playing cards with Maria. We had exhausted the French card game and invented plenty after that. We hardly enjoyed them anymore—we played mostly to cure the boredom. But right now I played them to keep me from smashing my fist against a window as I waited for our turn in the garden.

Commandant Avdeev finally retrieved us for our afternoon outing. I was the first on the stairs. The first out the door. The first to the swing.

And the first to see the indented patch of earth, empty of a paperweight.

It was gone. Someone had found it.

I whipped my gaze around, frantic. Avdeev was talking to a soldier. He didn't seem bothered. Neither Ivan nor Zash was on duty. Who had found it? Were they waiting to see what I'd do? I'd implicated myself by running to the swing. To the very spot the letter had landed.

"Next time you should use a smaller paperweight." Papa came up beside me and sat on the swing. "It will fly farther."

A gust of air released from my lungs. "You found it?"

He patted the spot on the swing beside him. We swung gently. "I do not fault you for trying, Nastya. But this was a bit messier than your usual impishness."

"I know." I watched my shoes smear the mud underfoot as we rocked back and forth. "I was caught up in hope. I think I'm losing some of my logic. I am growing desperate, Papa, and I cannot control it."

"You must."

And that was that. I had no choice. I *must* control my desperation. I must be more vigilant. I must be patient and wait for the Matryoshka doll to open and give me its spell. Why was it taking so long?

I stomped away the muddy indent from the paperweight. "Wait . . . how did you retrieve it?" We'd not been allowed into the garden yesterday. I was first out the door today.

"Some soldiers have grown more loyal to me than Avdeev. I do not expect their secrecy to hold under the pressure of a bribe, should Avdeev find out. But we are safe for now."

"Papa, you are a magician." How he managed to befriend the soldiers to such a sincere degree baffled me. It was taking me a full month to get through to Zash. But at the same time, as his loyal and adoring daughter, I wasn't surprised at all.

We returned inside to find the basket of food delivered by the sisters. My face grew warm, thinking of the nun who looked up at my window. Did she see my failed attempt? Did I endanger them?

The sight of their food must mean that they were safe, since they were still able to deliver it.

I took the basket to Kharitonov. He manned the tiny kitchen that we were sometimes allowed to cook in. "Thank you, Nastya. Would you like to help make the bread today?"

I always loved when he had to make bread—it gave me something productive to do. That felt as though I was providing for my family. It made me feel like I could survive in a cottage as a common working girl someday.

"Yes, please." I unloaded the basket of food, setting the eggs on the counter and the milk bottle in the cooler. I pulled out a long parcel wrapped in thick cloth. Inside rested a black loaf of rye. "Actually, I think the sisters sent some."

Kharitonov's thick eyebrows popped up. "They don't usually send us bread."

"That or it doesn't always make it to us. I think Avdeev takes it." I held the loaf to my nose and inhaled. Not warm, but very fresh. Likely baked this morning. I squeezed it lightly to hear the crunch of the crust, as Kharitonov had taught me, but something hard crinkled beneath my fingers. Something that I'd thought was a crease in the cloth.

I unwrapped the rest of the loaf and a small square of paper toppled into my palm. "What . . . what is this?" I unwrapped the paper to find a note written in red ink in French.

I scanned the letter, my breath quickening as I caught words and phrases like *friends* and *the hour has come*. I got to the end—to the signature line—but it held no name. All it said was, *From someone who is ready to die for you. Officer of the White Army.*

This letter . . . was a rescue.

12

"*Olga has the best handwriting.*" Tatiana bent over the letter as gingerly as she used to tend wounded Russian soldiers. "She should write the response."

My family encircled the note, reading and rereading it. The officer's letter said the White Army was only fifty miles away from Ekaterinburg. It told us to listen for any movement outside—to wait and hope. To be ready any time of day. It told us to send a reply—hidden in the cream bottle—with a mapped layout of our rooms. It was happening. Our rescue!

I had to stop myself from thinking too far ahead—from dreaming of me and my family living in a cottage; Papa sawing wood and me dabbling in spell ink to create words that would heal Alexei's pain.

Dr. Botkin sketched a quick map on the back because he had the steadiest hand, and Olga wrote a short reply in French, per Papa's dictation.

All our windows are shut and Alexei is too sick and unable to walk. No risk whatsoever must be taken without being absolutely certain of the result. We are almost always under close observation.

We couldn't afford a half-baked rescue attempt. Whoever this White officer was, his plan needed to be flawless. Foolproof. Perfect.

He was lucky that I was an expert in such things.

Three days passed with no response. We wore our jewel-encrusted clothing, and all of us except Mamma took shifts throughout the night to listen for any unusual sounds. The guards sensed our tension.

"Are you alright?" Ivan asked Maria during a garden excursion. He seemed truly concerned.

"Being shut inside the house takes its toll," she replied softly.

After another two days, we received a response. Papa read it first this time but shook his head when he got to the end. "He talks of an escape from an upstairs window. Did he not read that all our windows are sealed?"

"What else does it say?" I took it from him. Maria and Alexei read over my shoulder.

Would it be possible to tranquilize the little one in some way and lower him out the window without his feeling any pain?

"The *little one*?" Alexei scoffed. "Who is this general? If he's so loyal, why doesn't he use the proper titles?"

"Stop being so sensitive, little tsarevich," I teased, though the officer's choice of reference regarding Alexei peeved me as well.

Could I figure out some sort of spell with my remaining ink that would numb Alexei? Maybe another relief spell or two would help him enough to manage a window escape. But that still didn't change the fact our windows were sealed.

The bell from the landing rang and Maria shoved the note down her blouse. Commandant Avdeev entered and Papa rose from his chair. It was still an hour until our appointed recreation time in the garden. Did he see the concern—the guilt—on our faces? Had he found out about the letters?

"Everyone is to go into the garden—including the tsarina."

"Is there a reason for the extra time in the fresh air?" Papa put his hands in his pockets, likely to hide any sweating.

No other soldiers were with Avdeev, and he responded in the friendly manner that slipped out when he wasn't saving face. "I hope to have some good news for you."

We obeyed. Kharitonov carried Alexei into the fresh air and placed him on the swing. I tied a head scarf over my baldness, nervous about Zash seeing me since he'd mostly been on outdoor watch these past few days. Mamma came out in her wheelchair, pale with a hand to her head. We set her in the shade so the heat wouldn't aggravate her ache.

I wanted to go to her, but since sharing her secret about Rasputin's spell mastery, she had established an emotional distance from me.

Avdeev lined us up, stiff commandant once again now that his soldiers were present. "You will remain outside under close watch until you are summoned. The Committee for the Examination of the Question of Windows in the House of Special Purpose is here to inspect your quarters."

Papa gave a bow. "Thank you. Let us know how we can help."

Window inspection—were they checking to make sure they were secure? Had Avdeev seen the White Army's letter? He couldn't have. He said he hoped for some *good* news for us.

We did not see the committee, but we stayed outside through lunchtime. I didn't even mind the missed meal. We giggled and played chase with the dogs. With every moment of inhaled sunlight, I filled with sustenance far more valuable than food—the sustenance of hope, of light, of the sense of freedom.

Some of the guards joined in the laughter, though most stayed at their posts. Zash and Ivan patrolled across the garden. I avoided going near them, tugging my head scarf a little tighter.

Maria, however, seemed to overcome her self-consciousness. She fluttered her eyelashes at Ivan and Zash. "Will you push us on the swing?"

Before they could answer, she grabbed my hand and pulled me after her. My heart pattered faster than my feet as I ran with her to the swing. Toward Zash.

We sat close together, linking elbows. Ivan did the pushing. Zash stood by the tree trunk, arms folded, watching. I peeked his way as we swung. What did he see in me now? Why did I care?

His face betrayed nothing. He stood stiffer than the tree, all professional Bolshevik. With each back and forth, my grin grew because he remained so stoic. The longer he stayed serious, the funnier it became. Soon I was giggling just as hard as Maria. Zash wouldn't crack, though his eyes seemed to twinkle the way Papa's did when he hid a grin beneath his mustache.

On the next forward swing Maria released my arm and toppled backward off the swing with a squeal. Right into Ivan's arms. Oy, what an obvious flirtation! I would have rolled my eyes, but her abrupt departure from the swing sent me lurching since she had been the support on my right side.

The swing carried me upward, the momentum sending me straining for the other rope with my free arm. I would *not* allow my feet to go over my head the way Maria did. No soldier had the right to see *my* underclothes.

But gravity and momentum were against me. My fingers brushed the opposite rope, but not close enough to grip it. Off I went, balance lost, exhaling my pride and accepting the fact that this would hurt.

But it didn't. No crunch. No hard earth under my skull.

Instead, strong hands, an arm behind me. Not Papa's arms—I knew Papa's touch. The moment my mind registered *not Papa*, a delighted flutter pinched my stomach.

Zash.

I wasn't on the swing enough to haul myself up, but I wasn't off enough to get my feet under me. Instead, my traitorous hand gripped his uniform lapel. This was so awkward.

Zash hauled me off the swing and set me on my feet. My scarf had slipped, revealing my bald head. I released him immediately and reached for the scarf, but he scooped it up from the ground. My hand hung between us, waiting for the flowered square of material. Trembling.

He didn't give it to me right away. "You don't need this, you know."

I never knew how to take compliments, but my face warmed. I slid the fabric from his fingers, our skin brushing briefly. Then I jammed the scarf back onto my head and tried to resurrect my dignity. "I do if I don't want my head to turn into a sunburned tomato!"

"You're at no risk of that, with how frequently you wear the scarf—both inside *and* outside."

I finally looked into his face. His mouth held the closest thing to a grin I'd seen since the Chugwater play.

"You know what I meant," he said.

I could hardly catch my breath—though it had nothing to do with the swing. Emotions buzzed like a beehive in my brain. He was flirting. And I liked it—craved it. *Danger, danger, danger,* the bees hummed, to deter me.

Didn't they know I thrived on the thrill of danger?

I cleared my throat and stopped the lazy sway of the swing by grabbing the rope. "Thank you . . . Zash." Then, before he thought I was thanking him for the compliment, I added, "For catching me."

He winked.

In that moment I saw nothing else but his wink. Again and again and again, and with each mental repeat my stomach lurched as it had when I fell from the swing.

Maria might have feigned drama to catch the attention of Ivan, but I ended up with the true moment of rescue and flattery and winks.

I'd never felt so unsafe at the Ipatiev House as I did just then.

⁓

"Security has been increased." Avdeev paced in front of the sitting room window. "You are forbidden from putting your head outside or attempting to signal anyone . . . on pain of being shot."

He stopped his pacing. "After inspection, the Committee has agreed that we should unseal one window." He pushed against the window and it opened a small crack. The twitter of birdsong burst into our space.

The window had been unsealed—the entire window! The Window Committee—or whatever Avdeev had called them—had granted us fresh air. Already, our five-room prison smelled fresher. Cleaner. Like life had returned.

"Thank you," Papa said sincerely.

Avdeev nodded and left. None of us cheered, but we exchanged expressions of such astonishment and delight we might as well have been shouting, "Huzzah!"

Now we could send the White Army officer a reply. This rescue might really happen. What perfect timing for a window to be opened. Almost too perfect. "Papa," I whispered. "Do you think they know? About the rescue?"

"If they knew, Nastya, they would not have opened the window."

"But they increased security." I'd instigated enough sneaky escapades that I recognized the blare of warning in my mind. When things came too easily, that implied a catch. A danger.

"Our escape is being blessed," Papa said. "But we will proceed with the highest caution. I am counting on your analytical mind."

Once we deemed it safe, Olga sat to write the response to the White Army officer. We gave the details of the newly opened window and the locations of the upstairs guards. We explained the surprise inspections and how the soldiers had a system of alarm bells they could use at any moment. We also made sure to mention the guards across the street that we never saw but we knew about because they shot at me.

Lastly, we asked if the rescue included our friends—Dr. Botkin, Anna, Cook Kharitonov, etc. Papa asked Olga to also make a small note about his diaries and personal documents that still filled a crate in the outhouse. "Be certain to assure this officer of our composure. Make sure he knows we will remain poised and calm during the rescue and during correspondence."

It was our longest letter yet and made the rescue seem real. For all we knew we could be free within days!

I slipped away to pull the Matryoshka doll from my blouse. It seemed warmer but still no seam. More than ever, I expected it to open any day. And I would use it on the night of our escape. My mind wandered to the hidden spell ink. If we were to escape soon, I should fill a tin with relief spells for Alexei. For travel. It would be best to have them all formed and ready so I wouldn't have to make them during our rescue—especially since none of my family save Alexei knew I was secretly doing spell mastery.

Papa read us Scripture before bed as he did every night, and the room shrank as our hearts swelled with hope. What a wild day— almost four hours out in the garden, an unsealed window, a planned rescue, and . . . and a wink that wouldn't leave my consciousness.

I missed the last half of Papa's prayer as the wink replayed in my mind—like some sort of naughty reminder that my heart had dared to flutter when met by those long-lashed soldier eyes. I hadn't even looked in them long enough to know their color, though I was sure if I asked Maria she would be able to tell me. She paid attention to those things.

When she and I finally climbed onto our cots that night and the lights went out, I rolled to face her, about to ask if she knew the color of Zash's eyes. But she spoke first.

"I want to tell Ivan."

I gaped. "*What?*" To ensure I understood, I asked, "Tell him what?"

"About the rescue. I want him to come with us."

I reached for her hand. "Oh, Maria, you can't. Not yet. Not now. Wait until we've heard back from the White Army officer. Wait until a plan is more permanently in motion."

"Why should I wait?"

"Because to reveal such a risky endeavor so early puts us in danger."

"Like when you almost got shot?" she retorted.

The pain in that memory erased Zash's wink. "Yes. Exactly like that."

"Ivan is a good man. He will not harm me. He won't tell anyone."

"I can see that he is kind and gentle with you, but for the safety of our family—and you know Papa would agree—wait a little longer." She was silent for a long time. "Maria . . . I do not oppose your attraction to him. I *want* you to be happy."

"Do you?" She sounded teary. "You scolded Ivan the other day. *Scolded* him!"

I reached across the small gap of our cots and cupped both hands around her fist. "Oh, sweet Sister, I want you to be happy, but you must be careful in your interactions here. Don't you see that? You're endangering all of us. You're endangering Ivan. *He* is endangering you! For now, you must quiet your feelings." I lowered my voice to a bare breath. "Wait until the White Army rescues us. I'm *sure* Ivan will join us if this plan works."

"But what if they kill him first?" she whimpered. "What if the White Army arrives and they don't know he is gentle and kind and caring? What if they shoot him in the head and . . . and . . ." She started to sob.

Only then did I realize how deeply involved she and Ivan were. I'd seen her flirt before. I'd seen her wail over boys, but not like this. And I was sure our imprisonment and torment made every act of kindness feel that much more longed for.

I squeezed her fists. "We must trust that Iisus will protect us. Like Papa read tonight." I said it mostly for my benefit as well as hers. But my own traitorous heart started thumping its concern about Zash. What if *he* got injured—or even killed—during our rescue?

"Does Iisus protect Bolshevik soldiers?"

I wasn't sure how to respond to that. "Ivan is not a Bolshevik. You said so yourself. He is a soldier." He was here because of her. But if I told Maria that now, there'd be no stopping her from risking all our lives through her love for him.

He was not a Bolshevik. He was a boy in love. No Bolshevik would tell a lice-ridden former princess that she was beautiful.

No Bolshevik would risk his reputation with his commandant to push that girl on a swing.

And no Bolshevik would steady her on her feet, hold her close . . . and wink at her.

My heart flipped again. I tugged my hands away from Maria, feeling like a dreadful hypocrite.

13

JUNE 26

"S dnem rozhdeniya!" Everyone encircled Maria's bed and shouted the birthday greeting as loud as we could. Her eyes popped open and a smile quickly followed.

We cheered and danced around her bed. Well, all except Mamma. She sat in her wheelchair, trying to smile. Papa held Alexei and we shouted, "Huzzah!" so loud that the soldiers in the basement likely heard us.

Maria squealed and pulled the blanket over her head. Tatiana and I jumped forward to tickle her. None of us had any gifts, so we did what we could to pamper her. Mamma braided lace pieces together as a new ribbon for her head. Both Alexei and I gave her our servings of cocoa. Even Joy seemed to understand Maria deserved extra licks, rubs, and pouncing today.

Around noon, I snuck into our small kitchen to see what items we had in stock. I found nothing but a small bag of lentils and some broth. Nothing that could make a cake or even a sweet blini for her birthday. The basket from the sisters had not yet been brought up. When it did arrive, I'd be digging for far more than eggs and sugar. Was it too soon for the White Army officer to reply?

"What do you want to do today?" Papa asked Maria when I reentered the room. "More card games? I can read any book you like."

"Will you tell me how you and Mamma met?" Maria settled on the floor nearest the window, but her gaze flickered toward the main door. I didn't know which guards were on duty today, but she was likely thinking about Ivan. And romance.

I sat next to her, wanting to hear the story. Trying—and failing—not to think about Zash. Papa's eyes twinkled. "Ah, so you request a fairy tale!" He scratched Joy's furry head. "How can I resist?"

Even Mamma cracked a smile as her eyes took on a reminiscent shine.

"I was sixteen and first saw your mamma at the wedding of her sister. It was the way you always hope to meet your love—at a ball where I could ask for her hand dance after dance after dance."

All us girls sighed and sank deeper into the story. I pictured the Catherine Palace with its gold floors and tall windows. I imagined twirling in a lovely gown with hair still on my head—braided and pearled and assembled in a way that would make me appear graceful.

"It was a whirlwind meeting and we visited only long enough to know we both wished for more time. She went back to Hesse and I stayed in Russia. For five years we didn't get to see each other. We didn't get to write to each other. But then she visited for six weeks and I determined, during that time, to win her as my wife."

"Only I said no." Mamma covered her grin with a handkerchief.

We knew the story—she'd said no despite adoring him and despite being the courting age of seventeen.

"She may have said no, but she *did* agree to write me letters in secret when she went back home. Not only that, but she turned down all other marriage proposals—including one that would have made her the next queen of the United Kingdom!"

"That proposal was my grandmother, Queen Victoria's, doing. I don't even think *he* wanted to marry me."

"His loss." Papa waved a hand in the air. "Finally, another wedding brought us together in Coburg and I knew if I didn't win her then, I would not have another chance. So I declared my undying affection in the most romantic way possible—"

"You begged me through tears, if I recall," Mamma chirped.

"—in the most *romantic way possible*. And you know what she said?"

We all knew this part of the story and turned to Mamma to finish it. Her pale cheeks flushed and she gave Papa an apologetic pout. "I said, 'Very well. Who else is there to marry, anyway?'"

"Yes, you did say that. And all I heard was a resounding *yes*." He planted a kiss right on her lips. "There was no one else to marry because you had refused all the other princes."

A knock on the door interrupted us. The knock was so light I might have imagined it, but everyone stilled. Avdeev never knocked—he walked in. The knock did not repeat, but the knob turned slowly and the door inched open.

Our first sight was a nose and then brown hair. Ivan. He saw us and his freckled face broke into an enormous grin. "I hear there is a birthday to celebrate."

Maria bloomed pink as a pomegranate. Her hand fumbled for mine amidst the folds of our dresses and I squeezed it. Ivan didn't wait for an invitation. He stepped into the room and held before him a tiny decorated chocolate cake.

Everyone gasped. Cake. *Real* cake!

Ivan glanced over his shoulder back out into the hallway. Then he strode in and placed the cake on the table. He held Maria's gaze and reddened a little himself. "Happy birthday, Grand Duchess Maria."

His other hand deposited the basket of food from the sisters. With a little bow he left, and all of our astonished faces turned as one toward Maria. Her jaw hung open and she rose slowly, approaching the cake.

"There's a note," she whispered, lifting a small torn piece of paper from the top of the cake. "'May this cake be sweet, lovely, and unexpected . . . like you have been to me.'"

My heart melted right along with the thin frosting dripping down the side of the cake. And I decided never to scold her about Ivan again. We all hugged her and then divided up the small treat. I didn't know if he'd purchased it, baked it, or bribed someone for it, but it tasted like clouds and dreams.

"Nastya, take that basket in to Kharitonov," Papa said with a meaningful look.

I nodded and took it to the kitchen. By the time I arrived in the small cooking space, I'd found the letter from the White Army officer. I unfurled it and read it quickly. Enough to get an idea of its contents. This one wasn't asking for information.

This letter held the plan for our escape.

14

It was the worst rescue plan I'd ever read. "*I* could plan an escape better than this," I hissed to Papa.

"Joy could make a better plan," Alexei grumbled. The spaniel sniffed as though agreeing.

According to the letter, we were supposed to wait for a signal at night. Once that signal—whatever it was—came, we were to barricade the door with furniture and then climb out our one open window using a rope that we were supposed to make between now and then.

I couldn't imagine Mamma or Alexei strong enough to shimmy down a shoddy rope in the dark. And what about the night patrols who constantly guarded our windows? What about the guards who monitored the perimeter between the two palisades? What about the ones with machine guns on the ground floor who watched the area below us at all times ever since word came of the White Army's approach?

"We told them of all these dangers," Papa said. "This officer and his men don't wish to die. They will have thought through everything." He didn't sound confident.

That night we all waited, fully clothed, out of view of the

windows. My sisters and I had braided sheets into a rope with plenty of knots to hold on to. The tension caused by this flabby rescue plan had dampened Maria's birthday joy.

We sat the closest and she spent most of the time fidgeting with the note that Ivan had delivered with his little cake. "I need to tell him. I can't escape without him. I can't, Nastya."

I didn't know what to say. Everything felt too rushed. "The rescue probably won't happen tonight. It's too soon. They'll wait until tomorrow night."

"Do you think so?"

No. I didn't. I couldn't read this officer's thinking. I didn't trust it. It was too unpredictable. I'd spent the afternoon using up the last of Zash's spell ink and filling an empty butter tin with four relief spells. The minute we heard the signal, I would apply a spell to Alexei's knee and we'd escape.

But my body sat in unrest. The Matryoshka doll stayed resolutely sealed and this White Army officer lost my respect with every passing minute. His plan held barely any details. He was putting our lives in jeopardy.

And the lives of the Bolsheviks we'd come to love.

There was no way to alert Ivan, and I wasn't sure that was a good idea anyway. Though, as a guard, he could possibly help if we were to get stopped by another guard. The logic in my head said it was best to keep him out of it. But the drumming of my heart urged me to do the same as Maria—to warn Zash. To invite him to escape with us.

I focused on the message of my head. I would miss Zash. I would leave that part of my story unfinished if we escaped and I never saw or heard from him again. But my family's safety and survival were more important.

We waited. And waited. And waited.

Maria whispered for hours how sweet Ivan was. How thoughtful Ivan was. How caring Ivan was. I couldn't disagree, but it was a relief when she finally nodded off. Papa and Alexei remained the most vigilant. Mamma sat with her eyes closed, but I knew she wasn't asleep.

I slipped the Matryoshka doll free from my blouse. Having checked it so many times, I didn't expect to see anything different, but this time there was a slight glow around the middle of the faceless doll. Not quite a seam, but definitely magic.

I gasped a whisper. "Papa."

He moved to my side and I showed him the glow.

"The spell is almost ready." He grinned. "This is a sign. Whatever spell that doll is going to release will help us. Save us. I am certain."

Immense relief covered me. If this rescue attempt went awry, at least we had a backup plan. A spell from Dochkin, the great spell master.

The night passed without a signal. Neither Papa, Alexei, nor I slept. When breakfast came, I could hardly swallow the dry black bread. A basket of goods came from the sisters, but there was no new note. I was torn between longing for bed and longing for the sunlit garden to wake me up.

We'd had to untie the sheet rope and return the sheets to our beds so no soldiers suspected anything. My fingers hurt from picking at the knots. I dreaded reknotting the sheets tonight.

The time finally came for us to go outside. Alexei and Mamma stayed inside. Olga cared for them. Maria, red-eyed from a long night, burst into the sunlight and ran straight to Ivan. I didn't blame her. She was going to tell him everything.

And there was nothing I could do to stop her.

Papa noticed the same thing after yesterday's cake incident and, as a family, we agreed not to share any more fragile information with her. She had suffered the most in this house—being confined longer than the rest of us children without a companion.

Once I'd finally realized the rescue wasn't happening last night, I had spent the hours of picking at sheet knots thinking about Zash. Letting my heart and head war. I acknowledged that part of me sought out every small motion or twitch of an eye that might insinuate kindness. But really, I knew nothing about him. I wanted to know more. I wanted to talk to him more. And I couldn't bring myself to think of a good reason not to.

So when we were in the garden and Ivan and Maria whispered away in their tree corner by the swing, I approached Zash. Avdeev wasn't joining us today, so there was little risk of scolding. Soldiers muttered about his vodka supply. I'd heard the constant clink of glass on glass followed by a splash and a cough. Papa said that there was always a reason behind drink. Perhaps Avdeev was indulging more and more because the White Army was closing in. Or maybe because he was growing to like us and wasn't sure how to handle his position.

My heart felt for him. Even the soldiers took turns visiting his office or picking up some of his dropped duties.

Zash watched me cross the garden, right up until I stopped in front of him. "I heard your sister had an excellent birthday."

I smiled brightly, though the sun stung my dry eyes. "Better than any of us could have hoped for."

"I am glad to hear it." He broke eye contact. We both watched Ivan and Maria take a turn around the garden. Under the sunlight with her new head ribbon she looked radiant. Instinctively, my hand drifted up to my own head. It was prickly with tiny growth and I recalled Zash's and my last conversation.

"It becomes you," Zash said.

A laugh burst out of me. "Becomes me? *Baldness?*"

"It captures your strength, Nastya. That is what I meant."

"Oh." Every time he used my name, a different part of me melted.

Zash breathed out a long sigh. "What do you need? What can I—we—do for you to make you like"—he gestured toward Maria, a walking sunbeam of delight beside Ivan—"like that?"

My knee-jerk temptation was to respond in jest. But if we were leaving the Ipatiev House tonight, I wanted to be fearless in my conversation with Zash. "Why do you want me like that?" I lifted my eyes, nervous to see his reaction.

His gaze was open. Real. Not the stiff soldier persona, and it made every word skip my head and land on my heart. "You find joy in so many little things. For once . . . I want to see joy find *you*. Surprise you. You deserve it." His fingers brushed mine, ever so lightly. My breath caught and I found myself fighting the urge to move closer. To twine my fingers in his.

Instead, I stepped back. Because to lock my fingers with his would make it impossible to use them to descend a rope toward rescue. I had to be able to leave him behind. The very thought burned my throat and stole whatever magic had bloomed between us.

He saw the change and asked quietly, "What is it? What's wrong?"

My voice came out thick. "I can't . . ." I shook my head. "Ask me tomorrow, Zash." I turned away, chills sweeping down my arms despite the day's heat.

There would be no tomorrow for the two of us.

15

"*We can't do this.*" *Papa* paced in our bedroom as the tied sheets hung limp across Maria's and my laps. We were about to untie all the knots. Again.

Another sleepless night of pacing, wondering, sitting with muscles tense, ready to spring into action and pile furniture against the door. No signal. No rescue.

The more and more we thought about this plan, the more fool-hardy it seemed. Even if we did all safely descend the rope with our belongings and kept the dogs quiet, how could we get out the thick palisade gate? How would the White Army officer get *in*?

"People will die," Papa concluded. "Likely some of the soldiers here."

Maria released a shaky gasp. My own heart shrank. Zash. Ivan. Even Avdeev. I didn't want them injured or killed. We'd spent months befriending these soldiers, even though they were dutifully keeping us in exile.

"Their lives are more important than escape," Papa said. And that was the conclusion. We all knew it was true. I felt it in my heart—I would rather remain in exile than be the cause of these soldiers' deaths.

So that morning Mamma scribbled out a reply to the officer with a crayon since we were out of ink. She gave it to me to insert into the cream bottle to send with the sisters. Her words were brusque and no-nonsense.

> We do not want to, nor can we, escape. We can only be carried off
> by force, just as it was force that was used to carry us from Tobolsk.
> We have no wish for the commandant or the guards—who have
> been so kind to us—to suffer in any way as a result of our escape.
> We are too closely watched. If you still plan to perform a rescue,
> then, in the name of Iisus, avoid bloodshed above all.

We all signed it.

Our trek into the garden was a somber one. No one maintained enough energy to paste on a smile or summon joviality. Ivan hurried to meet Maria and they retreated to the small tree grove at the back corner. I knew by his intense muttered questions that he was inquiring about the rescue.

Maria burst into tears and he embraced her. As I passed them I caught him cupping her face in his hands and saying in low intensity, "I will *not* let you die here, Maria. I will get you out."

She sniffled and nodded.

I hurried on, my eyes searching for Zash. The urge to run to him as Maria had run to Ivan quickened my feet until I finally saw him. He strode toward me and, as though planned, we retreated to the shadows against the house wall for privacy. His stiff Bolshevik persona had been done away with days ago.

This was us. Zash and Nastya, learning what friendship looked like. I breathed his scent of earth and smoke—a mixture of his patrols outside and in.

"It's tomorrow," he said softly. "I can see that something is wrong."

I closed my eyes, closed out the sky. "Surely you know I can't tell you."

"I wish you would."

"Don't you already know?" He spent so much time with Ivan, no doubt he learned the information about our attempted rescue.

"I have my suspicions, but I'd rather hear truth from you."

I opened my eyes and cranked my head to face him. He sat with one knee up and his arm rested across it. Staring at me. Inviting me.

I gave in. "We've realized that we're going to die here." Once I said it, I knew that was why my heart hung so burdened. "We care about you. *I* care about you . . . and the other soldiers," I hurried on. "And that is more important to us than . . . well, than survival, I suppose."

"That's absurd." His soft tone turned sharp. "How can you possibly care for captors more than your own family?"

"That's not what I said." I pushed myself up, angry. "It's not about more or less. We care about every soldier. I am a Romanov, and I *will* value life—every person's life—above all else. There is nothing to gain from hatred of our fellow man."

Zash opened and closed his mouth several times until he finally shook his head with a small, stunned smile. "Don't you realize these soldiers would likely *let* you escape if you really gave forth an effort? They love you."

They. Not *we.*

He reached up and gently tugged the scarf from my head. He seemed closer. I wanted him closer. "They love you," he said again.

Somewhere, in the thin space between us, our hands found each other through the grass. A small touch—but enough to communicate that we both wanted more than captor and captive. Craved it.

His statement rested between us until the creak of the palisade gate caught our attention. An automobile trundled through the opening and pulled up in front of the house. I'd seen it before.

Zash jumped to his feet and resumed his post by the wall. My, how quickly he could adopt that stiff, obedient Bolshevik stance.

But now I could see through it. Now I knew the dark-haired man beneath. And my heart felt safe with him.

The automobile sprayed gravel as it stopped. The young, round-faced man who got out glanced our direction and then strode toward us, purposeful. Beloborodov—the chair of the Ural Regional Soviet.

A surprise inspection.

I pushed myself from the wall of the house and joined Papa to meet the entourage. Papa held out his hand, but Beloborodov did not shake it, nor did he address Papa at all. Instead, he marched past until he stood before Zash. "Where is your commandant, soldier?"

Zash bowed sharply. "Inside, sir."

Beloborodov surveyed the garden with narrowed eyes. "Where are the other prisoners?"

I spun to look, just as Zash did. Papa, Tatiana, Alexei, and I stood in a small clump on the edge of the garden.

"My wife is in bed, ill," Papa said. "And my eldest daughter is tending to her."

Beloborodov did not acknowledge that he had spoken. Instead, his scan stopped on the copse of trees holding the swing and his eyes turned to slits. Between the trees, in the back corner of the palisade, I caught movement.

My heart plummeted.

Maria.

Beloborodov stalked across the garden. It took a moment for me to recover the use of my legs, but once I did I stumbled after him, my mind sprinting far beyond the reach of my strides. I wanted to scream at Maria to come out of the trees. To hide herself. To separate herself from Ivan. That was the only reason she would still be in those trees.

But I couldn't squeeze out a word.

I rounded the tree mere seconds after Beloborodov to see Maria in a tight embrace with Ivan. Sharing a kiss. In a different life, a different situation, it would be sweet. There was nothing unseemly about it. Just a gentle sweetness.

"Maria!" I gasped—a warning, not a reprimand.

She and Ivan jumped apart and their eyes went straight to Beloborodov. Ivan paled and Maria's eyes widened. Papa arrived beside me, Zash at his side. I took Papa's hand. He squeezed mine tight.

Zash's mouth was a thin, grim line. He met my eyes and the resignation in his sent my stomach twisting. A crunch of footsteps announced Commandant Avdeev's arrival.

Beloborodov let the silence stretch out. No one dared break it. Then in a deadly voice, he said, "Girl, return to your father." His eyes remained on Ivan.

Maria, trembling, slunk to Papa. He did not embrace her. Instead, he took one of her arms and steered her back toward the house. I wasn't sure what to do. Follow? Stay?

Beloborodov jerked his head toward me. "See them back to their rooms."

Zash was the soldier to obey. As he escorted me after Papa, Beloborodov asked Commandant Avdeev, "Who is this traitor?"

"Ivan Skorokhodov, sir," Ivan responded. "I am no traitor. These prisoners are no danger to our country—"

Metal on leather preceded the cock of a pistol. I spun, but Zash dragged me on, his fingers pinching into my muscles. Maria, too, peered over her shoulder and seemed to see something in Ivan's grim gaze that I couldn't.

"Ivan," she gasped. "Ivan!" She fought Papa and Zash rushed forward to hold her. She thrashed, fighting the tangle of arms. "Ivan! *Ivan!*" A wild, terrorized thing. I'd never seen her like this. So desperate.

It was as though Ivan was the last of her hope being torn from her.

One of the Bolsheviks who had arrived with Beloborodov stepped away from his post by the automobile and slapped Maria. Papa pressed the soldier away with a single hand. The soldier lifted his gun, but Zash stepped between them. With a mighty force he grabbed Papa's arm in one hand, Maria's arm in the other, and dragged them both inside.

I ran after them, feeling as though there was not enough air in the world to calm my lungs. Through all of Maria's screaming and clawing and desperation, Ivan never said a word.

Moments before I rounded the corner to enter the house, I glanced back. Ivan still stared after us. Our eyes met. In that moment, I saw what Maria had seen: a crinkle-eyed, freckle-skinned farewell.

"Nastya." Zash returned to the base of the stairs. He held his hand out. "Please." He sounded broken.

I took his hand and he tugged me inside.

The gunshot followed.

16

The gunshot ricocheted in my skull like a never-ending echo.

Dead. They had shot Ivan.

Zash barely made it up the stairs to the landing before he fell against the wall and lifted a trembling hand to cover his anguished face. I couldn't breathe. I couldn't process.

Maria's screaming smashed through the walls until it entered every ear in Russia. But Zash's fall to his knees was the final blow that splintered my composure.

I dropped to my knees in front of him, weeping through my own confusion and shock. I pulled him into a tight embrace and he clung to me with one arm. I sent what comfort I could.

It lasted a mere second. A short, shuddering gasp, and then he shoved himself back up. "I . . . I can't," he croaked, taking gulping breaths. "He'll come." With a grimace he pulled me to my feet. "You . . ."

I nodded and forced my muscles to support me. "I understand." I squeezed his hand, so tight it likely pained him. But sometimes comfort needed to sting more than the sorrow for it to break into the grief.

We separated and I entered our prison. Zash needed to be a Bolshevik today. Otherwise he'd be the next one with a bullet in his head. I'd given what solace I could.

Inside the main room Maria writhed on the floor, wailing and clawing at the carpet. I knelt over her, shaking and hollow. What had just happened? "Papa . . . Papa, what do I do?"

But it wasn't Papa who came to me. It was Alexei. He was in Mamma's wheelchair and he pressed a hand to my shoulder. "Get her to bed." His young face hardened into a grim resilience. He'd seen death before when visiting the army with Papa before the revolution. Ivan's death cut his core, but he knew how to remain calm and be a leader.

I had no idea how to respond. How to process.

"There's no comfort any of us can bring," Alexei finished.

Papa carried Maria to her bed. I turned around to face the open door. Zash still rested against the wall on the landing, his face covered. The strength that often came when one of my siblings was crumbling hummed inside me. It felt so feeble. So distant.

I stumbled across the room to close the door to the landing, to free Zash from Maria's keening, but then angry footsteps entered the stairwell. I leapt back. Zash took a deep breath, drew a sleeve against his eyes, and stood at attention. He didn't quite manage the stoic Bolshevik demeanor, but I could see the energy it took for him to pull himself together.

I closed the door when I heard Beloborodov's voice, too frightened to face him. I prayed that he would not enter our space. That instead he was coming up to speak with Avdeev in the commandant's office.

The stomps reached the landing and Beloborodov barked out an order. "You, go bury that body."

"Of course, sir." Zash's cold reply could be taken as compliance . . . or hatred. I had an idea which one fueled it. He retreated down the steps, his footfalls heavier than I usually heard.

Beloborodov and Avdeev retreated to the office. I breathed out a relieved sigh and went to our opened window. I didn't want to see Ivan's body, but neither, I assumed, did Zash. It was as though lending him my gaze and my presence would help give him strength.

Though the whitewash still muted the glass, I could watch through the opening.

Zash stumbled across the lawn with a shovel. The only other Bolsheviks in the vicinity stood at their posts by the gate or by Beloborodov's car. Zash had to deal with the death of his friend alone.

He barely reached Ivan's corpse when Beloborodov stomped back out onto the grounds, entered his automobile, and sped away from the Ipaticv House. The moment the gates closed behind him, Zash fell to his knees and scooped Ivan's bloodied body into his arms.

As he rocked his friend into the afterlife, his weeping was silent but his anguish went deeper than sound. My heart could sense it . . . and it wept with him.

~

Maria no longer spoke. She did not play games. She ate the food as obediently as the three dogs did but with no enthusiasm. Almost as though sleeping. No attempts at conversation were met with a response. She was in a different world.

It was as though I'd already lost her to the Red Army.

When she wasn't eating, she lay in her bed like Mamma. None

of us blamed her. But neither could any of us comfort her. I sat and stroked the fuzz on her head. I rubbed her feet. I snuggled beside her and held her in a hug while sleeping. Because, though I knew not what to do, I had to do *something*. I was her sister. And whether or not she felt my tears or my love or my soft kisses on her cheek, it was what sisters did.

Two days later, Avdeev entered our quarters. His eyes and jowls sagged, his skin sickly and pale. "I am being replaced. The new commandant arrives this afternoon."

"Will you remain here to help him?" I asked, oddly hopeful.

"Likely not."

Papa shook his hand firmly. "Go with our blessings and love."

Avdeev's chin quivered. He nodded and then retreated into his office, defeated.

We did our best to straighten our living quarters, though there was little out of place since cleaning was one of the few ways with which we could pass the time. We mended our clothes for the rest of the day, and I made sure to look my best.

I didn't know why we did this—maybe because, even though Avdeev had been drunk and greedy and unforgiving in many ways, he still took care of us. He still bent for some requests. We had entered a rhythmic understanding of our roles, and he seemed to appreciate it as much as we did.

The new commandant wouldn't know us. We'd be starting our exile all over again. The fact that one of Avdeev's charges—a former grand duchess of Russia—had entertained a relationship with one of his own soldiers was an immense oversight. It meant that Avdeev had been too lenient. He had compromised the Red Army.

Ivan had been shot because of it. Because of a kiss.

I checked the Matryoshka doll in my corset, certain the spell would be ready by now. But the seam was still nothing more than a line of light—nothing I could open with my hands. Part of me hated the spell for taking so long. But the other part of me trusted Papa and the time it took for strong magic to age appropriately. Especially if this spell would be as powerful as Papa thought.

We finished our lunch and remained in the main dining room until the new commandant showed up. We heard the gate open. Heard the gate close. The crunch of tires preceded a crunch of boots.

A head came into view from the stairs. I straightened in my seat as he ascended. A brow. Two steely eyes met mine. Eyes I'd seen before. Eyes I'd winked at when I was on a train with his prize, thinking I was leaving him forever.

Yakov Yurovsky.

Yurovsky stopped in the entryway of our quarters. "Greetings, Citizens." He seemed to speak only to me. His eyes burned through me to the Matryoshka doll tucked into my bodice. He knew. He knew because my face betrayed me. In this moment I lost my ability to shield my emotions. My guard was down. My family broken. My will crumpled by the appearance of this man.

"Greetings, Commandant." Papa extended his hand.

Yurovsky shook it once. "How is the tsarevich's knee?"

Papa's eyebrows jumped at the inquiry. "Not yet well."

Yurovsky gave a singular nod and appraised the room. "There will be an inspection and recording of your belongings as well as your quarters." There was no question. We would comply. He was our new warden.

And with his arrival . . . everything changed.

We never saw Avdeev again. Yurovsky completed his inspection of our quarters and took note of our items that had been stolen by the guards. Papa commented on how thorough Yurovsky was. He seemed optimistic. I was not, especially as Yurovsky eyed me every time he crossed my path.

He knew I had the doll. And he wanted it back.

I grew edgy. During the change in command we were not allowed out in the garden and Zash was not on duty on the landing. I wanted to see him. I wanted to ensure he was okay since Ivan's death.

As dawn rose on Yurovsky's first full day in command, I woke to the sound of boots on the stairs. I crept from my bed, sliding my hand out of Maria's tense grip of sleep. I tiptoed to the door of the landing and listened. The boots stopped at what sounded like Yurovsky's office. A knock. A muffled, "Da." The door creaked. The boots clicked. The door shut.

Then silence.

I sat by the door, listening as I once did when Maria and Ivan were flirting out on the landing. Five minutes passed, the light brightened against the whitewash, and then the door opened. The footsteps left. Just a meeting. Possibly with a guard. Yurovsky was gathering intel as the new commandant, but why so early in the morning?

I was about to push myself from the floor and return to my room to change, but then another set of boots came up the stairs. Another knock. Another whisper. Another meeting. Every five minutes this happened. Every five minutes the pattern of boots was different. Different men meeting with Yurovsky. What were they telling him? Were they loyal to us?

The day went on and at breakfast we had our daily inspection and roll call. No cocoa was served. The time for our garden outing came. And went. Perhaps Yurovsky was not yet aware of our previous schedule.

My throat ached for the fresh air. My skin wept as it imagined the sun upon it. I needed light. I needed open sky. I'd not breathed fully since before Beloborodov pulled into the drive.

A half hour later, Yurovsky entered our space. Papa stood from his chair. "Are we to go into the garden?"

"Not today." Yurovsky consulted his pocket watch, then glanced at me. "The guards are being replaced. During this transition you are to stay in your quarters."

My heart lurched with an awful spasm. "Which guards? Why?"

His dark eyes narrowed. "All of the guards are being replaced. I expect you know why."

Maria sat with glassy eyes, untouched mending in her lap. Yurovsky was replacing the guards because he believed they'd been compromised. That meant they were leaving. Zash was leaving. He might already be gone.

I couldn't swallow. *No. Please don't let him take Zash from me.* I understood, to an extent, how Maria had felt when she looked at Ivan for the last time and what she must have seen. She must have known, in that moment, that she would never see him again.

Would I get a good-bye with Zash? Where were the soldiers being sent? If Yurovsky thought they were compromised, they might be sent to prison. Or even executed! We'd heard the gunshots in Ekaterinburg. Every day.

The rest of the afternoon passed in agony. Our food from the convent sisters was even more limited. Mamma's headache worsened. I sat by our one open window—far enough away to be safe from the eyes of the guards waiting to shoot at me but close enough to watch the string of soldiers tromp away from Ekaterinburg, group by group. The clank of their packing and the scuffle of their departure reached our ears through the floor.

I watched. And watched. And watched. Watching for his midnight hair. For his straight spine. For the elegant eyes that winked at me. For his glance over his shoulder toward my window. For a good-bye. But everyone wore budenovka hats. They left in groups too large and too swift for me to sift through.

By the end of the day, when the old guards were gone and the new ones had walked in carrying a chill in their posture strong enough to freeze out the July sweat, I knew I'd missed him. Zash had slipped away. We didn't get our good-bye. I had lost him in the madness.

I finally allowed myself to cry into my pillow. Until the sun had gone. Until my appetite had gone. Until my hope had gone.

17

"*You must come eat, Nastya.*" Alexei served food onto my plate and I crawled from my bed. I couldn't drift away like Maria had. Alexei needed me. My family needed me. Zash was not central enough in my life for me to allow him to derail it.

I needed to move on. To face forward.

So we ate—rather, we picked at our food because we were all so exhausted. But we'd starve without it. The moment the last fork was set down, Yurovsky entered our space. Avdeev had never come in after supper. What did Yurovsky want? I couldn't meet his eyes—not because of the doll, but because of Zash's departure.

"Citizen Nikolai, I will speak with you in my office, please." Yurovsky didn't wait for Papa's response. He left our rooms and entered his office. Papa followed. The rest of us sat at the table, staring after him.

"What does he want?" Alexei whispered.

"Likely to question him," I said. "Yurovsky inspected our belongings. It's time to inspect us." I didn't miss the fact that Yurovsky had waited until all our allies were sent from the Ipatiev

House and we were at our lowest morale. Hopelessness and exhaustion were part of his inspection—to place us under his spyglass when we were weakest.

"He will likely question all of us." Tatiana rubbed Ortipo behind the ears but didn't dare pass her any of our precious rations.

Mamma's head snapped up. "I cannot undergo an interrogation." She rose gingerly, her food untouched, and retired to her bed. "If he wishes to question me, he can come in here."

I stared at the closed door separating us from the opportunity to eavesdrop. My heart slammed against the Matryoshka doll. I needed to hide it. Or maybe Yurovsky would *expect* me to hide it, so I should leave it on my person. I still had Alexei's relief spells in my pocket.

Papa returned, escorted by a soldier I'd never seen before. Yurovsky stepped in, his gaze fixed on me. "Citizen Anastasia."

I rose slowly. He wasn't giving me time to hide the doll. My feet carried me after him as I tried to maintain a semblance of obedience and suppress my panic. As I passed Papa, he gave me a nod—a nod to be strong. To not cower before this man.

Yurovsky's office was the same mess Avdeev's had been. I didn't know if it was him or leftovers from Avdeev. Empty bottles lay everywhere with stacks of papers and latched boxes. Only the bed across the room had been cleared and replaced with Yurovsky's belongings. The same belongings I had ransacked before leaving Tobolsk.

Yurovsky gestured to a chair. To sit would be to humble myself. To lessen myself. To reduce my courage because sitting spanned half the distance to bowing. A princess never sat in submission.

But I sat because Yurovsky sought compliance. And any tickle of rebellion would do me no favors.

"We did not spend much time together in Tobolsk, but I feel I know you, Nastya." His use of my nickname pinched my throat. It felt too intimate—like he knew my secrets. Which he likely did.

"The feeling is mutual, Commandant."

"Where is the Matryoshka doll?"

He certainly didn't waste time. "Pardon?"

"The doll. You took it from my satchel. Don't deny it."

A flush rose to my face. I could barely hear through the blood in my ears. I swallowed hard. "I do not deny it, sir. It was wrong of me to take it."

He paced before me. "Where is it now?"

"It was confiscated when I arrived in Ekaterinburg, upon my first search." I tried to sound helpless, as though I wished I could help him more.

His pocket watch lay open on the desk in front of him and he examined it for a moment, as though wondering how to make me comply like the gears in his timepiece. "Do not lie to me, Citizen."

"I am not lying, Commandant." I was *so* lying.

As though to indulge me like a child, he gave a sickly smile. "Spells are illegal. Why did you want it enough to risk infuriating the Soviet?"

I let out a gust of breath. "I didn't know what the doll held, but I figured it could be helpful for Alexei's illness."

He rose from his desk. "Where is the doll, Nastya?"

My voice spiked up a notch. Insistent. "It was confiscated! We and our belongings were searched. A soldier took it. I assumed he reported it to Commandant Avdeev."

The lies felt like saltwater across my tongue. I was not in the habit of lying—my old mischief was more sophisticated than that. But truth was a gift that Yurovsky didn't deserve. My family was the one thing I would lie for. Especially if it saved them. *Forgive me, Iisus.*

Yurovsky stopped in front of me, snapping his pocket watch closed, then open, then closed. "There is no record of it."

"Perhaps you should ask your Bolsheviks." I stared at the opening and closing of his pocket watch, hypnotized. Only then did I realize why it captivated me so. The hour and minute hands were loose. Instead of telling the time, they pointed sharply as one toward the edge of the watch.

Toward me.

Yurovsky stepped so close, I smelled the disgust on his breath. "You are not as good a liar as you are a pickpocket." He gave me a mighty shove. My foot caught on a loose trunk and I sprawled onto the ground with a cry.

Yurovsky checked his watch and triumph crossed his face. I didn't need to see the face of the timepiece to know . . . its hands had followed my movement.

That pocket watch didn't tell time. It detected *spells.*

That was how Yurovsky found the doll in Tobolsk. That was how he knew I still had it on my person. All this time I thought he'd been checking the hour, to ensure his clockwork soldiers ticked and tocked and chimed to his will. But instead he was hunting for spells.

He shoved the watch in his pocket. Then he advanced. I scrambled backward, terror flowing through me. "Papa!"

I threw items in Yurovsky's path—boxes, vodka bottles, whatever my hand could reach. Then, when I'd crawled into a mess of papers and boxes and crates near a cabinet, I curled into a ball. The position brought a sense of safety, but mostly it allowed me to shove a hand into my corset and pull the Matryoshka doll free.

Yurovsky stopped beside me. "You're pathetic."

I uncurled and lay before him like an animal exposing its belly in submission. But in my movement, I let the doll loose underneath the worn cabinet. I adjusted my position among the crinkled paper to mask the sound of the doll rolling across the floor to the back of the cabinet shadows.

Yurovsky's nose wrinkled as he stared at me. "I could call a guard in here to tear every stitch of clothing off your body until we find the doll. No one would stop him. No one would stop me. You are nothing, Citizen. Nothing but an inconvenience to the Soviet."

He held out his hand. "Now. Would you rather give me the doll on your own, or do we need to see how many bruises it takes?"

I thought of Papa on his knees in front of Avdeev. I thought of Zash swallowing his sorrow to comply with Beloborodov's wishes. I clamped a fist down on my pride and slipped my hand into the pocket of my skirt. I allowed my fear and emotions to create tears. They weren't a facade—they were a shield.

"This . . . this is all I have, Commandant. Please." I held out the tin of relief spells.

He eyed the tin before snatching it from my hand. I scrambled to my feet and put distance between me and the doll. When Yurovsky looked at his pocket watch next, his eyebrows popped in the barest display of surprise.

So I was right—the pocket watch pointed toward spells. And since I no longer had a spell hidden on my person, it didn't point toward me. It pointed toward the tin in his hand. Maybe that meant it pointed to the spell nearest it?

I wanted to flee the room, but I needed Yurovsky to believe I was a frightened, obedient rabbit. I needed him to believe he broke me. Instead, I seemed to have broken him—or his composure, at least. He glanced back at the watch, then me, then the watch. Not very subtle, Mister Dark-Eyed Bolshevik.

He opened the tin, set the lid aside, and squinted to read the words. Wrong move.

The wiggly relief spells popped out of the tin, flopping to the ground like unnested birds, then bouncing into crevices and hidey-holes. He clapped a hand over the mouth of the tin with a curse, trapping what was left of the spells.

But several were already loose—wiggling their way to freedom where they'd possibly fade or expel their magic on some useless piece of wood. And they would send his pocket watch spinning.

"They are relief spells," I said meekly. "For Alexei's knee. That is all I have on me. He was in such pain . . . I couldn't help but try to relieve it."

Yurovsky set the tin on the cabinet shelf, beneath which the Matryoshka doll lay in hiding. Then he slipped his watch into his pocket. With a deep breath through his nose, he said, "You may go, Citizen."

I didn't wait for him to repeat the order.

18

Yurovsky confiscated our finery. All jewelry upon us—rings, bracelets, necklaces. Well, all jewelry except that in our corsets. Mamma was furious, but Yurovsky allowed Papa to watch him place the items in a box and lock it for safety. "This is standard for prisoners."

I wasn't bothered by any of it . . . except the doll. I eyed Yurovsky during his confiscations, watching for any sort of triumphant grin or sign that he'd found the doll. So far . . . nothing. It was safe in the enemy's lair. My family's salvation, a hairsbreadth away from being taken away. Not only that, but I'd lost the relief spells for Alexei's knee.

I needed to get the doll back, but not until I had a plan. Because if I retrieved it, his pocket watch would betray me again.

The second day of Yurovsky's command arrived, as well as the new schedules and rhythms of the guards. I didn't have the energy to befriend new Bolsheviks. I didn't have the will to hope for the arrival of the White Army. We'd heard nothing from the White Army officer since our declination of rescue.

A grey morning greeted us, feeling little different from the dark night. Storm clouds turned the whitewashed windows into dark drapes. The rain pattered against the glass. I moved to the open window and let the rain spray my face for a few seconds until Mamma beckoned me away before I got shot.

For a mere second, I felt life. Then it was gone.

I changed into day clothes and rang the bell to the landing to use the toilet. The door opened. I avoided eye contact with the new Bolshevik soldier. The soldier who would mock my fuzzy head, who would scratch nasty messages on the bathroom wall, who would whisper something about Papa that would turn my blood to angry embers.

So I entered the toilet and did my business, trying not to breathe in the stench of new and old soldiers. Trying not to think of the many times I had passed Zash on my way to this same location—a glimmer of hope and friendship inside a relentless prison. I missed him.

Did he think of me at all?

I could've used his help to sneak back into Yurovsky's office. But when was the right time to retrieve the doll? Papa said to use the spell at the last possible moment. That moment loomed closer and closer now that Yurovsky was at the helm.

The seam on the doll had started to show. It *wanted* to be used.

Despite Papa's strange advice, I'd always trusted him. But what if he'd been compromised? He'd been here a long time. Maria had been unable to think safely after her time here. She gave in to Ivan, causing this new mess. Mamma's headache had become her new cell and she showed no will left to live. Even I had cracked beneath the sorrow of losing Zash, losing Ivan, even losing Avdeev. And now Yurovsky was determined to find the doll. It was only a matter of time.

Could I trust Papa's advice? He'd shown humility to the commandants for so long, perhaps he was growing to accept our fate and imprisonment and death. He never asked for the Matryoshka doll back from me. He let me keep it, because he knew *I* could use it as the family's salvation.

When was I supposed to take it into my own hands? Surely it would be better to use it than to allow Yurovsky to take it from us. I imagined retrieving the doll from his office. I imagined opening it and seeing the spell. Saving us.

A fist pounded on the door. I jumped and finished my business. It had been nice to have a solitary space for a minute. My time was up, but my mind had been sparked with something new to dwell on. A new plan, perhaps.

I splashed water on my face and opened the door.

Zash stood before me.

My hands flew to my mouth to stifle a gasp. "Zash!" I almost jumped into his arms. But then I took in his appearance.

He wasn't smiling. His smooth brown eyes did not sparkle. He stood as rigid as when I'd first met him. And he wore a crisp new Bolshevik uniform.

"Zash?" It came out as a whisper this time.

"Return to your quarters, Citizen." His face betrayed no softness. I stared into it, searching for my friend. For the man who was the only one who could send my heart pounding in something other than fear.

No twitch. No blink. No kindness. The gears in my head whirred, connecting the pieces. He must be under watch. I must not cause a scene. I did not want him to get shot in the head like Ivan.

I nodded. "Of course, sir." He took my arm and led me through the door and back into our five-room cell.

Zash—*my* Zash—was here. At the Ipatiev House. He had not abandoned me. He might look like a Bolshevik, but he'd given me his spell ink. He'd caught me off the swing. He'd winked at me. He'd shown kindness. He cared about me and my family.

He played the role of Bolshevik well, but light could not be so swiftly overcome by darkness. Not when that light rested in a person's soul. So as the door closed, I sent him the smallest of smiles.

━━

That day we were allowed into the garden for a mere ten minutes. It was enough for a swing, a turn about the small space, and about seventy deep inhales. That was all we were allotted for the entire day. No second outing.

The next day we were let out again. This time Zash was on garden duty, but instead of standing with a friend, he stood with a rifle. He did not watch me. I did not go to him. It felt like a secret—our friendship. Even though he'd yet to reveal the Zash *I* knew, I faithfully held on to the knowledge he was in there. He was my new hope. And hope never abandoned us—only we could abandon it. Perhaps rescue would never come for us, but for now, I had friendship.

I would not die alone.

Joy trotted beside me as I walked the garden. She shook her head and her long ears flopped across her face like furry paddles. I took in the new guards and their machine guns set up on the edges of the palisade. They watched us like vultures. Waiting for us to die. Or waiting for the order to shoot. As we were ushered back inside, a truck arrived with enormous grates of metal. We were locked back in our quarters, but not before we saw them reinforcing the wooden gate with a metal one.

The next day Zash was on duty on the landing again. I spotted him when Olga took her morning bathroom visit. I sat at the breakfast table wavering back and forth on whether I should try talking to him again. But he was too close to the commandant's office.

Then I saw something through our window: Yurovsky leaving through the reinforced gate on horseback with two other soldiers. I watched the rhythmic trot of the horse's hindquarters take them along the path toward the wooded distance. Yurovsky faded from sight and there was only one guard on the landing.

I hopped up and rang the bell.

Zash answered the summons. I stepped out and closed the door behind me, then breathed his name. "Zash." I couldn't restrain myself. I embraced him, pulling his form—a form of safety—to me, never wanting to let go.

It was the most we'd ever touched beyond the brush of his fingers against mine and the embrace of grief after Ivan's death. But it didn't hold the same assurance as that previous touch. Because he did not return the embrace.

Instead, Zash placed two strong hands—the same hands that caught me from the swing—on my shoulders and pushed me back, not unkindly. "Do your duty, Citizen."

Confused, I glanced around—again—to ensure we were alone. Maybe he didn't understand. "Yurovsky is not here. He's left on horseback. We can converse safely!"

Something changed behind his eyes and my relief was swift. "Oh, you *are* there," I said like a silly girl. "I thought . . . I thought perhaps you'd . . ." My voice broke.

War entered his features. A war of ice and heat. Of morals. Of duty. I could see it play out and knew that if I let him stand there warring within himself long enough, he would choose the ice. It was safer for him to be a loyal Bolshevik.

I couldn't risk that. I couldn't lose him. I took his hand in mine. He startled, but I held fast. It was warm. It was comfort. "Zash, please. Don't leave me. I don't . . . I don't want to die alone."

I could see he understood. *Alone* didn't mean without someone by my side. It meant void of friendships. Completely at the mercy of the enemy.

His fingers tightened around my hand and I held on to the gesture as I would a lifeline. He swayed forward for a moment, then seemed to catch himself. He pulled his hand from mine and the ice won over. "I'm here. But you saw what they did to Ivan. I cannot abandon my duty and my future for"—he gestured at me—"*this*. There is nothing you can offer me that I should risk my life for."

My hand turned cold at my side. Words like *friendship* and *trust* and maybe even *love* sounded so foolish in my head. What could I say? That I'd been imprisoned for so long that I'd grasped on to his acceptance like a drowning girl to a straw of grass?

"You would risk your life for *them*? For the Bolsheviks who shot your friend in the head? Who attack cities and steal people's livelihoods? What do you live for, Zash, if not *others*?"

He gripped the barrel of his rifle and suddenly I was staring at a stranger. "Do your duty, Citizen."

I gaped like a beached fish. Gasping for air. Assurance. Neither came. So I closed my eyes and forced the breathing to even out. Zash . . . my Zash.

When I opened my eyes, I let my sorrow show. I let him know I was resigned to his coldness. "The only reason I came out here was to see you."

The statement chipped his ice, but not enough.

I channeled my heartache into a fresh rhythm of boldness. "But, if you insist . . ." I turned and pushed my way into Yurovsky's office. Let Zash try to stop me. Let's see how far his Bolshevik loyalty went.

"Nastya," he hissed, completely abandoning the use of the term *citizen*.

I didn't stop. The room was much tidier than when Yurovsky had interrogated me. No more empty bottles or boxes. He'd disposed of most of the loose papers and even dusted. I dropped to my knees by the cabinet. At first I saw only shadow. But then . . . the doll.

I snatched it and shoved it into my corset. Zash stepped into the office and watched me. Had he seen the doll? He stood rigid—I almost mistook it for anger, but the darting of his eyes betrayed his concern.

I pushed past him back onto the landing. "Report me if you must, but you instructed me to do my duty. And my duty is to protect my family." I waited a moment, on the off chance he would return to the Zash I knew.

He did not bend. Did not move. Did not soften. With a sigh I reentered our quarters.

So we had finally reached the end. There was no White Army coming for us. There was no Zash. My hand slipped up to the Matryoshka doll. Hope and life were up to me now.

19

I hid the doll in the corner of the main room, right up against the wall of Yurovsky's office and inside my spare pair of shoes. It wasn't safe—but nothing was safe these days. I had to hope that Yurovsky's pocket watch would point toward his office. I had to hope it would buy me some time.

None of the soldiers would talk to us. They were loyal to Yurovsky through and through. Even Papa stopped trying. I could tell each time he approached a new soldier his heart wasn't in it. He was giving up. We were all giving up. He barely got three words out before the soldiers leveled their guns at him.

There would be no alliances. It was rescue or death.

Three days in a row, Yurovsky rode out on a horse and did not return until late. On those days, we received our full time in the garden, but the laughs were subdued. Mamma never came out. Olga stayed inside to read to her. Maria was a glassy-eyed shell, and Alexei could only bear to be moved from his bed every other day.

My family was fading.

Anytime I saw Zash, he stood stiff as a statue. Chin raised. Rifle gripped. Encased in ice.

Gunshots echoed from the city, seeming more frequent than they ever were before. Louder now that we were outdoors instead of trapped in our five-room prison. Something was happening out there.

So on the third day, I left the garden early and returned to our rooms. Zash would be on landing duty once my family returned. For now I muttered to the current Bolshevik that it was too hot outside for me.

He didn't respond. I pushed myself into the main room. Mamma was asleep on her bed. Perfect. I retrieved the doll from my shoe, closed myself in my bedroom, and dropped to my knees at my bed-side. I knew what I had to do, and the only safe way to vent my concerns was through prayer. *Help me, Iisus.*

That was all I could manage. My family wasn't alone in their despair. I was fading, too. And perhaps soon I wouldn't have the strength to try to save my family. I needed to know what spell the Matryoshka doll held. I needed to know what weapons we had for survival.

The White Army wasn't coming. I had to do something while I could.

I held the doll in front of me. The seam was complete. A thick black line ringed the center of the doll, shining light no longer. My heart thundered in my chest and I managed to dig a thumbnail into the crack.

"Don't use it until the White Army arrives," Papa had said. *"Or at the last possible moment."*

I rubbed a thumb over the doll's face. The time spent against my sweaty skin and my rough corset had scraped away some of the paint. I gripped it in my fist as the pounding footsteps of my family ascended the stairs. They returned and took up whatever games or entertainment they'd been indulging in prior to the garden time.

I finished my prayer, waited a few extra moments, and then rang the bell on the landing.

Zash answered. I looked up at him, but he didn't meet my eyes. No one was in Yurovsky's office and, though I knew Zash would not receive it well, I still brushed a hand on his shoulder. *"Privyet,* Zash." It was a simple hello, spoken with all my heart. Trying to understand his turmoil.

After all, why *should* he maintain friendship with me? Simply because we didn't deserve to die yet? Or because we were friends? Those things could get him shot. It was best he separated himself from us. Yes. That was best.

I entered the toilet area and latched the door. Then I took the doll from my corset. My sweaty hands slid against the wood. I gripped the top half of the doll with one fist and the bottom half with the other. With a deep breath, I twisted.

The doll opened.

Inside rested a smaller doll. I didn't see a spell or a word like when Rasputin had used spells. Gingerly, I lifted the inner doll and slid it into the space in my corset. It felt too small and loose now that it was not encased by its senior.

There, in the bottom part of the largest doll, sat a word. Painted in the glimmering rainbow spell ink: *Ajnin.*

I had never seen that word before—not in Russian, English, German, or French. This gave me no information. What sort of power did this spell hold?

As I stared at the word, it detached itself from the inner wood of the doll layer. It floated in the air, up in front of my eyes, the letters flickering as though on an invisible ribbon. I grabbed the top of the doll to recapture the spell before it was somehow enacted.

But the word seemed to sense my intentions. It swooped down and slipped between my lips. I gasped and the spell settled onto my tongue. It burned like a flame but tasted like embers and power.

Somehow I knew that once I spoke the mysterious word, the spell would be enacted.

I'd never heard of a spell entering a person's mouth to be spoken. I'd never heard the word *ajnin* before. But this was a spell by Dochkin. This could save my family—and now it couldn't be taken from me.

A fist pounded on the bathroom door. I jumped. "A moment, please!" Then I clapped a hand over my mouth. The spell hadn't come out. I hadn't said the word. I was able to speak other words freely.

My breath returned, and I closed up the empty shell of the Matryoshka doll before leaning close to the small mirror. I stuck my tongue out. The letters rested in the very center of my tongue. Like an unswallowed line of sugar. Barely visible.

The pounding on the door repeated. Zash's voice came from the other side. "Nastya."

Now I'd done it. The spell was *in* me. Dare I use it without knowing what it did? Was this the time? I slipped the empty doll shell up my sleeve, shut my mouth, and opened the door.

"What were you doing?" Zash hissed. "Do you *want* to raise suspicion?"

I lifted my chin. "I was doing my duties, as you commanded me to do. Sir." Then I returned to our space and placed the now smaller Matryoshka doll back in my shoe.

It was a torrential day when the cleaning women came. We were sitting at our table, playing a family game of bezique. All of us but Mamma who lay in bed and Olga who read to her in the other room. Alexei sat in Mamma's wheelchair with Joy on his lap.

"*Zdravstvutye!*" We greeted the four cleaning women with bright smiles. It was nice to see new faces. Kind faces.

We hadn't had cleaning women before, but Yurovsky liked clockwork and cleanliness. He paced on the landing, eyeing us. Eyeing the cleaning ladies. His pocket bulged with his watch and I turned away. If he pulled it out, would it track me again? Would it detect the *ajnin* spell on my tongue?

None of the women returned the greeting beyond deep bows. We did not speak with them beyond the greeting, not wishing to bring trouble upon their heads.

We kept our quarters relatively clean, but I found myself staring after them longingly as they mopped and dusted and scraped bits of mud off the entryway. I wanted to put my hands to work. Not to play. I wanted purpose like they had purpose.

They continued to glance our way. A flicker here. A side-eye there. I couldn't stop my grin. They were curious about the royal family. We probably looked a fright compared to their expectations—all of us girls in our black skirts and white frocks that we'd mended more times than we cared to count. Practically bald.

The ladies finished the entryway and hoisted their cleaning buckets toward the bedrooms. Yurovsky must have seen enough because he reentered his office. I stuck out my tongue—just barely—at his retreating form.

One cleaning lady giggled. I caught her watching me. I giggled, too, and hopped up from the table to help move the cots so they could reach the floor beneath.

"Nyet, nyet," one lady said. "We can do it."

"Oh, we welcome this opportunity for physical exertion," I replied. Even Maria moved from the card game to help slide the beds. "At home we used to enjoy work of the hardest kind with the greatest of pleasure." I wanted to go into detail about sawing wood with Papa and stacking logs.

They let us help. I relished the strain on my feeble muscles. I hoarded the reward of *doing* something. Of helping someone. But these were women from outside. From the city. We rarely encountered people from the city, and I had to risk further conversation. I had to know the temperament of Ekaterinburg.

"What is happening out there?"

The lady nearest me paused in her scrubbing. She glanced over her shoulder toward the entryway, then shoved her stiff brush over the wood, sending bubbles in a spray at my knees. "Unrest." Her gaze met mine. Wide. Fierce. "The White Army is here."

20

JULY 16

It was too much to hope for. That the White Army was here! In Ekaterinburg! I might have doubted the cleaning lady long after she left, but Yurovsky's nervous pacing and constant in and out of his office the very next day affirmed her statement.

The White Army *must* be here.

Yurovsky's clockwork regiment was chiming off-time. His pendulum broke its rhythm. Olga—frail as she was—jumped into action, hemming and mending and stitching our jewel-encrusted camisoles and corsets to ensure their durability should we be rescued. She didn't join us in the garden that day, telling Yurovsky she was going to read to Mamma and "check the medicines."

That was code for sewing more jewels.

Alexei stayed inside, too, because he had woken with a cold. I took Joy out into the sunshine with me, per his request. "Maybe she will carry some back inside for me."

Once outside, I tried to listen for city sounds. Sounds of unrest and rescue. Sounds of war or panic. All I heard were engines. Automobile engines. Back and forth and back and forth along the road beside our house. Even the gunshots had stopped.

I paused by Zash during my walk. He didn't acknowledge me, but I spoke anyway.

"What is happening?" The words came stilted. In between each one, the Matryoshka spell tried to wiggle free. I swallowed, though it brought no change to the discomfort of the spell. I shouldn't have spoken. Each word out of my mouth became harder and harder to control.

I had opened the doll too early. I should have waited for the White Army like Papa commanded. I must not let it loose before it was time, especially now that rescue could be right on the other side of the gates.

"The city is evacuating." Zash's stiff Bolshevik obedience cracked. He seemed nervous, like he didn't know what was going on or what would happen to all of us—soldiers included—at the Ipatiev House. My breath hitched at the idea of him being attacked by the White Army. Killed, even.

I pressed my hand to his arm. I wanted to speak, but the spell chanted in my mind, thrummed against my tongue. *Ajnin. Ajnin. Ajnin.* It craved being released, but I forced other words out instead. The last words I'd likely speak to Zash until I used the spell. "Please." *Ajnin.* "Be careful." *Ajnin.*

He looked at me. Torn. "You, too."

When we returned to the house, Olga placed each of our jewel-encrusted camisoles—perfectly mended and reinforced with thread—beside our beds. We didn't put them on yet. That would alert Yurovsky to our preparation for a rescue.

He drove in and out of the palisade gates all day, leaving for a longer length in the evening and not returning until dinnertime. After dinner, the Ekaterinburg curfew sounded. Eight o'clock. A gunshot interrupted the curfew bells. I stepped to the window, but Papa pulled me back. "Best not stand by the window tonight, Nastya."

I nodded, still not speaking. The spell sat like a coal in my mouth. Where was the White Army? I couldn't hold this back much longer. I doubted I would even sleep! I wanted to tell Papa of the spell, but I couldn't risk releasing another word. Perhaps I should write him a letter?

"Come play bezique," Maria urged, and I indulged her. I imagined she was thinking of Ivan. If we were rescued, she and he likely would have spent life together. It would be a bittersweet escape for her. At least she'd woken somewhat from her dazed existence.

The guards changed at ten—our signal to retire for the evening. As we climbed into bed I still heard scuffles on the floors below. Whispered voices. Each show of Bolshevik nervousness emboldened me. Rescue was coming. This was it. I pressed my tongue to the roof of my mouth, letting the spell burn.

At 1:30 a.m. I startled awake. I'd heard something. What? What had I heard? It came again—the cling of the bell at the double doors that connected the landing to the sitting room. They weren't locked, so whoever was ringing it could come in if he wanted. No.

The bell was ringing to wake us up.

I launched out of bed, but Dr. Botkin beat me and Papa to the door. Probably for the best—how would I have kept the spell in if I'd answered?

Dr. Botkin opened the door. Yurovsky stood before him, fully dressed and looking more haggard than ever. "The situation in Ekaterinburg is now very unstable. The Whites might, at any moment, launch an artillery attack on the city."

Would they truly? Even if they knew we were here? An artillery attack could kill us! Did they know we were being kept here? I gripped Papa's arm and he reassured me with a squeeze of his hand.

"It is too dangerous for the family to remain on the upper floors." Yurovsky spotted Papa and me at the edge of the room. Olga joined us, a frail ghost in her nightgown. "Please wake the others. We must take you to the basement for your own safety."

Dr. Botkin nodded, bowed, and closed the door. Then faced us. Pale. But smiling. "It is time."

The mixture of terror and excitement was almost too much. *Ajnin. Ajnin. Ajnin.* My knees buckled, but I caught the doorframe. Tonight. It would end tonight. Surely.

The first person to come to mind was Zash. What would happen to him? Would he be captured by the Whites? Would he escape and return to the life of a simple worker? Would he think of me at all?

I dressed in my jeweled camisole first, the Matryoshka doll out of my shoe and back in its place. All covered by my typical long black skirt and white blouse. Everyone else took their time. Didn't they know we were probably going to be rescued? That or blown up. Or simply moved to a new place of exile by the Bolsheviks. Frankly, any of those options would be more desirable than another two months—or even two days—in this terrible place. Especially with Yurovsky in charge and Zash an obedient soldier.

We washed as best we could and grabbed a few belongings stuffed in pillowcases. I wanted to scream at them to hurry, but I kept my mouth tightly closed—something Alexei would have commented on had it been a normal day.

At last, after forty minutes, we exited our quarters and met Yurovsky on the landing.

Three soldiers stood with them—one of whom was Zash. I paused, startled, but then hurried forward to let the others out—all of the Romanovs and all of our servants. Dr. Botkin, Anna, Kharitonov, Papa's manservant.

Yurovsky didn't let us bring the dogs with us. I understood, as they could get excited or unmanageable during something so crazy as a rescue. They would behave better upstairs. But just in case, I left the door cracked so they could get out if we weren't able to come back for them.

Papa carried Alexei—both of them in their soldier uniforms. They looked so handsome, even in their frailty. I was proud to belong to them.

Yurovsky and the guards led us to the stairs. We lined ourselves up with proper protocol—like the days of old. Papa in front, carrying Alexei and accepting no assistance. Alexei sat as regally as he could manage in Papa's arms, even with his bandaged leg and the winces from each jostle. Mamma followed using a walking stick and leaning heavily on Olga. Then Tatiana, Maria, and me.

The servants were behind us—Trupp hauling blankets and Anna carrying pillows. Dr. Botkin lugged his small case of medical tools.

Zash placed himself at the back by me. He stared straight forward, not meeting my eyes, but sweat slid down his temple and I could practically hear his nerves scraping.

Please, Iisus, protect him. I took his hand in mine, but he yanked his away and met my gaze with a look of pure horror. I'd never seen such an expression on a man. Things must be worse than Yurovsky let on. The White Army must be in the city. Maybe even at the very palisade gate.

"What about our personal belongings?" Mamma asked as we descended.

"It's not necessary right now," Yurovsky said in what seemed to be a strained calm. "We'll get them later and bring them down."

We exited the house into the courtyard and I sucked in the night air. The midnight sun was below the horizon, for a couple hours at least. The darkness carried a threat and a tension I felt in the deepest shadows as we passed. We reentered the house through an adjacent door that led into the basement. My heart stalled. I didn't want to descend into such darkness. I didn't want to enter the tomb. What if the White Army did fire artillery and we were buried?

I stalled at the top of the stairs. Zash stopped beside me. He didn't nudge me forward. He didn't encourage me to enter. He stood there, trembling even more fiercely, then surveying the night as though searching for the enemy. His gaze finally landed back on me and he took a deep breath. "If you are hiding a spell, now is the time to use it."

I almost missed his words, he spoke them so quietly. So . . . he knew I had the doll? Perhaps he overheard me talking with Papa, or perhaps Yurovsky had alerted the soldiers, but Zash had just shown that he cared about me. About my safety. About my family.

I opened my mouth. *Ajnin.* I swallowed hard. I couldn't respond. I tried again, but the spell practically leapt free. I clamped my lips closed. I couldn't tell Zash that I had a spell. I couldn't tell him I wanted him to come with us. The frustration burned my eyes. *I can't speak,* I wanted to say.

Instead, I shook my head, trying to convey my predicament.

Zash's countenance fell in some sort of resignation. He misinterpreted my head shake, but there was nothing I could do about it now. He'd see soon enough. And I prayed—oh, I prayed—that he would be spared. That he would be safe. That he could escape with us.

With a deep breath he straightened. If he could be brave, so could I—despite the fact we were tightening our courage for opposite causes.

I descended the stairs, counting as I went. Twenty-three. The same number of years Papa had sat on the throne. We entered a room with a single naked lightbulb swinging from a cracked plaster ceiling, splashing yellow light from wall to wall.

Mamma stopped and gestured with her walking stick. "Why are there no chairs? No place to sit?" Did Yurovsky expect Mamma and Alexei to sit on the cold ground? How long would we be here?

"Of course." Yurovsky sent a Bolshevik to fetch a chair.

The man returned within minutes, muttering under his breath as he slammed a chair in front of Mamma and then Alexei. "If the heir wants to die in a chair, very well then. Let him have one."

This Bolshevik thought we were all going to die. Surely the White Army wouldn't murder us. They would see that we were captives. They would come here to save us.

Papa set Alexei in the chair. Alexei watched the guards with wide eyes, taking in their every movement. Their every whisper. Their every emotion. His brow wrinkled, seemingly confused by what he saw.

Mamma sank into the other chair.

"Please, everyone, take positions behind the tsar and tsarina." It was the first time Yurovsky had ever used Papa's title.

We moved behind our parents, and Papa situated himself in

front of Alexei. I didn't like the idea of him receiving the brunt of the White Army's arrival. But he was a soldier. He would know what to do and how to protect us.

I folded my arms and stood to the side, in full view of the door, showing Yurovsky I wasn't afraid. And I still didn't view him as my leader. Trupp and Kharitonov situated themselves in front of me. Protecting me.

"You will all wait here," Yurovsky said. "We have a truck coming to take you to safety." He left the room, leaving us with the three soldiers.

So Yurovsky was moving us. That would be my moment to use the spell. If the White Army didn't arrive before Yurovsky piled us into this truck he mentioned, then I would release the spell, whatever it was. The little coal leaped excitedly against my tongue, as though sensing my plan. I couldn't wait to set it free. To learn of its power. To help us escape.

We couldn't allow the Bolsheviks to take us away again. I looked to Papa. He sensed my gaze and met it. I raised my eyebrows and lifted my hand to my chest where the doll sat. He gave a slow nod. That was all I needed.

After about a half hour of shifting my weight and rolling my tongue against the spell, the sounds of machinery rumbled into earshot. It sounded like a truck. Gears ground. Then footsteps. Yurovsky had returned. Most of us had slumped against the wall by this point, but Zash remained rigid, looking sickly under the naked bulb.

I'd never seen him so pale or ill.

Yurovsky opened the door and led a group of soldiers into the room. Did we really need so many to escort us? I didn't recognize some of their faces.

"Well, here we all are." Papa faced the commandant. "What are you going to do now?" He was tired of the waiting. Tired of the slinking about.

Only then did I realize Yurovsky held a piece of paper in his left hand. "Please stand."

We all pushed off the wall and Mamma, with a grumble or two, hauled herself up from her seat. Alexei remained in his chair, unable to stand with or without help at this point.

Yurovsky cleared his throat and held the paper high. "'In view of the fact that your relatives in Europe continue their assault on Soviet Russia, the presidium of the Ural Regional Soviet has sentenced you to be shot.'"

Papa's head snapped up. "Wait." His face paled as though splashed with milk. *"What?"*

"'. . . the Regional Soviet, fulfilling the will of the revolution, has decreed that the former Tsar Nikolai Romanov, guilty of countless blood crimes against the people, should be shot.'"

Then Yurovsky pulled a Colt from his pocket and shot Papa in the chest.

21

Ringing.

Silence.

Papa fell to the ground, his uniform turning his impact into a soft *flump*. Blood pooled. Pulsed. Slower. Slower. Slower.

I heard it.

I heard its chant dying.

Romanov. Ro . . . manov. Ro . . . man . . . ov.

The soldiers all drew guns.

Not just on Papa. Us. All of us. My senses screamed. I couldn't think. What was happening? Wild panic reflected in Zash's eyes. He raised his own pistol.

Aimed at my chest.

I'd yet to take a breath. Papa's heart still pumped. I couldn't look away from Zash, even as his comrades pulled their triggers. Even as bullets slammed into plaster and bodies and wood. I was frozen. I was dead already.

Zash's hand trembled.

He looked away.

And he pulled the trigger.

22

My chest crumpled beneath the impact. I tumbled backward into the sea of gunshots, the smell of pistol smoke, the hot blood and cold cement. Screams were lost in the chaos. Glass shattered. Darkness smothered us. I felt myself dying. My hope, at last, snuffed.

Zash . . .

Zash had been my executioner.

My life flickered. I could not see. I could hear only Yurovsky screaming for everyone to stop, then the soldiers running up the stairs, sucking in the night air. Thinking they could escape what they'd done. Leaving us alone. Gasping corpses. Dying together.

In the momentary silence I heard moans from my sisters. A cry from Dr. Botkin. I wanted to weep. I wanted a hand to hold. I didn't want to die alone. But I couldn't move. Heat spread through my chest, numbing my body. Hitching my breath.

Footsteps returned and then a command to the soldiers.

To return.

To finish the job.

I finally let myself slip away.

23

Consciousness returned with a shard of pain in my spine. My body swayed. Back and forth. Rough arms under my armpits and others gripping my ankles. Then weightlessness. I landed hard on wood that shuddered from an engine.

Where?

What?

Help.

My eyes cracked open and I sucked a breath. It was lost in the sounds around me. I saw only darkness. I reached up and my hand brushed a canvas wall. Truck. The back of a covered truck. Voices everywhere. Scents of death and betrayal.

Something heavy landed beside me, causing the truck to quake. I turned my head. Moonlight filtered in from a place I couldn't see. The heavy thing beside me was a body.

Alexei. Still in his small uniform and half wrapped in one of our monogrammed sheets. His skin pale. Blood splashed on his neck. His eyes dead.

And I remembered.

Execution. They killed us. They had killed us all. Except I was alive. My Romanov blood pumped.

Alone. Alone. Alone.

Romanov. Romanov. Romanov.

No. Please. I didn't want to know what had happened. I didn't want to be alive. I didn't want Yurovsky to find me. To hurt me.

A hot tear slid down my temple and into my ear.

Then I heard a sweet but terrible sound. A soft moan from the cherished, ill boy beside me. My Alexei. I turned to face him. Saw his chest rise. I was not alone. He was not alone. With every effort of my will and body, I slid my hand and found his. Sticky and cold and heavy. I wrapped my fingers in his.

"Alexei," I tried to whisper. I wanted him to know I was here. I wanted him to hear my voice. But only a wheeze emerged from my throat. I took a breath. It burned and pinched and resisted. "Alexei."

But his name was not what slipped through my lips. Instead, a hot coal of a spell tumbled out as I unwillingly said, *"Ajnin."*

My pain evaporated. I turned weightless. I could no longer feel the vibration of the truck beneath me or Alexei's hand in mine. I was neither hot nor cold. Neutral. Completely healed of all wounds. Energized. Renewed.

My mind rose from the slog of slumber and pain. Sparked to life. If I was healed, I needed to get to my family—to *rescue* them. I had survived—the soldiers might be trying to kill the rest of my family as I lay here.

I forced away the weight of the situation, the fear of execution, the despair of reality. Instead, I opened my eyes and scanned the inverted world for the presence of soldiers. None. I tumbled backward out of the truck and rolled into a shadow. I didn't want to leave Alexei in there, but I didn't have time to think.

The rest of my family needed me.

The Ipatiev House glowed under the low half-moon, ghostly and pale as though ashamed of what had taken place in its belly. I kept flat along the palisade and slid toward the basement door. Soldiers emerged, carrying a body so riddled with bullet holes I only recognized Papa from his shredded uniform.

I fell back against the palisade, a hand to my heart. "Papa." My distraught croak seemed as loud as a bullfrog in the night, but no soldiers paid me any mind. They tossed him into the truck and took no notice of me.

As they returned to the house for another body I could not bear to identify, I rushed to the truck. To Papa. I couldn't make out his face beneath the blood, just his mustache. His chest didn't rise. Didn't fall. It didn't act like a chest at all, caved in from the impact of endless bullets.

I stumbled back and closed my eyes. No. Papa couldn't be dead. I used his spell. I did what he asked! He needed to wake up and tell me what to do. I reached to shake him. To tell him I'd obeyed his instructions.

But my hand didn't meet his shoulder. I couldn't seem to touch him. Had my fear numbed me?

"Nastya?" Alexei's scared, timid voice came like a bugle call from behind me. I spun, my heart galloping up my throat.

Alexei stood in the courtyard next to the truck, but he wasn't himself. He shimmered of silver and moonlight and a splash of dimmed rainbow. An ethereal creature, still in uniform, but transparent. I could see *through* him to the soldiers carrying another body out of the basement toward the truck.

I froze. What happened to him?

We needed to hide. I glanced back at the truck at Papa's body.

Beside him lay Alexei's injured body. And beside *him* lay a longer body in a black skirt and bloodstained blouse that clung to a jewel-lined camisole.

Me.

My body.

My knees buckled and I landed hard on the ground, holding my hands in front of my face. Moonlight glistened through my transparent palm. I was transparent, too. I was double. There were two of me—Nastya in the truck and Nastya on her knees. I was a terrifying duplicate of myself—a ghostlike copy that could move and think and see just like the unconscious body of me.

The soldiers paid me no mind as they tossed Tatiana's body into the truck, half on top of my physical one. I fell to all fours and sucked in deep breaths. They couldn't come fast enough. What happened? What *happened*?

"Nastya, are we dead?"

Alexei came up behind me, handling this odd state much better than I was. I used the back of the truck to claw myself to my feet. The machinery felt distant and less than sturdy beneath my touch. Alexei's physical body lay prone, solid, and bloodied in the bottom of the truck. But an ethereal copy of him stood—*stood*—beside me, uninjured, relying on me for an answer.

"I . . . don't know." I reached for Alexei's hand and we touched.

"They can't hear us or touch us. But I can touch you. Why?"

"I don't *know*, Alexei!" Panic sent my voice spiking, almost begging for a soldier to overhear and come explain the madness.

"If we're ghosts, Papa and the others must be, too. We need to find them." Like when he read Maria's letter a lifetime ago, telling us we were going to exile in Ekaterinburg, he remained calm. Only thirteen, but a soldier from skin to marrow . . . and even to transparent soul.

"You're right. If we're like this, Papa's soul, or ghost, or whatever we are must be somewhere." My ghost-heart lurched at the need to see my papa walking and moving and smiling again. To hear his voice. To run to him and find a semblance of normal.

I moved to steady Alexei, to help lead him away from the truck, but he held up his hands. "I can walk. I have no pain. Nothing holding me back." The awe in his voice buoyed me further. Whatever this state of existence was, it was freedom and healing and hope.

I took his hand. "Let's find our family."

The guards went about their work, hauling bodies from the cellar room to the truck. I couldn't look at the bodies—I searched only for the ghost forms. With each step I knew my physical family was dead. We had all been shot. Executed brutally.

Zash had taken part.

But I couldn't dwell on that now. Not yet.

Had my family's souls gathered somewhere? Were they waiting for us?

I quickened my step and ran past the guards—and sometimes *through* the guards—to the basement. All I had to do was follow the trickle of blood from the bodies they were carrying out. The trail led down. Down. Down to the basement that smelled of smoke and defeat. Plaster fell from the ceiling and walls in chunks from the bullet holes. Blood coated the floor like fresh paint.

I managed only one glance before I scrambled back up the steps, dry heaving into the darkness. I was dead—or something—but the raw emotions and horror still boiled in my chest.

They killed us. They *slaughtered* my family. "Papa!" I screamed, abandoning any caution. "Mamma! Olga! Tatiana! Maria!" I ran in the dark, Alexei keeping up behind me. "Dr. Botkin! Anna! Trupp! Kharitonov!" But I could not find their ethereal forms. Only their bodies. Their dead bodies, which the soldiers searched and manhandled and treated like sacks of garbage.

"Jewels." One soldier tapped Maria's body with the butt of his gun. "She had jewels in her clothing. That's why the bullets ricocheted. That's why it took so many tries to kill her."

My eyes burned, but my current incorporeal form would not allow tears. Only the burn. Only the emotions.

"Maybe they are in our rooms," I said in a last desperate attempt, leading Alexei in a sprint around the house, through the door, and up the stairs. We didn't need to touch the doors. They opened on their own, as though just for us, and then returned to their previous state, releasing no creaks or groans or slams. Did they open at all in the physical world, or was this merely the ghost world reacting?

Up in our rooms we found nothing but packed bags and our rooms as we left them. The only difference was Tatiana's dogs. Both of them lay dead near her bed.

"No!" Alexei cried, running into the room. He searched for his spaniel. "Joy! *Joy!* Come here, girl!" He ran from room to room. I had never seen him run like this before—not even on his healthiest days. "Joy! Where are you?"

No answer. No bark. No response from his beloved spaniel. I didn't help him search because I didn't want to find her body. We both knew that had she been in the room alive, she would not have ignored his calls.

"Perhaps she escaped," I suggested. "Or maybe she can't hear your ghost voice."

He bit his lip but didn't cry. Always the soldier. I would cry for him if I could. He slunk to me and wrapped his arms around my waist. I gripped him hard, clinging to the comfort. The safety of family.

"What are we, Nastya?" He sounded so small. "Why is it just us?"

And finally I acknowledged the answer that I'd pushed aside until this moment. "I used a spell, Alexei. A spell from Papa. He gave me the family Matryoshka doll and there was a spell in it he told me not to use until we were desperate. When I reached for your hand in the truck, the spell came out. And here we are."

"What does the spell do?"

I shook my head, a lump in my throat. "I thought it had healed me. But now . . . I don't know what it did to us. Papa said each spell was for the good of the Romanov family. He said it could be our salvation." It didn't seem right to have salvation without Papa. It was supposed to extend to him. To everyone. I'd waited like he told me. I didn't use the spell until the very end.

And it was too late.

Papa had been wrong.

"Maybe it is letting us escape." Alexei leaned away and stared up into my face.

I glanced out our open window at the truck below. It was filled with bodies now—ours included. Yurovsky hissed orders at the guards, threatening them at gunpoint to turn out their pockets and surrender the jewels they'd torn from Maria's clothing. Then he took a bayonet from one of the soldiers and speared a moving body in the back of the truck. I flinched. Had that been mine? Or Alexei's? Or someone else?

Would I feel it if they destroyed my physical form?

I couldn't handle the moment—the truth of our executions and the betrayal that came from our country, from the soldiers . . . from

Zash. So my mind turned blank—a defense against the emotions. It knew they were too much, so it allowed only a drop here and there. A drop that carried the weight of a broken and torn country.

"I think you're right," I said in a dead voice. "The spell is letting us escape." But I didn't know if I had the will to escape. To survive without my family. To run with the knowledge and memories of tonight.

Then I looked at Alexei, standing tall with his chin lifted. Emulating Papa's calm and ferocious strength. For him. For Alexei I would escape. I would not give up. We would survive . . . for our family.

———

Yurovsky was quick. He had the bodies in the truck and the soldiers in their vehicles within a half hour of having executed us. When he was the only one left to climb into a truck, he pulled out his pocket watch.

Alexei and I huddled near the truck but hadn't gotten in. We couldn't bear to sit among the dead bodies that no longer felt like family. They felt like tragedy and grief.

Yurovsky consulted the watch face. Then he walked toward the truck until he stood over my body. He stared down at me as though I were sleeping. In that moment I wished him dead. I wished to see him shot from behind, crumpled on the ground, devoid of all dreams and pursuits and hopes and honor.

Papa would be ashamed of my thoughts. Even Alexei would likely parrot Papa and say I ought to forgive this terrible man. But my will to forgive had died with the first bullet sent into Papa's chest.

Yurovsky patted down my physical body none too kindly.

First, he found the Matryoshka doll husk in my sleeve—the one I'd already used. Only a moment later, he found the rest of the doll tucked into my corset. He pulled it free, then snapped his pocket watch closed. I could do nothing but watch him steal from me.

He held the Matryoshka doll in front of him as though it were a priceless jewel. His eyes glowed with greed, his hands trembled with victory. "Clever little Nastya. You may have protected Dochkin for a little while, but now that you and your family are snuffed, you've been bested at your game." He examined the shell of the *ajnin* spell, then shoved it into his satchel.

My fingers lifted to my ghost clothing. I still felt the doll there, tucked into my camisole. But I also *saw* the doll—the physical version of it—in Yurovsky's hand. Reflected in his shining eyes. I couldn't pull mine from my camisole. I couldn't remove it from its spot. Who truly had it? Yurovsky or me?

He tucked the doll away. This item alone he did not place in his office or write a report on. He kept it for himself. He said something about finding Dochkin. That must be why he needed the doll. Somehow it led to the spell master. And Yurovsky would surely kill him.

Yurovsky climbed into the truck. Soldiers held the door open to the palisade and it rumbled through. Another truck with a bed of shovels and canvases and cartons of acid followed. Alexei and I climbed into the back just in time to ride after our family.

To ride after our enemy.

To ride away from our prison and into the deadly unknown.

As we passed through the gates, I caught one soldier muttering to the other, "So this is the end of the Romanov dynasty."

Alexei and I sat like two defiant ghosts, determined to live and prove them wrong.

24

I wish we hadn't followed.

Where did I think we would be taken? Yurovsky and the men transported our bodies not only to bury us but to destroy all evidence that we even existed. Now I knew where he went on horseback so often—to scout out a burial ground.

His choice of grave left me ill.

It was a mine shaft. Set in the muddy center of the dense Koptyaki forest. It had taken us over two hours to reach it because the trucks continued to get stuck in the mud. Yurovsky was furious. They took the bodies of my beloved family and stripped them of their clothes so as to burn them, then dumped them in the mine shaft.

Next came the acid, dumped down the shaft and sprayed all over them to destroy their names. Their legacy. There would be no royal burial. No mourning of the people still loyal to us. Perhaps the world would never even know we had died.

"I can't watch this," I croaked, only then realizing that we'd joined the entourage because I wasn't yet ready to bid farewell. But what good were we doing? "We must go, Alexei."

"What of our bodies?" Alexei stared at the men working over the mine. We heard Yurovsky shout that the mine wasn't deep enough. That they'd need to haul the bodies back up and find a new site.

"The spell will likely wear off." I squinted at the midnight sun now dipping back up over the horizon, even though it was not yet morning. The sickly light revealed Yurovsky's twisted attempts to conceal evidence. "And when it does I expect we will probably return to our physical forms. Or perhaps we will die." I shuddered at the idea of returning to my body at the bottom of that mine with the rest of my family's corpses.

"We need to lead the White Army here. To the grave." Alexei spun to face the forest. "Tell them what Yurovsky did, so the truth doesn't die with us. Yurovsky is trying to keep our execution a secret—probably because it will ignite the Whites."

"How can we do that when no one can hear or see us?"

He took my hand. "I have to try."

I remembered when he and I sat talking about his purpose, and how helpless he felt as an ill soldier. He'd trained to be a leader but had no one to lead. Now he did. Me. He may not have a throne, but he was the rightful heir to one if it existed.

And it was my duty to support my tsarevich. To help him find the White Army. To help him survive. "Lead the way."

We hurried into the forest back toward Ekaterinburg. Away from our family. No exhaustion came from our efforts. No resistance from the undergrowth of the forest. No splashes from the puddles of marshy floor. We ran and ran and ran, never tiring, hardly having to breathe. Despite our sobering and desperate situation, Alexei ran with a wild ferocity. This form was the healthiest he'd ever been.

"Look at my legs," he said as he leaped over a log. "Watch this." He attempted a terrible cartwheel. "And this!" He wove between trees like obstacles in a race.

"You are exquisite." It was all I could offer before the terror of our impending end reclaimed my mind. I didn't want to return to our physical bodies. I didn't want to wake trapped in that mine or back in Yurovsky's truck. I would rather we died. *Please, Iisus, let it be death.*

We had been running for well over an hour when the trees began to thin. This forest held none of the nostalgia of home. Instead of inviting me into a fresh, earthy embrace, the taiga felt more enemy than friend.

I slowed and my senses went into high alert. I threw out an arm to halt Alexei. "Listen."

By the time we stopped and focused on the sounds of the forest, the noise I thought I'd heard had faded. I didn't have to wait long until another sound came. A guttural groan. Human.

Ahead of us.

I ducked behind a tree but Alexei advanced. "Remember, we can't be heard. No one sees us."

We picked our way through the forest until, through the labyrinth of trees, I spotted a form. Though Alexei was right—we were unseen and unheard to the regular world—I still pressed against trees and peered around trunks.

Then I saw him.

Zash.

My executioner. He was on his knees at the base of a large tree, his head in his hands and his pistol in his lap. "Iisus," he said, hardly louder than a whisper. "Forgive me."

Iisus? Forgiveness? How *dare* Zash ask for forgiveness? He *shot* me! Nothing could undo what he'd done. His fingers clawed at his hair, as though trying to pull out the memories. As though the pain would drown out their screams.

Alexei gasped. "It's Zash!" He sounded excited. Hopeful.

"He shot me," I snapped. "We can't trust him."

Alexei went silent. I felt wrong watching Zash's sorrow as though it were a play. I didn't believe half of it. That was until he quieted and seemed to enter a new place of resignation. Of cold hopelessness as he reached into his lap and picked up his pistol. He looked at it as though he'd never seen one before.

Then he rotated the barrel until it pointed to his heart. Changed his mind and slid the tip up under his jaw.

"No!" Alexei shouted.

Even I was stunned. The old Nastya didn't wish Zash to be gone from this world. But the new Nastya didn't want Zash to exist anymore after what he'd done. It made me angry to see him taking such an escape. He didn't deserve to be free of whatever pain he was feeling. His suffering was penance for his decision to execute my family.

"Stop!" Alexei hollered near Zash's ear. Zash tensed. For a moment I thought he heard Alexei. But then he slid his finger over the trigger. "Nastya!" Alexei turned to me as though I could do something. The more panicked he grew, the harder my heart thumped.

This wasn't right. This wasn't *fair*.

"I don't know how to stop him, Alexei." My voice sounded dead.

Alexei tried to shove the gun out of Zash's hand, but his own thin limb went straight through it. Zash's hand trembled, but the gun barrel stayed fixed against his skin. He started muttering to himself in Russian. Swift and desperate. I caught *Iisus* again.

"What is the next spell from the doll?" Alexei screamed at me. "Use one of those!"

I snapped out of my numbness. Of course. Of *course* I had to stop Zash—for Alexei's sake. For mine. I couldn't watch him die. We had lived through a sea of blood. And though Zash shot us, Alexei still cared for him. I was tired of seeing Alexei in pain.

I grappled for the doll against my sternum, but I couldn't pull it out. It was trapped in the in-between land of physical and ethereal. In the ethereal world I had it. In the physical world Yurovsky had it. "The doll is stuck. I can't use it because Yurovsky has it!"

"Well, what was the first spell? Maybe it will turn Zash into a ghost like us." He placed his fingers around Zash's wrist, angling it as though he were touching him. Then he held out his free hand for me. I grabbed it and searched for the spell word, but already I knew it wouldn't work. The spell had been used. It was gone from my lips. I felt the emptiness.

I said it anyway. *"Ajnin."*

The change came like a rushing wind. My body grew heavy. Pain blossomed in my chest. My knees gave out and I dropped, catching myself on a log. The scene darkened and I blinked rapidly, trying to take it in as my eyes blurred and readjusted.

I was physical again.

Alexei kept his feet a moment longer, but he stiffened as though an electric shock had gone through him. His eyes slid to mine and a feeble plea escaped his lips. "Nas . . . tya . . ."

He fell headlong across Zash, his hand tearing the gun away from Zash's head. It went off, sending a bullet into the leaves above us. Zash cried out and fumbled for his dropped pistol. He scrambled out from beneath Alexei's body and then held the pistol like a shield between him and us.

"No!" I lurched to my feet. The underbrush grabbed at my skirt as I fought to reach my brother, finally flinging myself in front of him. Sharp pain stabbed me at all angles. I glared up at Zash and his trembling pistol. "He just saved your life, Zash. Don't you dare murder him."

Zash stood pale as the body of my dead papa. The gun tumbled from his hand and he crossed himself. "How . . . ? What *are* you?"

"Not four hours ago, you shot me in the chest. And now you don't recognize me?" I wasn't interested in explaining how I was alive or why the bullet ricocheted. And now that he no longer pointed a firearm at me, I twisted to my brother.

He lay with his eyes squeezed shut. Trembling. "Alexei?" I called softly.

"Ah," he groaned, reaching out with his hand. "I . . . h-h-hurt."

And I could see why. Beneath the now-risen sun I could finally take in his injuries—they'd not shown on his ethereal body. A bullet had gone clean through the palm of his left hand and half his face had swollen purple from the butt of a gun clubbing him down. Someone had speared his hip with a bayonet when Yurovsky commanded everyone to finish the job without bullets.

Of all people to survive an execution, I never would have guessed Alexei to be one of them. But at the rate he was bleeding and his head was swelling, he would not hold that title long. "Oh no." I grabbed his hand. "No, no, no. What have I done? Alexei, what did I do?"

Blood slipped from the wound at his hip, gurgling and bubbling lazily as though tired of leaking. How long had this been going on? How was his body here? How was *my* body here? If the spell reunited us with our bodies and moved our physical forms to this spot, that meant Yurovsky would know we were alive.

I pulled the Matryoshka doll from my shirt. It was as solid as the pain in my ribs.

Yurovsky would be coming for the doll.

No seam showed on the new layer of doll. No glowing spell. I shook the doll. "Open!" Nothing changed, so I shoved it back into my shirt.

It turned out I was wrong. Alexei and I didn't return *to* our physical state. Our physical forms returned to *us*—returned to our forms from the moment I used the spell. Whatever had happened to us in the back of the truck or when Yurovsky tossed our bodies down a mine shaft . . . had been undone.

I'd never seen—nor even *heard* of—a spell as powerful as this.

No wonder Yurovsky wanted the doll. No wonder Papa told me to find it and bring it to Ekaterinburg.

"Are you real?" Zash whispered.

I paid no attention to him. If he wanted to pick up his gun and finish the job he started, so be it. But my brother was perishing before my eyes and I was helpless.

Alexei's agony increased. Fear bubbled up in my chest. "What do I do?" I said softly to Alexei, who I doubted could hear me anymore through his pain. His eyes squeezed closed and his teeth ground against each other. "I don't know what to—"

"Nastya . . . let me help." Zash's plea came from over my shoulder. I hadn't even heard him move from his spot. "Tell me what you need."

"How can *you* help?" I shrieked, letting fury fill my words even though it emptied my logic. "Alexei is dying *because of you*!" It didn't matter that there had been an entire squad of Bolsheviks at the execution or that Yurovsky headed up the entire thing.

Zash betrayed us.

My family had grown fond of him and trusted him and he allowed them to die. Everything—*everything*—was his fault. I expected such darkness from Yurovsky. Not from Zash. Never from Zash.

Alexei strained against the pain, his bloodied hand gripping mine until I thought the small bones of my wrist would snap. It served as a sharp reminder that I needed help wherever I could get it. And currently, Zash was offering it. I could not allow my anger to push him away.

"How close are we to Ekaterinburg?" I asked in as forgiving a tone as I could muster.

"Only a few kilometers." Zash sounded embarrassed. Ashamed. "I did not join the transport to the gravesite."

I could put two and two together pretty easily. He shot us, felt convicted, and fled. Unwilling to help with the burial. Unwilling to see if any of us survived. He fled into the forest where he planned to take his life.

I wanted to feel relief from his regret, but I couldn't. I despised him. "Was Dr. Botkin killed?"

A pause. "Yes."

I expected as much. I stood. "We need to get to the Ipatiev House and find the spells Yurovsky has locked in his office. There's a small tin of relief spells in there. They might help Alexei." They'd ease the pain but not the injuries. Still, it was all I had.

I clawed my way up a tree trunk until I stood, wobbling. I started to tie my skirt into a knot so I could run without it flapping around my ankles, but Zash grabbed my arm. I glared, but he stared at my arm, as though surprised to find it real.

I jerked away. "Don't touch me. We don't have time to lose."

"Nastya . . ." Alexei called. "I think . . . I think I'm bleeding too much."

I almost broke into a run then and there. But Zash stepped in front of me. "You cannot go back there. If any guard remains, you will be recognized and likely shot. Especially if Beloborodov shows up. I will run. I will be fast. I am not injured."

"Fine, but *hurry!*" I sank down next to Alexei and bunched the hem of my skirt over his hip wound. "Check the lockboxes in Yurovsky's office for any spells you can find . . ." My words ground to a halt when I took in Zash's face.

This was *Zash.* Loyal Bolshevik soldier who'd gotten cold feet after a dirty job.

I took several deep breaths. Alexei had gone quiet—the pain too much. Or perhaps he was already dying. "Are you capable of helping us, Zash?"

"I am. Please. *Please* let me show you." I saw the hope in his eyes—hope of a second chance. That this would pay for his misdeeds. That his prayers for forgiveness had been answered.

I let him rest in the lie. If it would help Alexei, I'd let Zash believe whatever he wanted.

I nodded. He left at a sprint. Only then did I realize he'd asked no questions about our survival or our sudden appearance. He was willing to believe what he saw, to act on his second chance without questioning it. On a different day—a day before this one—I might have admired that.

But today I only hoped he'd be fast enough to save Alexei's life.

25

Being alone in the forest felt far more vulnerable as an injured physical being than as an agile ethereal one. The moment Zash's crashing run faded from my ears, my mind sprinted as though *it* were the one racing for medical supplies.

I had assumed the Ipatiev House would be empty now that we were not in it. But what if there were soldiers? What if Zash got caught? It would be easy for him to show up and tell them where Alexei and I were. Bring them back to us. Finish the job.

He might run into Yurovsky, who had likely noticed the disappearance of our bodies—and the Matryoshka doll—by now. What if he found Zash? What if he found us? What if his special watch could detect our location because of the doll in my corset and he was coming after us in the forest?

I rose from my spot by Alexei's side and found Zash's discarded pistol. I'd never held a pistol before, but it didn't seem that difficult. He'd simply lifted it to his head and put a finger on the trigger. I could do that if Yurovsky showed up. But then . . . even if he did appear, how terrible would it be to be killed?

Poor Alexei groaned with every breath. I'd stuffed cloth against his hip wound and pressed my knee against the hole in his hand, but since his blood didn't clot it wouldn't do much good.

These were the types of injuries Mamma had dreaded because there was little to do to combat them. These were the things that Rasputin could heal, sucking Mamma's health away.

My own chest throbbed with each breath—not from emotion, but from the strike of a bullet that had ricocheted off the jewels in my corset. How many times had I been struck? I hurt terribly.

The sun flickered through the leaves overhead, but the shade kept us cool. My throat burned for water. Why had I not asked Zash to get water, too? When he came back we would have to bandage Alexei and leave.

To go . . . where?

To the White Army? We didn't even know how to find them. Yurovsky said they'd been prepared to launch artillery upon the city. Surely they couldn't be far.

What was our life for now? Clearly Iisus had given us another chance, but I didn't know why. I wasn't sure I wanted it.

I smoothed hair away from Alexei's brow. Straightened his bloodied collar because he would want it that way, little soldier that he was. For now, my life existed for him. The final heir to the throne of a country that would never accept him. But more than that: He was my brother. And I would save his life.

No matter what it cost me, I would ensure he lived.

I looked at the Matryoshka doll, holding the last two mysterious spells. Yurovsky said the doll would help him find Dochkin. Did the spells lead to him? That must be why Yurovsky wanted the doll so badly. Not to use or confiscate the spells, but to find and kill Dochkin.

Perhaps if I could get Alexei to Dochkin, the spell master could heal him. How powerful was he? His *ajnin* spell sent us into the spirit realm. It defeated time by bringing our bodies back to us only as injured as they'd been the moment I used the spell.

He had reversed our injuries. With power like that, he could create a spell that could undo my family's execution. A time spell that reversed the slaughter. If I brought Alexei to him—as his tsarevich—I knew Dochkin would do it for him. For Russia. He was loyal to the Romanovs—there was proof enough of that in the Matryoshka doll.

The sound of something crashing through bushes came from ahead and I threw myself over Alexei's prone body, grappling for the pistol. As I aimed it toward the bushes, Zash appeared. He saw me, saw the pistol, and pulled up short.

The relief that expelled from my lungs said it all. Though my heart despised him, something in me still trusted him. Still felt safer around him than any other Bolshevik. My arm dropped to the earth and I let the gun fall from it.

"So you *are* real," he said softly.

I frowned. "What did you think?"

"I thought perhaps you were sent by Iisus to stop me from taking my life. And perhaps upon my leaving, you would return to heaven."

"Unfortunately, we're not angels—we're just the last two members of our entire family trying to survive."

Zash tossed me a canteen. "The Ipatiev House was empty except for a handful of soldiers cleaning up the . . . the basement." Scrubbing away our blood, he meant. "The sisters arrived at the gate almost as soon as I did, so I accepted the food and sent them on their way."

More rustling sounded from the bushes and I narrowed my eyes. "You brought someone." He had turned us in—told his soldiers.

The rustling grew louder, but it seemed too fast to be a soldier. Then a russet-and-white bundle of fur burst from the undergrowth and leaped into my lap, licking my face with ferocity.

"Joy!" My eyes burned as I snuggled the spaniel. Another survivor. Another sign of life and hope. "Oh, Joy, you're alive!" I pressed her face to mine, but she yapped too excitedly to sit still. Then I let her loose on Alexei.

Being the spectacular spaniel she was, she didn't leap on him, only sniffed around his body and touched her nose to his cheek. He remained still. Cold. No longer strong enough to speak.

"He's dying, Zash. We have to do something. What spells did you get?"

Joy licked Alexei's skin—cleaning and healing and showing love in the best way she could.

I beckoned impatiently. "Did you find the tin of relief spells?"

Zash hurried forward and dropped a bundle at my side. Only then did I see how much he was carrying—two packs over his shoulder stuffed with items, three canteens, two rolled-up sleeping mats, and a basket of food. The same basket the sisters would bring to us, only this one carried much more food than what we were ever given.

It was as though Zash knew we had a journey ahead of us. As though he planned to *join us* on that journey. If I could view him only as an asset—a body of muscle and protection—I was okay with that.

But I couldn't see him that way. I still saw him enshrouded in a cloud of mistrust. He betrayed us to the point of our deaths. Could a person feel remorse deep enough to undo that? Even if he did, it meant nothing to me. I would never forget what he did. I would never forgive.

"There was only the tin," he said in a low voice. "I could find no others." He pulled out a small bottle, barely the size of my thumb. "And some spell ink."

My hands stilled in their search of Dr. Botkin's things. "Nothing other than the relief spells?" I'd been hoping for something stronger. Relief spells were about as useful as a cup of cold tea right now. "You can't have searched very hard!" I should have gone. I should have done the job instead of letting him.

"I searched everywhere, Nastya. He cleared out his office. He must have done it the night before . . . before all of this."

I found the tin, but when I popped it open no spells wiggled inside. Empty. Either Yurovsky had used them all for some reason, or he'd lost them. "Give me the spell ink."

Zash handed over the bottle.

There was hardly enough for six spells. I forced my heart to calm so I could hum while painting the words on Alexei's skin. I used my own finger as the brush since I didn't have a paintbrush with me.

I painted four and stowed two in the tin for later. The spells were messy, but when I said, *"Oblegcheniye,"* two of the four spells melted into Alexei's skin as they'd always done.

"You're a spell master," Zash breathed. "All this time."

"No. I can make *one* spell. For my brother." I wasn't about to tell him I *wanted* to be a spell master.

Alexei's breathing evened out for a moment before the pain seemed to return. The spells had hardly helped. I considered using the last two relief spells, but then I saw a kit for stitches. I eyed Alexei's hip wound.

It was all I could do for now. I pulled out the curved needle. I unwound the thick thread. And I reminded myself of all the times I'd hemmed my skirt and sewn tight lines to keep the diamonds in my corset. I told myself the blood was batting and tangles, that the skin was two frayed edges of cloth.

And I reminded myself that I was a Romanov. I could do this.

26

By the time I finished sewing up Alexei, both Zash's and my fingers were stained red. We'd packed and bandaged Alexei's shot hand and then wrapped what was left of Botkin's cloth around Alexei's middle. Other than medical instructions, we didn't speak.

Joy had settled into a curled position near Alexei's swollen head. That swelling concerned me the most, but I didn't dare bleed it since he'd likely die from the extra blood loss and the inability to heal. The fact he was even still breathing proved Iisus' protection over us.

"Thank you for bringing Joy," I said to Zash.

"She would hardly let me leave without her." I caught a tentative grin in his voice as he rubbed his hands on a nearby patch of moss.

I didn't indulge him. Instead, I stared at my unconscious brother, stained red like the color our enemies wore. My throat clogged. "He's going to die. Probably within hours."

Zash stilled. "There is a hospital in Ekaterinburg."

"And there are Bolsheviks in Ekaterinburg. And the Red Army. And people on the lookout for bloodied and dying Romanovs." I shoved the medical supplies back into Dr. Botkin's bag. "You asked me to let you help, but if you're going to lead us right into the hands of your Bolshevik leaders, then get out of here before I shoot you."

He took a deep breath. "I'm not trying to lead you back into their hands, Nastya. I suggested the hospital because it is nearby and the tsarevich doesn't have long."

"He doesn't! Because of *you*!" My voice echoed through the trees, silencing us both with its intensity. And when my echo finally settled, a new sound met my ears that sent my blood draining. A distant holler. A search party.

Everything silenced—my thoughts, the forest, the world.

Yurovsky.

He was here. Hunting for us.

Zash scrambled to his feet, throwing our belongings over his shoulders. I grabbed a pack and scooped up Joy—all I could manage with my injuries. "What of Alexei?" I whispered, panicked. "You must carry him!"

Zash was already laden with travel supplies, but he didn't hesitate. He lifted Alexei gently but swiftly, and we began to run. It was awkward. Jostling. Painful.

And loud.

I was sure Yurovsky was moments behind us, but he'd been up all night, too. He'd been digging and disposing of bodies and planning and plotting and pacing. But he had bullets to catch us.

Wherever Zash was leading us, I followed, hiking up my skirt with my free hand. Every step sent pain shooting up my ribs. Joy kept quiet in my arms, banging against the Matryoshka doll and bruising my sternum. Oh heavens. The doll! We couldn't outrun Yurovsky when he had his pocket watch. He was after the doll, and the watch would always point him toward the nearest spell.

I couldn't give it up—not when it would save Alexei. And I couldn't hide it because Yurovsky would find it. *Iisus! What do I—?*

I gasped. "Zash! Stop!"

He slid to a stop in a marshy spot of moss. When I reached him, I dropped Joy. She ran around our ankles, happy to be free of my arms. Then I dove into one of the packs over Zash's shoulder.

"Nastya, what are you doing?" Zash hissed. We could hear them closer now. Their movements, not their voices.

"The spells," I panted. "His pocket watch detects them. He wants my doll." My fingers closed around the small tin of relief spells. I put one in the large Matryoshka doll shell and left the other in the tin. Then I threw the tin as far as I could to my left and the other relief spell to my right. "Okay, let's go. But quietly."

"We need to keep running."

"They'll *hear* us—"

"They'll find us, Nastya. If his watch does what you say it does, we need to get out of here." Without another consideration, he bolted forward, leaving me to catch up. I ran, too, letting Joy use her own four legs, and I prayed my plan worked. Those spells would lure Yurovsky in. Perhaps he'd think they were the doll or me hiding. And he would spend several minutes following his pocket watch until he found both spells.

Only then would he realize it was a diversion.

I tried to keep pace with Zash, but even carrying Alexei he managed to stay ahead of me. The jolt of each step sent a serrated spike of pain into my chest that grew and grew until I finally couldn't push myself any farther.

I had to walk—it went against every instinct. It went against every ounce of my willpower. But I couldn't push through the pain of the bullet that had bruised or possibly snapped my ribs. Zash must have sensed the change in my pace because he looked back and slowed. I wanted to apologize for my weakness, but how could I apologize to the soldier who caused my injuries?

"Keep running," I told him.

He maintained a walking pace I could match. "No. We will go together."

"For Alexei's sake, you must keep going!"

"If I leave you behind, you won't know where to find us."

I should shove the Matryoshka doll into his hand and force him to go, but the stubborn set of his jaw told me how successful that attempt would be. I returned the doll back to my camisole. "Where are you even leading us? The hospital?"

It scared me that I had followed blindly to this moment, putting my trust in him through instinct. I reined it back in to the spool of suspicion and growing bitterness in my mind. I must not relax. I must not trust Zash except for the moments that I had no other choice. Like now.

"I know someone who might be able to help."

Help who? Him? Alexei? All of us? I still hadn't caught my breath, so I didn't voice my questions. I just followed Zash through the forest toward the war-zone city of Ekaterinburg. Forced to place my trust in the man who helped execute my family.

We tromped through the forest, silent in speech but growing louder in footsteps due to exhaustion. I glanced over my shoulder every other step, certain I'd see Yurovsky on our trail.

"You have to remember he's been awake even longer than you," Zash panted, now carrying Alexei over his back like a turtle would its shell. "No matter his desire to persist in following us, his soldiers will be too tired."

"*You* are not too tired." I wanted to accept his logic, but my fear ushered in too many doubts. If Zash could persist for so long, so could Yurovsky.

"My energy is from a different source than mere willpower." He said this so quietly, I almost didn't hear. And when I did process it, I wasn't sure how to respond.

We walked for another hour before stopping at the tree line of a little village not far from Ekaterinburg. The sun hung low in the sky opposite us, sending the shadows of the small carved houses spiking toward our hideout. A long stretch of field rested between the trees and the village. To cross it would bring every eye turning our way.

"The house is not far in." Zash assessed my appearance. "But perhaps you should cover your head."

I used another strip from my skirt as a scarf for my baldness. "What about you?" I tried not to let my words sound cutting but didn't quite succeed. "You look like a Bolshevik."

"No one will question me for that."

"And Alexei?" Alexei still wore his tsarevich soldier uniform. Zash lowered him to the ground and we stripped off his coat and stuffed it into one of the packs. Even against the dark strips of skirt wrapping his hip wound, I could see the bloodstain that had soaked through. There was no time to waste. No time to fear. I took a deep breath. "Let's go."

Zash lifted Alexei and took off across the field. I pulled Joy into my arms and pushed my legs to carry me across the field, though not nearly as fast as Zash. Every muscle ached, every breath stung, but once Zash entered the shadow of a house, he stopped and waited for me.

No one filled the streets around us, but open windows and fluttering curtains betrayed the presence of a few observers. What did it matter? Let them see. Let them see that Anastasia and Alexei Romanov were alive, even if just barely. Maybe word would reach the White Army.

Zash led us down a side street, though there weren't many to choose from. We walked now, keeping our heads low, and passed a few cottages. He turned down a lane and we walked to the end where a classically quaint house of stone and stucco rose from the shadows.

Without even a knock Zash lifted the latch and entered the house. I had no choice but to follow. The interior smelled of old cotton and hot supper. An uneven wood floor creaked beneath our feet. Zash closed the door behind us, shutting out most of the light, and laid Alexei down on the floor, using Alexei's coat for a pillow.

I remained standing by the wall, tense against the strangeness of this house and the mystery of its owner. Where had he brought us?

"Babushka?" Zash called.

Babushka? This was his *grandmother's* house? I'd never entered a village house. My own grandmothers had been royalty and not at all the aged women depicted in the storybooks.

Joy squirmed in my arms, wanting to roam the new space and sniff it out. I set her down and she went straight to a large cushioned chair beside the fire and sniffed around it.

An open doorway led into another room from which the supper smell wafted. My stomach growled and I pressed a hand over it, not that it did much good. Perhaps Zash's babushka was not at home? As the thought crossed my mind, a low, dark voice met my ears.

"I smell magic." A short, thin form exited what I assumed to be the kitchen, a scarf around her neck and wrinkles weighing down her skin. Her dark-black hair was pulled into a low bun, and her old eyes supported so many wrinkles I could hardly tell where her gaze fell. She bore the same Siberian coloring as Zash.

The wooden spoon in her hand was stained crimson. The supper smell must be coming from borscht—a cabbage, beet, and beef soup that sent my stomach practically leaping from my body.

Her narrowed gaze struck Alexei first, flicking to his bloodied bandage. Then to Zash, whom she greeted with a brief nod, not quite the reception I would expect from a grandmother. And then to me. "You are hiding a spell." She smacked Zash with the soupy spoon. "And you brought her into my *home*? Reckless boy."

I took in this woman's displeasure. And as I looked to Alexei's weak and injured body, I realized she might not help us. Desperation filled me like it never had before, and I thought of Papa dropping to his knees in front of Avdeev, begging for an open window. I hadn't understood his humility then, but now I did. Now I knew that pride meant nothing when set against the life and well-being of a loved one.

"Please," I gasped. "He said you could help us. Help *him*. My brother." I gestured to Alexei. "Please do not send us away."

She did not acknowledge my plea but addressed Zash. "Who are these people? What have you done, Zash?"

27

Zash told her everything in a matter of minutes. How we were the last Romanovs, how he had helped guard us these past months. How Yurovsky's pocket watch detected spells. How Yurovsky assigned him to the firing squad. "I helped kill them, Babushka," he said in a low, torn voice.

"You did what you had to," she barked.

I balked at her lack of compassion. Did she not hear what he said? We were Romanovs! He helped *murder* my entire family. If that didn't move her, she certainly wouldn't help us.

"But I have a second chance—to help them now. And we need you." Zash removed the soup spoon from her hand, then pressed her fingers between his palms. "Please, Babushka. For me."

She rolled her eyes and her countenance seemed to change into something resigned but softer. "Of course I will, boy. You know that. Now, get some soup for you and the girl." Then she pointed to me. "*Sidyet.* I'll see to you next."

I plopped into the nearest chair, mostly out of relief. The impact stung and sent a ragged breath into my chest. Who was this woman who could help us?

She knelt by Alexei and assessed his wounds, her hands gliding but not touching. Sensing and reading. I caught a low mutter. "*This is our tsarevich?*"

I was glad Alexei was not conscious to hear that. His heart would break. "He has an illness that does not allow his blood to clot."

"Hemophilia."

"Da." Alexei's condition had been our family secret, but this woman barely flinched. Had she worked with it before?

"Do you know what I am, Grand Duchess?"

My throat constricted. She'd sensed the Matryoshka doll. She was the one person Zash thought could help Alexei. "You are a spell master."

She nodded. "Now I am just Vira, the old woman at the end of the lane. A Bolshevik commandant is after you. If your spells lead him here, I will be executed without a second thought. Probably shot in this very room."

"I thank you for risking your life—"

"It is not for you, Grand Duchess. I do this for Zash. And you must leave within an hour. You understand? I will do what I can for the tsarevich, but I can already tell you it will not be enough."

My hope fractured. "What do you mean?"

Zash returned to the room with two bowls of steaming borscht. He handed me one, and I took a long moment to breathe in the aroma of herbs and vegetables. The beet-red broth swirled over a mix of potatoes and beef and cabbage. This would be the most flavorful thing I'd eaten in months. No more black bread or broth with lentils.

Vira reached over to her empty fireplace grate and pulled out a brick, behind which sat a small clay bottle stoppered with a cork.

"Listen, child. I rid my house of all spells once the Bolsheviks came hunting. Spell masters had two choices: either turn themselves in to the Red Army to serve the new government or be killed. Personally, I think the Red Army is killing them anyway. I didn't like those options, so I chose to live a life as any other woman might. After all, I was just a simple village spell master."

She unstoppered the bottle and peered inside. "There's not much left."

"I was planning to bring you more, Babushka." Zash had given his spell ink to me. That's why he'd had it in his pack—for his grandmother.

She waved him away. "This will do." Then she returned to our conversation. "I am a local who used to create simple spells for colds and bruises and broken bones. A few spells of wisdom and memory stirring here and there. But nothing the likes of which might heal the tsarevich." She reached back inside the hole left from the brick and pulled out a silver pin. "Now eat your soup and let me work."

I couldn't tear my eyes away as she dipped the pin into the bottle and drew out a tiny drop of the glistening rainbow liquid. "But you've been hiding spell ink!"

"Your commandant may be able to detect spells, but nothing can detect spell ink. It is neutral when a spell master makes it and only activated once you blend your voice or blood with it."

"Spell masters make it? How?"

She eyed me through slits. "You're a bit curious for a grand duchess. Is this really the time to interrogate me about spell mastery?"

I shook my head and spooned some borscht into my mouth. It warmed me like an internal fire. Reminding me of life. "Was it hard to start a new life?" I asked quietly as she worked.

"It is if you separate the two—old life and new life. But once you learn that it's all one life and each day is a new page, it gets a bit easier to let your story take an unexpected path." She set out four squares of paper and bent over the first one, meticulously dotting out a word. A spell.

As she did this she hummed and occasionally sang in a weathered voice and a language I did not recognize. Alexei stirred but not in discomfort. He seemed to be soothed. Her humming went on for several minutes and did not appear to be stopping soon.

I ate my borscht.

She told me one hour. With each slurp of soup the seconds seemed to increase. My body ached to lie down and sleep. To remain seated on the cushioned chair. To test the fates and see if I would truly wake up to this same life and nightmare. But ticking in the back of my head was the knowledge we would be leaving. Soon. Most likely returning to the forest, and once we did that, I didn't know where we'd go. I couldn't follow Zash again. It was doubtful he had a second spell-master babushka hiding in a local village.

I didn't know when I'd finished the soup, but I still felt empty inside. Zash took my bowl and returned with it full again. This time he added a dollop of sour cream. It turned the red soup a light pink and brought the extra fat my stomach craved. In another lifetime—a more polite lifetime—I would have declined, knowing it had taken Vira hours to make it when she hadn't expected guests. But I accepted the soup and ate every last drop.

Alexei moaned and my head snapped up. His eyes fluttered. Vira continued humming but made eye contact with him. He frowned. Blinked a few times, and then his voice came out in a croak. "Spell woman . . ."

"Tishe, Tsarevich," she tried to soothe.

"Will you fight with me?"

She stopped creating the spells for a moment. A lump rose in my throat. Was he aware of what he was saying? He'd been unconscious for quite some time.

"I am making spells for you—to help you." Her voice remained in that soothing tone as when singing.

"Make a spell for the White Army. Join them. Help them . . . fight." His voice grew weaker, but his gaze remained fixed on hers.

She took a deep breath and I feared she would abandon helping him at all. "Tsarevich, if you come back to me healthy and ready to lead . . . then I will fight for you."

That seemed to be all Alexei needed. He returned to the darkness and Vira returned to her small paper squares with her bottle as though nothing had passed between them. But both Zash and I remained silent, soaking in the moment. No one could have missed the intensity of their exchange. They had understood each other in a way I'd never communicated with Alexei before. Even now, I wasn't sure what he had asked of her. Somehow she knew.

Vira's low singing filled the room. It went beyond my ears and into my very skin, soothing me. Swaying me. I relaxed. And the next thing I knew I'd folded in half and left the darkened little cottage in exchange for dreamless bliss.

⁓

I startled awake at the clatter of wood on wood. I'd dropped my soup bowl. The heaviness in my eyes and limbs told me I hadn't slept for long. But I'd slept enough for my ribs to scream in pain and demand I adjust my position.

Vira had finished her spell making. No more singing. Dim light came from the lowering of the sun. It had been longer than an hour. She and Zash spoke softly.

"You have chosen them, Zash. They are under your care now. You've made yourself their provider."

"But what of you?"

She snorted. "I will manage."

Zash shook his head. "How?"

"Don't press me, boy. I've been saving your soldier pay, not squandering it. It's enough to get me by. You have new duties now." She handed him one paper square. "Use this one on the girl. Her ribs are broken. This will set them, but they will still pain her for some time. These other three are for the tsarevich."

"I'll take them." I pushed myself up to a sitting position and held out my hand.

"I know my boy. I don't know you, even if you are the grand duchess." She passed the squares to Zash. "One will close up his wounds, but it must sit in the paper for an hour before it is mature enough. Neither spell will stop the internal bleeding. It was all I could do and I've already used an extra hour to write it. The other two spells are identical—they numb his pain. This should allow him to wake and to function enough to walk. Each lasts for twenty-four hours, but there is no healing power in them."

"Oh thank you. Thank you." I clasped my hands over my mouth. "Can we use one of those now?" Zash tucked the spells into his pocket.

"Don't you dare," Vira said. "I already used a spell to renew his blood loss. His body needs to soak that one up before you give him another." She pointed to the maturing spell in Zash's hand. "Use that in an hour. Don't wait any longer. I've bought the tsarevich time. It is *your* duty to ensure it isn't wasted." Her hand stroked Alexei's brow without her seeming to notice the movement.

"His head wound is bad." She returned the clay bottle and silver pin to the hole in the fireplace. "The blood inside is spreading and may take his life at any time." Her eyes lifted to mine. "You need a stronger spell master."

Alexei looked so fragile lying there, half his head swollen and purple. His breathing shallow. His knee hadn't even healed yet from his small fall upon our arrival at the Ipatiev House. How could the bleeding in his head wound abate enough for him to survive? There must be another answer. Another solution. "What if we took him to the White Army?"

"Girl, those soldiers would drop their weapons and surrender to the Bolsheviks the moment they saw the tsarevich in this condition. The fire in their bosoms is lit by the *idea* of what he is and could be. A feeble, dying boy does not align with that idea. You would crush the hope of the people if they saw him in this state."

Because my family had always hidden Alexei's condition from the people, the people created their own image of him—one he could never live up to, no matter the embers of passion in his heart.

"But we could disguise him. We could approach the army as simple peasants. They are in Ekaterinburg!"

"No, they're not, Nastya." Zash's statement was almost lost on me, he spoke it so quietly.

"What do you mean?"

"They were not close enough to rescue you. Yes, they are approaching Ekaterinburg, but Yurovsky used them as . . . as an excuse to plan his . . . execution."

I gripped the arm of my chair. "You're wrong. We were contacted by a White Army officer planning a rescue. A rescue that we *refused* because we didn't want it to result in the deaths of any of our Bolshevik friends."

He shook his head slowly. "That White Army officer is dead. Avdeev intercepted the first letter. Beloborodov demanded that he forge responses in the hopes of capturing you and your family in an escape attempt—to speed up the order for an execution."

Every word he spoke blotted out drop after drop of hope I'd been clinging to. All those letters we'd written and received, with the terrible escape plan . . . all those late nights weaving bedsheets together into a rope and hoping for rescue . . . had been a hoax?

"You knew about all this?" I breathed.

"I only learned of it these past few days."

"Now is not the time!" Vira shoved a pile of white and grey costumes, trimmed with fur, into my hands. "You need to change and be on your way."

I stared at the material, trying to recover from what Zash just told me.

"Stop gawking and put them on," Vira barked. "They are traditional reindeer-skin clothing."

That explained Vira's and Zash's coloring. They must have been from one of the seminomadic people groups of Siberia. What had brought Zash into the Bolshevik army? What brought them into a village at all?

"Will these not bring more attention?" I asked.

"You've been shut up in a prison. You don't know what will bring attention in this area or not. This will be far better than your ragged skirt."

Zash took the reindeer clothing from me and held out the coat. I allowed him to help me into it, mainly because my ribs ached too much to do it myself. The reindeer skin rested against my body like a blanket of comfort. It alone almost soothed some of my pain.

We were about to leave, for Vira's safety, but to where? "What can you tell me of . . . Dochkin?"

Vira rose from the floor, her knees creaking and popping like a fresh log in a fire. "What do you know?"

My hand was tempted to stray to the Matryoshka doll, but I kept it firmly at my side. "I know the Red Army never found Vasily Dochkin."

"Trust me, girl. If the Red Army couldn't find him with all their gadgets and commandants and persistence, you have no chance." She avoided my gaze.

"You might be surprised what I know," I responded. She busied herself brushing off her skirt and adjusting her head scarf. "But you are also not ignorant. You know something."

She looked up, no surprise or guilt on her face. "All spell masters know of his renown. I've heard it said the only way to find Dochkin is through his spells, of which he is *very* selective to bestow. That is all I know."

That lined up with what Yurovsky had said when he claimed the doll. It may be a wives' tale, but it was one worth pursuing. "Thank you for your help." I reached into my corset, slit through some threads with my thumbnail, and handed her a small pearl. "Is this sufficient payment?"

She pushed it back toward me. "Serving the tsarevich and grand duchess is sufficient enough for me."

"I would like to pay you. To thank you."

Vira handed Zash a bundle of items that had not been in the room prior to my falling asleep. "The thanks is accepted. You may pay me by leaving this house and not returning." She tossed me a flowered head scarf. "A pearl like that could get me shot. To a village woman it is as useless as it is lovely."

I'd never had to deal with money or payment, so I tucked the pearl back into its spot, my face warm. I hadn't meant to insult her. I tied the new scarf around my bald head. "Thank you again. Your kindness will never be forgotten."

"Babushka . . . will you be safe?"

Vira shook her head. "Likely not, but who is in these times?" She kissed Zash's forehead, then saw us to the door.

Before we exited, she turned to me. "You are right, Grand Duchess. Dochkin *could* save your brother. He is likely your only hope. But finding him will be like searching for a strawberry in a field of blood."

28

Vira sent a stretcher with us, on which we carried Alexei once we made it back into the forest. It was a long piece of cloth with two wooden poles sewn into each side. We balanced them on our shoulders, but I was significantly shorter than Zash, so poor Alexei slipped every time we jostled too much.

"We should head toward Revda," Zash said from ahead of me. Joy trotted around his ankles. "We could board a train there."

"We?"

"To get you away from Ekaterinburg."

I knew nothing about the surrounding villages. My life had been in western Russia. The Bolsheviks had kept any new information from us once we were exiled. "How far is that?"

"About a day's walk. Ten hours, perhaps." The wood pressed into my shoulders, already forming bruises. At this moment—after a night of bloodshed and walking and grieving and worrying for my brother—ten hours might as well have been ten years.

But what logic remained in my brain reminded me that it wasn't impossible. I could do it for Alexei. It would make Papa proud.

We walked for an hour. There were no stars by which to navigate due to the midnight sun, but Zash had a compass. Again, I was forced to follow. And to trust. I stared at the back of Zash's head and let the anger bubble. I recalled his face as he lifted his pistol. The sweat—the nerves—sliding down his brow. What had gone through his head when he shot me?

He stopped and lowered the stretcher. "It's time for Alexei's spell."

Every step had been agony to both my body and my mind. I understood the importance of waiting for Vira's spell to mature, but marching while aching and watching my brother bleed weighed me down far more than any stretcher could.

Zash pulled the spells from his pocket—each one labeled. Joy popped into my lap, curling up to rest the moment her paws were off the ground.

"Do you think Yurovsky has stopped to rest? Perhaps he is no longer hunting us?" The pattering of my heart told me otherwise. It told me not to stop. To run. *Run.* RUN.

"We can only hope." Zash's fingers shook and his eyes drooped as he peeled open a paper. "Once we use these, we should walk until the sun dips. Push ourselves as far as we can and then stop to sleep."

The word *sleep* struck my mind like a spell of its own. A golden reward I would do anything to win.

Zash handed me the spells for Alexei. I was too tired to pay mind to my bitterness toward him, but not too tired to feel gratitude for him handing over the spells. He knew what it meant to me to help my brother.

I sent the stitching spell onto Alexei's hip and hand wound. "*Stezhok.*" The spell glowed and then the skin over the wounds came together, meeting in the middle and bonding as though entwining miniature fingers. It left a messy scar in its wake, but was far more efficient than my sewing had been.

Alexei groaned and twisted. I took his hand. "It'll be okay. This will help you." For now. "I will save you." Maybe. "I love you." Always.

The next spell—the numbing one—was less visible but far more comforting. The moment I spoke it, Alexei's entire body relaxed and he breathed the most contented sigh I'd ever heard exit his lips. He looked, almost, to be merely resting. Oftentimes quality rest was a body's best healer.

"Let's go." I reached down to lift the stretcher. I wanted to get to the end of our day so Alexei and I could sleep. My own body craved the same sigh Alexei just gave.

"There's a spell for you, Nastya." Zash held out another square. "We need to do that one first. Babushka said you were injured?"

I took it and turned my back. "Thank you. I'll do it." As if he didn't *know* I was injured. *He* sent a bullet into my torso. I checked over my shoulder to ensure his back was turned before untucking my shirt and releasing my corset enough to reveal my skin. Each movement stiff. Each breath more painful than the last.

A blossom of purple spread across my ribs, with a dark spot in the center like something I might see in the night sky when watching for the aurora borealis with Papa. Only now it was on my skin. And Papa would not wish to see it.

I let the spell slither onto my finger and then pressed it to my ribs with a wince. I whispered its name and it sank into my skin. The bruise did not change, but something shifted inside my body with a dull *pop*. I cried out and steadied myself on a tree.

"Nastya, are you—?"

"Stay away!" I flung my free hand toward Zash, palm out. The pain had lessened but not completely abated. I straightened, returned my corset to its place, and tucked my shirt back in. "I'm ready to go."

He nodded and allowed me to lift my side of Alexei's stretcher before he lifted his own. We placed Joy on the stretcher with Alexei, then heaved it onto our shoulders and continued into the forest.

Darkness took years to arrive. By the time it did, I was walking with my eyes closed. Tripping and catching myself, sweating beneath the reindeer clothing. Finally we stopped and I didn't care how near or far Yurovsky was. I lowered Alexei to the ground and curled up beside him.

The air was chilled, already preparing for the upcoming August frosts. I'd take that over the mosquitoes. Soggy ground gave way beneath our movements. Zash rolled out the two soldier bedrolls he'd been carrying. He moved Alexei to one. "Take the other. You will sleep better without the wetness of the ground."

I didn't want his kindness. I didn't want his sacrifice. And a dark part of me thought that, yes, of course I should have the last bedroll and Zash should sleep on the damp marshy ground. But the human part of me—the part that loved Papa and now heard his voice in my heart—asked, "What of you?"

"The cloth of the stretcher is sufficient. I will keep watch for a time."

Keep watch. How could he possibly imagine keeping his eyes open? Even Joy had already snuggled beside Alexei and drifted off. "We are the safest we'll ever be. Sleep now. Tomorrow and every night after is when we will need to be on alert the most."

He didn't argue. As one, we all accepted the embrace of darkness and weariness. A sleep that comforted and revived the saint, the sinner, and every being in between. A night that would finally separate us from the longest and blackest day of our lives.

29

I woke coughing on the thick, wet fog rising from the forest ground and then grinding my teeth from the pain it caused to my ribs. The sun was up and warming the day. Joy licked my face. I petted her head and sat up. That was when the wave of reality struck me in the throat as I recalled the previous day's events.

Papa.

Mamma.

Olga.

Tatiana.

Maria.

Their names flowed in my chanting blood. Boiling. Bubbling until they sent me scrambling away from our little camp and heaving yesterday's borscht into the bushes.

Romanov. Romanov. Romanov.

My blood was lonely. I couldn't do this without them. Without my family. All the hope we had clung to had been held as a family. Every dream, dreamed as a family. We planned to live together or die together.

But I was left behind.

The tears came swift and hot. I dug my fingernails into the ground and wept. Wept for the life ripped from me. "The bond . . . of our hearts . . ." I gasped.

Maria wasn't here to finish it for me. I pictured her voice. Her face. Her smile. ". . . *spans miles, memory, and time.*"

But what about death? Did it span death?

I stayed in that spot. Weeping the names of my family. Weeping for my loss. Weeping for my helplessness and confusion. Until, finally, I managed to shove the sorrow away. Not forever, but for today.

I'd spent so long waking to joyless days that it was easier to move forward than to look back.

Back at our spot in the woods, both Alexei and Zash still slept. Joy whimpered and licked my hand, as though she knew where I'd gone.

I allowed tiny thoughts to trickle back in. Alexei's wounds. Vira the grandmother. The Matryoshka doll. Dochkin. I pulled the doll from my corset and stared at it. No new seam. The gold and red swirls gleamed against the black body. Such elegant mockery. It was as solid as the previous layer before it had been used prior to my using it to escape our execution.

I gripped it tight. "I need you," I hissed to the doll, thinking of Dochkin. "I need this spell to heal Alexei. To reverse time and bring my family back. I need to find him." I twisted the doll. When in the Ipatiev House, I had thought the seam appeared because of our need. That's what Papa hinted at. I'd used it and it saved Alexei and me. But now Alexei was dying and I needed it more than ever. Why wouldn't it open?

"Would you like me to try?" Zash asked softly, pushing himself into a sitting position from his place on the stretcher. "I could—"

"No," I snapped. "It was entrusted to me."

"Perhaps a different person has to alternate spells."

"Then I'll wait for Alexei to wake." I tucked the doll back into my corset. Alexei hadn't moaned or expressed pain since Vira's spells. But my eyes strayed to the purple bruise on his head. Was I at risk of letting my anger at Zash hinder getting help for Alexei?

I tossed Zash the doll. "Fine. Go ahead and try. We need all the help we can get."

He examined the doll just as I did. I turned back to Alexei and covered him with my reindeer overcoat to make sure he was warm enough. Hunger and injuries were likely taking a toll on his body temperature.

"Oh, here's the seam." Zash held the doll close to his face and slid his thumbnail along a tiny line around the center.

No! That definitely had not been there when I tried. He gripped the top and bottom in his fists. I reached for it. "Wait. Let me—"

The doll popped open, and before either of us could react, a shimmering rainbow light sped from the inside of the doll and disappeared into the trees like a startled pixie.

"The spell!" I squeaked, scrambling to my feet. "You let it escape!" Joy ran after it, yapping as though it were a squirrel. I stumbled a few feet, but the streak of light was long gone. Joy disappeared into the underbrush, but soon her barks communicated that she'd lost it, too. "Wasted!" I threw up my hands. "Did you even see what the word was?"

I spun to face Zash, but he stared at his compass. "The spell went west. Exactly west. Like a shot arrow."

My mouth formed a silent O. "It's leading us to Dochkin." *That* was the spell. That's what I'd asked for when I tried to open it this morning—for help finding Dochkin. It wasn't wasted. It was directing us. Finally, we had a destination. Or, at least, a direction.

"Nastya? Nastya!" Alexei woke in a panic, shoving the reindeer coat off of him.

I knelt at his side. "I'm right here." I recalled how I felt upon waking this morning—not ready to remember. Not ready to grieve. "How are you feeling?"

His gaze locked onto mine and he held it, as though it was the only offer of safety. "I feel . . . strange. I know that I'm hurt, but I don't feel much of it." He lifted his shot hand and examined the now-closed wound. "Are we ghosts again?"

I took his hand. "No. We visited Zash's babushka—a village spell master—and she managed to gift us some spells to help us."

"How long do I have?"

"If we use the final numbing spell tonight, you have until tomorrow evening. About thirty hours." That didn't sound like much. I prayed that Dochkin wasn't *too* far west. We were on the edge of Siberia. Cities like Moscow and St. Petersburg were days away. "How's your head?"

"It doesn't hurt right now, but I feel . . . sluggish. I can't seem to focus my vision." He lifted his head. "I'm likely dying. Will you be alright with that, Nastya?"

I jerked back. "Nyet! No, I will not!" He asked me so calmly that it stirred my anger. "You are all I have left, Alexei!"

"Well, what are our options?"

Once I caught my breath again, I filled him in on our recent discoveries. How Yurovsky could track spells with his watch, how Dochkin was the only one who could help with Alexei's injuries, how the Matryoshka doll sent a spell that pointed the direction we needed to travel.

"We should go." Alexei hauled himself to his feet, using the trunk of a tree for leverage. "It is lucky Dochkin lives in the west, since the train can take us that same direction."

"Are you certain you can walk?"

"For now." I admired his push to be strong, his will to be a soldier and leader. But also his willingness to admit when he needed us. He knew stubbornness only hindered. "Besides, the stretcher is soggy."

There was, indeed, an imprint from where Zash's body had pressed the material into the wet ground.

Joy returned to our spot, saw Alexei up and moving, and ran circles around his feet. "Joy!" Alexei scooped her into his arms. "Joy, you crazy pup! You're alive!" For the first time Alexei showed a crack in his armor to stay strong.

"Zash found her." I didn't want to give him credit. I didn't want to stir any gratefulness in Alexei's heart toward my executioner, but Zash was helping us. He seemed as though he cared about our survival and I didn't understand it. I wasn't ready to understand it, because to accept it meant to move past what he did. I could picture Papa telling me to care for the soldiers.

But he didn't care for me!

Joy's barks echoed through the forest and I couldn't stop the heightened alertness that tingled my ears. If Yurovsky was anywhere close, he'd hear us.

"Tishe. Let's go." I took the bedrolls and carried them over my shoulder. After a bit of protest, Zash gave me a pack of goods and he took the stretcher since it was too awkward for me to carry.

Off we went. West toward Revda.

This time as we walked, there was less panic. Less pain. Less distraction from our predicament. Zash led the way with his compass, keeping us due west, though picking the paths of least resistance, like game trails. Alexei trudged behind with Joy. His walking seemed awkward and tentative. It kept our going slow, but it left us with more energy since we weren't carrying him. We picked some bilberries as we walked, the dark, sweet fruit reminding me painfully of other days.

I let the silence continue for a while, though Alexei tossed a stick for Joy to fetch every few steps. Eventually, the silence grew heavier than the packs and even the stretcher. I never used to back down from a challenge. So I willed myself to quicken my pace until I was level with Zash. He raised his eyebrows as though surprised I'd come this near him. He wouldn't be happy to discover why.

I chewed on my lip for a moment. It pained me to speak with him and show . . . vulnerability. "Why?" I cleared my throat and tried again for a stronger voice. "Why did you shoot us, Zash?"

He stumbled on a fallen stick and it cracked in half with a snap. "I . . . shot only the one bullet—the one you saw."

"The one at me." Did he think that excused him?

"Da."

"Did you know my camisole held jewels in it? Did you know the bullet would ricochet?" A small part of me clung to this hope that might redeem him.

He shook his head. "Nyet. I did not know."

So he'd intended to kill me. I almost lost hold of my voice completely. "You know, shooting one bullet instead of ten doesn't make you any less guilty of what you've done."

"I know what I've done, Nastya." He choked on an inhale. "And I don't know what to tell you. I don't think . . . I don't think you'll understand."

"I want to understand!" As if there was any reason he could give that would make his choice acceptable.

"You're . . . you're not in a place to hear it yet."

"You don't know me!" I practically screamed. "You don't know where I am or what I'm feeling."

He dragged a hand down his face. "*I'm* not in a place where I can talk about it yet."

As if it were hard for him. As if *he* hurt. I wanted to scoff at his hurt—to dismiss it as inconsequential. But I couldn't. Everyone's heart had its own aches—and that was not something I could scoff at.

"Very well. But please . . . please explain soon." I wanted my ache to disappear. I highly doubted Zash's words could do that. But Dochkin could. With a reversing spell that would undo the execution, he could heal my ache. He could even fix Zash.

Dochkin could return us to that night. I could catch Zash before he tied himself to Yurovsky and tell him what was about to happen. And then I could kill Yurovsky.

We could all heal once we found Dochkin.

"I'm sorry I can't tell you yet, Nastya. Truly. I can barely even ask your forgiveness."

"Which I cannot give," I said in a low voice. "You know that, don't you?" Forgiveness. What did that even mean in a time like this? Papa always told us to forgive our captors. To show them love. Would he apply that to Zash? To Yurovsky? I could forgive the soldiers for doing their duty and guarding us. I could forgive them for not knowing us and for being deceived by propaganda.

But Zash knew us. Zash knew *me*. He'd given the impression he . . . possibly loved me.

"I can't expect you to forgive me, but I can still ask. Perhaps your heart will change."

"This has nothing to do with my heart. This is about your actions." Some things were not forgivable. At least not by me. He could plead with Iisus as much as he desired. But I was human. And my heart was broken. All my forgiveness had leaked away.

"Is there nothing I can do?" he whispered.

I lifted my chin. "You can save Alexei's life. And then disappear from mine."

He nodded and we continued in silence. Resigned. His humility ate at me—causing an odd mixture of regret and disgust. He had no right to be humble. He had no right to ask for forgiveness. He *owed* the help he was giving. It was not charity. It was not kindness.

It was penance.

So then why did I feel as though I not only had caused him more sorrow and myself more sorrow . . . but also had grieved Papa's heart?

Papa's dead, my bitterness reminded me. *He can't grieve or rejoice any longer.*

30

"Yurovsky will be watching the train stations." Alexei sank onto a log as Zash pulled a loaf of bread from one of the packs—the last loaf brought to the Ipatiev House by the sisters. I recalled the rescue notes between us and the White Army officer. The forged letters that Zash claimed had been penned by Bolsheviks.

Zash broke the loaf into thirds and handed out the pieces. I was pleased to see he gave the greatest third to Alexei. "He's too busy hunting us."

The bruise on Alexei's head had spread and the swelling seemed to have grown. We needed to get to Dochkin as soon as possible.

"If not him, there will at least be guards," Alexei said.

I tore off a corner of the bread. Dry and dissatisfying . . . like my bitterness. "Could we go in disguise?" Revda was only a few hours away. My feet ached and my knees trembled at the idea of walking again. I'd not had enough sustenance to withstand this type of physical exertion.

Zash scooped the soft middle from his piece of bread. "Alexei's right. If they are watching for us, they will find us."

I waited for one of them to offer an alternative. A better idea. It didn't come. "We can't *walk* to Dochkin. We have no way of knowing how far west he lives." Not for the first time, I silently sent up a thank-you that Zash had had the sense to pull out his compass when the spell disappeared.

"Disguises won't work, but I agree that we still need to take the train." Alexei nibbled at his loaf. "But speaking of disguise . . . what is Nastya wearing?"

I straightened my reindeer clothing, imagining how much softer it would be without my bejeweled corset underneath. "It's from Vira."

"It's from our tribe," Zash said.

"Your tribe?" Alexei snapped his fingers. "That explains your good looks. Siberian."

"You're one of very few who would think so positively of the Siberian coloring." Zash finished his bread and picked the crumbs off his lap.

"So . . . your family was nomadic?" Alexei asked. I forgot he hadn't been awake when Vira and Zash gave me the clothing.

"Seminomadic. I was, too, until the revolution. Vira did spell mastery for the tribe and I worked with the other men, breeding reindeer, trading pelts for spell ink and other needs. Working with my hands . . ." He glanced at his palms as if their lines now held shame. "But when spell mastery was made illegal and spell masters were being hunted, I joined the ranks."

"Why would you—?" Alexei let out a hiss of pain and bent over his bread. I gripped my log to keep myself from rushing to his side. Years of hearing his groans and agony had taught me that I could not help take it away. But I could help him keep his honor. Alexei hated coddling, so I remained in my seat.

"What hurts?" I asked.

"My head," he croaked. "The throbs grow sharper. And each time, I can't . . . can't seem to think."

I took in the sun's location in the sky. It had been almost eighteen hours since we'd left Vira's house. "The numbing spell is likely wearing off—"

"I know!" he snapped. "You think I can't feel it?"

I recoiled. Alexei never snapped—at least not at me.

"*Prosti.* Forgive me." He lifted his head and tenderly tapped his head wound with the tips of his fingers. "I'm irritable."

"Of course." I moved to him this time. "We do not have long. Can you manage another hour or two without the spell?"

He nodded, but it seemed sluggish.

"Perhaps you should ride in the stretcher. It's dry now." Zash looked helpless across from us, watching our pain.

"No, I like watching you carry it." Alexei smirked, feeding Joy a piece of bread.

Zash rolled his eyes. "But of course, Your Imperial Highness." He gathered our belongings and pointed forward. "Onward to Revda!" He led us at a march—a pretty good one, too.

"Back straight, soldier!" Alexei marched after him. "Joy! Nastya! Get in line!" Joy circled their ankles, her tongue hanging out as she panted in delight.

I couldn't stop the grin as I took up the rear. Alexei was so much like Papa—only with more humor. In a situation such as this, I didn't know how he managed it.

We walked and I ached. My stomach still felt empty, but at least the horizon held the hope of a train ride—movement and forward motion with promised rest.

Our silly march lost its posture pretty quickly, weighed down by packs and pain. Alexei slowed, so I slowed, so Zash slowed. Zash stayed at the front—the trailblazer. Joy trotted by his heels now and Alexei and I walked side by side.

"You're having a hard time with Zash, aren't you?" Alexei asked. The slap and sway of undergrowth muffled most of our conversation.

I shoved a little branch out of our way. "How can you be so amiable with him? He was part of the firing squad."

"I suppose I've seen a lot more soldiers than you. I understand that they are often ordered to do things they don't want to do."

"But kill us? Kill *me*?"

He took his time stepping over a log, ensuring good placement for his feet before committing. A single fall could send him back onto that stretcher—or even dead before we reached Dochkin. "I don't think he wanted to do it, Nastya."

"So why did he? I thought he loved us!" We'd shared something precious.

"I think he still does. He's broken, too. I can see it as clearly as I see yours and feel mine. The Bolsheviks killed his best friend, whom he then had to bury. And then they asked him to murder people he had grown to care about. It broke him so much that he's no longer with the Bolsheviks. He's left his post—abandoned Yurovsky. Do you know what that could cost him?"

I shook my head. "I hadn't really thought of it that way."

"It could cost him his family. His livelihood. If caught, his life. That should say plenty about how much he regrets taking part in the slaughter."

Alexei's perspective didn't ease my hurt. Of course I didn't want Zash's family—Vira—to suffer. And I didn't want him dead. I didn't know what I wanted. I wanted all of this undone. That was the only thing that could fix me.

"We need him," Alexei said.

"I know," my lips said.

I know, my head said.

I want him, my heart said. I wanted him back—the way things were before Ivan died and Yurovsky took over.

As we walked I couldn't help but glance over my shoulder now and again. A presence whispered up and down my spine, threatening failure. Clawing at us. Yurovsky was not far off. I could feel him catching up.

The train whistle met our ears before the station. Zash had led us around the town, keeping to the forest, until we stood opposite the train station. It was situated at the edge of Revda with the tracks between it and the forest, where we currently hid.

Two Bolshevik soldiers sat on a bench near the platform, sharing a smoke and scanning the passersby every few minutes.

"You and Alexei will not be able to board from the platform. It seems Yurovsky has sent a telegram to every train station." Zash pressed against a tree trunk, several trees deep from the tracks, with enough view. "You must travel up the tracks and board once it's moving."

Alexei seemed to barely be listening. He crouched on the ground, curled in on himself, wheezing through the discomfort. It had been only an hour, but the swelling in his head seemed to have spread even farther, bulging over his temple and forehead.

"What of his numbing spell?" I asked. "I can't lift him onto the train. He needs to be able to do it on his own."

"Use it when the train whistles for the first time. That will give it enough time to take effect. Once I purchase tickets, I will come find you and we'll board together."

My heart pounded with the familiar thrill of danger and mischief, but it sent a rain of nausea into my stomach—the same feeling that came when I examined a plan filled with flaws. Nastya the shvibzik never enacted plans that could fail. She thought through every angle and abandoned them if needed. That always kept the mischief successful and of the best quality.

But with the train, we had no other plan. We had no way to avoid the Bolsheviks or board the train without arousing suspicion. We needed to get on it while it was moving because if one whisper of our presence made its way to the conductor, he would stop the locomotive. We would be caught.

And killed.

Zash's plan was all we had, and I didn't like it one bit.

He and I hoisted Alexei up on the stretcher and headed through the forest up the tracks. As we walked the steam engine pulled into the Revda platform and stopped with a deafening hiss. We walked until we were several train lengths up the tracks.

"You will have to run to board," Zash said. "We will load Alexei and Joy first and then I will help you, Nastya."

I nodded, swallowing hard, as we eased Alexei to the ground. Then Zash walked away from us. Back toward the platform to risk his neck. I couldn't find my bitterness in this moment, not when I thought of all he'd been doing for us and the things Alexei said.

Instead of seeing the mental picture of Zash pulling the trigger on me, now I saw a flash of him holding Ivan's dead body and weeping. He wanted to save us as badly as we wanted to be saved.

Perhaps I'd been clinging to my bitterness because it felt like a betrayal to my family to forgive Zash. To thank him. To enjoy his company. I wasn't ready to let go yet, but something inside me was softening. Was growing thankful that he had these ideas to go buy us tickets and risk being recognized.

I remembered him on his knees, the pistol under his chin. He really must have changed. Because to help Alexei and me was to turn against his duties as a soldier. To turn against his very country—at least in the eyes of the Bolsheviks.

Time passed slowly. I stared along the tree line long after Zash had disappeared beyond a curve of the tracks. I couldn't see the train. I couldn't see the platform. I felt blind and foolish and endangered.

"Nastya . . ." Alexei's soft plea startled me. Joy rushed to his side and licked his face.

"What do you need?"

"The spell." His whisper barely rose above the soft breath of wind. "Please."

I peered back down the tracks. "Soon, Alexei. Any moment." I pulled the spell from Zash's pack. He said to use it when the train released its first whistle. But Alexei didn't ask for relief unless he truly needed it.

I picked at the folded piece of paper that held the numbing spell. Alexei would need to be able to help us load him into the train. The spell needed time to assuage the pain. And the last time I had waited to use a spell—per the request of Papa—my family had been shot.

So I unpeeled the piece of paper, slipped the spell from the parchment with my finger, and pressed it to Alexei's skin. The effects were immediate, just like last time. A balm to my heart as his tense form relaxed.

No sooner had he pushed himself upright than the train

whistle blew. I shot to my feet. Did that mean it would be leaving? Where was Zash? I peered down the way, but no steam rose over the trees. Soon, though, it would.

We needed to be ready to board that train with or without Zash. If he had been caught . . . My throat closed. We couldn't leave without him. I couldn't abandon him to be murdered by an angry Bolshevik. That realization frightened me.

"Where's Zash?" Alexei asked through deep breaths.

"He'll be here soon." I bounced on my toes and kept to the tree line, sticking my head out as far as I dared. It didn't provide me with much more view.

The train whistle blew again, and this time an explosion of steam burst into the sky.

"Where is he?" Alexei pushed himself to his feet, testing his movements. "You can't lift me into the train on your own."

"I will have to."

"We don't even have to board. We'll wait for the next one."

"Yurovsky could be close behind us. We *have* to take this chance." But what if Zash didn't make it? Was Alexei's safety worth sacrificing for the sake of Zash's? What was my duty here?

Then I knew.

It was Alexei. It would always be Alexei. "Come. Let's get ready."

I grabbed what packs I could—the ones with the food and a bedroll. I left the stretcher. It would be useless without Zash to help me carry it. Still, I prayed he would appear. I wasn't ready to face survival alone. And we needed those train tickets.

The chug of the locomotive started slow. Distant. Then it grew closer.

We stepped up to the edge of the trees, ready to run. Alexei held Joy tight in his arms. The very moment the train engine crawled into view around the distant curve, Zash burst through the underbrush.

"*Spasibo*, Iisus!" I gasped. "Where have you *been*?"

He barely paused but snatched up the remaining belongings. "They were selling no tickets," he panted. "We will have to board anyway and bribe the conductor."

The train came closer. Louder. Drowning out sound and thought until Zash's voice cut the air. "Nastya."

I turned to him. He already had Alexei in his arms, but his face was pale. "Yurovsky's here."

The train crawled past us and Zash began to run. I stood stunned for a long moment, car after car passing me. Then panic sent me running after him.

Yurovsky. Here. He knew we were here. What good was boarding the train now? He'd only come after it and stop it! He'd send Bolsheviks after us. He'd telegram the next station. There was nothing we could do.

The locomotive picked up speed and Zash ran parallel to a hitch between train cars with a small landing. Alexei reached for the support pole with his free hand and Zash tossed him onto the landing, stumbling moments after. I ran faster than the train, catching up to them, but my energy wouldn't last long.

I pulled a pack off my shoulder as I reached the hitch and tossed it to Alexei. Joy pressed against the train car, trying to keep her feet.

"Get on!" Zash shouted from behind me.

I reached for the bar, but my skirt tangled around my knees. I hoisted it up and tried again. My fingers wrapped around the warm metal. Alexei reached for me from his spot by the closed door—a gesture of help with no promise of success. He was too weak.

My other hand managed to find a hold, then hands lifted me from behind—just the momentum I needed to land awkwardly on the bumpy hitch between the two cars. I gained my balance and spun to grab the stretcher from Zash. His arms and legs pumped and his chest heaved. Even so, the train started inching beyond him.

"Climb on!" I cried.

He reached for the bar but couldn't seem to keep up. I looped my left arm through it and then reached for him with my right, stretched until my ribs screamed. He grabbed my forearm and I pulled. My shoulder strained and threatened to pop from its socket. Zash put on a burst of speed.

A gunshot split the air, mixing with the whistle of the train.

Zash dropped like a stone.

His body tumbled away from the train. Beyond him rode two Bolsheviks on horseback, and four soldiers ran on foot. The rider with the smoking pistol was Yurovsky.

31

I didn't scream. I didn't panic. Instead, my mind entered that cool calm that came when everything went wrong. A sharp, almost painful clarity.

Yurovsky shouted something to his Bolshevik companion and pointed up to the train. The soldier took off, toward us. Even from this distance I could tell his eyes were focused ahead—toward the engine. He was going to stop the train.

I yanked the rolled-up stretcher from its place lodged against the door, gripping the long wooden poles with my shaking hands. I leaned back so the rider wouldn't see me, straining my ears for his hoofbeats over the chugging of the train.

Just as he came into view, I swung the stretcher poles in an arc. They collided with his chin with a loud *crack*, jarring my entire body. I almost dropped the stretcher as the soldier went tumbling off his horse. A thunk of metal told me he'd had an unfortunate collision with the spinning train gears. I didn't have time to feel sick to my stomach.

I shoved the stretcher into Alexei's hands. "Stay here!" Then

I leaped like a wild woman from the train to the horse. I landed on my stomach over her saddle and almost vomited from the pain it sent to my ribs. *Sorry, Vira.* The horse still galloped, but not as ferociously as when she'd been pushed by the soldier's relentless heels.

I straddled the saddle and turned her around. Yurovsky and Zash were still in view. Things had happened that fast. The saddle held a pistol in a holster near my knee.

I urged the horse back into her frantic gallop, back toward Yurovsky, averting my eyes from the bloodied form of her previous rider. Then I rode. I rode faster than I'd ever ridden—galloping like the cowmen shown in the Western moving pictures that used to come in from America.

Wind yanked Vira's scarf from my head.

Yurovsky sat mounted beside Zash's body. Zash pushed himself weakly to his hands and knees in the gravel beside the tracks, surrounded by Bolsheviks. Yurovsky leaned down and grabbed Zash by the hair. His gaze lifted at my advance. I didn't slow. Instead, I pulled out the saddle pistol and leveled it on the forearm of my hand holding the reins. Yurovsky's eyes widened.

Let him see how it felt to have the barrel facing his direction. Let his heart thunk with a defeated realization that a bullet was coming for him.

I aimed poorly but still pulled the trigger. The Bolsheviks surrounding Zash scattered. My bullet hit Yurovsky's horse. Poor beast. It reared. Yurovsky tried to hang on, but the horse was dead before its hooves returned to the earth.

It collapsed backward, pinning Yurovsky beneath its mass.

Zash stumbled to his feet, a patch of blood marking the gravel beneath him. I yanked my horse around him, sending pebbles skittering into the faces of the enemy. I held out my hand. Zash took it and nearly wrenched me off the horse's back with his effort to mount behind me.

Once situated, I steered the horse into the woods so Yurovsky and his soldiers couldn't shoot us. We dodged trees and headed after the train, branches whipping my face and thunder in my ears. Finally out of range, we returned to the open and entered a full gallop. We reached the back of the train, passed it, and found the gap between the two cars where Alexei stood, lodged against the exterior with the stretcher poles, holding Zash's pistol in his hand, ready to fight like a soldier.

But no one was coming after us. No one *could* come after us. Not with Yurovsky's horse now dead and me riding the other one.

Zash hauled himself from horse to train hitch and held his hand out for me. I shook my head. "I'll ride her a bit longer!" I hollered. "We can't have her returning to Yurovsky." I reached into my corset and pulled out the pearl Vira had refused to accept. "Bribe the conductor with this." I also held out a diamond. "And tell him he can have the diamond if he blows through the next station."

Zash grinned. "Let no one ever call you tame!" He managed to take the treasures from me. Blood gurgled from a hole in his upper left arm, but besides that he seemed uninjured. He and Alexei opened the door and entered the train.

And I rode. Wild. Free. Untamed.

32

The horse tired quickly. Only another few minutes of riding alongside the train and foam formed at the edge of her saddle and bit. She wouldn't keep the train's pace for much longer. But if I dismounted, would she return to Yurovsky?

The ground sloped away and I veered farther from the tracks to keep a clear riding path. The forest line grew tight ahead and I risked losing the train if I remained astride the horse. The slope ended so I reined her near the train again. With one hand I unbuckled her bridle. Next I pulled at the saddle's cinch. I undid what I could without completely unseating myself.

I steered her to the train and reached for the rail. It was farther than I thought. It'd be nice to have Zash's help.

No. I could do this on my own. *"Let no one call you tame."*

I released the reins and committed to the transfer, gripping the rail with both hands. The horse veered away from the locomotive and I pushed off her flanks with my feet to send me fully onto the center hitch between cars. Success. The horse immediately abandoned the gallop, drifted into the trees, and started nibbling grass.

The bit slipped out of her mouth and she shook herself free of the bridle before a curve in the tracks took her from my view.

I gave a little wave before I turned to the door. Neither Zash nor Alexei had come out to check on me, which struck me as odd. I hauled my weight against the door lever until my ribs reminded me that I'd just slammed them against a saddle horn. With a hissing inhale I tried the door again and the lever slid down. When I opened the door, I understood why Zash had not come back outside.

He sat at gunpoint, cornered by three workmen. Alexei formed a rigid shield between them.

My entrance drew everyone's attention. This boxcar had no seats—only crates of goods and some scattered luggage. One of the armed men lifted his gun and pointed it at me. I wasn't in the mood to be intimidated—not after escaping Yurovsky. So I raised an eyebrow. "*Zdravstvutye*, gentlemen."

"Not another word," said the man who aimed at me. It could have been the shudder of the train, but did I detect a tremble? "Who are you and who are these men?"

I knew I looked a wreck—thin and ragged from traveling and meager rations. My shaved head didn't buy me any favors. I shoved the rib pain out of my mind and produced an impish smile. "Which would you prefer: that I don't speak another word or that I answer your inquiries?"

He gaped at the others. One man gave a *"Go ahead"* type of nod. So he turned back to me, though his gun arm had drooped a bit. "Answer."

During his moment of indecision, I took in the situation and urged my brain to stay sharp. These men wore regular clothing and seemed nervous, which implied they weren't Bolsheviks. Their guns aimed mostly at Zash, who *was* dressed as a Bolshevik, and no one aimed directly at Alexei, who still wore part of his tsarevich uniform. These men weren't enemies. They were frightened that *we* were.

And the best rule of thumb was to tell the truth unless you absolutely had to lie. Truth was easier to keep track of, and no matter how good one was at lying, it could often be detected.

"I am Grand Duchess Anastasia Nikolaevna Romanova. This"— I gestured to Alexei—"is my brother, Tsarevich Alexei Nikolaevich Romanov. We have been imprisoned at the Ipatiev House in Ekaterinburg by the Red Army. Two days ago Commandant Yakov Yurovsky of the Red Army slaughtered"—I forced past the sudden quiver in my voice—"our family without trial. We are the only survivors."

My response earned the reaction I had intended. Slack jaws. Wide eyes. Sinking pistols. "And what about him?" One of the other men jutted his barrel toward Zash.

Zash's head hung low. I took a breath. "He was a guard at the Ipatiev House who helped us escape and is continuing to aid us."

Zash looked up, hope in his eyes. Relief in his posture.

"He's dressed like a Bolshevik," one of the men said.

"And for that, I'm glad, because he is far less conspicuous in public than we are." I folded my arms. "Do you have any other questions, or may I bandage his arm now?"

The men lowered their guns and backed away enough for me to approach Zash. He'd been disarmed but not mistreated. Yurovsky's bullet had grazed his arm and torn through his shirt, so I ripped the rest of the sleeve off and used it as a bandage. I tried not to tense knowing the three men stood behind me. But so did Alexei, and he'd keep us safe.

"You were telling the truth," one man said to Alexei.

Alexei lifted his chin. "I do not lie to my people." Such a bold statement coming from the mouth of a thirteen-year-old boy was enough to defuse the tension. The men seated themselves on crates. Only once they sat did Alexei sit himself. I was glad we'd given him the numbing spell, otherwise no one would likely listen to him.

"So who are you? Part of the White Army, I presume?" Alexei sat upright but not stiff. Like a soldier. Like a leader.

The two quieter men deferred to the first man who had pointed his gun at me. He seemed to be their spokesman, but I wasn't sure about leader. "I am Kostya. Yes, we are with the White Army."

I tied off the bandage on Zash's arm. "Thank you," he said softly. I nodded and smoothed out a wrinkle. Then I sat on the floor next to him.

Alexei questioned the men. He had a way with words and a way of making them feel comfortable sharing. I'd never seen this side of him. From all the times he joined Papa with the soldiers, I had pictured him sitting and watching. But not actually *being* a soldier. Not actually leading. I never thought he'd get the opportunity. Yet here it was. He guided these men and their conversation as though he were already their tsar.

"We have been hiding in this boxcar for days," Kostya said. "Trying to get to Perm. The Red Army is hunting spell masters and killing most of them. Our mission is to find them. To convince them to join us."

"You place a lot of stock in a handful of people," Alexei said. "What if they don't join you? What is the White Army's plan? Who is your officer?"

Kostya shrugged. "We don't really have an officer."

"You must," I broke in. "You come from Ekaterinburg, do you not?" Kostya nodded. "So then who was your officer? He sent a plan of rescue to us. It was intercepted by the Bolsheviks, but this officer was in communication with the convent sisters."

Kostya glanced from Alexei to me and back again. "If the Bolsheviks intercepted his letter, they likely killed him. We did not spend enough time in Ekaterinburg to know this officer."

"So . . . where is the White Army?"

"A division of us was sent to Ekaterinburg. We feigned an assault to disperse the Red Army, but then we split to search for spell masters."

So they were never here to rescue us.

"The bulk of the White Army is in the west," Kostya said. "But there is no one man in charge of the Whites." He gestured to his friends. "We have come to find the remaining spell masters and encourage them to fight with us—against the Bolsheviks."

Zash squirmed under the gaze the other two men gave him.

"We are going west, too," Alexei shared. "To find Vasily Dochkin, Russia's most skilled spell master."

Kostya laughed in disbelief. "How can you find such a man? He is as untouchable as royalty."

Alexei pushed himself to his feet and rested a hand on Kostya's shoulder. "I am royalty, yet you are touching me."

Kostya clamped his mouth shut and a sense of awe permeated his features.

"I am the tsarevich. I have a way to find Dochkin, and when I do, I will bring either him or his power back to the White Army and join the fight."

"As our leader?" one man scoffed.

"As our tsar?" the third man asked with hope in his gaze.

"As your fellow soldier," Alexei replied. "The throne has been abdicated. I will fight beside those who wish to restore traditional Russia—who wish to oppose the actions of Lenin and the Red Army. The people will decide upon their monarch."

Steel hung in his gaze and admiration in the gazes of the three Whites. I swelled with pride for my little Alexei, but a shadow of concern blossomed in the back of my mind. What would happen when his numbing spell wore off? We needed to get him to Dochkin, and we couldn't let these men know why.

"What will we do at the next station?" I asked. It was clear Kostya and his men hadn't allowed Zash or Alexei to bribe the conductor—or even get to him. "Yurovsky could be waiting for us there. It puts all of us in danger."

Zash grew rigid. "We can't let this train stop. If Yurovsky found a horse or an automobile, he will be at the station. Even if he's not there, he will have sent a telegram. There would be no escaping him this time, Nastya."

I nodded. And though my brain spun for solutions, I did not speak them. I waited for Alexei. His mind spun as fast as mine—despite his head wound that turned his thoughts sluggish. He needed every opportunity to lead while he was still conscious enough to do so.

The three Whites awaited Alexei's response. Zash opened his mouth, then caught my eye and closed it again.

"We must deal with the conductor directly," Alexei finally said.

Kostya snapped his fingers. "We have four pistols—that's plenty to threaten him and the other workers in the engine."

"First, we will *ask* him." Alexei folded his arms. "If that doesn't work, we will offer him compensation. Nastya?"

"Of course." I discreetly withdrew a necklace of pearls and

handed them to him. Zash also passed over the two pieces I'd given him.

"If he will not be swayed even then, we will resort to force and threats. But we will not kill the man unless in self-defense. He is a citizen of Russia."

"What of the other passengers?" Zash asked. "They will notice if we blow through a station—especially if some of them wish to disembark."

Alexei didn't hesitate. "I'm glad you asked, Zash."

~

"Everyone disembark!" Zash's shout blasted through the closed doors of the stopped train. Alexei and two Whites had caused the conductor to stop the locomotive one mile from our first stop. And Zash had reentered the train in full-on Bolshevik mode. Head high, coat buttoned, and commands echoing like a relentless battering ram against everyone's ears.

Not a single passenger hesitated.

"This train is to be searched!" he hollered. "All luggage and passengers must disembark!"

Kostya tossed luggage out of the baggage compartment, not too roughly. The last thing we needed were angry passengers coming up to us. I stayed hidden—there was no way I could blend in as a worker or even a passenger. But I listened. Zash's forcefulness frightened me a little. I'd never heard him shout.

He played his role well.

The moment the passengers and luggage had been removed from the train, the engine started back up. Passengers stared at each other, confused, as car after car inched past them. But no one tried to board again. Within minutes we were gone, leaving them alone with their piles of luggage to haul the remaining two kilometers to the station.

I didn't know if the conductor had acted under honor, bribe, or threat. All that mattered was that it worked. We were on our way to Moscow.

33

Zash and I were alone—finally alone—in the passenger car.

Alexei and the Whites were forward with the conductor and the coalmen. This train had nothing like the Imperial Train's wide, open, and airy compartments. This car was filled with chairs with their cushioned backs against the walls, passengers facing inward toward each other. With just the two of us, it still felt roomy, but I couldn't imagine how it might feel if every seat were filled.

Zash sat in a chair opposite me, his injured arm held tightly across his middle. I suspected he was in pain but not sharing it. I couldn't let that stop me from doing what I must.

"May I ask you something, Zash?"

"Okay," he grunted, adjusting his position to bend over his arm a bit more.

"Why did you join the Bolsheviks?" The first time I met him, he seemed so loyal. He hated me and my family. He'd told Alexei he'd joined to provide for Vira, but that didn't explain his initial anger toward my family. So much had changed since then. I wanted to understand where he came from.

He released a gust of a sigh, then squinted at me as though to assess how vulnerable he could be. The only emotion I felt toward Zash in that moment was curiosity. It was a blessed relief not to feel the thrum of hatred just then.

"Everything seems tied together. I'm not sure where to start."

I waited, allowing him to sift through his own memories—which were likely equally as painful to recall as my own, this side of Yurovsky's slaughter.

"My papa and mama died when I was a boy—Mama from an illness in her stomach, and then Papa was trampled only weeks later when the tribe was trying to gather wild reindeer to breed. Accidents like that happened often. My babushka—Vira—took me in. But she had no livelihood. So she took up spell mastery and I gathered items and supplies she needed. She became particularly good at healing spells, as you've seen. After the revolution began, we moved to the city so as not to draw any attention to our tribe. They've since relocated and we have no way of finding them again."

Having grown up traveling and cherishing every broad forest or stretch of countryside, I imagined the move from the wild to the city had been hard on Zash. It would have been difficult for me.

"By that point I'd learned of the unrest in St. Petersburg." He glanced up, almost as an apology.

"Rasputin," I filled in.

"The people were afraid of spell masters because of him. They blamed the tsar."

"It wasn't Papa's fault," I jumped in, determined to preserve his memory and character.

Zash shrugged. "I don't believe it was any one person's fault. But when the people assassinated Rasputin and your father abdicated the throne, I blamed him. Everything changed. It cost my babushka her livelihood. Imagine having all your passions stripped from you because of a decision from someone with more authority than you."

"I don't have to imagine," I said softly. "Our freedom, our lives, our home—everything was stripped from us, too."

He grimaced. "I guess you're right."

"Go on." I sensed where his story was going, but I wanted to hear it from his mouth while he was willing to tell it.

"I was practically forced to serve in the army. Babushka had no other income, and with the Red Army growing, I could be shot if I didn't choose a side. So I chose the Bolsheviks. They promised provision. They promised freedom. They paid well and Babushka was taken care of. The more Bolshevik I became, the less anyone would ever suspect Babushka of spell mastery. I was keeping her safe, trying to convince myself that I was also a Bolshevik because of my beliefs. Only once I started guarding your family did I start to see . . . to see things differently."

I reached for him. "I'm glad you did." He moved to take my hand, but then a grunt of pain escaped his lips and he curled in on himself. I lurched forward in my chair. "Zash, are you alright?"

He remained bent over his midsection, fists clenched.

"Does your arm hurt?" It had been only a bullet graze and he'd not even bled through his bandage. Could it have wounded him that severely?

"It's something else. My insides are . . . tearing themselves apart."

"Are you motion sick?" That happened to me on a boat once. It felt terrible.

"No." Each word came through a gasp.

What could I do? I had no remedy to offer and conversation seemed to be the last thing to provide comfort.

"I think . . . maybe it's Dochkin's spell?" He managed to tilt his head and look up at me.

"But we haven't used any spells on you. Unless . . . Dochkin's spell did something to you when it escaped and sped west?" It *had* flown in his face. "Do you think maybe this feeling is a clue that we're going the wrong way?"

"I don't know. I don't know, Nastya."

I pulled the Matryoshka doll from my shirt. Only the tiny nugget of the doll was left with an actual spell. The last little doll, so small I wasn't sure it would actually open. I pulled it from the larger layer and held it in my hand—the size of a black bean. It shimmered a little under the light flashing past the windows. But no seam appeared. No word appeared. It was the last spell. Perhaps it glowed brighter the closer we got to Dochkin?

Alexei returned to our car, unescorted and bedraggled. "Kostya and the others will stop the conductor near Perm for them to find the spell master. After that, it's up to us." He sank onto a bench chair and leaned against the armrest. Then he noticed Zash. "What happened?"

Zash shook his head and I explained his discomfort to Alexei.

Alexei seemed barely awake enough to listen. "I am sorry for you, Zash. Perhaps you need rest."

I handed Alexei a balled-up coat and he was out. Rest wouldn't help Zash. "Is there nothing I can do?" I felt so helpless, watching the men suffer while I sat with no answers.

"Perhaps this sounds crazy, but I think moving to the back of the train will help."

I eyed him. "That does sound a bit odd." I pushed myself up. "But if you think it will help, then let's go."

Zash got to his feet, his good arm around his middle. He

walked in a half crouch to the back of the car. I opened the door and he managed to cross the hitching well enough. It was only four cars back, but when we arrived in the end car, Zash sank onto a filled burlap sack and gave a sigh. "There is a little relief."

"So it has to do with our traveling." My heart sank. "It's Dochkin's spell. We must be going the wrong way."

"If so, then why did it start hurting only now? Why didn't it direct us sooner?"

"Maybe we were going the right direction at the start, but once we boarded the train it was wrong?" I had barely interacted with spells—let alone powerful, confusing ones like Dochkin's. "I don't know, Zash."

"Neither do I. We are all at a loss here."

We sat in silence, rocking to the rhythm of the train. I stared at the ex-Bolshevik before me. Hate and bitterness simmered beneath the surface of my mind, wanting to be acknowledged. I managed to ignore them. Maybe I was starting to forgive him? I still didn't know how. I had never had to try as hard as now.

"Zash . . . tell me about the night of the execution." The question slipped through my lips softly, as though part of my voice tried to keep it from coming out at all.

He looked up and I held his gaze. I needed to know why he made the decisions he did. He tried to explain before, but I wouldn't listen. Now . . . I would try harder.

"When Yurovsky was removing all the soldiers who had served under Avdeev, he asked me if I would be willing to shoot one of the prisoners." He balled his hands together. "I told him I would do it without hesitation. So he let me stay."

"Because you wanted to stay . . ."

"Because I wanted to stay. And that was the answer I knew

he needed. I didn't think he'd actually do it. Avdeev had never received orders having anything to do with execution. At least not that we knew of. But then a few days in, Yurovsky started assembling a firing squad. He commanded us to arm ourselves and he instructed each man to target a different . . . victim."

"Why did you agree?" My heart and voice cracked under my hurt. "Why didn't you stand up to him? Say no?" This was the part I hated the most. The cowardice. The cowardice that led him to help execute my family. The cowardice that kept him bowing to Yurovsky's will.

"The soldiers who refused—and there were several—were locked in the shed." His fingers twisted and tightened and cracked under his tension. "What good could they have done? They've likely been shot by now."

"A worthy death," I breathed.

"I agree." He dropped his gaze and we both managed to take a breath. "But I couldn't do that, Nastya. I don't expect this to make sense to you, but I kept thinking of you and your family being lined up and shot without warning. I imagined you staring into the cold faces of Bolsheviks who did not care about taking life. And . . . I wanted to be the one to do it. I wanted to be there for you."

His hands slid to his face and I barely caught his words. "You told me you didn't want to die alone. I figured that if you were going to be killed, perhaps it would bring you some comfort to be shot by a friend. By someone who didn't do it out of hate or malice." He shook his head. "Now, saying this, it doesn't make sense. I see it was the nervous mindset of a fool. But on that day, when everything was moving so fast and I feared for both our lives . . . it made sense to me. I suppose because that's how *I* would wish to die."

"It makes sense, Zash." In a way it brought me a pinprick of comfort. Not enough to erase my pain, but enough to erase my confusion. At least now I knew Zash did not take part in the execution because he wished to see us dead.

"That was the only bullet I shot, Nastya. And in that moment my soul fractured."

"I know what will heal you, Zash . . . and I'm trying. I'm trying to forgive you." If that didn't work, I had the spell I was going to demand from Dochkin. The one that would take us back and allow Zash to choose a different path.

His mouth opened in a vulnerable show of disbelief. "That is . . . Nastya, that is far more than I could ever ask."

My lips slid up in a half smile—an acknowledgment that we were both broken and this new life of an ex-princess with an ex-Bolshevik was scary and dangerous and dark for us both. But there was still light—we were just learning how to find it.

~

Sleep came for us all, navigating us through the night and into the dawn when the train brakes squealed. I jolted upright out of the burlap bags. Zash was curled like a turtle in his own spot in the burlap across from me. I wasn't sure if he'd slept. When he lifted his head, he didn't seem as though he had.

"We've reached Perm." I pushed myself to my feet.

Zash followed suit and let out a long breath. "Nastya, it's getting better."

"Bravo! You just needed sleep!"

"No. I didn't sleep. What I mean is the pain—that ripping feeling—is subsiding as we slow down." He didn't seem happy about it, and neither was I. Because that meant that if his pain *was* from the Dochkin spell, we were traveling the wrong way.

Alexei had mere hours before his agony returned, and we might be days from finding Dochkin.

The train stopped and Zash stumbled free of the train carriage. I joined him, basking in the nature. Zash breathed in the relief for a moment, then strolled away from the train—back the way we came. He walked for about a minute, stopped, then turned perpendicular to the train and walked into the forest on the right.

"What are you doing?" I called when he reappeared.

He tromped across the tracks to the other side of the forest. "Assessing which direction hurts the least." He finished his experiment and then rejoined me.

"Verdict?"

"East." His mouth formed a grim line. "Dochkin must live a lot closer to Ekaterinburg than we thought. We might have already passed his village."

All this running. All this danger and bribing and escaping . . . wasted. "That means we have to head back toward Yurovsky."

"This might actually be a good thing. The last thing he'll expect is for us to turn around and travel back the way we came."

My spirits lifted. "You're right. Let's find Alexei."

Before explaining to Alexei, we bid farewell to the Whites. They headed into Perm to find their spell master. Would the spell master be like Vira? Unwilling to join either side of the fight?

Once they were gone, it took some long explaining to share our conclusions with Alexei. In the end he agreed that we should return. "It seems we'll be on foot. The conductor cannot send the train in reverse for a long period of time—it is meant only for fine adjustments." He swayed on his feet.

"How are you feeling?" I asked.

"Unlike myself. I feel as though I've expended the last of my energy—for Kostya and the others. But just because I can't feel the pain doesn't mean my body doesn't feel the wear and tear."

Practical. Matter-of-fact. Alexei.

"We will get you to Dochkin." I gritted my teeth and climbed back onto a train hitch. "Let's get our things. Not a minute to lose." As we dispersed belongings, set Joy on the ground, and prepared ourselves for walking, I kept thinking, *Soon. Soon this will be over. It is misery now, but not for long.* We would find Dochkin. He would heal Alexei, reverse the execution, and the pain would be over.

Alexei settled things with the conductor and we left. "He thinks we're heading to Perm, too. That way, if Yurovsky questions him, he won't have accurate information."

"Well done, Alexei."

He pulled his coat tight around himself, even though we walked under the heat of the July sun. "Let's hope the Whites find their spell master and get out of there before Yurovsky goes digging."

Once again we set off following Zash. Trusting him with our lives and hearts and futures. Only this time it didn't frighten me so much. We'd been through enough that I knew he was on our side . . . and I didn't want to lose him.

If Dochkin reversed our execution, would that change Zash? Would he forget everything we had gone through? What if he resumed being a Bolshevik? Yet how could I allow the deaths of my family? I could not continue living with the knowledge I could have saved them all. This action of finding Dochkin was me saving them as I should have in the first place.

We walked inside the tree line—for both shade and cover, the pace slow for all our sakes. Every few minutes Zash would veer one direction or another to continue testing his spell's reaction. It kept us due east. I hated the feeling of traveling back toward Siberia. That place held only captivity and death for us.

But at least we were doing it under the open sky. Every step brought a breath of freedom with it—a snub at the whitewashed shoe box that was the Ipatiev House. We were back in nature—the same place we had spent the majority of our childhood. Even though Siberia was Siberia, nature was always connected to itself. In that sense, we could always find home.

The sun flirted with the horizon, torturing us with its endless summer glow. Alexei stumbled, gripping a tree trunk and clapping a hand over his head. "I hope we're not far," he groaned.

"Can you sense anything, Zash?" I asked.

He shook his head. "All I know is that relief comes with each step we take east."

It wasn't long before we unrolled the stretcher again to give Alexei a break. "This isn't humiliating at all," he said with his eyes closed as we lifted him.

"Not around us, it shouldn't be." I settled the two wooden rods onto my shoulders and old bruises reminded me to bunch the fur of the reindeer coat beneath the rods. "Now, if we were carrying you like this through a party of lovely young girls . . ."

"Then I'd find the one girl who didn't snicker at me and I'd make her my tsarina," Alexei replied.

I giggled. "That's all it takes to win a proposal from you?"

"That and a proper pastry. That might even get her a ring."

Zash nodded serenely. "You can't overlook a well-made pastry. May you dream of nongiddy girls with arms full of *vatrushka*."

"What sort of girl would win *your* favor, Zash?" Alexei asked with a grin in his voice. My throat cinched. Alexei, you little snoop! I would pinch his foot if it wouldn't bruise him for a week.

"Oh, I'm *very* picky," Zash said.

"As your invalid former tsarevich, I demand that you reveal."

"But of course, Your Imperial Highness."

If anyone asked me in that moment if I was curious about his answer, I would lie and say absolutely not. But in truth I barely allowed myself to breathe as I awaited his response. I knew how I had felt about him in the Ipatiev House. Even now, with forgiveness on the cusp of my heart, my pulse galloped faster than Yurovsky's horse when Zash looked at me. When he talked of his remorse or his reasons behind obeying Yurovsky's orders.

Zash adjusted his grip on the stretcher. "I only accept advances from ex-princesses. Particularly bald ones."

Alexei snorted. My face burned. When I finally glanced up, Alexei had pushed himself onto his elbows enough to make eye contact with me . . . and to waggle his eyebrows.

I was pleased to see the backs of Zash's ears were red.

After a long, awkward silence of crunching leaves and labored breaths, Alexei lay back down, folded his arms over his chest, and said, "I approve, peasant."

34

Zash called an end to our march first. He'd had the least sleep of us all, so I didn't blame him. My feet and shoulders ached. Alexei grew heavier with each step, so I gladly set down the stretcher.

Zash unrolled the two bedrolls and placed them next to each other. Alexei crawled onto one, not yet ready to be moved to it by external help. But I pushed the second bedroll toward Zash. "You need more sleep than I do."

"Absolutely not." He lay down on the stretcher, bunching his Bolshevik coat under him like a pillow.

I kicked his foot. "The bald ex-princess would like you a lot more if you took the bedroll."

"As tempting as that is . . ." He gave a giant yawn. "It's too late. I'm already . . . drifting . . . off . . ." He released a giant snore and I turned away to muffle my laugh.

"Shvibzik," I muttered.

His second snore rattled the branches around us. As fake as a snore could be. But as he continued to pretend, the snores toned down and morphed into heavy breathing with a few real snores here and there. He was out. Alexei was out. Joy was out.

The midnight sun was a sleepy light, hanging on to the horizon with sharp nails, refusing to dip and allow our eyes a reprieve of darkness. But we were all too tired to let it triumph.

I was alone.

So I pulled out the Matryoshka doll's final spell.

The little nugget of a doll glowed in my palm, a shimmering gold and purple, pulsing magic. It hadn't glowed this much the last time I examined it. We must be getting closer to Dochkin.

I turned the little doll over in my hand. No seam. No spell word. Just glowing and pulsing. I expected the spell to appear any moment now. Somehow I knew that spell would be our missing piece. It would be the name of the town Dochkin lived in or the final direction to go. Or a place to meet him.

I lay back on my bedroll, Joy snoozing at my feet, and rolled the doll around and around in my fingers above my head, until its shimmering light melded with the twinkle of stars peeking through the leaves and branches. Until its glow became a lullaby and I drifted off.

I was hardly rested when Joy barked a low, throaty warning. I bolted upright at the sound, blinking through the darkness to see. It wasn't fully dark anymore. The midnight sun had set and risen again, pale and cold.

None of us had kept watch! None of us had even thought of it.

Zash was already on his feet. Perhaps Joy barked at him? But no, he looked as startled and disheveled as I felt. Alexei hadn't moved. In fact . . . I wasn't sure he was breathing.

I scrambled to Alexei's side. "Zash! Alexei's not—"

"Nastya," Zash hissed. "Someone's here."

"Alexei's not breathing!" We both seemed to register the other's statement at the same time. He swiveled toward Alexei, and I stiffened at his warning.

Alexei groaned, weak. I released a relieved cry. His chest barely moved, but he was still alive. The numbing spell had worn off and I finally took in how swollen his head was. It pushed his forehead out like a shelf, and the skin around his eyes hung yellow and bruised.

Dying.

A crunch of leaves interrupted the tense silence. Joy's barks increased. Zash drew his pistol, but a gunshot split the air and his pistol went flying out of his hand.

Alexei's eyes fluttered open at that, bloodshot with pain. He tried to raise himself to one elbow but grimaced. "What's . . . happening?"

I tried to tug him up so we could run. "I don't—"

"You really made this far too easy, soldier." Yurovsky stepped out from behind a tree. He was no longer the sleek, clean, dark-eyed man. His hair was mixed with foliage and ruffled like a wild beast. Dirt smeared his cheeks and holes dotted his uniform as if nature had gnawed on him in his sleep.

Unseen footsteps continued around us in the thickness of the trees. He'd brought Bolsheviks with him. I darted my gaze to Zash. Had he helped Yurovsky?

"I don't know what you're talking about." Zash waved a hand behind his back, signaling for me to run. But how could I leave Alexei lying helpless? And Zash without a weapon?

"You walked right into my hands." Yurovsky twirled his pistol around his finger.

Zash's eyes closed slowly. "The spell inside me . . . that was from you. At the Revda train station."

"A tether spell. The last spell your dear babushka ever made, I'm afraid."

Zash paled and he clung to a tree for support. I fumbled at my throat for the Matryoshka doll, but Yurovsky darted his pistol toward me. "Ah, ah, ah. You'll hand those spells over to me or I'll send a bullet into the body of that boy."

That boy. Alexei. The tsarevich of Russia. I planted myself between Alexei and Yurovsky, but Yurovsky only laughed. "I can tell by your face that you know I'm not the only one here."

The *click, click, click* of other pistols behind us, around us, thrust my hopes deeper into darkness. *Iisus, what do we do?*

"Give me the doll."

I shook my head before he even finished demanding it. I would give up any spell he wanted, if only to keep Alexei safe. But this final spell was the only way to heal Alexei. If I gave it up, Yurovsky would kill us anyway.

"I don't ask twice." Yurovsky stepped left and fired. Alexei jerked and flumped onto his back. I screamed. Yurovsky fired again into Alexei's stomach.

I threw myself over Alexei. "No! *No, no no!*"

"Give me the doll!" Yurovsky shrieked, brandishing his pistol. I was too busy trying to plug the two holes in Alexei's abdomen to care if he shot me in the back.

"Alexei! *Alexei!*" My body yearned to collapse. My mind ached to shut down. But beneath the panic flowing over me came the calm logic that had guided so much of my life. It sped through my brain so quickly it was as though time stopped.

The only way out of this was to get us to Dochkin. And the only way to do that was with a tiny glowing bean of a carved doll I'd dropped in my sleep last night. It sat half buried by leaves beside Alexei's ear, calling to me. *Romanov. Romanov. Romanov.*

There was still no seam. No word. But finally, there was clarity.

I inched my bloody hand toward the piece and wrapped my fingers around it as if physically grasping a final hope.

"Give him the doll, Nastya." Zash's voice crawled into the forest, bringing with it a cold silence.

"N . . . No . . . ," Alexei whimpered beside me, beneath a blanket of blood.

I gripped the little doll even tighter. So this was it. Yurovsky was back—the main contender for Zash's loyalty. And Zash was choosing him. Again.

We were always meant to be on opposite sides of a pistol.

"Give it to him!" Zash yelled.

"No!" I curled in on myself, hunched over Alexei's body. In the darkness of my own shadow, I slipped the small doll into my mouth. It tasted of metal and was salty from the blood. But there was also the bright burn of magic. I fought a gag and forced a swallow. Down it went, leaving the spell in its wake on my tongue.

Yurovsky cocked his pistol, but Zash strode to me and yanked my arms away. "Give it to him or you'll be shot!"

Didn't he realize Yurovsky would shoot us anyway?

But then Zash snatched the bigger Matryoshka doll—the empty husk from the last spell—out of my sleeve and threw it toward Yurovsky. In the noise of Yurovsky scrambling for the doll, Zash whispered, "Now."

He hadn't been betraying me. He'd been using it as an excuse to get near me. To hold my hand so when I used the new spell, whatever it did would happen to all of us.

He took my left hand and I gripped Alexei with my right. But Joy still stood guard over Alexei's head and I didn't have a free hand. "Zash," I gasped. "Joy."

By this point Yurovsky had opened the doll husk and found it empty. "Not so fast," he growled.

Zash grabbed Joy by the ear just as Yurovsky lunged forward. Pistols fired and pain exploded in my neck.

Drenched in my brother's blood, I screamed out the final spell. A name. *"Dochkin!"*

35

The world dissolved around us.

We were falling. Flying. Spinning through darkness and it was all I could do to keep my grip on Alexei and Zash. My body grew thin and weightless, then heavy and sluggish, then finally balanced back out. The spinning stopped. And I blinked color back into the world.

Bright greens, flickering blue, startling sunlight.

We were still in the woods, but no longer in the wild.

We'd been moved to a flourishing garden of trimmed grass, twisted rosebushes, and a stone-laid brook winding through it all. Gravel dug into my knees. Alexei lay in a heap on the ground before me, Joy swaying drunkenly at his swollen head. My hands pressed on Alexei's chest as his blood seeped into the rocks beneath us.

Behind me, Zash grappled with another body—an angry, disheveled Bolshevik body.

Yurovsky had come with us.

Zash needed help. But one name chanted from the blood around my knees louder than the rest. *Romanov. Romanov. Romanov.*

Alexei lay paler than a snowfall. The world turned to silence around me. Through the haze of my panic, I saw the gravel path led to a carved house of wood and I knew where we were—not through recognition, but because the spoken spell had woven the answer with the threads of my veins.

Dochkin's home. He was here. *We* were here.

"Nastya!" Zash croaked from behind. I spun, halfway to my feet before I caught his next strained words. "Get him . . . to . . . Dochkin."

Just like that, the conflict in my soul between staying and helping Zash and saving my brother was loosed like a snapped rope. I gathered Alexei into my shaking arms, his blood sliding across my skin. His breath undetectable.

Though he weighed hardly more than the shoulder pack I'd carried the past few days, my knees threatened to buckle as I rose. My ribs screamed. I stumbled through the gravel, small stones jamming between the worn cloth of my shoes and my tender skin.

I reached the door, hefted Alexei over my shoulder, and lifted the latch. Before I entered, I looked back over my shoulder. Zash was on the ground, a hunting knife clenched in his fist, pinned beneath Yurovsky.

Iisus, help him.

I entered the house. "Help!" I blinked against the sudden dimness, willing my eyes to adjust. "Help! Help! Please, Vasily Dochkin!" The first thing that came into view was a quilted bed across the room. I managed two steps toward it before my legs gave out. I slammed into the wood floor, clutching Alexei close so he wouldn't bruise.

But then he was weightless. Lifted from my arms and transported to the bed by two weathered arms of an old man. He had a long mustache and a bald head.

A sob rose in my throat. "Save him . . . please." I pressed a fist against my chest and stared at the blood—the life—flowing out of my brother. Already dripping from the quilt onto the wood floor.

Dochkin bent over Alexei, tearing open Alexei's uniform—buttons flying everywhere. "Come press on this wound."

I was on my feet mere seconds after the word *come*. I pressed the palms of my hands over a bubbling red wound in Alexei's abdomen. The moment I plugged the hole, Dochkin rushed to the kitchen.

His home was a wide one-space cottage. To my right rested a kitchen of sorts, covered in scraps of food but also bottles of ink and pieces of parchment. A double window lay propped open and birds pecked at seed on the sill, some hopping into the house and others flying around in the rafters.

Dochkin sifted through the bottles and jars. Alexei gave a shuddering gasp. I swung my attention back to him. His gasp turned to a gurgle. A wet cough. "Dochkin!" I screamed, pressing harder. But Alexei had more than one wound. I couldn't stop them all. His body was a cracked dam, leaking and growing weaker. About to crumble entirely.

My scream echoed in the still house, mixing with the noise of clattering bottles and the scuffle outside. I twisted toward the kitchen. "Doch—" I choked.

Yurovsky had entered, silent as a cougar. He leaped at Dochkin from behind and pressed his knife to the spell master's throat. Dochkin clutched a black jar in one hand, its stopper stained with silver-rainbow smears. Spell ink.

Where was Zash?

"Release the jar and surrender," Yurovsky growled. "You are a traitor to your country."

With a shaking hand Dochkin passed the jar to Yurovsky. The moment it passed from old weathered fingers to bloodstained ones, Zash stumbled into the cottage. Half his face was bashed in and a nasty gash across his hairline poured blood down his face. He held a river rock and rubbed a fist against his eyes as he took in the scene.

Alexei's body stilled beneath my hands. "Alexei." I freed one hand only to plug another wound. "Don't give up! Alexei!"

Zash swayed but lifted the river rock, setting his gaze on Yurovsky. But Yurovsky threw first. The ink jar sailed across the room and smashed against Zash's temple, glistening spell ink splashing everywhere. Zash collapsed to the floor, blood like a halo rippling around him. No. *No!*

The ink from the smashed jar rolled in a thick stream toward my boots.

"It knows your blood." Dochkin pinned me in place with the intensity of his stare.

"Silence, old man!" Yurovsky gripped him tighter.

Dochkin's throat bobbed against the knife blade and he spoke again. To me. "The ink is loyal to the Romanov—"

Slice. Splash. Fall.

Dochkin sank in a shredded heap, his throat split open like a seam. Time slowed. Even my scream of dismay seemed to take thrice as long to escape my mouth.

Our one hope. Our spell master. Our *life*. Gone.

My body processed the hopelessness before my mind did. My hand slipped from Alexei's wound. My eyes blinked against the flash of sun on Yurovsky's raised knife. My knees slammed into the silver of the spell ink.

The ink mixed with blood—mine, Zash's, Alexei's, Dochkin's.

Yurovsky turned a murderous gaze to me. My heart barely beat enough to process my end, let alone my smothered hope. There was peace in an end. Death would come as a relief . . .

. . . but not at Yurovsky's hand. I couldn't let him take that from me—not after he'd taken everything else.

Yurovsky stepped over Dochkin's body—using it as though it were a mat for him to wipe his shoes. Dochkin let out a gurgle under the pressure of Yurovsky's step.

Yurovsky's boots splashed into the shimmering spell ink that still held its rainbow color despite the blood everywhere. The blood that chanted my name. *Romanov. Romanov. Romanov.*

The reminder startled me awake. The emotions and heartbreak flowed back into my body and I let them—I let them fuel me.

I was Romanov.

I would not kneel while this man cut me down. I had never surrendered to failure, and I wouldn't start today. Yurovsky's shadow fell over me, he was so close. I closed my eyes and hummed the hymn that Mamma and my sisters would sing each night. It wasn't a spell song, but it was the only song I had.

I plunged my hand into the spell ink that had gathered in small pools in the cracks of the floor. Light awoke in my mind, like a flickering star falling closer and closer to earth, growing brighter and more stunning even though it fell to its death. The spell ink warmed between my fingers, like gloves on a winter day.

"The Romanov line is ended." Yurovsky's voice came as though through a pool of water. Muffled and distant, even though I felt the energy from his body hovering over mine.

A streak of white and red burst through the open door and launched itself at Yurovsky. Joy, sporting her own battle wounds, clamped down on Yurovsky's meaty thigh. He roared, but I barely heard it over the song that now seemed to be singing itself in my mind.

I dove for Zash's hand and yanked him closer. His body slid easily across all the blood. Joy yelped. I tangled my other fingers with Alexei's limp ones. In a last thought, I pulled Dochkin's arm out from where it was lodged under his body and clamped his and Zash's together in mine.

Joy went silent.

Yurovsky dug his nails into the skin of my fuzzy scalp and a wet blade hit my throat. I let the spell ink turn to fire on my skin. I didn't know what I was doing, just that I was doing it with all the hope and faith left in my body.

I yanked free of Yurovsky's touch. And as his blade cut into my neck, I whispered a final word. The only word I had.

"Ajnin."

36

I saw my body fall.

I watched my own blood join the mixture of three dying souls.

But it had not been silenced. I could still hear it. *Romanov. Romanov. Romanov.*

Yurovsky stood over me, his arm still raised, his knife still slick, his face still manic. As though he had not yet realized it was over. He'd cut the life out of me. I was at his feet—the way he'd always wanted me.

But I was also standing at his side. Tall. Ethereal. Alive.

It had worked. The spell worked—on me, at least. I didn't know how. I didn't understand why. But I rushed to Alexei's side. I tried to shake his shoulder, but my hand went through his body. No. *No.* I needed his ethereal form. I needed him alive! This was my last hope.

Yurovsky stumbled away from his battlefield and plopped into one of the few kitchen chairs. He stared at our bodies. "It is done," he said quietly. "I am most loyal."

Let him revel in his victory. Let him think he'd won. Meanwhile, my heart was crumbling.

Zash's own ghostly form raised itself to all fours, staring at his bashed body beneath him. My first breath of relief expelled from my lungs. He stumbled to his feet, a confused and terrified frown on his face.

Then he saw my fallen form—the one that Yurovsky had cut. And he fell to his knees beside it with a strangled cry. He moved to gently lift my head, but his hands went straight through me.

"I'm right here," I choked, stepping from beside Alexei.

Zash's head snapped up, his eyes wide as saucers. He pulled himself upright and I barely made it into his arms before the sobs came. "The spell worked. We're ethereal. But . . . but I was too late. Alexei. He's . . . he's . . ."

"He's not feeling too well," came the young sarcastic voice.

I gasped and spun. Alexei's ghost form sat up from his dying physical body. He swung his ghost legs over the edge of the bed and grimaced. "It's not quite like last time, Nastya. I feel very weak this time."

"Well, I should expect so." Dochkin's form rose from its lump of a body. "I'm surprised you're alive at all."

There was nothing else to do. I shrieked. Not in fright. Not yet in joy—the shock was still too new. But in . . . hope, maybe? "You're all alive!"

Dochkin nodded. "For now. And only thanks to your quick thinking."

I held tightly to Zash's hand and took Alexei's in the other. "How did I do that?"

"Well, I wasn't exactly paying attention to what you were doing—since I was bleeding out, you know—but I told you the ink is loyal to the Romanov name, because *I* am loyal to the Romanov name . . . and I crafted the ink."

"So . . . it just obeyed?"

"It is like the ink inside the Matryoshka doll. Do you know how my doll worked?"

"It released the next spell at certain times," I said. "I couldn't figure out if there was a pattern."

"The doll *created* spells according to your need. The ink in each was not formed into a spell until it was needed. Each layer heard your pleas, sensed the needs of the Romanov family, and then became the spell you needed at the time. *That* is why I hide away in my little cottage. Only I have ever been able to set such a spell as that. I use my own language—known to no other spell master. My Matryoshka spells are the closest thing to a wish. That is why the commandant wanted to find me so terribly. I'm too powerful an enemy to the Soviets."

Zash seemed to have swallowed his confusion enough to join the conversation. "But the spell that zoomed west. How did that help us? It gave us nothing other than to head west—no specifics on how to find you."

Dochkin's mustache crinkled. "It was not intended to give you directions. If you recall"—his gaze slid to meet mine—"you were whispering your needs to the doll. That spell brought those desires to me so I could start on the spells for your arrival."

It took three swallows to dislodge my voice. "So . . . you have the spells I wished for?" I thought about my desires that I'd proclaimed to the doll—that Alexei would be healed and that Dochkin would reverse the pain of my family's deaths. That he would undo the entire event.

A clatter startled all four of us as Yurovsky tossed the bloodied knife onto the floor. He seemed to have caught his breath and stood from his chair. He then faced the many bottles on Dochkin's table.

Dochkin took a deep breath, watching Yurovsky pick up one bottle and examine the handwritten label. "Yes, Nastya. I have the spells you asked for, but they will not be what you expect."

I shifted my gaze from Yurovsky and his greedy fingers and landed on Alexei. The spells weren't what I expected? Why didn't that surprise me? "You can save Alexei, can't you?"

"I've managed to make a spell that will restore his body to a state without bruises or bleeding or wounds, but his hemophilia will remain."

"Nothing I haven't dealt with before," Alexei croaked from the bed. "And that's far more healing than I've ever had before." He fixed Dochkin with a serious look. "Do you think you can apply the spell in time for me?"

Dochkin shook his head and my heart might as well have stopped. "I cannot, my tsarevich. But your sister, the grand duchess, will be the one who might."

"Because you won't heal in time to apply it," I concluded.

He gave me a grim smile. "I'm not going to heal at all, Grand Duchess. I will not survive the return. A throat slit is a race between suffocation and bleeding out. I suspect your spell caught me with mere seconds left." He patted my arm. "It's time for you to go."

I stumbled back. "But . . . we need you!"

"I'm old, and I did what I could for my tsar." He toyed with his mustache like Papa used to, hiding a sad smile.

Alexei looked even more distraught. "I'd hoped you would join me . . . and help in the war."

"I am sorry, my tsarevich. I would have liked that." Dochkin adopted a serious tone. A soldier-like tone that returned Alexei to a state of strength. "The most I can do now is heal your body."

Dochkin's eyes flicked to where Yurovsky stuffed a spell bottle into his coat. "It's time to go, Nastya. You need to keep him from destroying or taking those spells—those are the spells that might save you. Let me show you where they are."

He directed me past Yurovsky. I still squeezed my body tight so I wouldn't touch him, even though I would have passed through him. Dochkin pointed to a metal tin beside a half-eaten loaf of bread. "Those are minor healing spells. They can help with pain."

He pointed to a cupboard opposite us. "There is a pistol on the second shelf, but I ran out of bullets after the last commandant hunted me." He gestured to the bullet straps crossing Yurovsky's chest. "Those should work, but you have no chance of retrieving both pistol and bullet before he stops you. You don't want the pistol to fall into his hands either. Use that as a last resort."

I nodded, though a pistol sounded awfully handy just now.

He stopped by the windowsill where two glass vials sat pushed against the wood frame, soaking up the light. He pointed to the larger one. "This is for Alexei. You must pour it over his bare skin. All of it. There is no spell word. Just say *Romanov* and the spell will do the rest. It must soak into his skin, so do not let his body be disturbed after you've applied it."

I nodded, my heart thundering at each clink of Yurovsky thumbing through spells and vials and jars. Any second he could turn and find these. Smash them.

"There was another request that came with that Matryoshka spell," Dochkin said softly. Zash stilled from across the room.

"Mine," I breathed. "The one that will reverse this tragedy—that will take us back to that night so I can save my family." Tears sprang to my eyes. "Please. Tell me you've made it." I scanned the windowsill and captured the smaller vial with my gaze. I wanted to erase the pain. Erase the loss. This man had created a spell to heal Alexei. He could do it. I knew he could.

Dochkin rested his hand by the smaller vial.

"Nastya . . ." Zash's meek voice came from behind me.

"It is not what you think." Dochkin's hand dropped to his side. "I cannot reverse time."

I backed from the window. "But the first spell I used . . . *this* spell that we are in. It reversed the attacks on our bodies!" I was very careful not to say the word *ajnin* because that would send us back to the physical realm.

"That was not reversing time. That was reversing the actions taken on your body *after* the spell was used. It is a very different thing."

"Can't you reverse what Yurovsky did? The firing squad? The massacre?"

His expression showed that he wished he had a different answer for me. "Unless the proper spell was enacted beforehand, there is nothing I can do."

I gestured halfheartedly at the little glass vial. "Then what is this for?"

"That is for you, Grand Duchess. And it is only because you *are* my grand duchess that I made it. For anyone else, I would have refused."

I sensed Zash behind us but didn't turn.

Dochkin knew my desires—that spell of his had whispered my secrets to him and he'd made me this new spell. "What does it do?" I peered into the liquid and caught some dark letters floating around.

"I used a Russian spell word for this one—*pustoy*," Dochkin said.

"Blank," I translated, entranced by the liquid.

"It will erase your pain."

I tore my eyes away from the vial. "How? How can anything do that?"

"It will erase your story. Your memories. You will not know of the hurt—therefore you can never feel it." He nodded as though officially passing the spell to me. To keep and to use as I willed.

Blank. It was exactly what I wished . . . for myself. To never have to think of Papa's face again with a stab of loss. To never revive memories of my sisters being bayoneted and dumped down a mine shaft. I would never have to remember Zash's betrayal or the fear that came from Yurovsky's pursuit.

I would be free.

Free to start over. To start fresh.

"Nastya, wait." Zash reached for my hand, as though to stop me from using the spell then and there, even though my ghost form couldn't touch it. "You . . . can't."

"Why shouldn't I, Zash?" I asked softly.

Dochkin raised an eyebrow at Zash. "It is her right. You have been part of her pain. It is not your choice to deny her healing."

Zash's hand slid from mine. Defeated. "But . . . Nastya, I want to be part of your healing. I want to be part of your *life*."

"You need to go, Nastya," Dochkin urged. "Remember that wherever you're standing when you reverse the *ajnin* spell is where your body will join you."

I turned from the windowsill to find Yurovsky stuffing bottle after bottle into his pack. I strode past Zash, not strong enough to meet his eyes after what Dochkin had given me.

"That spell does not carry over," Dochkin warned. "It can be used on only one person—it's not strong enough for two."

"Nastya, please . . ." Zash jogged after me.

"I have to go." My heart was breaking. "I can't think about that right now. I have to save Alexei."

Zash closed his mouth and nodded.

I didn't want to silence him. But I meant what I said. I couldn't think about that spell yet. I had to get this right. Once I returned, I would have mere seconds to try to save Alexei. My gaze slid to Dochkin's body.

How could I leave him there to die? He was alive for the moment . . . and Alexei so craved Dochkin's knowledge and guidance. I needed him to teach me spell mastery. Otherwise, what future did we have? Even if we stopped Yurovsky?

"You cannot save me," Dochkin said, as though reading my thoughts.

"You should know," Alexei said. "Nastya doesn't really like when people tell her she can't do something."

I kissed Dochkin's cheek. Then I ran and gave Alexei a tight hug, even though he'd yet to stand this entire time. "Please . . . hold on as long as you can."

"I will, Sister."

I took his face in my hands and stared hard into it. Painting it into my memory. A desperate flutter in my heart whispered that this was the last time I'd see his brave smile. *No.* No. I couldn't acknowledge that. I *had* to cling to hope.

Finally, I faced the room. I faced Zash. He strode up to me as though to embrace me. But instead, he grabbed my shoulders and steered me to the river stone on the ground beside his body. The stone he'd dropped when Yurovsky smashed the spell ink jar against his head.

"Wake up here and use this to defend yourself. He's too close to the hunting knife for you to start there."

I nodded, trying to muster up the courage that used to come so easily when planning something risky.

Yurovsky examined a bottle of spell ink from the big table, sneered, and then threw it into the brick fireplace where it smashed to pieces. He reached for another, but then his eyes alighted on the windowsill—on Alexei's healing spell.

My nerves spasmed. "I have to go." I knelt by Zash's unconscious body, my hand poised over the stone.

"Aim while his back is turned."

I nodded and took a breath to say the spell. At the same time I said, *"Ajnin,"* Zash whispered with a desperate edge, "Don't leave without letting me say good-bye."

I was glad I didn't have a chance to give an answer.

37

This time, there was no disorientation. I was back and instantly my hand gripped the river rock. Yurovsky's back was to me. Though Zash, Dochkin, and Alexei had returned to their dying bodies, I still felt as though Zash was behind me—in my ear—whispering strength into my limbs.

My neck stung from Yurovsky's knife prick before the *ajnin* spell was enacted. But it was only a prick. A nervous swallow proved that my throat was intact. I straightened, my heart beating to the rhythm of a chant. *Alexei, Alexei, Alexei.*

I cocked my arm back and let the stone fly. Unlike with Papa's paperweight, my aim was perfect this time.

Maybe it was my intake of breath, or the whoosh of stone through air, or the prickle of defeat flying his way . . . but something alerted Yurovsky. His soldier instincts sent him ducking.

The stone whizzed past his head and sailed through the window above the two spells, clipping the top of the vial holding my memory spell. The glass vial teetered . . . and then toppled off the sill, disappearing into the garden shrubs outside.

I didn't stand or gape at my failure. I'd known there was a chance I'd miss, so by the time Yurovsky straightened and spun to face his attacker, I had scrambled to the space near his feet and risen with the knife in my hand.

Alexei, Alexei, Alexei.

"How?" Yurovsky growled. "Why won't you die?"

"Because I have a story I was meant to live. And not even *you* can unwrite it."

Wild and feral, Yurovsky dove at me. I swept the knife in front of me. It met flesh but then spun from my hand. He slammed me to the ground. His weight crushed the air from my lungs and he straightened, keeping me pinned. "I don't know what spell you used to survive, but I *will* finish you."

His fist connected with my face and a flash of black blocked my vision.

I dug my fingernails into the skin of his forehead, but he hit me again. All the while, my mind kept screaming, *Alexei's dying!*

Yurovsky got his meaty hands around my throat and squeezed as though to snap me in two. He trapped what was left of my breath in my lungs. My chest heaved. But with his two hands occupied, mine were now free.

I could go for his hands.

I could go for his eyes. But his wild fury told me no amount of pain would distract him from his mission.

So I went for the knife.

I threw my hands over my head and sent my fingers searching, my mind praying, my feet kicking. If I didn't find it within the next seconds, my muscles would liquefy. My mind would shut off. My brother would die.

Yurovsky squeezed harder. Spots swam across my vision.

I made it halfway through a prayer before my fingers felt metal instead of wood.

I gripped the blade with both hands and slammed it against Yurovsky's face.

No one could withstand a knifepoint to the eye. Yurovsky screamed and reeled backward. My own hands still gripped the blade, gushing blood of their own, though I didn't feel the wounds yet.

I scrambled to my feet, unable to fully see the room, but I stumbled toward Yurovsky's scream as I sucked in air through a pinched windpipe. He pulled at the edges of my skirt, clawed at my ankles, trying to bring me down. I tore my foot free and stomped on his temple with my heel. He went limp as a blini.

I wanted to retrieve the knife. To plunge it into his heaving chest. To watch his blood leak out of him the way Alexei's had. But that would be a false victory. Yurovsky's death was not the end goal. Not yet.

Alexei, Alexei, Alexei.

I tripped over his body to the windowsill, grabbed the spell for Alexei, and then sprinted to Alexei's spot on the bed, unstoppering the spell as I ran. His shirt lay open, but blood created a vest of death over what should have been his skin. I upended the bottle and sent the spell ink dribbling up and down his torso.

In a last frantic moment, I stopped the pour so there was only a tiny splash of spell left. Everything in me wanted to dump the rest onto Alexei, but I heard Alexei's voice in my head. Demanding I do what I could for Dochkin.

I spread the spell across Alexei's body and his wounds with my palms, making sure it touched all the skin it could. "Romanov, Romanov, Romanov," I muttered, hoping to feel some sort of magic pull in my chest from the spell working.

I felt nothing except blackened hope.

I hurried to Dochkin's body and rolled him onto his back, not sure he was even alive. Then I poured the last bit of this powerful healing spell directly on his slit throat. "Romanov."

Please, Iisus. That seemed to be the only prayer coming from my mouth these days. I left Dochkin to the will of the spell and returned to my brother. I hovered over his body—*prayed* over his body—but nothing seemed to be happening. No increased breathing. No action from the spell ink. Alexei lay with his mouth open but no inhale.

"Work," I croaked.

I bounced on my toes for a moment longer before tearing myself away to the other healing spells. I had more injuries to take care of. I unscrewed the tin that Dochkin had pointed out and applied one to Zash, then one to Dochkin in case that would couple with the last splash of the healing spell. I also applied one to Joy, who still lay limp against the wall. I didn't know how spells worked on animals, but it was worth a shot.

Lastly, I applied one to myself.

The slices on my palms stung as they sealed but didn't fully heal. Other parts of my body—my neck, my ribs, my feet, my face—snapped in protest too. Once I finished, I returned to Alexei. No visible change. The spell ink hadn't even sunk into his body. It floated among his blood like a film of oil.

I slid to my knees and moved to take his hand but then remembered that Dochkin said not to disturb his body. So I pressed my forehead to the bedcover beside him and closed my eyes. "Please, oh please. Don't leave me."

Scuffles of cloth on wood came from behind me. I spun and scrabbled for where I'd left the dagger. But the movement wasn't from Yurovsky. It was Zash, climbing gingerly to his feet.

I was no longer alone.

And I was no longer strong.

He took one look at me, his eyes shining, and opened his arms wide. "You did it."

I stumbled into his embrace and pressed into the tight safety that came from his presence. The tears came and I tried to muffle them against his coat. He didn't ask me what was wrong. He didn't ask if I was okay.

"I d-didn't. Zash, I . . . I failed."

"No," he said forcefully. "No, you didn't. *You* are alive. *I* am alive. Yurovsky is dead. That's because of you."

I shook my head. "He's not dead." I wished he was. With all the blood gushing from his eye wound, he *should* be dead.

Zash held me at arm's length. "I should tie him up, then. We don't want him waking." I shuddered and let him bend over Yurovsky's body. He loosed his belt and wound it around Yurovsky's ankles.

"I think . . . I think Alexei's gone," I said.

Zash's hands stilled, but he didn't look up. Not at me. Not at Alexei. "Don't give up hope yet, Nastya."

Words. Just words. There was no reason—no extra knowledge—behind his assurance. Empty soothing.

The grief in my heart welled as it did moments after my family's execution. The double feeling of being hollowed out and refilled with all things shadow and darkness. The pressure climbed from my midsection to my lungs. Up my throat and demanded release. I didn't have the strength to swallow it. An aching groan tore from me and I doubled over.

I couldn't handle this. I couldn't live with this.

I needed to pour my sorrow somewhere else—into another

vessel. My tight gaze found Yurovsky's body. And I released my sorrow into a vessel of fury. He hadn't killed me, but he'd still won. I wanted Yurovsky dead. I wanted him to bleed out and decay under the open sky where vultures could turn up their beaks at the disgusting meal he would make.

"We need to kill him," I growled.

Zash faltered in his tying.

I didn't care if he disapproved. "He'll wake soon and might escape his bonds—"

"Not likely."

"Even if he doesn't, what will we do with him? Take him with us?" I talked as if we had a future. As if Zash and I would walk away from here and start a new life. But my mind had drifted through the window and started searching the bushes for the memory spell that Dochkin had made me. *That* was my end. That was my future. "We can't let him continue hunting spell masters."

"I agree."

I strode across the room and pulled Dochkin's pistol from the cupboard. Once back over Yurovsky's body, I slipped a bullet from the strap on Yurovsky's belt, loaded it, and aimed toward his head. My heart pounded with the anticipated relief the gunshot would bring.

Nastya. Papa's voice echoed in my mind, and I remembered how he abandoned the Ipatiev House rescue plan because he refused to risk the lives of any of the soldiers. Any of our enemies.

But this was Yurovsky. This was a leader. He murdered spell masters. Zash's grandmother. He murdered my family. And yet . . . Papa would tell me to forgive him. Even my own words from a lifetime ago echoed in my head. *"I am a Romanov, and I will value life."*

I clenched the pistol, my finger tightening around the trigger—half wishing I would accidentally pull it and blow him to pieces.

"Nastya." Zash placed his hand on my arm and pushed until I lowered the gun. "Let me do it." His own hands trembled as he took the pistol from me. He held it in his lap for a long moment. "Perhaps you should go outside."

And there was my release. My opportunity to go find my spell—my freedom. To let someone else do the dirty work.

I wanted to see if the *blank* spell had broken. I wanted to hold that opportunity in my hands. It was Dochkin's gift to me. Everything would be erased the moment I used it. I would be pain-free.

I nodded and moved toward the door, but not before Zash said quietly, "Come back to me."

He knew I was going to search for the spell. I couldn't bring myself to respond. The door creaked on its hinges as I shut it behind me.

38

Resting in a bed of grass beneath the sill of the open window lay the vial. Whole. Shining. Beautiful and full of promises.

I scooped it up and relief mixed with the sorrow swirling in my heart. Straightening, I took in the garden. The sun hung in the sky like a newly blossomed daffodil. My surroundings were like stepping back home. Back into Papa's arms. A small trimmed lawn of flowers and a creek bed lined with stones. Around all of this—forest. But not the brown taiga forest we'd been traveling through the past three days. No, *this* forest glistened under the sun, reaching for the sky and embracing it the way I wished I could.

Life hung on every leaf and sprout. I wasn't afraid. Perhaps it was because I felt as though I'd finally reached the end—the crossroads of my new life and my old. I sat by the creek and pulled off my boots. I slipped my feet into the icy water and let it wash over my jumbled thoughts.

If I remained how I was—with my family's slaughter in my mind and all the agony of the past months—how could I move forward? How could I do anything without aching? Without Alexei?

To live with my memories meant I would have to forgive Yurovsky, even once Zash killed him. Papa would ask that of me. But did he know how impossible that was?

Then again, I'd thought it would be impossible to soften toward Zash.

Papa. What would you have me do? The question hung in the light summer sky, but I couldn't imagine his voice. I couldn't hear his words. He was slipping away. My eyes burned. *Don't leave me.*

If I applied the *pustoy* spell, he would be gone from my mind forever.

Iisus?

If I used this spell, I wouldn't have to forgive Yurovsky. I wouldn't have to forgive anyone because I wouldn't be hurt by their actions. But this would be a false victory. A shortcut. And though it sounded tempting right now, it would have its own trials.

I inspected the vial again. What right did I have to such a spell? It would be selfish for me to take it for myself—I'd be abandoning Zash. Zash who had given up everything to help us—who had just lost his babushka. Who was preparing to kill Yurovsky this very moment.

I should offer the spell to him.

But that would leave *me* hurting. It would leave me behind, carrying all the memories on my own.

I lay back in the grass, allowing my thoughts to drift to more vulnerable places. Zash had made it clear how he felt about me. I felt something for him, too, tied up in the confused emotions of his betrayal. I wanted to be with him and he wanted to be with me. If I took the spell, would he be willing to help me start over? To build new memories with me?

Could I ask him to do that? Could I ask him to keep his memories and never share them with me? To let me live a happy and free life while he wallowed in his own lonely story?

I couldn't. It was as simple as that.

I'd told him I was trying to forgive him. As I lay in the grass next to the spell that could rid me of heart pain, I realized that a part of forgiveness was accepting the things someone had done—and the pain that came with that—and moving on with love. Forgiveness was a personal battle that must always be fought in my heart. Daily. And though I was tired of running and surviving and fighting . . . I wasn't ready to surrender that battle yet.

Zash had lost as much as I had. He deserved the spell.

I couldn't take the easy way out. Not if it would leave more pain in my wake for others. In this, I thought Papa would have been proud. If I used the spell for Zash, I could be strong enough to help him rebuild his life. I wouldn't bring up his past. I wouldn't remind him of his pain.

But I didn't like the idea of him losing his memories of me. Losing his *love* for me, even though love could be rebuilt.

I lay in the grass waiting for the gunshot. Waiting for the end of Yurovsky. My heart grew sick thinking of Zash shooting his unconscious commandant. Alone. In a house of dead allies. And I'd left him there.

Suddenly everything became clear, like the blast of sunlight when the breeze blew away the tree branch: the selfishness of my escape. The injustice of me using the memory spell for myself. The fact I'd completely given up on Alexei and let hopelessness win.

I shoved myself to my feet, leaving my shoes by the creek. I'd reached my conclusion. The spell was not for me. But neither would I waste it. I knew what I needed to do. If I waited any longer, I wouldn't be strong enough to do it.

I burst through the door, letting in a spill of sunlight—a source of strength.

Zash stood over Yurovsky's body, still holding the cocked pistol. His hand trembled like a rattling carriage. Yurovsky's chest still rose and fell.

At my entrance, Zash broke from his terrorized trance. "Nastya?" My name from his lips sounded both alarmed and hopeful.

"I'm still here," I whispered.

Sweat lined his pale forehead and his face bore a twist of torment. He opened his mouth once. Twice. His chin trembled and finally he managed to force out tremulous words. "I . . . I can't."

His hand dropped to his side. "All I can think of is the last time I shot a pistol. At . . . at you. It fractured my heart—my very soul. If I take this life, I'll shatter." He shook his head. "I'm so, so sorry. I . . . failed you."

I took the pistol from his hand and set it back on the kitchen table. "You didn't fail me. You were *stronger* than me, Zash. I finally realized why Papa always asked me to forgive. Because it takes more strength and courage to forgive than it does to enact revenge."

I twined my fingers with his. "Revenge would have shattered us both. But you've given us the opportunity to be strong. To mend our hearts instead of break them further. And I want you to know . . . I forgive you. For everything."

A wash of freedom overtook his features. Like he'd stepped into daylight for the first time. He barely maintained his composure as he asked through thick emotion, "Really?"

I nodded.

He took my face in his hands with a fierce joy. As he pressed his forehead to mine, he whispered fervently, "You've freed me."

So then why was I the one who felt freed?

"Don't you *dare* kiss when I'm in the room," came a feeble voice.

I jerked away from Zash so forcefully we both lost our balance. But as I landed hard on my elbows, I had eyes only for Alexei. He'd hardly moved from his supine position. But his head now angled toward me and he managed a weak wink.

"Alexei!" I screeched. I bolted to his side, careful not to touch him, not wanting to interfere with the spell. The ink was nowhere to be seen. It had soaked into his body just as Dochkin had said. "You're alive! You're alive!"

"Well, you *did* tell him to hang on." Zash grinned, coming up beside me.

Alexei frowned at me. "Someone hit you in the face. You look like a plum."

"I won't even tell you what *you* look like."

His gaze moved to Dochkin's body on the floor. "Is he . . . ?"

I knelt beside Dochkin. "I did what I could." I placed a hand on his chest but felt no movement. The slice in his neck had sealed. "I think he's gone."

"Wait." Zash joined me and held Yurovsky's blade under Dochkin's nose.

"What are you—?" A tiny cloud fogged the knife blade. I gasped. "Is that . . . breath?" The cloud came again. Another breath. "He's alive!"

"Why is it taking him so long to wake?" Alexei asked.

I racked my brain for my meager knowledge of spell mastery. "Likely because he was so close to death, he's old, and I used only a tiny splash of your healing spell on him. Let's be careful not to move him."

The swelling in Alexei's head had mostly gone. All his wounds were closed. "How are you feeling?"

"Better by the minute. Weak, though."

"You're prolonging the inevitable," Yurovsky rasped through swollen and cracked lips from his spot on the floor.

Zash recoiled, despite Yurovsky's bonds. Even I backed up a step, Yurovsky's voice as threatening as his fists or blade or bullets had been.

"Well, let's all wake up at the same time, shall we?" Alexei said.

"He's been sickly his whole life—never able to rule." Yurovsky wouldn't even address Alexei as his own person.

"I don't *need* to rule," Alexei retorted. "That is not my future. I'm not trying to get the throne back—I listen to the demands of my people, even if they demand my disappearance."

"They demanded your *death*."

"No, that was you," Alexei said calmly. "You received an order to disobey the laws of our Russia. No trial. No proper burial. You slaughtered the royal family and tried to defile our stories."

"Your story is ended, little tsar. What future can you have without your family? Without your papa to carry you around?"

"Can someone please gag him?" Alexei asked.

I threw a spare blanket onto Yurovsky's head and enjoyed watching him writhe with bound hands and legs to get out from under the itchy material. None of us were willing to go close enough to gag him.

Dochkin's breaths grew stronger. His chest visibly rose and fell now. My risk taking had worked. When, finally, his eyes opened, they crinkled into a frown. "Wasn't I supposed to die?"

"Something you should learn about us Romanovs is that we like to defy *supposed to*s."

"Indeed." He struggled to sit up and Zash helped prop him against the bed frame. "Well done, Grand Duchess."

"Thank you," I whispered. "But there is one last thing I must do." I pulled the memory spell from my dress pocket and unstoppered it. My breath quickened.

"What's that?" Alexei asked.

"This spell . . . Dochkin made for me."

Zash watched the unstoppered spell tremble in my hands. "Please don't do this," he said softly. "Let me help you heal. Let me help you understand. We can heal together."

Yurovsky had escaped the smothering blanket and squinted at me through the dried blood with his good eye. "With every spell you use, you condemn yourself further. The Red Army *will* find you all and finish the job."

"Isn't it interesting how the Red Army focuses all their efforts on murdering the noncompliant rather than actually serving the people?" Dochkin mused.

"Dochkin, you are to hand yourself in to the Soviets."

"You have no way to take me in, little Bolshevik," Dochkin said, not even giving him a glance. "And your slice with that knife proved the Soviet has no interest in negotiation."

"If I die, you will be hunted!" Yurovsky shrieked.

"I've been hunted my whole life."

Yurovsky's and Dochkin's voices passed through my consciousness like a distant echo. I stared at the memory spell. It flickered. Flowed. Called my name. *Romanov. Romanov. Romanov.*

It wanted to serve me. I gripped the vial with resolve.

"Nastya, what are you doing?" Alexei asked quietly.

Zash reached for the spell. "Wait. Please."

I yanked it back. My throat burned. My eyes stung. The spell gurgled and climbed its way toward the opening, as though sensing

I was ready. "None of us deserves to live with the pain and grief that is now woven in our stories."

I couldn't wait a second longer. I walked past Zash, and Yurovsky's dark gaze finally slid to mine. "But at least we can stop you from causing more." I choked on tears. "You don't deserve this mercy."

He sneered. "Mercies won't stop me from hunting you and killing—"

I splashed the spell onto Yurovsky's startled face. My own tears fell with it as I choked on the word. *"Pustoy."*

39

"What are you doing?" Zash grabbed my wrist.

I dropped the vial and it shattered on the plank floor, but the spell had been poured. The ink sank into Yurovsky's skin and a thick film of peace took its place. His features relaxed and he slumped backward into a deep sleep.

I cried harder. He didn't deserve it. He didn't deserve peace or freedom from the things he'd done. Whether he wanted it or not, he deserved to drown under those weights.

Zash took several deep breaths and wrapped an arm around me. "I . . . don't understand."

"Don't you see?" I rubbed my sleeve across my face. "He will never hunt us any longer. He will have no vendetta against us . . . or against the spell masters he's been killing. He is no longer a commandant or Bolshevik."

We were free.

"Don't *do* that to me!" Alexei hollered from his bed. "You left me lying here, helpless. Wondering if you were going to use that spell on yourself and turn into a hollow-head."

I managed a grin for my brother, who raised himself up on one elbow. "Apologies, my tsar."

He rolled his eyes and then turned somber at Yurovsky's sleeping form. "We are free of him." He gave me a firm nod of approval. "Papa would be pleased."

My heart warmed. This was my first step toward forgiving Yurovsky. Releasing him from his actions. Tearing his claws from my heart and smashing them to powder. No matter if he was ever repentant or ever regretted murdering my family that night, I had to forgive him. Otherwise I would perish from the inside out.

Faced with releasing my hatred of Yurovsky, my forgiveness of Zash was a light of hope and freedom in my heart instead of a burden.

"I'm proud of you," Zash said.

Dochkin said nothing of my choice or my use of his spell. "We will dress him in peasant's clothing, give him a pouch of rubles, and deposit him in a village far away from here. For now, though, that spell should keep him sleeping a few hours."

Dochkin held out a hand toward Zash. Zash helped him to his feet, both grunting from the effort. Dochkin felt his healed throat, then popped his neck. "Not to sound self-praising, but I made a mighty fine spell." He brushed his hands together and surveyed the scene.

Blood stained his wood floor in a crimson lake with channels of red branching off into the cracks. Glass shards decorated the kitchen from smashed spell bottles.

"Shall we clean it up?" I suggested, not really having the energy to dive back into the sticky blood with a bar of soap.

"Before anything else, we all need rest . . . and food, I think."

"Food first," Alexei chirped, rising fully into a sitting position. My, how he'd healed!

A patter of small feet came from around the base of the bed in a broken rhythm. Joy limped into view, panting. She gave a small yap. All I could do was laugh. "You resilient little spaniel, you." I picked her up and deposited her onto Alexei's lap, joining him on the bed.

So many hours of our relationship had been spent with him in a bed and me at his side. But today he would finally rise in good health, not on borrowed time.

Zash and I—being the most recovered of the group—helped Alexei and Dochkin outside, per Dochkin's instructions. We all washed our hands in the creek as best we could, then rounded the house where a carved table stretched along the back wall. It faced a lovely view of a small pasture with a low fence. Inside the pasture a few goats nibbled at flowers, two horses meandered by the creek, and chickens clucked around a coop.

More pens and a vegetable garden could be spotted beyond the coop. Dochkin sat at the table and gestured to a tin bucket by the pasture fence. "Zash, could you—"

"Say no more." Zash grabbed the bucket and strode out to the pasture.

Less than a quarter hour later, we munched on fresh carrots, tomatoes, and bowls of berries in milk. I could have cried over the simple luxury of it. Joy caught herself a squirrel and made her own meal.

I tried not to stare at Dochkin throughout the meal. He struggled to swallow a piece of carrot and abandoned the root for his bowl of milk. Perhaps his spell hadn't completed the job as thoroughly as hoped.

"How long have you lived here, Dochkin?" I popped a cowberry into my mouth.

"Longer than you've been alive, at least." His long mustache hid his smile like Papa's used to, but I knew how to recognize the crinkles around the eyes.

"And no one has ever discovered you?"

"Without a locate spell, like what you used to get here, it's impossible to find. I spent half my time here crafting spells that erased any traceability."

"Yurovsky had a pocket watch that could detect spells. Even that wouldn't have found you?"

"Even that."

Tension leaked out of my bones and I plopped my elbows on the table. "It seems a wonderful place to study spell mastery." And to live. "Do you never get lonely?"

"There's a village not far—a few hours' walk. I venture there at least twice a month." He opened his arms to gesture to the landscape around us. "Peace, quiet, and safety are all well. But community and relationship are what truly fill a person's life. Of course I use an alias when in the village, but the people there are good. I help them where I can." He tossed part of his carrot toward Joy, who sniffed it once and turned away in disgust. "Tell me, Grand Duchess . . . why so many questions?"

I flicked my gaze to Alexei. He knew my aspirations and dreams. But would telling Dochkin imply that I wanted to act on them? I played with the berries remaining in my bowl. "I've always . . . always wanted to be a spell master. And this type of life—learning and farming and serving the people—is similar to the dreams Papa would speak of for our family. I can't help thinking about how much he would love it here."

Alexei nodded sadly, setting aside his now-finished second helping of berries and milk. "He would have loved it, but he wouldn't have stayed. Not with the current unrest."

"Please expound." Dochkin folded his hands on the table in front of him.

Alexei lifted his head. "I want to entreat your help, Spell Master. You have healed me, which shows you are loyal. Would you consider serving with me?"

Dochkin looked politely interested. "How so, my tsarevich?"

"I would like to rendezvous with the White Army. They are gathering as many spell masters to help them as will join. You know many spell masters across the country. And you are the most powerful. I invite you to take up the fight. Though I am not your tsar, I am a soldier of the people. And I know you are, too."

I couldn't read the expression on Dochkin's face. But I was more interested in understanding Alexei. He was ready to return to the front lines. To help his fellow soldiers and his country in the only way left to him. In the way he was designed to do.

I was not designed for that. The very notion of returning to battle and leaving this place made me want to crawl into the nearest bedroll.

"I've been waiting many years for you to enter my home," Dochkin said. "I always knew that once you came, it would be time for me to leave."

"So . . . you will join me?"

"At your command."

"No, at my request. I will not command you to leave your life and follow me."

"That is why I shall join you, young Tsar."

"Alexei."

Dochkin's eyes twinkled. "Alexei."

They shook hands and shared grins. I saw a bond form—between an old spell master and a young boy who never let his illness hold him back from his dreams and duties.

~

We were allowed back in the house long enough to grab thick blankets to spread out on the grass. Dochkin gathered some peasant clothes from his dresser for Yurovsky while Zash set to bandaging Yurovsky's wounds. I looked forward to dumping him in an alleyway. It didn't seem fair that he'd be able to start a new life. Not when I wasn't sure what I would do with mine yet.

"Take those blankets and get outside," Dochkin barked.

Alexei and I scrambled back out into the light. I still tensed watching him move with such ease, having seen him bedridden for the past several months. It could happen again in a second—with a single trip or accident. But I had to let him live and risk and bruise.

Because we were all at risk of accidents. Pain could strike us all in a moment. And just because it could strike Alexei more severely and more swiftly didn't turn him timid.

We spread the blankets on the grass and rested. Truly rested. Dochkin would not allow us back into the house until we'd done so and I was only too happy to oblige, lying side by side with my healthy brother, soaking up the sun in a way we were never allowed to do at the Ipatiev House or even Tobolsk.

Clouds passed. Time passed. I didn't count either. I just watched. Zash and Dochkin worked inside the house. I didn't allow myself to imagine what chores they were tackling or conversations they were having.

Alexei propped himself up on his elbows. "Nastya?"

"Mmm?" I responded sleepily.

"What do *you* wish to do, Sister?"

I opened my eyes fully. "I want to stay with you, of course."

Alexei shook his head. "This is your crossroad. This is where you get to make your own way. Do not let me be a tether."

I pushed myself up until I sat cross-legged. A tether. Like the spell Yurovsky had used on Zash—the one that ate at his insides the farther he got from Yurovsky. "You're not a tether. I go with you willingly."

Alexei gave me a stern frown. "You know what I'm asking."

I picked at a snag in the blanket beneath me. "You know better than anyone else that I wish to learn spell mastery."

"Ask Dochkin to teach you. Who better to instruct you?"

I shrugged. "He has a different mission . . . young Tsar."

A shadow fell across us. I spun to face Dochkin. His wrinkled face held warmth in every crease. "There is no greater joy than to pass on one's passion to an eager student."

I gulped down a breath. Dochkin sat with us. Across the way Zash pushed a wheelbarrow of soiled cleaning cloths and dumped the contents in a burn pile. He seemed too far. I yearned for him to take part in this conversation, so when he turned our way, I gave a little head jerk. An invitation to sit with us.

"I am old, Grand Duchess Anastasia," Dochkin went on. "And I will be joining your brother in war. There will come a time when only *you* will know how to make the spells that will enable your brother to heal when he needs to."

It was as though he'd ingested my hopes and spoke them out in complete understanding. "Would you teach me?" I breathed.

"I would be honored."

Alexei scooted to the side as Zash arrived and gingerly lowered himself across from me.

"But what of this place?" I asked. "What of your home? Your spell work?"

"Your animals?" Zash added. "Who will care for them when you leave, Spell Master?" I could see the longing in Zash's face as he gazed toward the pasture.

"If the tsarevich will permit me to lend some advice . . ." Dochkin faced Alexei, who nodded in encouragement. "This is not a war that will end in a week. We must enter it prepared for a long journey. I believe we will need a base. A base to gather spells. A base to which we can send injured spell masters, injured White soldiers. Somewhere safe."

Alexei nodded, somber but determined. "You mean here."

"Da. If there should be those willing to stay behind and care for it."

The opportunity swam before me like the berries in my bowl of milk earlier. I could stay here. I could *stay.* "I cannot leave my brother."

"It's not leaving me, Nastya. It's letting me leave." Alexei picked at a stray thread on the blanket. "You are fearsome, but you are not a soldier for the battlefield. Your talents and passions were not meant for the thick of war. They were meant for the side of it. The healing side. The side that renews the spirit of hope."

My little brother was instructing me—not commanding, but guiding me toward a solution that he wanted me to choose on my own.

"But what would I do here?" It almost seemed cruel to allow

myself to dream of walking in the forest and picking berries or gardening like I once did with Papa. It was the life Papa always wanted for us if we left exile. It felt wrong to take it all for myself.

"You could run the base," Dochkin offered.

I took in all the animals and the garden and pictured the well-kept home. "I think Zash would be better suited for that."

"You don't see it yet, Sister." Alexei smiled. "Zash works with his hands. *You* work with your mind."

I knew what he was trying to say. Spell mastery. "How would I learn spell mastery if Dochkin is gone?"

"First, through my journals," Dochkin said. "Second, through visits. I have an entire pouch of those locate spells that will bring us back to this house when needed—when Alexei needs a healing spell or when I need to replenish my stock. It will be up to you to learn the spells that heal his injuries so he can continue serving Russia. You must pass on this legacy."

A legacy of life. A legacy of hope.

This time, it was a choice to be left behind. No, not left behind . . . a choice to determine my future. And to let Alexei determine his. This was our new life—free of crowns and thrones. Free of hunters and Bolsheviks and exile.

We were finally free to live anew.

The same thrill that sparked in my heart shone in Alexei's eyes. "Do it, Nastya."

I dared to imagine life not as Grand Duchess Anastasia Nikolaevna Romanova, but as Nastya. A Russian girl who happened to have royal blood. A spell master in training, who would help her people through her voice, her blood, and magic.

"Of course I will." I was being handed my dreams—the opportunity to help my brother, to help my country, and to help my heart. I was finally going to learn spell mastery at the instruction of Russia's mightiest teacher.

But I didn't want to do it alone. While Dochkin and Alexei clapped each other on the back and entered a new conversation about the future, I watched Zash out of the corner of my eye. No one had offered him a future. No one had invited him to stay or leave.

Perhaps . . . that was up to me.

40

"The first step to spell mastery is the spell ink." Dochkin handed me a stoppered jar.

I took it gingerly, the first lesson of our new day in Dochkin's house. I was amazed at what a passing night's sleep could refresh in my mind. It tamed the high emotions of the previous day, sent another drop of healing into our souls, and woke us up fresh and optimistic.

Dochkin's house wasn't completely cleaned—the wood floor still had a giant stain of blood—but almost all evidence of the fight that took place yesterday had been scrubbed away.

Yurovsky lay against the wall in a shadowed corner, still asleep. Dochkin had applied a sleeping spell to him to ensure he did not wake up until deposited in the chosen village. Now in peasant dress, Yurovsky looked less shadowed and sinister.

I focused on the jar of spell ink in my hands. "I've searched and searched to learn how to make it." My pulse quickened at the thought of finally having the answer.

"That is the secret no spell master reveals . . . until they are with their student." Dochkin tapped the jar in my hand. "You can *only* create spell ink once a spell master has gifted you with ink of his own. That ensures spell mastery is passed on through discretion and passion. You had my Matryoshka doll, but this ink is my first gift to you, Grand Duchess."

I gawked. "That's why it was never recorded in spell books." Dochkin nodded. "And please, Master Dochkin, call me Nastya. I am not your princess anymore. I am your student."

He plopped a stack of three black journals on the kitchen table, similar to Papa's. "Start with these. Now that you have the base of your spell ink, you can read how it works and connects with the spell master. Keep a list of your questions for when I return. Once you've mastered these journals, I'll give you the next set."

I nodded.

"I'm almost ready!" Alexei strode into the kitchen wearing regular clothing. His face bore a healthy glow after all the rest and healing he'd received.

My spirit spasmed and I almost dropped the spell ink. They were leaving so soon. Today. I wasn't ready to say good-bye.

"Such a scowl, Sister!" Alexei held out his arms. "Does my common clothing look that bad?"

I dropped the scowl I hadn't known had made its way to my face. "You are too handsome to ever look fully common, I'm afraid." I swallowed hard. "It's difficult to say good-bye."

He took my hands in his and I only just realized he almost matched me in height. "The bond of our hearts . . ."

My eyes burned. ". . . spans miles, memory, and time."

"We will return soon—for Dochkin to further your training, and I'm sure I'll get into a scrape and need a spell sooner rather than later."

Dochkin loaded tins and bottles of spells into his shoulder pack. "I have plenty that will sustain you until our return, Tsarevich." He still couldn't drop the formal titles—he'd have to work on that before they got into the village.

Movement through the door caught my eye. Zash knelt by the little brook in the distance. He had barely spoken a word since yesterday's conversation on the grass. Afterward, he'd poured every moment into cleaning, caring for the animals, and preparing the wagon in which Alexei, Dochkin, and Yurovsky would depart.

He was the one untied thread to the fabric of my new story.

I'd wanted to speak with him yesterday, in the aftermath. But the conversations and exhaustion and emotion weighing us all down did not allow me to cross that threshold. Now . . . I was procrastinating. Why was I so hesitant when I had such hopes?

Alexei squeezed my hand. "Go to him, Sister."

"I'm nervous," I whispered.

Alexei grinned. "That's a good sign." I nudged him playfully and obeyed, but not before I caught a last word from him. "His future is in your hands, not mine, Nastya."

I found Zash out in the garden across from the brook. He sat on his knees beside a pile of stones and worked on twining two sticks together in a cross. His hands worked gently, weaving memories and sorrows into the thick cord.

I knelt beside him in the grass. "I am sorry about Vira."

His hands stilled. "She knew the risk."

I held the twine in place while he tied a knot. "I'm sorry all the same."

"I feared for her life so many times, it's as though I've lived this moment already. A hundred times over. She tried to prepare me.

Every time I left home, she made me bid a final farewell." He held the cross in his lap and stared at it.

"I think she'd be proud of us."

He nodded. "I was afraid that once she left this world I would feel empty. Alone."

"You're . . . not alone."

He stabbed the cross in the grass, in the center of a bed of flowers. We pushed scoops of dirt around the base to keep it upright. This was how my family should have been buried. Perhaps someday I would be able to give them a proper burial.

"If anything ever happens to me or Alexei . . . will you make sure we're buried with our family?" My question came after a long silence, but Zash seemed to understand why I asked it.

"Of course." He stacked stones around the base of the cross. I didn't help too much, allowing him this closure.

As we sat before the cross, it reminded me of the many times Papa read to us and led us in prayer. It reminded me of the hope and the life that Papa so strongly instilled in us.

Zash helped me to my feet and we brushed the dirt from our clothing. We stood in the garden together—a reminder of the days at Ipatiev, but with a new freedom pointing to our futures.

What did Zash want to do now? Would he return to Ekaterinburg? Search for his tribe of people? Alexei said I held Zash's future in my hands. I didn't want that duty. I wanted Zash to feel the same freedom of choice I had. So I asked the same question Alexei had posed to me.

"What do you want, Zash?"

He was quiet for a long time. "I want to love rightly."

That wasn't what I'd expected to come out of his mouth.

"All my life I was driven by the loyalty of caring for the people

I loved. Caring for fellow herders, caring for Vira. I was taught that nothing was more important than such care. But your family showed me differently. You cared equally as much about those you loved—you would do anything for them. But you also allowed yourselves to love . . . more. You loved your enemies. You loved your friends. You loved the Bolsheviks enough to sacrifice an opportunity to escape."

My throat pinched the longer he talked. I never felt as though I'd loved well, but Papa certainly did. And Papa was our example. We all wanted to love how he loved.

"Once I finally opened myself up to love like that, I found myself caring about you. And Alexei. And it's changed who I am. I'm . . . a better person now, I think. I have a better frame of spirit."

His vulnerability invited me to be vulnerable, too, and it refreshed me. "I like who you are, Zash. As do Alexei and Dochkin, so much so that they want you to stay here. To use your hands as you did with your people and to . . . help me help them."

"Is this what you wish, Nastya?"

To affirm him would be to share a deep, confused, raw part of myself. I wanted to say yes. To *yell* yes. "I can't do this alone. Will you stay? And help me?"

It was a cheap way out. A coward's way out. Inviting him for his benefits instead of inviting him to help me because I wanted *him*.

Still, it seemed enough for him. "Of course I will stay. Of course I'll help." The vulnerability had left his voice. It was my fault.

What could I say? How could I make it clear to him what I was feeling? Even *I* didn't know. I opened my mouth and closed it several times. But he changed the subject before I could say anything more. "Thank you for not using the memory spell on yourself. I don't imagine it was for my sake."

"It was for Alexei's sake," I said, and he nodded. "And Papa's sake. And *my* sake." I took his calloused hand and placed it in mine. "And yes, a big part of it was for your sake, too, Zash."

He looked up.

"I couldn't abandon you to these memories alone. I'm . . . I'm here." His breath hitched. But I didn't dare hope just yet.

"I'm here for you, too, Nastya. I know a lot about the struggles spell masters live with. I would be honored to serve Alexei, Dochkin, and you as . . . as whatever you need from me. The way I should have from the beginning."

"All I want from you . . . is you." There. I'd said it. The words broke through my hesitation like a galloping horse through a fence. "I want exactly who you are, Zash."

He looked stunned. Frozen in time. "You mean . . . ?"

I grinned. "You said you like bald ex-princesses. And I'm afraid I only know one. She wants to live life and fight the fight and learn spell mastery with *you*. She's wondering if you'll have her."

He touched my face lightly, tracing my cheekbone. "Is she certain she wants *me*? Could she even bring herself to trust me?"

To trust Zash was to believe there was still hope—in humanity, in my future. That frightened me. I wanted to hope, but I still couldn't think back to a time that hope carried me through. We had saved Alexei, but Yurovsky was going free. Papa had hoped in rescue and life, but he'd been shot. I'd hoped in Zash's friendship and he'd betrayed me.

But then he repented. He'd asked forgiveness and I dared to set aside my pain and let him in. Partly out of desperation and partly because I couldn't bear to give up hope fully. Papa never had—not even in the worst of times.

"Yes. With all of my broken Romanov heart." I peered up into

Zash's face as he drew me closer. His eyes reflected the same caution—the same fear—I felt. But also the same hope. And through that, we were bound.

He twined his fingers with mine and leaned forward with a whispered question. "Is this okay?"

I breathed in the moment, forcing myself to process the question. I was not yet okay, and I knew Zash was not okay yet either. But this—us—was a step toward that. "Yes."

Then softly, gently, he kissed me. His free hand held me steady, and I knew that this—this moment at least—could not be taken from me. It was fully ours. No matter our futures. No matter our pasts.

We made our way back to the house, back toward Alexei and Dochkin, where we would support each other's new pursuits. It wasn't a new mission . . . it was a new lifestyle. We were no longer fighting to preserve our old ways of living. Instead, we were all trailblazing forward into a new life. A life in a war-torn country. A life under the regime of the Soviets who may or may not be overthrown.

But it was a life together. A life anew. And we were finally ready.

As we crossed the lawn, Zash held out his hand for mine.

I stared at it for a long moment, seeing not just the calluses or the strength or the earth in the creases, but instead seeing all the promises it held. Healing. Forgiveness. A shared story. The promise of walking through life with someone who knew my bloodied past. A hand willing to touch the skin of a Romanov and feel only joy.

So I allowed Zash to take my hand—no, I *gave* him my hand. Willingly. Hopefully. And with no plans of ever letting go.

AUTHOR'S NOTE

Phew! We made it! I know this book was drastically different from the movie we all love and quote, so I want to thank you first and foremost for letting me take you on a *new* journey down the actual paths of history.

When drafting this manuscript, I could only tackle it for a couple of hours at a time because the true story was too heavy for my soul. But as I explored the depth of character of the Romanov family, their kindness, and the true caring they had for their people, I grew thankful I got to discover their story on such a level. And I'm even more thankful I get to share it with you.

I wanted to tell Anastasia's story—the true, historical tale of what she went through at the end of her family line, and then the fictional story of how I think she might have lived after that horrible night of July 16–17, 1918. Knowing her upbringing under a caring father and a devoted family, I think she would have struggled with forgiveness, but her desire to live a joyous and impish life would have won out in the end. She really was nicknamed *shvibzik* and, yes, she really pulled pranks all the time and performed silly plays.

Having spent part of my childhood in Alaska, studying the

Russian language, growing up with Russians in my home since before I can remember, and then traveling to Russia several times, I always hoped I'd have a chance to pen a story that would honor the Russian history and the people I have come to love who live there.

So with that, let's jump into fact and fiction.

What's True

So much research went into this book—particularly the first half—that I would never be able to list all the things that are true in this story, but I'll touch on a few:

The Romanov family was transferred from Tobolsk to Ekaterinburg for exile, and it was an extremely trying time. But they drew strength from their faith and from their relationships as a family. The order for their executions was carried out by Yurovsky and they were given no trial.

For almost ninety years, people suspected that Anastasia and Alexei could have survived. In 2007, their bodies were discovered in a separate grave near the rest of the family. I like to think that Nastya and Alexei went on to live out new adventures and were eventually buried with their family, as Zash promised they would be.

The attempted rescue mission from the White Army officer actually happened, but many historians suspect that it was a ploy by the Bolsheviks to catch the Romanovs in the act of escaping. Ex-Tsar Nikolai truly did call it off for the safety of their captors.

Ivan Skorokhodov was a real person. He and Maria shared an attraction, and we don't know what happened to him. He was caught with Maria and some say he could have been sent to prison. Others suspect he was shot. There's no known answer. But, in a way, it brings me comfort knowing Maria did have that source of joy during her time of exile.

Rasputin was also a real person and played a huge role—though unintentional—in the revolution of the Russian people. His relationship with the tsarina and the Romanov family is, to this day, still analyzed by historians. Unfortunately, the Romanovs' leaning toward constant secrecy did them very few favors.

Yakov Yurovsky was a watchmaker and a Bolshevik commandant when the Romanovs were killed. Though he had no role in Tobolsk (that was a stretch on my part), he was Avdeev's replacement commandant after the episode with Maria and Ivan. Yurovsky went on to live several years after the Romanovs' deaths and was loyal to the Soviet Union.

Oh, and finally: Joy the spaniel really existed and survived the execution of her masters.

WHAT'S STRETCHED

Zash is a fictional character, but the turmoil in his heart as a Bolshevik represents what many of the Bolshevik guards went through. The Romanov family befriended so many that the guards on duty were replaced again and again to keep them from growing too sympathetic. (And yes, they really did build the Romanovs a swing.) Though Zash is a creation of my imagination, the semi-nomadic people inhabiting Siberia are not. When the Romanov children saw people wearing reindeer skin and representing the east side of their country, they found it intriguing because they had not been educated thoroughly regarding the population of their country. They had always wanted to know their people on a deeper level, and I wanted to capture that desire through Zash's backstory and relationship with Nastya.

Vasily Dochkin is actually Vasily Zvyozdochkin—but the last name was just too much of a mouthful to make it all the way into the book, so I shortened it. (You're welcome.) He is the first known maker of the Matryoshka doll, and that's about all we know about him. To my knowledge he had no relation with the Romanov family, nor did he live in a little old cabin in the woods. I like to imagine that he would have been secreted away, making spells to save his tsar and his country. I loved giving him a bit of story woven with magic in *Romanov*.

The Romanov sisters did not shave their heads due to the lice infestation but instead due to a bout with measles a year prior. I fiddled with those dates and combined the two events.

If you want to do your own digging and learn about the Romanov family, I recommend reading any book on the Romanov family written by Helen Rappaport. I spent most of my time scouring the pages of *The Romanov Sisters* and *The Last Days of the Romanovs*.

DISCUSSION QUESTIONS

1. Nastya spends a lot of time in this book struggling with forgiveness. What do you understand forgiveness to mean?
2. Zash became a Bolshevik to help protect his babushka (Vira). How far would you go to protect those you love? And what do you think about his decision to join the Bolsheviks?
3. Nastya seeks to understand why Zash thinks and acts the way he does. Do you think it's important to strive to understand an opposing perspective? How do you go about doing so?
4. Zash has a moment when he thinks it will be better to take his own life than to live with what he's done. What do you think that would accomplish? Do you think that is ever the right answer? Why or why not?
5. Nastya had the chance to erase her memories and to erase her hurt. Have you ever wished you could do that? If so, why does it sound appealing? What might the repercussions be?

6. Why do you think Nastya chose not to use the memory spell in the end?

7. At the end of the book, the war is still raging. No one knows when it will end or who will win, but they are able to still live their lives. Do you ever struggle with focusing on your day-to-day when the bigger picture of your culture is caught up in unresolved issues?

8. The Romanov family had very strong values and this affected their ability to hope and forgive. Which values can you identify and how do you think those empowered the family?

ACKNOWLEDGMENTS

No story is written—or lived—alone. My writing journey is filled with soul friends and supporters who have cheered me through the bogs and over the mountains. Here are only some (of the thousands) of thank-yous I wish I could give in person every day of my life:

Always first is the One who saves me daily and brings purpose to my life and writing: Iisus. I've experienced the power of your hope and forgiveness. Life, writing, breathing . . . is nothing without you. Thank you for creating my storytelling mind.

Mister Ninja: my one love. My fellow adventurer. The one who is always encouraging me to go tell stories and who takes me out to dinner to celebrate every completed draft, edit, and milestone. Thank you will never be enough.

My agent, Steve Laube: you are my hero. Truly.

My fantastic publishing team: Amanda Bostic: for answering my constant questions and for hailing a cab like a boss in New York so we could get to BookCon. Becky Monds: for keeping me sane and encouraged while I tried to meet deadlines through morning sickness, and for all your passion for history and the Romanovs.

Kristen Ingebretson and Jeff Miller: for the mind-blowing cover. I'm speechless every time I look at it. Julee Schwarzburg and Jodi Hughes: for helping get this story squeaky clean. Paul, Allison, Matt, Savannah, and the rest of the TN crew: for all the marketing, brainstorming, and support you show my books. ♥

To my papa: for taking me on my first trip to Russia, teaching me to be a traveler, and then cheering me on through the many trips afterward. To my sweet mom: for delighting in every little step I take with this publishing journey. To Melanie: for calling me before every nerve-wracking bookish event, Binsk for always reading early drafts, and Liza for giving my books as gifts to strangers. I love you all dearly.

To my YA sisters: Mary Weber: you cry with me and rejoice with me and I truly don't know how I'd navigate this writing journey without our voxes. Sara Ella: for putting this idea in my head way back at ACFW . . . and fangirling when I told you I was going to write it. You're my favorite fairy-tale princess.

Ashley Townsend: you have no idea how precious all our 2018 adventures were. The boba tea, silent discos, and spontaneous Disney trips . . . you've been a listening ear through every step of this writing journey. I thank God for you. Karen Ball: you always hear my heart and believe in the journey behind each story I pen.

My beta readers, Ashley and Rosalie: for reading this book on such a tight deadline, even while hospitalized, and giving me some of the most helpful feedback ever. To Katie Grace, Tricia Mingerink, Stephanie Warner, Lindsay Franklin, S. D. Grimm, Emilie Hendryx, and all my other dear author friends who seem to live and breathe encouragement my way.

To my family in Russia: for the many visits, lessons in Russian, meals of *borscht* and *pelmeni*, and hours of fellowship. I thank

God every time I think of you. You are constant joy and eternal family. Thank you for the trip to St. Petersburg and the tour of the Alexander Palace grounds. I will never forget standing where Anastasia stood, jotting down notes so I could tell her story.

To my Ninjas: for sending me Oreos even when I went silent trying to meet these deadlines. Thank you for your constant excitement and encouragement. (Hidden Ninja hint: sometimes ninjas need to look backward to move forward.) To the Mitchtams: my writing community and word warriors *forever*. Thank you OYANers, Enclave Authors, Biola family, and CCH students for being my people. And thank you, Brandes family, for always understanding when my deadlines fall on holidays.

And of course, to every single reader and fan who gives my books a chance, who sends me fan art, fan mail, fan jewelry, all the fan things . . . I think your goal must be to keep me in tears and you're doing spectacularly. And to all the amazing readers on Instagram/bookstagram who bring me joy and encouragement every single day. You are all so precious to me—whether my books are your thing or not. ;-)

The bonds of our hearts . . .

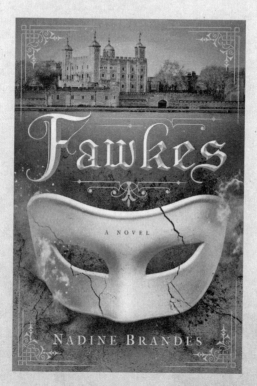

ABOUT THE AUTHOR

Photo by Emilie Hendryx from
E. A. Creative Photography

Nadine Brandes once spent four days as a sea cook in the name of book research. She is the author of *Fawkes* and the award-winning Out of Time series. Her inner fangirl perks up at the mention of soul-talk, Quidditch, bookstagram, and Oreos. When she's not busy writing novels about bold living, she's adventuring through Middle Earth or taste-testing a new chai. Nadine, her Auror husband, and their Halfling son are building a Tiny House on wheels. Current mission: paint the world in shalom.

NadineBrandes.com
Instagram: NadineBrandes
YouTube: Nadine Brandes
Twitter: @NadineBrandes
Facebook: NadineBrandesAuthor